The Necromancer Legacies

The
Gravekeeper

A. N. Anderson

I0590241

Published in Knoxville, Tennessee, by A. N. Anderson

ISBN 979-8-9992605-0-5

Cover Design by Mikayla Williams

Artwork by A. N. Anderson

To Patrick, my brother,
who listened to my stories
and encouraged me to write them.

Definitions and Terminology

Banshee ~ A spirit who foretells death and has power in her voice. She typically appears as a red-haired woman.

Contract ~ A formalized agreement. With spirits, this is a document that allow for quick summons.

Fiend ~ An unspecific evil spirit or entity.

Ghoul ~ A type of undead zombie that devours corpses. They lurk in graveyards and will arise from failed rituals or improper burials.

Lich ~ An evil, undead creature born of a necromancer. Through the sacrifice of many lives and imprisonment of many spirits, they transform and gain immense power and immortality.

Necromancer ~ A wizard with a rare affinity to dark magic and the ties between the dead and living realms. This affinity typically passes down through bloodlines.

Poltergeist ~ A spirit that creates freezing temperatures and has telekinesis. Unexplained thrown objects are often times attributed to poltergeist activity.

Revenant ~ A type of zombie created from a vetala. It has large claws and is very violent. Once its host body is damaged beyond use, it will revert to a Vetala and find another host.

Vetala ~ A violent, evil spirit that possesses corpses. Once it has a host, it becomes a revenant. Destroying the host does not destroy the vetala. They can only be summoned into the living world.

Will O Wisp ~ A mischievous trickster spirit with fire elemental properties. Often appearing in marshes or mazes, the Will O Wisp is known for leading travelers or those lost astray. Their true forms are unknown, and they are masters of illusions and deceit.

Wraith ~ A cursed spirit tethered to the living realm. Wraiths drain life-force through touch, and can be detected by the death of surrounding flora. They are typically bound to their graves with chains and cannot roam freely; breaking these chains frees them to pass on.

Zombie ~ An animated corpse. Zombies vary widely. The characteristics of a zombie depends upon how it was created and who controls them.

One

The Hill

"You are late," a spirit whispered in Benjamin Stone's ear as he stumbled down the steep stairs to the base of the hill, passing the dense thicket of ancient trees that twisted and moaned with the presence of the dead. The necromancer apprentice's shoes clattered across a length of mossy stairs, laces loosely trailing behind. He had slept in, and a late start was nothing short of an ill omen.

A sharp pitched voice jeered, *"Don't slip on your descent- ha HA!"*

Ben reached the end of the halfmoon stone landing and approached a grand wrought-iron gate. He pulled a heavy silver key from his pocket, pausing at the lock. He watched as a few kids stood across the road, whilst staring back at him, discussing something serious with hushed voices.

A small group of spirits had followed Ben to the base of the hill, and their voices mimicked the children, telling Ben what they were saying if Ben could trust the whispers of the dead.

"Look, he's opening the gate," one boy said while nudging another. *"You should go up there if you think you can make it back!"*

"Oh, that little lad is scared witless he hee! He's saying- ahem... 'I heard necromancers live there. Heeee is one of them – he he hee!"

"Is he even alive? What if he is a ghost?!" An actual ghost jeered. This comment encouraged an eruption of laughter amongst the spirits while the children argued in terror, each casting Ben a look more fearful than the last, before running off to school. Ben grimaced and looked down at his disheveled suit. Sure, he was as pale as a ghost and his face a little gaunt, but Ben was very much alive. He was just overworked and severely haunted.

Teeth clenched, Ben unlocked the gate and swung the heavy iron bars inward. *CLICK*. Ben hiked up the stairs back to the hill, pushing aside the spirit's jeers and the fearful attitude of St. Vincent's residents.

As Ben reached the top of the stairs, he witnessed the sunrise in full force. The tombstones and grass glistened with the early morning dew, and a gentle mist swirled through the landscape. Freshly placed roses dappled each grave with brilliant amber and scarlet. Ben spotted songbirds flittering about the tree line, and he imagined them singing too, but Ben could never hear them.

The air was thick with the sound of the dead. A long hollow voice wailed in the distance, laughter sporadically echoed, traversing through the graveyard like a trailing murder of crows. Not so far from Ben, just behind him to his left, he could hear a muttering of curses born from ancient grudges. Teeth gnashed, a tongue pressed on the back of the teeth, producing sharp *sss* and clicks of the *T*'s. Ben paused and closed his eyes, stilling his breath as his mind focused solely on that voice. It could have been a person muttering behind him- but as he concentrated, the voice projected not to his ears, but into his mind, making it undeniably the sound of a spirit. With his focus, the words morphed, carrying not just speech but the spirit's very thoughts, until they became an indecipherable rabble.

Ben's eyes opened with a glimmer of hope. He shifted and turned his neck to look towards the source of the brooding spirit's sound. A granite tombstone, glistening under the pale rays of dawn. Blades of grass twitched and swayed. A thick fog caressed the physical plane, but there was not a single specter to be seen.

The apprentice released a long-winded sigh. The spirit's curses slowly faded into a bleak memory as he trudged towards the house and up the porch.

He pulled open a large wooden door with iron ribbings and stepped through a silver framed threshold. The moment he entered the house, the lingering babble of conversation, screams, and laughter ceased. Ben's hand slid on the door's silver frame, fingers trailing over the twisted engravings. He could not see the barrier made from his grandfather's spell, but he could feel the faintest crackle of energy. For the sake of privacy, if not sanity, Grandfather did not allow the undead in the house.

There was only one exception.

Ben paused and sniffed the air, but as he breathed, the nauseating scent of burning flesh stung his nose and lungs. Ben gasped and spun on his heel, running into the kitchen. The apprentice gagged and grabbed his mouth, looking at the source. Smoke curled up from the stove where a maid stood, witfully cooking both a pan of eggs and her hand.

"Mely!" Ben cried as he shoved the maid aside. She swung her arm, whooshing the skillet right above his head, skimming the ends of his red hair and splattering the cabinets with half cooked eggs. Ben grabbed Mely's free hand and yelped, retracting his scalding fingers.

While nursing his hand, Ben cried, "What did I tell you about using the stove?!"

The maid tilted her head, allowing a strand of black hair to loosen from her bun and fall beside her pale blue cheek. "To not burn anything," she croaked.

"That includes yourself, Mely. Yourself!"

Ben carefully took her hand and inspected the burn. The charred, rotten flesh looked and smelled horrible, but it was not impossible to fix. A potion or two, depending on what Grandfather had in stock, would return it to a semi-lively state.

Ben sighed and let go of the maid. Being mad at her was pointless. Mely would not care if he yelled at her. Zombies were both emotionless and clumsy, and their standards of what was clean were on par with a rat. He did not understand Grandfather's desire to have a zombie maid to begin with, but Grandfather always argued that no sane or living person would want to work at the Hill. He was not entirely wrong.

"Let me fetch you a remedy." He shook his head as he left the kitchen, followed by the lingering scent of burned flesh.

The apprentice looked down the hallway and back towards the kitchen. He needed a potion from Grandfather's study. Surely he could spare one? The apprentice hurried down the hallway, mission in mind. The sooner he cured Mely's hand, the sooner the stink would vanish.

Ben opened the door to his grandfather's study and froze in the doorway. *You aren't allowed to be here*, a voice nagged in the back of his mind. It was too late to cater to inhibitions.

The office was a grand hexagonal room. Bookshelves lined the walls, each filled with necromantic tomes and a multitude of artifacts from Grandfather's journeys. An iron candelabra hung from the ceiling, hosting a myriad of thick white candles, burning brilliantly. Just to the left sat a massive wooden desk brimming with scrolls, ready to topple upon the floor from the faintest whisper. And at the desk sat Ernest Stone, the Gravekeeper and head necromancer of the Stone family, and most importantly, Benjamin's grandfather.

"What are you doing in here, Benjamin?" he growled, not looking up from one of his many ledgers as he fervently marked through it. His nostrils curled. "You're letting that *stench* in, whatever that is."

"Mely had an accident. I-I need a potion for her."

Grandfather sighed and looked up. "Benjamin, this isn't the time... is the gate open?"

"Yes, Grandfather. But Mely's hand-"

"Ugh, that *will* linger. This won't do..." Grandfather pinched the bridge of his nose, closed the ledger, and stood. "Benjamin, I must depart and gather our guests. Clean up whatever *that* is before I return."

"It's Mely, Grandfather... Where is the potion for her? Or the chirurgeon kit?" Ben pled as Grandfather sifted through a pile of ledgers, picking up a silver hand mirror. Obsidians and amethysts embedded the back of the mirror, and ornate runes were etched everywhere in between. Ben took a wary step away from the mirror as Grandfather scooped up the pile of ledgers and scrolls. "Mely burned her hand. It needs treatment."

Just as Grandfather was about to angle his face towards the mirror, he twitched his neck towards a trunk and said, "What you need is in there. If not, check up on the shelf behind it. We had a shipment of potions not long ago from the alchemist. Everything for Mely should be there... somewhere. Don't waste too much time and be sure to close the gate and get everything in order- swiftly! I will be returning with our guests before noon."

"What guests? I just *opened* the gate," Ben protested, but in a heartbeat, Grandfather had vanished. The apprentice stared at the spot Grandfather had stood only a second prior with a deep longing. One day, he too could use the mirror and traverse through the planes.

As the air settled, he realized he was alone in Grandfather's study, and there were more important things to think about. There were things far more important than Mely's hand. Would he ever have a more opportune time to dive into the knowledge of necromancy forbidden to him?

Every lick of information on necromancy Ben could possibly want to know was in this very room. If he wanted to know how to travel through the planes of the underworld without the mirror or see spirits without spectral specters, this room held the answer. With Grandfather's promise of a swift return, Ben knew he did not have a moment to spare.

Forgetting about Mely's potion, the knowledge-hungry apprentice's attention fell to the many scrolls scattered about the study. It would take hours to sort through them and find items of explicit interest. His eyes lifted to the more organized bookshelves and landed on a shelf filled with necromancy volumes right above the chest Grandfather had pointed to. Amongst the tomes, he recognized a few books he had read years ago, and others he had finished only months ago. His eyes flitted ahead to a gap in the wall, stuffed with a box of wax candles, and the next series of study material prepared for him for the months leading up to his rite.

'*1000 Uses for Ectoplasm*'

Ben's lips curled into a sneer. If Grandfather organized these books based on his curriculum, he would be studying how to brew potions and develop alchemical elements for the next month. And it would be... his hand slid along the worn spines of a myriad of textbooks until it landed on maybe... a year until he learned how to summon a spirit. That was a year too late. He would fail his rite.

Ben's hand trembled as he pulled on a two inch thick red textbook titled, '*advanced contracts and summoning.*' The book snagged on the edge of the shelf and toppled forward.

THUD

"Curses!"

Ben crouched down, picking up the damaged, ancient textbook. The back cover had ripped along the spine, and several pages had fallen all over the rug. Ben scrambled to gather the pages, but something odd caught his eye.

Chalk powder, salt, and ash speckled the rug, making parts of it pink and others maroon. The rug was disgusting, but it was not *just* filthy. Constant summonings had marred its plush fabric. And where the book had fallen, the edge of the frayed rug had furled itself upward, revealing surprisingly clean floorboards.

Ben set the book and its torn pages aside and crawled off the rug, crouching down to examine its edge. The cleanliness of the floor was no coincidence. He lifted the corner and, just as Ben thought his curiosity was causing him to imagine things, something silver glinted in the shadows. Ben pulled the rug back further, revealing a meticulously crafted silver trapdoor.

Ben's heart raced. He always knew about the contents of Grandfather's study and everything else about the house but not this. If Ben told him about this discovery, would Grandfather tell him what was beneath the hatch, or would he kick Ben out and punish him for digging around without permission? He imagined Grandfather reappearing into the room, standing behind him, and he jerked his neck to look about. The study was still, quiet, and empty. Ben gulped, knowing he would never get a chance to find out what was under the hatch unless he investigated it now.

He heaved the rug to one side and crouched over the trapdoor. It depicted a curled up dragon, sleeping above a nest of amethysts. His fingers traced along the silver carvings until they hooked into the dragon's mouth. The lizard's tongue curved like a trigger, and he pulled it upward.

Click

The silver door opened with ease. An iron ladder led down into a deep, shadowy, and unfamiliar tunnel. Ben looked around the study for a candle and spotted a lantern sitting atop Grandfather's desk. He shuffled around the desk and eventually found a small package of matchsticks. The boy eagerly snatched the lantern and lit it with a match. The moment the match's flame transferred to the lantern's wick, it turned a pale blue reminiscent of a spirit's essence.

The apprentice hooked the lantern in the crook of his elbow and climbed down into the chase. The tiny tunnel leading down to wherever he was going was a tight fit, and the back of his coat snagged and scraped against the cold, dusty stone throughout the descent.

With each step, an intensifying chill seeped from his skin to his bones. The iron rungs felt like ice, burning his palms. An eerie, hollow breeze breathed through the chase, ruffling his jacket and hair. His heart raced. Finally, the apprentice's shoes tapped down on solid earth. Ben turned around and waved the lantern forward to illuminate his discovery.

Beautiful stone and silver etched arches curved along the walls, hosting caskets stacked beneath the arches. Ben's mouth hung agape. A crypt! Grandfather never told him about a crypt beneath the house! The apprentice took a few eager steps and then froze. Was he alone? Where were the ghosts? The space was suffocatingly full of a silence that amplified the echoes of his footsteps and the rapid beat of his heart.

Why were there no spirits here?

He approached the nearest casket and examined the epitaph written on its side, tracing his fingers along the dusty engravings.

'Jackeline Raylin Stone. 1492-1654. A brilliant woman for her time.' Ben's eyes narrowed. He approached the next casket, quickly scanning the epitaph. *'Henry Ray Stone. 1494-1520. Still kicking.'* Another Stone. Ben's heart skipped a beat. This was *his* family's gravesite.

His hand slid along the silver engraved arches, sweeping away dust and webs. Grandfather never mentioned where their family was buried, but now he knew. Ben's eyes wandered down the dark, curving catacombs. Would *she* be down here?

He continued along the crypt, brushing away the occasional cobweb. The tunnels spiraled down a gentle slope, and after several turns, Ben was more than ready to end his adventure. All the arches were the same and all the caskets looked identical. The longer he explored, the more likely Grandfather would return and catch him in this forbidden place.

Just as he decided it would be best to end his search, he came into a square hall with a stone casket set in the center, unlike any other space in the crypt discovered thus far. He stooped down and walked around it, searching for a name, but there were none. Sighing, he made a sweeping investigation of the epitaphs along the walls and found her.

"Susan Blair Stone. May her heart be full and her soul rest in peace"

A foreign hollowness filled Ben's chest. His fingers shakily slid down to the bottom lip of the epitaph's engravings. He always imagined his mother's grave to contain a lively spirit. One that would talk to him and act just like all the other motherly ghosts on the Hill. He would one day have a conversation with her, one filled with memories even if they were forged postmortem.

Instead, her casket was cold and quiet. Ben's shoulders slumped. Grandfather had forewarned him of one thing about deceased relatives: it was dangerous for a necromancer to talk to those they once knew as the living.

Still, Ben had no memory of his mother. If anything, her memory only lived on within Grandfather's lectures focused on the responsibility of the Stone household that Ben had to live up to. He had to be a Gravekeeper- a responsibility she did not take on.

And now her silent grave served as a painful reminder that it was time to return to his duties above ground.

Casting one last look at her casket, Ben turned and treaded through the crypt back towards the ladder. Looping the lantern onto his elbow, he scaled up its iron rungs. As he neared the hatch, a bearded face poked through the gleaming exit, glaring down at Ben with vicious golden eyes. The boy gasped and nearly let go of the ladder.

"What are you doing?! Why are you down there?! What are you doing with that lantern, Benjamin?!" Grandfather roared. His voice echoed down the tunnel and reverberated back up, making Ben tremble.

"I... I was looking for a potion for Mely?"

Grandfather's face turned red, and Ben expected the necromancer to slam the exit off to the crypt and leave him trapped inside. Instead, he shook his head and moved aside, allowing Ben to climb up. Grandfather growled, "This isn't the time for nonsense. Hurry out of there, boy! And put out that damn lantern!"

Ben clambered out of the crypt, and before he could get on his feet, Grandfather snatched the lantern from the crook of his fingers. He cradled the lantern and blew out the flame with extra precaution. Ben brushed off lingering cobwebs from his suit while watching Grandfather stow away the lantern within the confines of his desk.

"Come along," Grandfather growled, opening the study door and waving Ben through. He followed the necromancer through the house, wondering what punishment his grandfather had in store and why he had not immediately received it.

"What is happening?" Ben asked, face stark white with fear and nose scrunching with disgust. Mely's burned stench had indeed permeated through the halls.

"That revolting odor is filling the house! You should have fixed Mely by now or at the very least closed the gate!" Grandfather grumbled as he shook his head and ignored Ben's question. He rested a hand on the front door's silver doorknob and turned around to face Ben. His soft face hardened, and the old man leaned forward so that he and his grandson were nose to nose. "Now whatever you do, don't speak. Understood? This is a brief introduction, nothing more. It *cannot* be more."

Ben squeaked, "Yes, sir."

Grandfather snorted and turned towards the door. He paused, straightened his shoulders as best he could, and opened the front door. The Gravekeeper stepped onto the porch, motioning for his apprentice to follow him, but Ben was frozen stiff. He stood at the threshold and gawked at a group of men and women assembled at the base of the house. They were all cloaked in long black robes, but they were no funeral party. Ten of the most powerful necromancers stood before him.

The Council of the Dead.

Two

The Council of the Dead

Benjamin Stone did not know what to do. Grandfather's warnings fled from his mind, and he resisted a powerful urge to flee into the house and back into the crypt. This was the council Grandfather met with every month to discuss the affairs of the undead. The council that reigned over any magical involvement with the netherworld. The Council of the Dead.

Ben counted ten council members- eleven, including Grandfather. They stood in a half-moon, hosting a mixture of expressions on their cowled faces. There was no immediate way of telling who they were, but Ben imagined the leaders of each great necromancy family standing before him, and his stomach twisted with sheer horror.

The Hill's silence fell on Ben's shoulders like a bag of bricks. Not a single spirit dared to whisper or whine. Ben trembled. His feet shuffled backwards ever so slightly, but a firm hand shifted from his collar to his shoulder and gave him an affirmative pat.

"This is the next Gravekeeper, Benjamin Stone." Grandfather's declaration carried like a cold gale, sending chills up Ben's spine. Ben's mouth hung open as confusion and terror contorted his face. He was an apprentice, but why did that matter to the Council of the Dead?

"A pleasure to meet you, Benjamin," a blonde woman said, lowering her cowl. She had vibrant green eyes and a twisted scar on her full lips. Isabella Nightshade- the head of the Council of the Dead and the Nightshade family. A necromancer capable of commanding an army of skeletons and raising a graveyard with the snap of her fingers. Ben had read plenty enough about her to shake in his shoes.

A few necromancers nodded their greetings to Ben, but most of them focused their attention on their host and fellow council members. A necromancer tilted his head so Ben could see a sharp jaw and eyes that glowed like rubies over flames. "Stone, shall we carry on with our meeting?"

"Ah yes, let us proceed to the garden," Grandfather declared. "There is a pavilion that will suit our needs nicely." Grandfather waved his hand towards a stone arch separating a row of rose hedges and marking the entrance to the gardens.

Grandfather's grip on Ben's shoulder tightened for a second, and he leaned down to hiss, "Go take care of Mely but first clean that up-" Grandfather waved his free hand at the pile of gardening tools Ben had left near the arch the day prior. "-We will discuss... where you were... later." He descended the porch stairs to guide the necromancers into the garden.

The council followed Grandfather's direction, but the man with the glowing red eyes stayed back and lowered his cowl, revealing short, peppered hair, angular features, and the full light of his crimson eyes.

"It is a pleasure, Stone. I am Jacob Withertomb," the necromancer said, holding out a hand to Ben. Ben looked at it and hesitated, staring after Grandfather's back. The old man seemed to notice the exchange and looked at Ben with a steady gaze in his eye before passing beneath the arch.

Ben gulped, and before delaying too long, he stepped down the porch's stairs and grabbed Withertomb's hand. The moment their fingers touched Ben could feel a heavy, hungry power buzzing from Withertomb's fingertips. The energy emanated up to Ben's wrist with a burning fervor- Ben jerked his hand away. Withertomb smirked.

"I understand you are to be the next Gravekeeper, but you are still a student of the necromantic arts. If you ever choose to study as a proper necromancer, my academy will always welcome the progeny of a council member with open arms."

Ben's face flushed. He had never heard of a school for necromancy, but the idea sounded thrilling. On the Hill, his company was the dead, and Grandfather's teaching methods were so slow and mundane, he doubted he would ever become a proper necromancer at this rate. Grandfather had put it correctly. He was just an apprentice.

But he was Grandfather's apprentice. Ben shook away the uneasy feeling of the necromancer's presence. This was another family, and one Grandfather was not on best terms with. It would be foolish to accept any offer from him without Grandfather's permission. "That is a decision for Grandfather," Ben said firmly. He paused, wondering the council member had some ploy against Grandfather and added, "I am the next Gravekeeper, not just a student of the necromantic arts."

Jacob Withertomb smiled although the smile did not meet his gaze. He reached into his pocket and pulled out a small slip of paper. "It looks to me you are a groundskeeper, not a Gravekeeper." Ben gritted his teeth. "Ah, I digress. If you deem your education is lacking, you know what to do." He stepped forward and pressed the paper in Ben's hand. He then turned and walked away, leaving Ben alone with his blood boiling.

Ben glared at Withertomb's back as he followed the remaining council members through the archway, black cloaks flapping at their heels. As his anger resided, he noticed an uncomfortable burning sensation in his hand. He looked down at the paper. He expected a flyer, but instead it was a charcoal drawing of a

A. N. Anderson

large building nestled on a plateau in the mountains. There was a lingering sickly energy attached to the paper, and Ben quickly shoved the drawing into his pocket. He had bigger things to worry about than the conflict between their two families.

Once the council meeting adjourned, Grandfather would surely punish him for delving into the crypt. Maybe he would have to go to the academy just to flee Grandfather's wrath?

Face flushed, Ben gathered the gardening tools and headed towards the garden. Everyone was likely arriving at the rotunda in the heart of the garden. The apprentice stored the supplies in the shed and locked it with his iron ring of keys. His forehead pressed against the shed's wooden door, and his eyes closed, yearning for a semblance of peace. The few spirits who enjoyed spending their days following Ben found delight in the council's arrival and Ben's newfound confrontation.

"You should join them," a spirit whispered with a soft, sweet voice.

A chorus followed, causing Ben to clench his teeth and sharply open his eyes.

"Why wouldn't you join them?" *"You are one of them?"* *"Oh he is just a groundskeeper, don't count him amongst thaaaat bunch…"*

"They are probably laughing at you," another spirit moaned right in Ben's ear to ensure his voice would not carry. It was clear the Hill's residents were still on edge with the powerful necromancers being in the vicinity but not on edge enough to stray from stirring up trouble.

The apprentice swatted his hand as if the spirit was a sweat bee and gazed off towards the rotunda. Ben had read about the history of the different necromancer councils in past eras. Everything they did greatly impacted the practice of necromancy and the society of necromancers. Grandfather had never hosted a meeting with the council on the Hill before, and Ben wondered if this would be his only chance to witness the world's most powerful necromancers in action.

Intrigued, and persuaded by the eager encouragement from the Hill's residents, Ben started down the garden's gravel path. He squeezed his way through a gap in the hedges into an unofficial dirt path nestled between two rows of rose bushes with brilliant red blossoms. Ben hunched his shoulders forward and carefully treaded along the path, trying to avoid being pricked by the stray branches.

As Ben progressed closer to the rotunda, the snickering in his ears faded to a faint murmur. The hill's residents did not need any introductions to know how powerful the people at the rotunda were. They had no desire to stick around and risk getting caught eavesdropping on the Council of the Dead.

Ben told himself he would not stay for long. He could listen long enough just to hear the agenda and if there was a reason Grandfather had introduced him to the council. Despite his curiosity, it would not be wise to stay for the whole conversation, that much he knew for certain.

He slowed his pace down to a creep when the roof of the rotunda came in sight. He froze. The spirits' whispers subsided into a deep silence and the sound of the living prickled his ears. The council gathered behind the shrubs on Ben's right. The rose bushes were thick enough to conceal Ben, but he crouched down anyway.

Grandfather's enchantments on the Hill would surely stop the necromancers from using any of their own tricks. There were already enough spirits around to throw off their senses, so Ben grew comfortable knowing he would not be detected by the council. The only person he had to worry about was Grandfather.

But Grandfather would already punish him for the crypt. What was the worst that could happen if he were caught here? The apprentice sneered. It was either this or studying the rudimentary rules of contracts while waiting to be punished. He could dig his grave a little deeper.

"-How many necromancers are on the blacklist?" someone asked. She had a high-pitched voice.

A calm, smooth voice that could have belonged to a nurse said, "Three necromancers have been added to the list this year excluding the ones that have been terminated."

"And of the ones-"

"An Ellandor became a lich," Grandfather's familiar voice interjected.

The conversations ceased as a thick silence spread amongst the council. It did not sound like anyone was surprised, but Ben had to suck in his own shock. Becoming a lich had been banned for over five hundred years, and as far as Ben knew, it was still a forbidden act of necromancy. To become such a being required the sacrifice of hundreds of lives, and somehow, the council failed to prevent it.

"The Ellandors will be discussed later," Isabella Nightshade's voice rang out like a grave's bell.

"What of your students, Withertomb? I heard several died in the past year," Grandfather added. "Is it all unrelated from the li-"

"Several students fell short of their exams. It is unfortunate but not unexpected." Jacob Withertomb's voice was familiar enough to make Ben shiver.

"What of their corpses? Their spirits?" someone else asked.

"They received their appropriate portraits. They are in safe keeping," Withertomb curtly replied. "Until the lich is destroyed, many of them cannot be recovered."

"Speaking of, when will the Gravekeeper's training be complete?"

There was a long silence, or perhaps time had simply frozen. Ben forgot to breathe.

"He is learning," Grandfather said with an irritated tone. "It takes time. I suggest we extend his rite out until-"

"The Gravekeeper is blind," Jacob said.

There was an uproar amongst the necromancers that made all of the conversation unintelligible until a single sentence popped out louder than the rest.

"How can a Gravekeeper not see the dead?! There's no such thing as a blind necromancer!"

Ben felt like his heart had stopped.

Grandfather roared, "And there's no such thing as a dead necromancer, but we still have liches running around. Do you want to explain to me what the Wraithrights have been doing lately? Have you been keeping in check the Ellandors while they rob the souls of unfortunate wizards and innocents? What about the headmaster of your school, Withertomb?!"

"No matter the taboo at hand, a lich is far more valuable than a ghost whisperer," Jacob Withertomb laughed.

Isabella Nightshade's voice grew cold. "Withertomb is correct, Stone. No matter what taboo is at hand, the Gravekeeper's sole purpose is to manage it. How could he monitor and prevent the creation of a lich if he cannot even perform a summons or see what haunts him?"

"He is learning," Grandfather growled. "It is taking some time. Naturally, it requires more time to raise a necromancer to ensure they do not target and kill wizards for their own gains. If only some would learn from this and teach their pupils accordingly, we may not need a Gravekeeper."

There was a sharp silence and a thud. Someone coughed and Jacob Withertomb, albeit muffled, said, "I only teach what must be taught. It is far more dangerous to allow those gifted to be necromancers not learn to control their gifts or be guided solely by curiosity. Much unlike trying to force a useless waste to invoke any hint of talent."

"What are you implying?" Grandfather growled.

"Perhaps, for your apprentice, there is potential-"

"My apprentice, mind you, has all the potential a Gravekeeper needs."

"You have already lost a generation. Shouldn't the training of this Gravekeeper be accelerated? Especially with his handicap? The boy can't stop a single grave robber if he can't see what he is protecting."

"You create the graverobbers."

Ben's mind raced as the conversation continued. His face burned red with embarrassment. He always believed his inability to see spirits was a secret only Grandfather and the residents of the Hill knew. The whole Council of the Dead knew it as well. He was as good as an outcast, a nobody.

Yet somehow, they were talking about his tasks as a Gravekeeper beyond ghost whispering and groundskeeping. A Gravekeeper actually could summon and perform just like a necromancer. Or at least, a Gravekeeper was supposed to be capable of such things. It was clear to everyone, Ben was not competent enough to be an ideal choice.

"What of your daughter. Is she not eligible?" the old man with the voice that sounded like sandpaper being rubbed on glass asked. "She was an excellent necromancer."

"She is dead," Grandfather snapped. "Benjamin is the only one who can inherit the position."

"Not if he can't perform." Nightshade's words slapped Ben's pride. "The dead can always awaken if need be."

Grandfather's voice followed with the killing blow. "If there is even the slightest chance he is deemed incapable of being the next Gravekeeper, we shall discuss alternate options for a new heir-"

Ben pinched himself to hold back from screaming at Grandfather and exposing himself to the entire council. He had heard enough. The boy crept back towards the house, his face burning a bright red. The moment he stepped out of earshot, he ran. Rogue rose branches snagged his jacket and tore at his face. Ben left the garden in a whirlwind of leaves, petals, and snickering spirits.

The conversation swirled in Ben's head, but he did not need a good memory to replay it. A couple of spirits made it their duty to repeat the discussion in mocking tones, laughing in Ben's ears between each impersonation. Ben blindly swatted at them and fled into the house, slamming the door behind him.

Ben fumbled around in the foyer, wondering what to do and where to go. His heart raced, and his mind felt as if it were buzzing with a swarm of flies. Tears stung his eyes as he replayed the council's conversation in his mind, and a bitter taste clung to his tongue. Did the entire necromancer society know about his secret? Did Grandfather tell everyone? Or was it Withertomb?

He sat at the base of the stairs facing the front door and dropped his head into his hands. Staring at his shoes, Ben allowed his thoughts to spiral. He was only an apprentice, but clearly the council knew he was behind the status quo.

Ben shook his head, eyes wide. His vision blurred with tears. Grandfather did not actually expect him to be capable of becoming a necromancer. He would be stuck doing basic graveyard maintenance forever! He never had a chance to learn true magic. Grandfather was delaying the verdict for the sake of his very own pride.

Ben's heart raced as the discussion replayed in his mind. How long would it be before Grandfather declared him unfit? Would he send him away from the Hill or adopt an apprentice worthy of becoming the next head of the Stone family? Was the transgression he made by entering the crypt the final strike?

Ben imagined returning to his room to study contracts. No matter what he did now, it was not good enough if he ever wanted to be the Gravekeeper. Not even becoming a necromancer seemed within reach. The Council of the Dead knew Ben could not see spirits. Naturally, they wanted a replacement. Ben's aspirations to inherit his legacy unraveled before his eyes.

He would never be the Gravekeeper.

Three

The Lantern

Hours passed. The sky shifted from a pale blue to a deep maroon, teetering on the brink of pitch. Ben forced his eyes to stare upon pages and pages of summoning circles for a multitude of spirits. His vision swam with runes and circles while his mind replayed the council's conversation.

The house's main door creaked open and slammed shut. Ben jolted in his chair. He shuddered at the thought of facing Grandfather and pressed his forehead against his palms. What would he say to him over dinner? Was it wise to confess on what he heard in exchange for an explanation? Ben felt his mouth go dry as scenarios of what might happen to him if Grandfather knew what he had done play through his mind. No matter how hurt he was, Ben figured revealing his own transgressions would only cause more trouble.

Knock

The doorknob rattled and clicked. Grandfather stepped into Ben's room.

A swirling feeling of fear and despair froze Ben in his seat. He could not bear to look at Grandfather, but as Grandfather stepped towards him, he could not ignore his looming presence.

Grandfather paused, standing behind Ben. Chills went up the apprentice's spine as he watched Grandfather's shadow move with an unnatural fluidity, covering his piling books and notes in an eerily thick darkness. "It is due time we begin today's lesson. Come with me," Grandfather said. His voice was soft for a necromancer who had a failing apprentice.

Anger filled Ben's chest, making it hard to breathe and properly respond to Grandfather. He raised his face from his hands and could not help but give Grandfather the coldest gaze he could muster.

Grandfather ignored every signal Ben put off completely, waving his hand towards the hallway in the direction of his study. "Your lesson must begin promptly before the sun sets."

Grandfather was never one to rush into one of Ben's lessons. He took his time, teaching Ben whenever he remembered or whenever Ben announced he was out of things to read. Most of Ben's days lately were filled with maintaining the graveyard and writing out contracts, so it had been weeks since Grandfather last taught anything spectacular. And the last time, Ben remembered with distaste, was how to stitch a zombie's wounds.

"What lesson needs to be taught at dusk? Am I going to test out one of my contracts?" Ben asked, voice low and level. He remained at his desk and slid his hand on one of the rolled up sheets of parchment. He was itching to summon a spirit and see if his contracts had any true merit. Ben, however, already knew Grandfather had no intention of teaching him how to summon so long as he could not see spirits.

"No, no contracts, no summons," Grandfather said, waving his hand and shaking his head. He motioned for Ben to follow him. "You will see soon enough. This night will be a long one."

"Is this about the crypt?" Ben asked warily. Some lessons were taught on the topic of morality and punishment rather than spells and summonings. He shivered, fearing Grandfather knew about his eavesdropping. What was worse? The crypt or the council.

"No, forget about the crypt." Grandfather said, shaking his head again.

Ben's heart skipped a beat. Grandfather was going to forget about him going into his crypt?! A weight of dread lifted from his heart until he remembered the piercing words of the Council of the Dead. Why punish a failed apprentice anyway? His heart sank. "Wh- what do you-"

"We are running out of time!" Grandfather roared, halting Ben's spiral of thoughts. Before Ben could make sense of things, Grandfather rushed ahead, grabbing the apprentice by the elbow. He pulled him out of his room and towards the stairs.

"It is imperative we *fix* you immediately," Grandfather hissed as they walked. They reached the study, and he opened the door, ushering Ben to follow him. "The council is not convinced you have the potential to be the Gravekeeper."

Ben yanked his arm out of Grandfather's grasp. Golden eyes glowing with anger, Ben snapped, "*You* aren't convinced I can even be a necromancer!"

Grandfather froze and looked down at Ben, calculating. Ben gulped, fearing he had just given himself away. He thought about what Grandfather *knew* and stammered, "I could be l-learning from Withertomb. At least *he* would teach me how to do something beyond clean a tombstone!"

Grandfather straightened his posture, gaining a foot in height. His eyes leered down on Ben, and the boy was sure he had just sealed his fate. "You want to be taught by the Withertombs. By another family? Do you know what it means to be a Stone? What your responsibilities are?!"

"What difference does it make if you won't teach me to even be a *measly* Gravekeeper," Ben spat. His face burned red with anger. He knew Grandfather had no intention of teaching him how to be a true necromancer. Only because of the council was he now addressing Ben's lack of sight!

"If you want to learn to be a Gravekeeper, you follow me now," Grandfather growled. He stormed past Ben and snatched the lantern from his desk. He then spun around and stepped towards Ben, causing the apprentice to flinch and shuffle backwards. Before Ben could react, Grandfather grabbed him by the sleeve and dragged him out of the study towards the front door.

"So, you want to see spirits? That is not all there is to necromancy or being a Gravekeeper, but I can teach you! I can teach you far beyond what the Academia Di Morti can do. If only you had the slightest inclination to what transpires there! There, you would be just another corpse at their disposal. Another painting to display. Enough of this nonsense asking for Withertomb's tutorship. He is nothing but a grave robbing fraud."

They stepped out into the graveyard and headed towards the gardens while Grandfather grumbled the whole while. Ben knew his resentment for Jacob Withertomb went deep to the bones, but he did not know why. Although, from Withertomb exposing Ben to the whole council, Ben had developed a sliver of unignorable resentment reserved just for the red-eyed necromancer.

The two stopped at a circular clearing at the core of a parterre in the flower gardens. In the center was a large circular fountain made of stone with a statue of a woman holding a bucket with water pouring from it. The water bubbled, and the air was fresh with the scent of flowers, mulch, and the late-afternoon sun. The parterre was a place of peace, but Ben's heart churned with anger. He wished the whole garden would just burn.

Grandfather lifted the silver lantern, drawing Ben's attention to its glimmering, ornate frame. "This *is* about the crypt," Ben said through his teeth. Of course, Grandfather only meant to punish him for trespassing into the crypt.

"No," Grandfather growled, clearly still upset about Ben's behavior. He rubbed his forehead, looking down at his apprentice with disappointment. "It is high time you developed the ability to see spirits so pay close attention. This here belonged to a will-o-wisp. There are-"

"Are the skillets made of ectoplasm?" Ben asked, eyeing the lantern with distaste.

"No, they are made of iron," Grandfather groaned while lighting the lamp with a snap of his fingers. He handed the lantern to Ben who begrudgingly took it. The flame was cold and emitted an eerie, pale blue light.

"Can you teach me how to make a flame like that?" Ben asked.

"Not yet."

Grandfather took several steps away from Ben. Rather quickly, he fretfully noted. He was convinced, despite what Grandfather said, this was still related to his discovery of the crypt.

"There are few things normal ghosts can carry and interact with, typically being anything made with ectoplasm. A Will O Wisp lantern is one of such things. Spirits can use it to leave their graves and places of haunting so long as it is lit and so long as it is night. There are plenty of the Hill's residents who wish to have this, so," Grandfather pressed the lantern in Ben's hands, "you are going to hold onto it and make sure none of them take it."

"Why not I kill the light?" Ben suggested, stepping away from the fountain and closer to the path leading back to the house. He did not like where this lesson was going. The idea of the Hill's residents seeing this object as their one-way ticket out of the Hill was a dreadful one. They would have no qualms with harassing him and doing whatever it took to retrieve the lantern. He did not see how this would improve his sight. If this was the only way, he figured he just wear a pair of spectral spectacles.

"Benjamin, if you want to be a proper Gravekeeper, you *must* do this. As they attempt to steal the lantern, they'll react to you more as will you react to them. It will become increasingly difficult to not see the ghosts, even if it is for a short length of time. But for your own sake, I advise you not to leave the garden. *Do not lose or blow out the lantern either*. The flame will naturally go out at dawn, and they will tell me if you blow it out even a second sooner."

"D-dawn?" Ben stammered, but the necromancer was already trotting away, fleeing the garden, and leaving Ben alone amidst the watchful eyes of the Hill's residents.

The apprentice listened to the trickling sound of the fountain and the soft rustling of rose bushes in the breeze. The spirits were oddly hushed, making Ben feel as if something was very wrong.

Ben stared at the lantern with dismay. It emitted a strange aura that sent goosebumps across his skin. This eerie feeling made Ben's heart skip a beat and face flush. In a way, this was Grandfather redeeming himself for what he said. Perhaps he would not abandon Ben and planned to teach him how to use magic, summon the dead, and progress into an actual necromancer. A deep ache in his heart made him doubtful, but he did not have time to be wrapped up in his emotions.

As an apprentice necromancer, Ben was not afraid of ghosts. Such a fear would be the bane of his career! However, he jumped when a spirit cooed, *"Ben, would you be a dear and hand that to me?"*

The fog that had clung to the garden's edges and hedges swirled and morphed into shapes, some taking humanoid forms for brief seconds. Ben looked down to the fountain and yelped, seeing four ghosts with eerie smiles etched across their ghastly faces.

"What is that?"

"Ooooh, I know what THAT is! That is a will-O-wisp lantern, isn't it?" One of those smiling faces laughed.

"I heard Ernest. He won't stop us from taking it," another ghost rasped, each word sounding like it would be the spirit's last.

The air grew frigid. Ben watched with eyes the size of saucers as pale hands emerged from nothing and grabbed hold of the lantern. He jerked away from them and stumbled backwards, pressing his heels against the concrete edge of the fountain. A multitude of hands grabbed Ben's arms and the lantern, pulling him back to his feet.

The length of the white hands extended, revealing transparent arms and flowing ethereal sleeves. Ben stopped worrying about the lantern as his gaze lifted to the ghosts. He could see through them, but they were there. Transparent bodies of all shapes and sizes, hair and clothes that flowed with intangible winds, and faces that moved when the voices occurred.

A slender spirit with droopy eyes moaned, *"Hand ooooover the lantern."*

A not so jolly looking ghost with a top hat propped over his head and a curly beard flowing onto his suit grumbled, *"Give me that lantern, boy. I've got a quack to haunt!"*

Ben pulled the lantern closer to himself and brushed away the hands. Some of the images faded when he moved the lantern away from them, but others managed to touch it making their apparitions appear. Ben quickly realized it was not his ability to see being amplified, but the spirits' energy being amplified by the lantern's magic.

As the night dragged on, the ghosts learned this as well and grew violent. Ben had no chance to hide and ran from the restless spirits. Cold ghastly hands snatched at the lantern, clawing Ben's arms. They could not grab him, but their hands felt as cold as ice, making his own grip on the lantern weaken. The spirits, however, discovered they could touch the ectoplasmic artifact and thus move Ben with it.

A group of ghosts snatched the lantern and pulled it from Ben like a game of tug-of-war. In sync, they screamed, *"One, two, threeeee!"*

They flew upwards with Ben in tow. Ben released a startled cry as his feet left the ground. He hung in the air by his weakening grasp on the lantern's handle. Dangling several feet in the air, he cried, "Put me back down or no flowers for a month!"

The spirits conjoined efforts faltered, and they dropped the lantern. And Ben.

A scream bubbled in Ben's throat as he fell to the ground. He landed on his shoulder and tumbled into the thorny branches of a rose bush. He groaned and rolled to his side, onto the gravel path, rubbing his rear and swiping foliage off his jacket. In that moment, a ghost snatched the lantern and flew one second before Ben sprung forward, falling through the spirit, and grasped the handle.

The spirit spat and screamed while the others observed and learned a new method to wrangle the lantern out of Ben's hands. They carried the lantern about, pulling it one way and the next. Worst of all, they found lifting Ben in the air incredibly amusing. So much so, it seemed as if they aimed just to throw him and did not care about getting the lantern at all!

When salmon rays of light stretched across the sky, Ben was about to topple over from pain and exhaustion. The blue light flickered and died under the daylight. At long last, the frenzy stopped. The ghosts scowled and sighed with disappointment.

"Now it's useless," a child wailed before kicking a bunch of lilies.

"Relight it! Relight it!" three women sang in soprano.

Ben's eyes widened. The lantern no longer was lit and none of the ghosts were touching it, but he could see the spirits' bodies perfectly.

Excitement filled Ben. He would become a necromancer! He sprinted out of the garden and past several floating spirits. He rushed through the house, sprinted up the stairs and barged into Grandfather's bedroom. The old man was still in bed, snoring loudly.

"Grandfather!" Ben cried, dropping the lantern on the bed. The old man snorted and sat up, grabbing his ruffled beard and crooked nightcap.

"Grandfather, it worked! I can see them!"

"What?" Grandfather grumbled. He wiped his face, paused, and then jumped out of bed. "You can see them?!"

Ben eagerly nodded and pointed. "The one in the window is an old woman with a beehive hairstyle."

"What?!" Grandfather turned around, gasped, and quickly closed the curtains. He tossed aside his nightcap. Ben's smile sank as the old man snapped. "Stop grinning like a fool! Go put away the lantern, you'll be using it again tonight. Make sure to your tasks before your rest."

"What?"

"Bah! Do you think gaining the spectral sight is that easy? The gate needs to be opened. Now off with you!" He waved his hand and flung himself back down onto the comfortable folds of his blankets. "Shoo, shoo!" Grandfather moaned, waving his hand for the apprentice to leave before unleashing a heavy snore.

Ben scooped up the lantern and scrambled out of the bedroom. He closed the door behind him and a heavy breath left his chest, leaving behind a sullen emptiness. He had hoped just maybe his success would allow him a smidgen of pride, but instead his hopes had been squandered. So the lantern did not work? But he could see the spirits clearly!

Exhaustion trickled back into Ben's system as the excitement of seeing spirits died. He returned the lantern to the study, eyes lingering on the tall shelf of study material before heading outside. Like the past few days, there was not a cloud in the sky. But a great fog had overwhelmed the graveyard, making it nearly impossible to see the trees' canopies.

He shivered, watching them run through him and through anything else in their path. He then shivered when he noticed a group of about fifteen ghosts were floating around him, following him. What did Grandfather mean? How was this not a success?!

The spirits could tell something had changed and floated around Ben waving their hands, waggling their rears, and making a mockery of faces in front of Ben's.

Before Ben got halfway through the graveyard, he turned and yelled, "Stop it!"

"*Stop what?*" Five asked in unison.

"*I told you! He can see us!*" A man with a curled mustache bellowed.

"*Oh no! I didn't fix my hair!*" a ghost that appeared around Ben's age cried.

"*You can't fix your hair, sweetie. You're dead,*" the plump female spirit replied.

Ben gawked at the group. He recognized all of their voices. These were the ones he heard most often. He never thought they would actually be stalking him! "Stop following me," Ben whispered, his words holding no effect.

"Our Benny is growing up!" two women cooed.

Ben shivered with disgust and looked away from the spirits. He closed his bloodshot eyes and cursed under his breath before descending the stairs and opening the gate. At the gate, they were louder than ever. As he ascended the hill, their voices grew in volume and excitement.

Spirits swirled at the corners of his eyes between the trees, and their voices flowed in and out like a multitude of radio stations being played all at once. The cacophony had never been so loud, and it pierced into his mind, causing him to feel ill.

As Ben reached the top of the stairs, a ghost popped his head through Ben's chest, showing off a big goofy grin. "Cut that out!" Ben yelled, swatting the spirit away.

"HA HA HA!" a myriad of voices rang.

The apprentice kicked the nearest tombstone in front of him. A crowd of spirits gasped in shock, but Ben was already halfway back to the house. He swatted at the spirits in front of him like flies and charged back inside, slamming the front door behind him. From the living room windows, he watched a crowd of confused and hurt faces, and he sharply drew the curtains shut.

As his anger slowly ebbed away, Ben peered through the curtains. Not a single sign hinted that the Hill was haunted. The apprentice wished Grandfather would be wrong just once.

Four

The Subject of Sight

Ben tried to eat lunch, but his appetite could not be satiated as his attention focused solely on the Hill's residents. Through the window, he watched a horde of ghosts occupying the Hill, meandering about and basking under the brilliant summer heat. And then slowly, and with great agony, he watched them disappear. It started with the fine details. Facial features washed away into orbs of pale light. Their limbs morphed from hands hosting fingers and dangling toes into ethereal whisps dancing like sheets in the wind. Then their bodies fully dissipated into a fog, and that too, drifted away.

Ben sighed and dropped his sandwich as the last hints of the hauntings disappeared from his sight.

"It is a temporary curse, Benjamin. It has everything to do with the potency of the lantern's energy. If you continue this training, eventually it may stick," Grandfather tried to explain.

Ben tilted his jaw and looked at his grandfather. He was certainly trying to improve Ben's sight, but Ben had a feeling it was all for nothing. Grandfather only helped him now because Withertomb had exposed the Stone family secret. There was no rightful heir to the Gravekeeper title. "How long is this going to take?" Ben pled.

"It should have taken only three days with your amount of exposure. Perhaps another week?" Grandfather did not look hopeful as his face bore a deep grimace. If Grandfather thought the exposure therapy would work by now, and it hadn't, there was no chance it would work in a week.

Ben dropped his head on the dining table. What was even the point?

An ordinary person would gain the ability to easily spot spirits after such horrific and constant encounters with the Hill's residents over the past few nights. Given the Hill was full of spirits, Ben already naturally had a great deal of exposure to the dead. Spirits transformed into an indiscernible fog for no other reason than him being completely inept!

"It's always so foggy when I do see them. Why is there so much fog?" Ben mumbled against the table's wooden surface, "What's the point of seeing nothing but fog?"

"Benjamin." Grandfather's expression darkened.

"What? Is that bad?" Ben asked.

Grandfather looked aside and sighed causing Ben's stomach to twist. "Seeing fog after using the lantern is not very promising. It may be tied to your lack of ability to see spirits along with the sheer number of spirits on the Hill. Perhaps it is overstimulating... but I think not."

"Wonderful," Ben groaned. According to Grandfather, his ability to see spirits was only based on the exposure of the dead in the moment, and hardly anything the lantern did would have a lasting impact.

Ben prodded at the remainder of his food with unease. He held onto the hope Grandfather wanted him to be the Gravekeeper just as badly as he did, but that hope was fading away like the spirits at noon. He wondered if Grandfather was trying to help him or if he was just passing time while searching for an alternate heir. If he could never see spirits, he was just wasting Grandfather's time.

Giving up on the idea of naturally seeing spirits, Ben brought up a forbidden topic with a spark of hope. "Isn't there another way? Can't I just wear the spectral specters?"

Grandfather scoffed. "What happens when your glasses break or when you have no light? You cannot see spirits in the dark with the glasses. Some spirits do not appear through their lenses. They are trinkets for amateurs and for ordinary folk to communicate with the dead."

"Wouldn't it help my vision?"

"It is not just about vision. It is about feeling their presence, seeing their very essence, and knowing when they are there when they do not wish to be seen. What you need is a higher exposure to the dead," Grandfather grumbled as he poured himself a cup of tea. "It might knock some sense into you if nothing else."

"W-what if I have no ability to see spirits... at all?" Ben asked, voice cracking.

Grandfather set the tea pot down with a sharp *clack*. He glared at Ben harshly, forcing the boy to look back down at his half eaten meal.

Ben doubted Grandfather was right. He had lived amongst the undead his whole life. How much more could he be exposed to ghosts? Over the years, he had researched on what could be done about his sight, and there were few solutions available. Being a necromancer was never a career choice for the average person. It was all about lineage or severe circumstances. Without inheriting the ability to see spirits, Ben knew his calling was not that of a necromancer. No one ever *learned* how to see spirits.

His only true option was to wear the spectral specters. But to Grandfather, they were the equivalence of giving up. His only other alternative would be to transform into some form of undead- this was not an option!

If he were undead, he'd be able to clearly see the ghosts. It was not uncommon for necromancer families to have a few undead family members lurking around. Usually, they were in the thrall-like form of zombies, but those family members could never become necromancers. Only liches maintained control of their necromantic abilities and could still be considered undead. Life would be better if Ben were just allowed to wear the darn glasses!

"Can't I focus on learning summoning? Perhaps if I used magic, it would awaken the inner eye?" Ben inquired in a fervor of desperation.

Grandfather rose a thick eyebrow, revealing the light of one of his golden eyes. "You think you can summon when you can't see what you are summoning?"

"I know all of the steps and all of the creatures! I am sure I could do it. I can summon something not ethereal like a ghoul or animate a skeleton. What if I practiced conjuring and dispelling revenants?!"

SMACK!

Grandfather's hand slammed against the table. He leaned over the table and spoke with a cold, low voice, "Do you know what happens to those who summon revenants and ghouls unprepared? They will shred you apart and eat you at best. It is impossible! You cannot contract with such beings. What would you gain from entertaining such thoughts?"

Ben bit his lip. "I can practice summoning them and sending them back. I never said I would attempt to contract with them."

"You cannot just send such creatures back. Without summoning and contracting with a familiar first, you will never be able to do such a summons safely. Listen, Benjamin. A necromancer is powerless without a contract. Do not ever believe you have power over any creature that is not bound to your soul."

Ben looked away and muttered, "Other necromancers have done it."

"Our family bloodline is not *other* necromancers. We are Gravekeepers. In order to be one, you must be able to fully support the Hill's residents." Grandfather stood and picked up his dishes. "Another week should do you good. If that doesn't work, I have another lesson prepared."

Ben already knew there was nothing else to do. Another week would not make any difference other than increase the risk of Ben breaking a bone. At this rate, the ghosts had a good method of throwing Ben around in the air, and he doubted his body could handle much more of their violence.

Ben wondered if there was something he could do differently without relying upon Grandfather's guidance. Maybe he could get magic flowing through his veins, maybe he could awaken what was missing? A subtle feeling deep inside him faded whenever he lost his vision. It was that thing he needed to hold onto, and using magic just might give him the ability to grasp onto it harder.

Otherwise, Ben would have to settle for wearing a pair of spectacles for the rest of his life.

Five

Summonings

That evening, Ben went into Grandfather's study to grab the lantern. Grandfather was already asleep, and he had entrusted Ben to take the lantern to the garden and light it himself. Ben picked up the lantern along with a box of matches and walked towards the door. He paused at the threshold, looking back at the unoccupied study. Was another night of torment worth it? Was this really the answer?

He set the lantern back on the desk and closed the study door softly. He locked the bolt just in case Mely came snooping around. Why waste his time being tormented by the Hill's residents? If time was a sensitive matter, it would be better spent learning how to use the ability to see spirits, not just how to see them.

Ben looked at the stacks of scrolls, his heart racing. They were all contracts belonging to the Stone family. The perk of boasting the lineage of an old necromancer family was the endless amount of contracts he had inherited. The contracts signed by his great great grandfather's blood were also bound to him. He gritted his teeth imagining someone else inheriting such precious documents. These were the sources of power the Stone family Grandfather always highlighted. An unfathomable power available to Ben if only Grandfather granted him permission to summon the spirits. But Grandfather was asleep upstairs. Nothing was stopping him from tapping into that legacy now.

Ben snooped around, tapping at scrolls and prodding at

tomes. He scooped up a pyramid of old scrolls from a bookshelf and allowed them to tumble upon Grandfather's desk in a heap. A cloud of dust plumed into his face. The apprentice recoiled and turned away in a coughing fit.

Face burning and eyes stinging, Ben wiped his nose and turned back to the stack of scrolls. He picked up a brittle yellowed roll of parchment and unfurled it. Ink covered the inside of the page with only hints of exposed, yellowing paper webbing at the edges. There were no words clearly legible to Ben, marking this document as an unordinary contract. Perhaps it was created by the dead, or maybe it was something Grandfather had acquired during his trips. Maybe it was not even a contract at all. Ben gulped and rolled it back up, careful not to touch the ink. It was best not to mess with such a thing.

The next scroll was indeed a classic, ordinary contract. It could have originated from one of Ben's many textbooks. A date marked the top right corner- *1732*- over two hundred years ago. The contract hosted three simple clauses and two signatures on the bottom. One of the signatures was written neatly in cursive with tight loops and a slightly right-angled font, belonging to Ben's relative Edward E. Stone. The other signature was something far more jagged and sporadic as if it took effort to sign. *Elaine.*

The letters mimicked the scribble of an elementary student, growing and shrinking in thickness and careening atop each other. Most likely, it belonged to a poltergeist, Ben noted. Contracts rarely directly said the creatures they were being contracted with, but the dead's signatures always gave them away. Every type of undead had certain characteristics in their signatures and markings. Beasts had hoof marks, claw marks, splatters of substances. Spirits had signatures written in ectoplasm that reflected their signatures when they were alive. The more peaceful the spirit, the more natural the signature. Other undead, the kind Ben would not dare summon, had more volatile signatures and eventually some resembled the markings of beasts or things that could only be described as monsters. Some scrolls oozed shadows, hosted dripping blood splatters, and sometimes contracts were in forms that could not be written on paper but were instead felt or heard or needed to be poured in a bottle.

A poltergeist would be the perfect spirit for Ben to summon. They were powerful but also simple and strongly maintained their sense of self. He furled up the scroll and tucked it into his inner coat pocket. He then began a search for summoning supplies.

Despite the subjective tidiness of the study, nothing was organized. Every shelf had books from different eras and varied on subjects. Behind books were trinkets, between books were skulls and stranger artifacts. Grandfather's desk drawers contained a plethora of trinkets and baubles ranging from coins to knives, keys, and greasy pastry wrappers. Ben held up one of the wrappers and sneered, allowing it to fall back into the large base drawer of the desk. It fluttered and dipped, changing course midair and falling on a rather deep wooden chest aside the desk before slipping over its curved lid and landing upon the floor.

Ben reluctantly picked up the wrapper between the tips of his thumb and pinky while he examined the wooden chest. It was so dull, he never imagined it would have anything of value, but just perhaps it had what the apprentice needed.

He tossed the wrapper back into the desk drawer and approached the chest. He lifted the heavy wooden lid while sucking in a deep breath. The trunk revealed a plethora of summoning supplies: candles, rolls of blank parchment, match boxes, a bag of salt, iron chains, silver dust, chalk, a few knives by the looks of it, some jewelry, and a few small jars of disturbing things suspended in formaldehyde. He doubted Grandfather would notice if a few of the simpler items went missing. He gathered in a bag what he needed to summon the poltergeist, snatched the lantern, and left the study.

By the time Ben stepped outside, the moon lit the sky with a pearlescent light. Ben knew he needed to endure fighting the Hill's residents just long enough to develop a sense to see to safely summon the poltergeist. Grandfather was not awake to stop him, but Ben knew his advice was not just hot air. If he were aware of Ben's plans, he would stop him immediately. To ensure Grandfather would not stop him, he had no intention of letting him know about the change in his lesson plan.

He arrived at the garden's fountain and set the bag of supplies at the foot of the fountain on top of a small patch of weeds. He then pulled out a match and reluctantly lit the lantern.

The wick flared a brilliant orange for a second before turning into a chilling blue. The tiny flame's transformation came with the sound of anxious voices. The spirits had been plotting how they would take the lantern from Ben all day, and just like the previous night and the night before that, they were certain of their success.

But Ben also had a plan after a week of torment. He stepped into the fountain. The water went up to just below his knees, soaking his pants and making his shoes weigh down like two bricks. He plodded towards the statue and wrapped his arms around it, holding on for dear life. The spirits all were watching as he did this strange act, but soon he felt their cold touch and knew they had decided to wait no longer.

The lantern hooked around Ben's elbow jerked back and forth like a bell ringing in a maelstrom. His grip on the fountain's statue tightened as the ghosts furiously tried to pull the lantern away.

"He won't budge!"

"He will tire eventually!"

Ben clenched his teeth and held onto the fountain for sheer life. So long as he was able to stay still, the spirits had no means to throw him around and successfully steal the lantern.

However, the icy water paired with the chill of the ghosts, causing Ben to shiver and feel an unbearable wave of cold envelop him. He could withstand the tugging of the lantern, but how long could he ignore the numbness in his legs and toes?

A couple of hours passed with Ben holding onto the statue for dear life. At some point, he could see foggy figures with swirling faces and wispy tails reaching out to snatch the lantern. It was surely faint and would not last until noon, but it was enough sight for now. He released the fountain hoping to blow out the lantern's light

A spirit spoke with a sly, soothing voice. *"Give us the lantern and we won't tell about your collection there, Benny boy."*

Ben's eyes darted to the pile of summoning supplies and panic rose in his chest. A spirit yanked the lantern, knocking Ben backwards and into the shallow pool of freezing water.

Ben tried to pull the lantern with him into the water, but enough spirits held onto it, keeping the flame safe from being snuffed out. Another force shoved his shoulders beneath the surface. The spirits were becoming so agitated their manifestations were strong enough to touch him. A ghastly hand with gnarled fingers grabbed his face and pressed his head underwater. He spluttered and gasped as several hands grabbed the arm holding the lantern.

The ghosts continued to push Ben's head and torso underwater. He tried kicking at the ghosts, but there were too many of them. Ben's lungs screamed in agony as a foggy hand pressed on his face, forcing his head beneath the surface. With the last of his strength, he gave up on resurfacing and grabbed the lantern with both hands and pulled it into the fountain.

The pale blue light vanished. The phantom frenzy ceased.

Ben's head broke the surface, and he gasped for air. He clambered out of the freezing fountain, cradling the cursed lantern and glaring at the ghosts. The group of spirits drifted around him in a state of dismay and confusion. Some were pouting, others were cursing, but a few just hung their heads and slumped their shoulders, aimlessly drifting around in defeat.

They were not as clear as Ben normally could see them by the end of the night, but his spectral sight was good enough. He could see the spirits but without details, hinting at only a couple of hours of sight.

This would be enough sight to conjure the poltergeist. Whilst shivering, Ben grabbed his bag and trudged through the gardens. Each step squelched with the sound of water and crunching gravel under his soaked dress shoes. Ben could not feel his feet, and as he arrived at the rotunda, he kicked off his shoes and socks to possibly save his toes from freezing.

The apprentice made quick work of setting up the summoning circle, fearing the passing of time.

"I'll tell Ernest everything," a ghost whispered as it watched Ben organize his supplies.

Ben looked over his shoulder at a small crowd of disgruntled onlookers. "Don't you want me to be your Gravekeeper?" Ben asked.

"Pah!"

"Not really..."

A sharp pain pranged Ben's heart at the betrayal, but the

Hill's residents were never so kind anyway. He groaned in frustration. What would he do with them? Ben scraped his mind for a solution, and then a brilliant idea came to mind. He stood and faced the onlooking spirits. Ben lifted the lantern and dangled it before them.

"If you stay quiet, I will hand this over to you. If you tell Grandfather, you will never get your hands on this."

If ghosts could breathe, they all would have stopped. Their eyes bugged out and their mouths hung open with thirsty anticipation. Ben smirked and set the lantern down before continuing to organize his items and thoughts. That would certainly keep the spirits silent.

Ben laid out a ring of candles around the rotunda, adjusting them again and again to ensure a perfect circle. Some necromancers used large compasses, but Ben could only rely on the pavilion's round roof for guidance. He sprinkled a ring of salt just inside the candles and drew as quickly as he could. He had drawn a standard summoning circle on paper hundreds of times, but drawing it in full scale with chalk on wooden boards was something different entirely.

Once the circle was complete, Ben set the bag of salt aside and picked up the knife. The leather handle was worn and well used, comfortably fitting in Ben's grasp. His fingers tightened, knowing what would be required of him. The true source of a necromancer's magic.

The apprentice lifted the poltergeist contract, placing it near one of the lit candles, and quickly read it. Summoning with a contract was far safer than without. He already knew the spirit, and the spirit was already bound to honor its word with the Stone family. He was at no risk of danger even if the circle was messed up or if Ben stumbled over his own words. It would be a test to see if he could summon anything at all before diving into the discovery of the unknown.

If he were to conjure a spirit without a contract, he would have had to recite a chant for the specific undead he desired, draw a specific circle, and present a particular offering depending on the type of undead. With a contract, all he had to do was present his blood in the middle of the basic summoning circle and read off the contract. There was no chance of failure.

Ben walked into the center of the circle and pulled back his sleeve. It was still soaking wet, making his arm clammy. He brought out the knife and looked away as he sliced the side of his wrist. A stinging sensation went across his wrist as the blade nicked into his skin. Blood dripped on the circle. He took several steps back until he was out of the circle, opened the contract and read it out as loud and clear as he could in the dim, flickering candlelight.

He knew he fumbled on a few words. Once he finished, he breathed a heavy shaky breath and raised the knife. Its blade glinted in the candlelight, and through the reflection, Ben spotted the pale light of the Hill's residents watching him from a guarded distance. He sighed and lowered the blade, focusing on the circle before him and the task at hand. Despite his determination, the boy winced as the blade sliced his palm. Blood streamed down his hand, dripping onto the circle. Following one breath shakier than the last, he finished reading the contract.

The air drew colder. So cold, it felt like the middle of winter. Fog left Ben's lips, and his body shivered as if he were encrusted in ice. All the hairs on the back of his neck stood. An icy wind swirled around him.

"Elaine!" Ben yelled, finishing the summons. The wind stopped dead. In the middle of the circle a rather typical ghost hovered. He gasped and wiped sweat off his forehead. It was a success!

The spirit's arms were a little wispy, and her legs were hidden in the folds of her skirts that faded in the air like a watercolor painting. The wind had stopped, but her hair and skirts still ruffled and flowed as if she were in the torrent of a tornado yet frozen in time. Ben could not see the details of her face, but her energy was so strong he could see her better than the Hill's onlooking ghosts.

The poltergeist tilted her head. *"Stone... You are younger."*

"I am Benjamin Stone, inheritor of this contract," Ben boasted, unable to hide the pride in his voice. She was the first spirit he had ever summoned, and it was a success! He could not believe it as he stared at the poltergeist. She looked just like all the other hill residents, but signs of her uniqueness made it clear she was a poltergeist. A cold wind filled with inherent power radiated from her being. A true success.

"Why have you called?" She asked.

Ben bit on his lip, holding back his excitement. He did not want to be rude to the spirit. "Please tell me if there are any flaws with the summoning circle."

Elaine curiously tilted her head but gave no complaint. She drifted about within the circle, her head cocked forty five degrees as she studied the chalk drawings and the salt ring. The spirit froze on the opposite end, facing away from Ben.

"This is... off. The circle is subsiding," the poltergeist calmly explained, pointing her hand at the ground. Ben could just barely see her pointer finger, but he could feel her energy focused on the chalk drawing. Ben gulped and felt his mouth go dry as he saw his footprints mar the chalk. His clothes were wet, and the water had dripped onto the circle, damaging its integrity.

"Your circle still holds. I cannot go elsewhere... this is not necessary." Ben nodded. He did not need to summon the

contracted spirit with a circle, but this guaranteed he could do so with another spirit safely.

"So I can't tell you to go over there?" Ben pointed to a bunch of hedges to his left.

"No. I cannot."

"A-anything else?" Ben asked. Soft purple rays of the morning sun were clawing their way over the hedge line.

The spirit shook her head and drifted back towards the center. She was slow and elegant despite the torrent that tormented her. If Ben were to meet a poltergeist in any other conditions, it would be the opposite situation. She would be a maelstrom itself. The poltergeist shook her head.

"Thank you for your help, Elaine." Ben rolled the contract up. "Until next time. Farewell." Elaine gave another nod as her body dissipated like snow being blown away in the stray breeze of an ice storm.

Ben walked over to the damaged circle and studied it more closely. He had also drawn a symbol wrong, and a candle was out of place. Thankfully, everything was correct enough that the summons was a success, but Ben doubted he would have been safe summoning a poltergeist without an existing contract. It could have easily broken through the flawed ring and wreaked havoc upon Ben.

The apprentice did not waste any time cleaning up. He pulled off his sopping wet jacket and brushed away the chalk and salt. He picked up the candles, blowing out each succinctly and stuffing them into a makeshift sack from his ruined jacket. Ben jumped off the rotunda and grabbed the rest of the supplies. He considered running them back to Grandfather's study, but it was clear the bag of salt was rather empty, and the chalk and candles were worn down. He instead shoved the sack of summoning supplies under a rose bush. Grandfather never tended to the garden, so he would never notice the pile.

As streaks of salmon and crimson hues painted the sky, Ben ran out of the garden, lantern in hand, feeling more awake than he had in months. He finally summoned a spirit. An actual spirit!

Six

The Revenant

When the sun rose and Grandfather came outside to check on Ben's progress, Ben's mind was entirely focused on his successful summons. He could not help but grin from ear to ear. He had summoned a poltergeist! It was proof he had enough magical potential to be a necromancer even if he could not see ghosts. Not everyone could summon a poltergeist or have a chat with one. Summoning and dismissing Elaine was undeniably an accomplishment worth celebrating. If only he could tell Grandfather.

As Grandfather took the lantern from Ben, the boy shifted uncomfortably. A sense of guilt flooded him, and he feared somehow Grandfather would know when he touched the lantern that something was different about last night. When he grabbed hold of it, he paused, and Ben's blood froze. Grandfather looked Ben up and down with growing discontent.

"You'll need a new suit," he said, eyeing his grandson's damaged attire. Ben's pant legs and jacket sleeves were torn, revealing fresh scrapes covering him from head to toe.

Ben exhaled and nodded with a smile.

"What are you grinning about?" Grandfather asked, eyes narrowed.

Ben went rigid and his grin flattened. "I- I can see them," he said, looking aside at a group of ghosts smirking with knowing, threatening gazes. Ben glared at the spirits, daring them to snitch on him, while Grandfather sighed, shaking his head.

"Enough nonsense. Go wash up."

As Ben trotted back to the house, his grin returned. Grandfather did not suspect a thing!

Ben knew Grandfather would learn about his summons eventually, and he wanted so desperately to tell him now. But summoning the poltergeist with a contract was not enough to prove he could be a necromancer. If he wanted to prove he could be a necromancer, he had to do so before Grandfather moved on to another method to *develop* his sight. Who was to say the next lesson would be a successful one or if there would be another lesson at all?

Ben also feared he would not have such easy access to Grandfather's study for long. It was now or never.

That evening, Ben fished out several contracts from Grandfather's study along with more summoning supplies. He was careful to hide the contracts in his room within the stacks of books. He then took the bag of summoning supplies into the garden and stowed it under the rotunda, between its lattice base and the rose bushes.

Through the following nights, Ben attempted summoning multiple contracted spirits. It was not hard to procure spiritual entities with the contracts, but it was easy to make mistakes. Ben realized with each night's results how desperately he needed more time to practice, and he wished for Grandfather's guidance.

The days passed swiftly. Ben spent the mornings tending the graves, slept through the middle of the days up until dinner, allowing for just enough time to review the type of summons he would perform that evening from the books he had robbed from the advanced study material shelf. He then proceeded with

Grandfather's training just until he was able to see spirits before shifting his focus to his personal agenda.

By the sixth night, Ben felt confident enough to attempt to create his own contract. Or rather, he knew he had to be ready. There was a high chance Grandfather would witness the last evening of him fending off the ghosts from the lantern, and Ben doubted he would be so lucky as to sneak one more attempt at summoning. He needed any spare time to hide away the materials and make it look as if he had never performed a single summons.

Even if Ben did have the chance to summon another spirit in the following days, he woefully realized he would not be able to. The results of every evening's fight with the Hill's residents always led to Ben's ability to see spirits. Yet, Ben noticed he could never see them so clearly compared to the first night. And with each passing day, his vision faded faster, leaving him blind before midday or mid-morning. The lantern's trick was quickly expiring.

He had to make the contract tonight.

+**X**+

As dusk arrived, Grandfather met Ben at the garden fountain. The boy was firmly holding the lantern in both hands, looking at Grandfather with a determined gaze despite the number of bruises that made his face swell.

"This shall be the last night with the will-o-wisp lantern," Grandfather said softly as he took the lantern from Ben's hands. Concern covered his face as he looked over Ben's fresh welts and wounds.

Ben's heart skipped a beat. "Why? I can continue this for

another day!"

"No, Benjamin. You have learned enough about how to handle fighting a horde of spirits and the dangers an object like this can create. I fear this is not a solution for your sight, and that is more concerning than anything else."

Ben looked aside, grimacing, but he could not help but feel relieved for already having planned to perform the summons tonight. Just a single evening's delay and he would have lost his chance.

"I learned a lot," Ben said. "This wasn't a waste."

Grandfather nodded, patting Ben on the shoulder. The boy winced and Grandfather jerkily retracted his hand, concerned for the apprentice's wellbeing. "No, this was not a wasted effort, Benjamin. I have another lesson for you tomorrow. Every necromancer should know how to heal themselves from mortal or menial wounds. I will teach you the basics tomorrow even if you may not be able to perform the spells yet."

Ben's heart skipped a beat, and he nearly tossed aside his plans to summon. Grandfather was going to teach him spells?! And healing magic on top of that! He could not hide the glimmer in his eyes or withhold a smile, until a look of pity traced its way across Grandfather's face, setting him back in his place.

Ben withdrew his emotions and looked down. Of course, the only reason Grandfather cared to teach him was out of pity.

"Yes, Grandfather."

Grandfather gave Ben a long look over before lighting the lantern. Without another word, he handed Ben the lantern and walked away, looking back only once just as Ben began his flight from the horde of spirits.

Ben ran as quickly as he could towards the rotunda, but he

could not outrun the horde of the Hill's ghosts. Icy hands pulled on his sleeves and pant legs, and spirits flew around him, acting like torrents of arctic winds. Ben stumbled as he ran to the rotunda, struggling to fight against the Hill's spirits after several nights of torment.

He made it into the clearing with the pavilion just as a couple of spirits managed to catch his ankles and flip him in the air. The boy summersaulted, cradling the lantern to his chest. His back smacked the wooden stairs, knocking the wind out of his lungs. He stared up at the starry sky in a daze. Ursa Major was spinning.

A white aura wafted through the sky, and Ben curled up in a ball, wishing for just enough exposure to see the spirits but the exposure only came at the cost of hours of torment.

The Hill's ghosts screamed in Ben's ears, howling and laughing and screeching like banshees. A multitude of hands clawed at Ben from every direction, yanking on his clothes, grabbing his face, smothering his mouth. The apprentice forced himself to stay still and hold onto the lantern for sheer life, knowing if he reacted in any way to the spirits, they would only see it as weakness.

Several hands pulled on Ben from under the rotunda stairs. The boy hurriedly scrambled to his feet, only to be heaved in the air and dropped on the ground.

The boy fell to his feet, witnessing the ghastly faces of the frenzied spirits surrounding him. His golden eyes widened, and he reached his hand around the blue flame.

"NOOOOO," the spirits wailed as Ben snuffed the lantern's flame. Their arms reached for him, but the lantern's effect was gone. Their hands slipped through Ben harmlessly like gentle breezes. The spirits drifted around Ben confused and frustrated.

"So close, so close," one of the ghosts moaned, grabbing her

face and looking to the sky.

"*Next time,*" another wailed.

"I'm afraid this is the last time," Ben said as he set the lantern beside the rotunda and wiped blood from a busted lip. He crouched down and pulled out the supplies needed for his final summons. He sorted the supplies into piles, tapping and counting each needed candle while listening to an uproar of complaints. "Surely you heard Grandfather."

"*Bah!*"

"*You promised to give us the lantern!*" another spirit cried followed by an encore of protest.

Ben stood, shining a flashlight on the ghosts, causing their ethereal figures to vanish in the light. "Figure out who deserves the lantern for the evening, and it is all yours." He turned to scoop up an armful of candles and set up his summoning circle, listening to the uproar of debate with a smirk.

Facing the rotunda, Ben's smirk was replaced by a stern frown and knit brows. Unlike the previous summons, this one would harbor the greatest risk. If he failed to perform properly, anything could happen. Despite everything he studied, reading could never fully prepare him for practicing in the field, and every contract he summoned previously could not prepare him for a random summons. Summoning a spirit without an explicit contract was like a raffle. He could aim to summon a specific type of spirit, but he would never know its temperament or strength, and if he made a mistake, he could not predict what would come through the circle or if it would stay.

The looming accomplishment of creating a spirit contract and showing it to Grandfather as proof of his abilities was enough for Ben to accept the risks. As Ben gulped down his fears and forced himself to step onto the rotunda's platform, he hoped his preparations would serve him well.

Drops of dried wax and stubborn dashes of chalk reminded Ben where to place his candles. He set them down in the centers of thick rings of wax. He paced around, rubbing his chin, as he paused to study his placements. He meticulously adjusted a few candles, circled around again, and adjusted them once again back into their original positions. He waved the flashlight about, casting long shadows into the rose bushes and causing the surrounding spirits' forms to shift and fade. This time, everything had to be perfect.

Once Ben was certain the candles were in their correct places, he pulled out a thick piece of chalk and began drawing. The apprentice created little circles around each candle and connected them, looping large, smooth arcs that intertwined with small rings. If he were not working in secret, he could have used Grandfather's massive protractor to make perfect circles, but he had to rely on the curvature of the flashlight's light as a guide.

Ben continued, analyzing the chalk rings until he was dizzy. The boy stepped back, breathed, and examined the whole of his work. Pride filled his chest.

This was by far the best summoning sigil he had drawn yet. The exterior circle was naturally round and thick to guarantee no breakage. Then there were three inner circles, looping together and encased by one final inner circle with a thin ring of chalk. Each were drawn with strong, smooth strokes, bearing the confidence a necromancer must have. The binding text of the empty contract Ben had forged weaved itself along the curving lines, integrating words and runes. It was not just a conjuring circle. It was a work of art!

The finishing touch, Ben moved around the outer boundary, hands gently shaking out a carton of salt. The salt line was a final line of defense if something went horribly wrong. No spirit could cross such a barrier. Once the sigil was complete, Ben set the carton aside in his bag of supplies. Crouching, he gazed over the circle and breathed in a steady breath of satisfaction. It was time.

Ben pulled a crinkled sheet of folded parchment from his inner coat pocket. It was a special parchment made from paper and ectoplasm, and with his newfound sight, he could see a faint ethereal energy emanating from the sheet. Sighing, his fingers fumbled with the page as he unfurled it and raised the document to his face.

Directing the flashlight over the page, he read the glistening ink several times, whispering fractions of the contract's terms under his breath until he felt ready to take the summons to the next stage.

He out a handful of matches and paced around the circle, carefully lighting each candle. When he returned to the front of the sigil, he crouched down near the stairs, at the head of the conjuring circle, and laid the contract down at his feet just on the inside of the barrier. His hand trembled as he released the document and stepped back, observing the whole of his work in the dancing candlelight and feeling a cold shift in the air as the surrounding spirits watched with quiet anticipation.

Ben breathed and unsheathed an obsidian knife. He winced as he pushed up his jacket sleeve, revealing several scabbed and bandaged wounds. Purple and blue with bruises from the constant battles for the lantern blotted his arm. The thin cuts from the summonings did not aid his recovery either. Each cut hardly had healed, making his arm look worse for wear. When the sleeve cuffed around his elbow, Ben winced from where the lantern had consistently been yanked against the crux of his elbow. There was not a single spot of undamaged flesh on his arms, but this was the path of a necromancer.

Ben's teeth clenched as he sliced his arm over an existing

wound. He froze, cringing from the stinging pain. He sucked in a sharp breath and blinked back fresh tears stinging the corners of his eyes. This was nothing compared to the pain of being abandoned.

Around the circle he walked, dripping his blood in one massive ring from the tip of the blade. Ben tiptoed within the outer barrier, careful to not step on anything, and allowed a shallow pool to form at the center before he wrapped a tight bandage around his forearm and painfully pulled down his sleeve, concealing the fresh wound.

He then stepped behind the contract and announced the summons from memory. He continued chanting for what felt like an hour. His voice wavered slightly as he could not help but shiver, but Ben managed to not stutter or garble his words. When he finished, he stood in silence and waited. He started to doubt if anything would show. Perhaps he was only capable of summoning spirits already tied to contracts? If that were true, he had no magical abilities or talent to speak of. This would be the end of his apprenticeship.

Fwoosh.

The faintest glimmer of hope. A candle in the right corner furthest from Ben blew out, producing only a shaky stream of smoke.

Then another, opposite the first, flickered out. Then the candle next to Ben on his right! Ben's heart raced while he scraped his mind over what was happening. The candles going out was textbook for an ill omen. Some books argued necromancers typically wanted such signs, but Ben could not help but feel uneasy. He did not have the experience to know which source to trust! He shuddered and lowered his voice, wondering if the summons had been a fluke.

Ben shivered and ducked his chin, looking down at the

contract. Perhaps it was best to stop before something unpleasant appeared.

The air drew cold. Colder than a midwinter gust. It was too late for him to change his mind. Something was already coming.

Ben eagerly watched the sigil's center where the entity would appear. What would it be? Another poltergeist? A banshee? Maybe a trickster? The chalk circles became animated and slithered across the ground. *It's reacting to the blood,* Ben anxiously thought, mind racing. Ben wanted to grab a notepad and scrawl down the blood's new forms as it twisted and constricted into a better trap for the arriving spirit. It was the core of his magic and both the lock and key to the summoning circle.

The blood in the center of the circle shuddered and rippled as if something was dripping from within. Time slowed down, the wind halted, and Ben forgot how to breathe as the garden sank into a deep silence except for the subtle, insidious dripping from the central pool of blood.

And there it was, like a gut-wrenching piece of dread incarnate.

A hand sprung out of the pool. It was inhuman. Long bony fingers with sharp black nails that curled and hooked, ready to kill. The flesh was blood red as if stained by the portal through which it came through. It reached upwards until a sharp elbow erupted from the pool. The arm smacked down on the ground, causing another candle flame to sputter and die.

Ben's heart fluttered with terror.

In the shadows, Ben watched another long, gaunt arm reach out of the ground like a fast-growing tree. With the sound of a branch snapping, it twisted back onto the ground at an unhealthy angle. The arms then straightened themselves, snapping and creaking whilst lifting a lowered head and torso.

The apprentice's knees weakened, and his lungs tightened. Tears burned the rims of his eyes.

The skeletal head faced the ground. It was covered in that same elastic thin red flesh. The torso was a skeleton wrapped in the same flesh, exposing enlarged sharp rib bones that stabbed through the visceral matter and somehow resembled the tusks of a monster. Ben's heart raced as the creature finished its ascent and crouched on the inner circle in an inverted fetal position. It kept its head low, and Ben dreaded looking at its eyes. The thing looked like a ghoul, but Ben could slightly see through it. The creature was indeed a spirit, but it was nothing Ben had witnessed on the Hill. It was not a wraith, nor was it a banshee. Ben listed all the spirit types in his head until one type stuck out. Only one spirit looked so inhuman and incomplete. A spirit that created revenants.

A vetala.

Ben crouched down, knees trembling. He carefully pulled out the box of matches and attempted to light the candle nearest to him. His hand shook something violent, causing a couple of matches to die before the boy could ignite the candle's wick. There were three other candles that had gone out, making Ben sweat. He could see a few spirits flying nearby, watching the summoning with equal amounts of terror plastered across their faces. They moved through the air with ill ease, wheezing and breathing heavily despite their lack of need to breathe. The Hill did not host evil spirits. The vetala, albeit an invited arrival, was an unwelcome guest.

Grandfather would be furious if he made a contract with a vetala. It went against everything the Stone family believed in. Such a creature used other corpses and disturbed graveyards, and if it were set loose on the Hill, it would wreak havoc amongst the residents. The parasite of a spirit needed to return to the underworld with no signatures signed. It needed no attachment to the living realm.

Ben looked down at the contract and felt the blood leave his face. He had not written a dismissal on the contract. He had thought once the contract was signed, a dismissal could be formed. Ben looked back at the hulking figure of bones. He did not know of any other way to banish such a creature. He would have to complete the contract to safely dismiss the spirit. Ben withheld a groan.

"I am Benjamin Stone. I have summoned you to create a contract. What is your name?"

Ben held his breath as the creature slowly lifted its head. Its spine creaked and popped as it moved, and its eyes haughtily glared at Ben. They were sunken deep into its skull and black with tiny red lights like gleaming rubies. There was an emptiness to its gaze as if they were full of hunger. This was a creature of nightmares.

"Benjaminnn Stoneeee... I have no name. I have no place."

Ben gulped and scraped his mind on everything he had read. '*Dealing with the Dead 101*' and '*How to communicate with spirits*' were only so helpful. The authors did not discuss evil spirits. But Ben knew enough from Grandfather's rants and lectures when it came to vetalas, ghouls, and revenants that they were not spirits he wanted to *deal* with at all.

"You have a hand, you have a face," Ben said with a grimace, matching the riddle in '*Dealing with the Dead 101*' that was supposed to help in these situations. Riddles and rhyming always helped. "You can see the contract and sign to be bound by my name and my place."

The spirit cocked its head and reached out an arm. It

extended its body and covered half of the circle. A hand reached for the contract and attempted to pick it up, but the contract did not move. The spirit hissed and slinked closer to Ben to address the paper.

The spindly hands were just a foot away from Ben. Long bony claws as sharp as knives grew out of them. Ben gulped and did his best not to take a step backwards. In this setting, he was a necromancer. He could not show fear.

The creature twitched and tapped the contract. *"What do you have to offer?"*

"The opportunity to come to the living realm," Ben said, his gut twisting at his own proposition. The spirit looked disinterested. Unlike another necromancer family, the Stone family valued mutual agreements and respect in their contracts. Ben had to give something to the spirit, not simply demand something from the spirit. His blood was only an agent to the summoning, not a deal maker. He did not have anything to give a vetala. If it were an ordinary ghost, he could offer it closure, offer to tend its grave perhaps, speak to a family member, or summon the spirit in a location that the spirit may experience nostalgia. He could just be nice. But this... There were no niceties with a vetala.

The creature growled from deep within its long skeletal throat. A thin arm slashed towards Ben. Ben instinctively yelped and jumped backwards. The vetala's arm retracted, burning. The creature hissed and stepped back towards the inner circle.

"I will send you back if you refuse. There will be no deal for you!"

"This isss no deal. Grant me freedom. I can smell the death in the air. I taste it." It smiled wickedly. The spirit wanted nothing more than to possess a corpse and wreak havoc on the sleepy town of St. Vincent. It had no intention of signing the contract

and making things simple.

"Then I shall send you back to the netherworld," Ben said through his teeth. He did not have a written down chant, but his words still held weight. This was a negotiation, and even bad negotiations came to conclusions.

"Return to the underworld. Your time in the land of the living has come to an end! Begone!" Ben yelled, feeling energy manifest in his words and desperately watching as the circle moved with their weight. He repeated himself again and again, but they were the wrong words, and the spirit was not crawling back through the circle's center.

It jumped at Ben again, claws reaching to rip off his head. Ben yelped mid chant and stumbled backwards, hitting the backs of his knees on the bench behind him and collapsing. He could hear the vetala growling and hissing in front of him, wanting to strike again. As long as Ben maintained the circle, it would never succeed, but Ben had to finish closing the summons.

"R-return to the underworld. Our negotiation has ended. Be... Be gone!" Ben roared, stumbling over his words. He could see something happening at the base of the circle, but the spirit was fighting it. It thrashed about and jumped at the invisible wall of salt and runes despite the burns that seared into its ethereal flesh.

Ben chanted louder. He picked different phrases typically used to dispel a summons. Something had to work. He just needed to know what! The spirit continued to fight until it suddenly faded like smoke dissipating in the wind. Ben shuddered as beads of cold sweat rolled down his forehead. Was it truly gone? Half the candles were no longer lit, but surely the barrier still held. He regretted summoning the spirit. He did not mean to do something so dangerous. How was he supposed to know such a horrid entity would appear with his first true summons?

The apprentice reached for the contract when his ears prickled to the sound of a low snarl. He barely had time to react. A clawed hand ripped his sleeve to ribbons, scraping over bandages and tearing into his already injured flesh. He cried and retracted his arm, tumbling away from the circle.

The spirit growled again with a hint of laughter in its voice. Ben did not spend enough time with the lantern, and his vision had faded too soon. Now he was facing a violent spirit he could not see and had no means of returning to the netherworld.

Ben scrambled to his feet as best as he could. He tightly held his injured arm, feeling hot blood soak through his shredded sleeve and trickle down to his hand. He could not feel his hand at all. The apprentice looked around with wide eyes, heart racing with terror.

Where was the spirit? He heard terrified whispers. All of the Hill's ghosts watching knew the situation had turned sour. "Someone go get Grandfather!" Ben yelled.

"We can't. He won't hear us inside the house," one of the spirits moaned.

Ben groaned. They were not wrong. If he wanted Grandfather to come, he would have to wait until it was long past dawn and the necromancer came outside. By then, Ben would be out of energy, have bled too much, and the spirit would have either broken through the circle and escaped, killed Ben, or both.

"Find Mely and tell her to get Grandfather!" Ben cried.

The spirits spoke amongst themselves and then went silent. Ben trembled and decided it was best to just keep chanting the vetala away for the time being. It would hold it off if nothing else! He still sensed its presence through a strange red fog that made the air ripple like a wave of heat. A sinister laugh as soft as a whisper, as deadly as a viper, penetrated the quiet. He had to dispel this fiend.

After what felt like hours, with Ben having no success, a spirit returned and cried, *"We can't find her! She may be in the house!"*

Despair filled Ben's chest, making his chanting falter. His heart fluttered weakly as his mind failed to produce a solution. If the circle broke, the vetala would kill him with vengeance and probably possess his corpse. Or any corpse in the graveyard. No matter what, the outlook was bleak.

Ben looked down the garden's gravel path towards the house. He had never heard of a necromancer leaving their summoning circle with a spirit inside, but there was a possibility it would have to happen. His blood still maintained the barrier. The salt would hold the vetala at bay. The circle was still intact.

But everything Ben had read dictated against it. The circle required him to be present as the summoner. With him gone, the negotiation would be considered complete, and the spirit still not dismissed would no longer be held by the negotiation. His only true options were to get the spirit to sign- which obviously was not going to happen- or send it back. Neither were possible.

He closed his eyes and breathed in and out in a mantra. He was shivering, his head was heavy, and pain ripped through his arm in wobbly waves. He continued to breathe in and out in and in again and then out until he was calm enough to listen to the rumble of the spirit's guttural snarls.

Despite his frailty, Ben recalled the words he read in his books and spoke in a low, heavy tone. *"Return to the realm without light. Be gone from the world of life. Hunger naught. In the darkest black, shut your eyes. Return to an eternal slumber."*

The growling ceased the moment Ben finished. The apprentice took a step towards the circle and paused, worried the silence was just a ruse. He studied the circle. Most of the candles were out, but two were still alit, dancing strongly in the subtle evening breeze. Shadows cascaded over the intertwining chalk lines.

Blood was splattered all over the rotunda. Ghastly inhuman handprints splattered the ground, wiping away at text that dictated the contract. The contract itself was torn in half, and Ben's blood obscured most of the contents, leaving a manilla page stained dark red. The whole time Ben had been chanting, the spirit was attacking the circle with all its might. The barrier was broken.

Ben could not stay forever. Maybe the vetala was gone, but he could not be perfectly sure.

"Can someone tell me if it is gone?" Ben called.

The Hill's residents remained silent.

"Anyone?" the apprentice cried. Of course, they were useless the only time Ben needed them! Only crickets chirped far off in the distance. The surrounding rose bushes faintly rustled with a midnight breeze. There was not a trace of the vetala's presence.

Right as Ben lowered to pick up the contract, a spirit called, "*I found Melly! She is alerting Ernest!*"

If there was any color left in Ben's face, it surely drained away. He wanted to scream at the spirit, but the severity of the situation loomed over his shoulders like the kiss of death itself. Grandfather would be in the garden in a matter of minutes, and possibly sooner if he believed a vetala to be loose. The horror scene that painted the rotunda could not be cleaned in time. No matter what, Grandfather would know what Ben had done.

Feeling defeated, Ben crouched down over the contract. Blood soaked the majority of the page, obscuring the words Ben had written. It was painful to see his first contract unsigned. This may have been a successful summons, but the lack of a signature made Ben's failure clear. Ben released his injured arm and felt it fall limp to his side. There was no hiding his injury from Grandfather or the state of the rotunda, but he could hide the contract.

Ben ripped the contract in half. He ripped it again, and again. Hot tears streamed down his face. He shoved the shreds in his pocket to be fully disposed of in the fireplace later. Even if Grandfather knew he had summoned something wicked, it was better than him showing proof of attempting his rite on his own and ahead of schedule. If this were that pinnacle moment, he would undoubtedly become an outcast in the necromancer society or already be dead.

Ben slid on his shoes and stepped away from the rotunda, expecting Grandfather to appear any second now. He picked up the lantern and trudged back towards the fountain, hoping to run into Grandfather halfway. Maybe he would not feel the need to investigate the rotunda, and Ben could somehow clean it and say the lantern had caused such a nasty spirit to appear.

A sense of bitter resignation in Ben's heart told him it was too late for dishonesty to provide any less painful of a resolution.

Thud thud thud...

Ben listened to fast approaching footsteps. The boy trembled. Grandfather would see his condition and maybe take pity. Hopefully, it would be a big enough distraction to direct Grandfather's attention away from the summoning circle on the rotunda, but Ben knew better.

The footsteps came to a sudden stop. He shut his eyes, fearing what Grandfather would say.

THUD THUD THUD...

He froze. The steps neared rapidly, coming from behind him. Not the direction of the house where Grandfather should have been.

Ben slowly twisted his torso and looked back down the gravel path. Halfway down the line of hedges stood a shadowy figure. The figure tipped sideways and blurred before Ben's vision focused on its twisted form.

A scream bubbled in his throat as a painful chill ran down his spine.

A mangled corpse stood on the other end of the path, figure outlined only by starlight and the red glow emanating from its rotten flesh. The vetala had indeed left the summoning circle, but it never returned to the underworld. Instead, it fled into the earth and found a host.

The Revenant shrieked and charged.

Seven

Failure

Stray branches snagged at Ben's jacket as he sprinted, stumbling and swerving into the rose bushes as he ran. Behind him, the revenant screeched and howled, thrilled with the vocal chords it had acquired as it announced its hunt. It had a bone to pick with Ben and would not stop until he was dead.

Ben did not think the revenant would have to try too hard as his vision blurred and doubled. The urge to vomit overwhelmed him, and he choked it down as he charged through the gardens. Behind him, feet crunched on gravel and stray rose bush twigs snapped. The footsteps drew closer and closer no matter how hard Ben ran. He wheezed in terror as he realized the revenant was merely steps away.

The boy looped around a corner of hedges, feet skidding across the gravel. He entered a round patch of tulips. The tall stems of the flowers snagged at his feet as his shoes crunched over ripened bulbs through the field. He just needed to make it to the house. If he could just get inside, the revenant would not be able to follow.

Behind him, another screech erupted from the fiend. Ben twisted to look back. His foot hooked around the thick stems of the tulips, and he stumbled, flying into the flowers and rolling flat onto his stomach with the edge of the lantern jabbing his ribs. Breathing through his teeth, withholding a sharp groan, he lifted his head and watched the revenant through the hedge line. It stood in a crooked manner just a few yards away, looking out onto the flower field. Ben ducked his head lower into the tulips, forcing himself to stare through the stems of the flowers and the dark shades of violets and yellow skimmed the skyline above.

Clack... Clack....

Ben lifted his head just enough to peer past the tulip buds at the revenant. The fiend jauntily stepped over flowers, jerking its head to every minute sound. Its teeth grated against each other rapidly, and its arms swayed violently with each motion, ready to attack the slightest breeze.

Ben held his breath as the revenant neared, feet crunching on trampled flowers. He was not fast enough to run away. He could not fight the spirit empty handed- he did not know how to manipulate the dead to stop it! His shoulders trembled, and his breaths stopped as the spirit closed in the distance with another step. There was nothing he could do other than hide and wait.

"Yoohoo, bone breath!"

Ben's head jerked to the sound, and his eyes landed on a pale blue shimmer appearing twenty feet to his left. In fact, the whole field seemed to be shimmering with the ethereal presence of the Hill's ghosts.

"You selected the wrong body to take. You are so ugly," another spirit called on the opposite side of the fiend.

The revenant growled at the spirits, jerking its head back and forth.

Ben's eyes replicated two moons as he watched the revenant react to the heckles of the Hill's ghosts. The air seemed to shimmer around the fiend, and it swiped out at the air in anger.

"Come on, use your words you fool!" another spirit cackled and was joined by a chorus of haunting laughter Ben so often heard targeted towards him. The revenant roared an unearthly

rattling sound that made Ben's heart quiver with terror.

Then, a familiar voice belonging to one of the Hill's many ghosts hissed in Ben's ear, *"Run!"*

Ben took his chances. He sprang to his feet and sprinted to his left, towards another pocket of hedges and back to the house. Just on the edge of the field, he heard the pounding of footsteps whooshing over trampled flowers and the cries of the Hill's ghosts.

He sprang back onto the gravel path and sprinted down a line of hedges. At the end of the path, the apprentice arrived at the clearing with the fountain. He ran up to the storage shed and snatched a shovel leaning against it. He looped the lantern in the crook of his good arm and held the shovel with both hands, gritting his teeth in agony.

Off in the distance, the fiend howled and screeched, drawing closer and growing louder. His grip on the shovel tightened, and he raised it for the moment the revenant would pop out of the hedges. He would only get one chance to swing the spade, and he knew he could only stun the revenant at best.

The screeching grew louder. Footsteps thudded on the ground, and shrubs rustled. Behind Ben, the fountain mirthfully trickled, acting as a metronome of serenity in the madness. Ben's heel pressed against the edge of the fountain, and a cold breeze tickled the back of his neck.

A set of footsteps neared behind him, just behind the fountain's spring. Ben jumped sideways and screamed, swinging the shovel. It connected with an arm that smacked the shovel away like it was nothing. He stabbed the shovel forward, piercing rotten flesh.

"Ben?!"

Ben's eyes widened, and his grip on the shovel laxed. Mely

was holding the spade against her abdomen. The blade's sharp edge pierced into her stomach, but the zombie merely yanked it out and tossed the shovel aside as if it were just a mere nuisance.

"Mely! I- I thought you were the revenant!" Ben looked about, listening for the monster, but he could only hear the fountain and his haggard breaths. "Is Grandfather here?"

Mely shook her head and pointed towards where the screaming had ceased. "He is dealing with the intruder." Her finger pointed at Ben's arm. "You are severely injured, Ben. I must tend to your wounds."

Ben blinked, collecting his thoughts, and nodded. He followed the zombie out of the garden and to the house. As they walked, he could not stop shaking. Maybe it was the cold or blood loss, the pain, or the fear of what Grandfather would do after he took care of the revenant. Ben blinked away tears. Grandfather was taking care of the revenant, the most horrific creature he had ever seen. To him, the revenant would be nothing more than a pest.

Ben struggled to walk up the front porch's stairs. Each step rippled and flowed as if it were driftwood in the sea. His knees wobbled as his body careened to the side, leaning heavily against the handrails. Mely turned and grabbed him by the shoulder, pulling him along. Her grip was so strong, she nearly lifted him off the ground.

They stopped on the front porch. Ben looked back over the graveyard. It could have been any other night. The sky was a deep black speckled with starlight. Not a single spirit tainted the air, and the graves sat solemnly across the hill. By the looks of it, the revenant had not disturbed the main graveyard, giving Ben the slightest feeling of peace.

"I *must* treat your wounds," Mely said, grabbing Ben once again and pulling him inside.

Inside, Ben sat down in the living room and took off his jacket. He did not really want a zombie to tend to his wounds, but one look at his arm in the light made his stomach do flips. He vomited into a vase next to the couch, head spinning. When Mely entered the living room with a box of medical supplies labeled 'medicine for the living,' Ben was already unconscious.

+X+

Ben's eyes flashed open, and pain flooded through his body. His legs felt like lead, breathing felt like inhaling knives, and a pounding headache emerged at the back of his skull. Worst of all was the pain in Ben's arm. It felt like something were crawling up and down his skin, biting into his flesh with every step. Ben shifted his arm uncomfortably, but it did not move. He tucked his chin, lifting his head just enough to see his arm from shoulder to pinky wrapped in a massive set of white bandages.

Mely sat in the corner of the room on Ben's desk chair, staring intently at Ben. Zombies did not need to sleep, so she turned her entire attention on every single one of Ben's movements.

"You have awakened," she said and stood, sounding as robotic as ever. She approached Ben,

Ben dropped his head back down and closed his eyes. He wished he could fall back asleep, but it was too late. The fear and dread of the consequences of his actions were sinking in along with the feeling of his arm going through a harvester.

"Did Grandfather... catch the revenant?"

"Yes, I did," Grandfather said, standing in the doorway.

Ben's eyes shot open, and he jerked himself up into a halfway sitting position.

Grandfather brought forward a taped-up roll of paper stained a deep red. He unfurled the parchment, revealing the incomplete contract Ben had left behind. Most of the words were smeared and the document had been ripped to ribbons before being re-assembled by Grandfather. "Care to explain this?"

He lifted a half-melted candle in his other hand. Grandfather's eyes glimmered something wicked. "Or why I found a bunch of these in the gardens?"

"I..." Ben choked on his words. Tears welled in his eyes. No matter what he said, the results would be the same. He forced himself to sit up all the way to face Grandfather. He gritted his teeth. "I wanted to prove I can be a necromancer."

"You thought you could be a necromancer by creating a revenant," Grandfather said, repeating Ben's explanation with a soft voice unbefitting the situation. He set the candle on Ben's bedside table. Grandfather placed the damaged contract beside it. "Do you know what happened when you summoned the vetala? Tell me, Benjamin, what is the one thing a vetala desires?"

Ben looked away.

"Benjamin," Grandfather growled.

"A corpse," Ben croaked.

"Whose corpse?" Grandfather pressed.

Ben looked down. "I- I don't know."

Grandfather crouched down, resting an arm on Ben's nightstand and forcing his apprentice to look directly in his eyes. "Henry Jefferson. He was once a hunter renowned for his enchantments on gear and weaponry. Do you think part of his agreement to be buried on the Hill included having his remains be defiled by a vetala? He is no longer a resident of the Hill, Benjamin."

"Of all places to perform a summoning, and you create the perfect concoction for a revenant. Not only that, but you do it with your very own blood!" Grandfather smacked his forehead with bewilderment.

"I didn't know that would happen!" Ben protested. "I just wanted to show you that I can be a necromancer! I successfully performed a summons. I even made-"

"You can successfully summon anything with your blood, Benjamin. You have the blood of a Gravekeeper!"

Ben shook his head and winced as a sharp pain flashed down his arm. "It doesn't matter what blood I have. You plan to replace me!"

Grandfather scoffed. "Replace you?! I can't replace blood! I'll have more to worry about replacing you after you get yourself devoured by the very monster your foolishly created!"

Ben's face burned, and he looked away from Grandfather. He could not deny the fact that he had nearly gotten himself killed.

Grandfather shook his head, muttering to himself. He rubbed his forehead and then stroked his short beard, glancing at the poor excuse of a contract on Ben's side table. "Your contract was correct, but you mustn't perform summonings of any sort. You aren't prepared for that."

"I'll never be prepared," Ben said. "That's why I have to do it."

"No, Benjamin. You can't fulfill a contract. It is too-"

"Why can't I?" Ben asked, looking up at Grandfather with a sharp gaze. "Because I can't perform magic? The only thing stopping me from learning is you teaching me. I could have finished the contract with the vetala or even dismissed the spirit if I had the ability to cast spells."

"You can't."

"Because you won't tea-"

"No, Benjamin," Grandfather shook his head, causing Ben to go silent while his heart filled with rage. "You do not have the ability to use magic. The only power you have is in your blood."

Ben glowered at Grandfather as his words sank in. "Then what about healing my wounds?" Ben asked.

"There are many ways to heal yourself, and your own blood has magical properties, so this is something possible for you," Grandfather explained.

Ben's eyes darted back and forth. So there was a true reason he could not dismiss the spirit. He did not have the ability to actually send back the spirit at all. What else could he not do?! He blurted, "then what about the candles?!"

"That is beyond your reach... Just what to do about your sight..." Grandfather mused while his apprentice stared at him in horror. Grandfather had never eluded to the fact that Ben could not perform magic at all. It was always a lesson for another time; Ben now knew why.

The boy looked down at his hands. They were marred with scrapes and small yet painful bruises from a week of fighting the Hill's residents. All that effort to gain the sight with a minuscule amount of results, and now he was being told after years of study that magic was not a possibility worth conceiving.

"I can show you I can do a proper summons," Ben said.

"Benjamin. Anger does not define my disappointment for your impertinence," Grandfather said. "You have ransacked my study and stole from it. You have summoned spirits knowing full well that you are not allowed to do so."

"But I did it," Ben choked, barely finding any strength in his voice. But if he were to speak, it had to be now. "I *did* summon them. Successfully. It was only the ve-"

"NO. You have done far enough. So, it appears you have suffered enough for your mistakes. I find it only right you heal from your wounds naturally and think upon the consequences of your actions." Grandfather stepped away from Ben. He paused at the door, motioning for Mely to follow him.

Grandfather walked out of Ben's room with Mely trailing in his shadow. She closed the door as gently as a zombie could. Ben could almost see the pity in her lifeless eyes. The boy trembled, imagining what would have happened to him if Grandfather had not stepped in to fight the revenant. It only took one swipe from the vetala to mangle his arm. If he had to fight the creature head on as a full-blown undead horror, he knew he would be far worse than dead.

He pulled up his knees and dropped his forehead as tears welled in his eyes. Ben felt stupid, humiliated, and utterly useless. No matter what he did, he could not prove he was capable. The revenant itself was proof Ben was far from earning the title as a Gravekeeper. Defeat weighed down his shaking shoulders until they slumped, and the boy's mind slipped from the thoughts of his failings and succumbed to the haunting nightmares of the revenant.

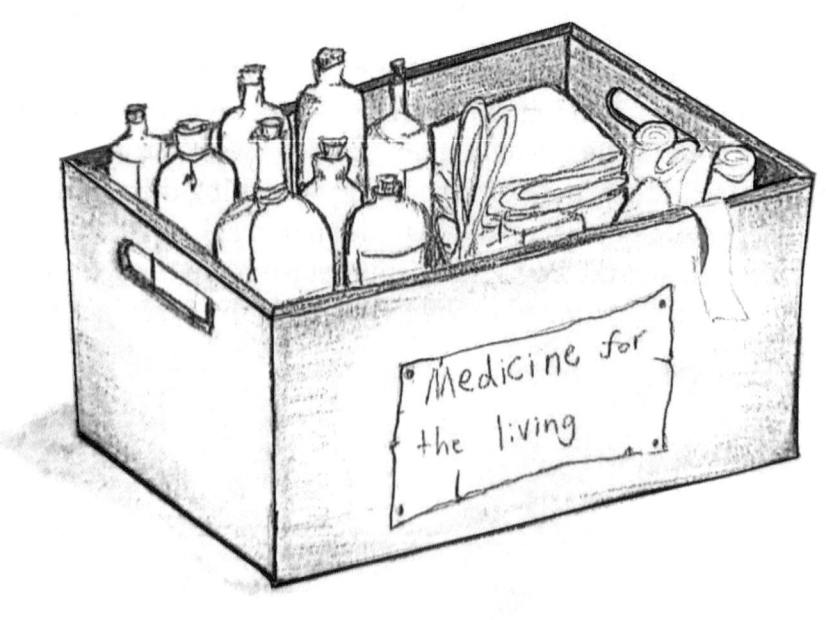

Eight

The Soul Weaver

Knock knock

Ben stirred awake as Mely entered his room, carrying the box of medical supplies assigned to the living. She placed it on his nightstand and crouched down to redress his arm and tend to his other injuries.

"I can do it myself," Ben said, looking away from the zombie maid.

"Ernest said otherwise." Mely took Ben's wrapped arm. He did not have the strength to protest and adjusted into an upright sitting position while she peeled away the bandages.

It did not take long for most of Ben's wounds to heal. His bruises and scrapes were minor, and the cuts he created for the summonings were slowly healing. The wound on his arm from the vetala was an entire other matter and one he wished Grandfather would change his mind about.

As the last bandage unraveled from his arm, a rotting stench assaulted his nose. He cringed and turned away from the putrid odor. Although Mely was a zombie, her body was in a frozen state of decay. It should not smell that horribly, he thought, but as he looked down at his arm, he realized it was not Mely that reeked.

Three gashes on his arm expanded from his wrist to his shoulder. The wounds had been closed with stitches, but despite them, it looked as if an oozing rotting green flesh was holding in a growing wealth of black feathers. Ben's stomach twisted, and he turned his head, grabbing his mouth to withhold vomiting.

It had only been a few days since the incident, but the wounds had clearly worsened to a state of irreparable decay.

"I believe I must report this to Ernest," Mely said, inspecting Ben's arm closely and daring to raise her own arm and compare the two. "Your arm is necrotizing."

Ben gulped and nodded.

She gathered the old bandages and left Ben alone in his room. He carefully started cleaning the wound with the supplies she left behind, but there was little he could do. Something about the injury was unnerving and unnatural not to mention it was too painful to touch.

Mely re-entered the room, followed by Grandfather. She stepped aside and waved her hand to Ben. "I cannot treat this," Mely said before standing very still.

Grandfather approached his grandson and examined his arm. Saying nothing, he scowled and left, sharply closing the door behind him.

Ben shivered, watching as Mely stared at the door for a long moment before returning to Ben and proceeding to redress the wound. Ben looked at his arm as white bandages wrapped around it, concealing the horror. Did Grandfather have no intent on helping him? Surely he knew the wound was necrotizing and, if they did not treat it soon with magic, his arm would fall off.

Ben shivered at the thought.

After Mely left, he sat alone in his room and sighed. It had been three days since the incident, and he had yet to have the heart to step outside. He had failed the Hill's residents and knew they would be mad at him for losing one of their own. Not only that, but Ben did not want to step foot in the graveyard. He did not see the reason to continue tending the graves and acting like the Gravekeeper when that never would be his path. He could not see spirits or cast spells. Why would Grandfather pretend to want him as an apprentice?!

The boy did not see a reason to try aiming to prove himself to Grandfather. All he proved was that he was a complete failure. It would be better to sit in his room and rot.

Another day passed, and Ben's arm was unbearably aching. He sat at his desk and stared outside. Rain heavily pattered against the windowpane, and the wind howled and shook the house's shingles to its trusses. Ben laid his head on his desk, wishing the burning sensation in his arm would stop.

Knock knock

The door opened.

"I don't need your help, Mely," Ben said as he sat up.

Mely softly shuffled forward in her typical zombie-like manner. She turned on the lights to Ben's room, revealing an old woman whom Ben had never met before. Grandfather strolled in behind the woman, looking incredibly displeased as if he were staring at a bug on his shoe. *He must still be mad*, Ben thought with disappointment even though he had resolved to no longer care about what Grandfather thought.

Ben could not help but be curious about the guest as she approached. She wore a dark red shawl over a long brown dress adorned in randomly sewn beads and other trinkets. Ben noted what looked like possibly a whole bird's wing in the folds of her skirts, but they swayed as she walked and covered the feathers completely. In the crook of her elbow, she carried a massive canvas bag stuffed full of trinkets. Stray strands of red yarn hung out of the bag, and Ben could see what looked like a pair of silver knitting needles poking out at the top.

"Erwys, this is Benjamin," Grandfather said, closing the door behind them. "Benjamin, this is Erwys Ellandor."

He stood, and his vision blackened for a moment in the process. Before he could find the words to greet her, Erwys Ellandor waved her hand for Ben to sit. "Take a seat, child. I am not your adversary." She turned her head to look at Grandfather and remarked, "What tales have you told this child to make him look at me as if he's seen a ghost?!"

Grandfather looked aside with an expression of guilt. He looked almost scared of the woman, but Ben was not entirely sure. He, on the other hand, was terrified. Moving with stiff limbs, he exchanged his desk chair to sitting on the edge of his bed, cradling his wrapped arm in agony. Ben looked up at Erwys Ellandor with a million thoughts sprinting through his mind.

There could be nothing good for an Ellandor to be on the Hill let alone in Ben's room! The Ellandors were another necromancer family, and remembering the Council of the Dead's conversation, they were a family that had recently procured a lich. Ben wondered why, of all people, Grandfather felt the need to bring someone like that to the Hill. A lich was far worse than any revenant! Having her before him made Ben fear Grandfather was paying her to get rid of him. Perhaps she had come to punish him for summoning the vetala at Grandfather's request. A shiver went down the boy's spine as he realized he had no chance of escaping the two necromancers.

"Benjamin, calm down." Grandfather noticed the fright in Ben's demeanor. "Erwys is going to fix your arm," Grandfather added, pinching the bridge of his nose as the boy looked at him with narrowed eyes. "That wound on your arm is necrotizing because it is cursed."

"Cursed?!" If there was any color left in Ben's face, it vanished in that instant.

"Don't frighten the child," Erwys said, glowering at Grandfather even though Ben was deadly afraid of her. Grandfather glared back at her. Ben did not need any special sight to see the tension between the two.

"There, there," Erwys cooed as she grabbed the desk chair and pulled it near the corner of his bed. Ben was frozen stiff as she did this, his mind screaming for him to run away. She was related to a lich, perhaps she was the lich. Any necromancy family with a lich could only be bad news, especially for a Gravekeeper. While his mind ran rampant, Erwys waved her hand at Grandfather to shoo him away. "Some privacy is appreciated. Soul weaving is a sensitive craft," she said.

Grandfather rolled his eyes. "If you say so-" Erwys shot Grandfather a murderous glare, "-once she is done, Benjamin, come find me," Grandfather said before departing.

Erwys waved a hand at Mely, "Follow your master." The zombie paused only a moment before following in Grandfather's footsteps. She slammed the door behind her, and the whole wall shuddered.

"Now then, isn't that better?" Erwys said, drawing Ben's attention back to her. Ben wanted to shake his head. He strongly preferred Grandfather being in the room. The head of the Ellandor family laid her deep purple eyes on Ben. "Calm yourself, child. I am here as your healer." She looked down and shuffled through her bag. "I have always been the one your family calls, and that shall never change. You have nothing to fear."

Finished inventorying her belongings, she set her bag aside and motioned for Ben to hold out his arm. "Let's take a look, shall we?" Ben hesitated, but the pain in his arm made him doubt she would do anything to make him feel worse than how he already felt. He held it out to her, and she helped Ben unroll the tightly wound bandages.

Erwys had to peel off the last few strips of gauze. A thick black ooze glued them to his arm.

"Tsk, tsk, Ernest should have called for me sooner," she said while clicking her tongue as if she were only looking at a sprained wrist. Nasty gashes tore down the length of his arm. There were three large claw marks in total and the subtle hints of a fourth from when the vetala had clawed at Ben. Without the bandages, Ben could see his skin around the wounds was shriveled and ashy grey now. The gashes themselves looked like the black feathers had expanded beyond the inner wound, opening it up and oozing out black blood.

Erwys tsk'd again as she picked up a silver case out of her canvas bag. She opened the case to reveal a singular silver needle. "Hold out your arm and stay very still, child."

Ben shivered. "W-what are you going to do?"

"You were attacked by a powerful, vengeful spirit, child. It has left a curse on you that must be removed to salvage your arm. Until it is removed, I'm afraid no traditional medical treatment, spell, or even a potion from a high caliber alchemist will heal you." Her purple eyes lifted to Ben's. There was a slight glimmer of kindness, or so Ben imagined. "Don't worry, as a Soulweaver, there is no one better at removing curses than myself."

She held Ben's hand and brought the needle to her lips. Ben watched with curiosity as the necromancer licked the needle and a silver thread seemed to appear from her tongue. She then lowered the needle and Ben looked away in fright.

It felt like his arm was being washed in a pool of ice as Erwys worked on sewing up the wounds. After several painful moments, Ben peaked at his arm to see one of the gashes sealed by a silver web. There was a strange silver fog glowing over his arm, and

Ben knew if he could just see better, he may have been able to see the details of the spell the head of the Ellandors was casting. Her actions were in the form of sewing, but Ben could not see the power within the threads. He simply knew it was there.

While Erwys sewed the wounds on Ben's arms closed, she whispered what sounded like a lullaby in Greek. When she finished, she stopped whispering and stowed away the needle, eyes sparkling. The color of the wound had returned to red tones, and the gashes were sealed with a shining silver web of stitches. The intense burning pain in Ben's arm now only emitted a subtle ache.

"What kind of necromancy is this?" Ben asked, studying the lingering silver fog that wrapped around his arm like an ethereal bandage.

"Ernest tells you very little," Erwys said with a roll of her purple eyes and a growl in her voice. She softly smiled at Ben and patted his injured hand. "Your family is that of the Gravekeepers. Mine is that of Soulweavers. We are not so different. You must know of the fates, child. My bloodline originates from the netherworld itself."

Ben shuddered under Erwys Ellandor's gaze. It was as if she could read into his soul and unravel it. Her eyes glimmered, and Ben knew she was looking well beyond his face. "I can see your sight fails you," Erwys said softly.

Ben gulped and refrained from looking away. "It is not just my sight," he blurted. What hope did he have left with Grandfather? He could not even cast spells!

"If I may," Erwys said, pulling out a small, bone sewing needle. Ben eyed it for a moment before gulping down his fears and nodding. He did not care what she did if it granted a hint of hope.

Erwys Ellandor lowered the needle and pricked Ben's finger, and the boy flinched, but his finger never bled. A faint golden thread lifted with the needle, but as it raised, Ben's vision faltered and it looked as if Erwys were merely raising a needle slowly and imaginatively as she twisted it around, scribbling in the air.

She then finished and stowed away the needle. The necromancer took Ben's hands and patted them endearingly. Ben watched her gaze, wondering what she saw that he could not. "Your fate is not what it was written to be... It is a damning thing, being born with your potential blocked," Erwys said. "They seep through the seams, but you cannot access the realms of magic and the boundaries of life and death."

"Is there anything I can do to fix it?" he asked, not knowing of the danger behind his question nor caring.

Erwys Ellandor looked down at her canvas bag and paused. "There is a way... but it is something Ernest would never allow." The left corner of her lips lifted. She dug into the bag. "Now where is it..."

"Here it is!" She presented a small charm made of red yarn from her bag and pressed it into Ben's good hand, curling his fingers around it. "This is no easy path. Consider your actions carefully. If you ever wish to regain control of your own fate, burn this."

She patted Ben's hand one final time before standing. "Now rest that arm, child. My threads will heal it quickly but refrain from dealing with the dead until that properly heals." The necromancer winked at Ben with a faint smile as she gathered her heaping canvas bag. Ben watched as Erwys Ellandor drifted out of the room, noting that the bird-like thing in her skirt definitely was a whole real bird wing, and watched as she closed the door, leaving him alone with his thoughts and the strange charm.

Nine

The Responsibilities of a Gravekeeper

Ben held the charm in his hand, studying the intricate knots of the red yarn. All he needed to do was burn this item, and he would be able to see spirits. Ben found it hard to believe that the answer to his problems rested in the palm of his hand, but a gut feeling told him Erwys Ellandor could not be trusted. Even though she had healed him, she still had a lich in her family. Given she said Grandfather would not be pleased, he doubted burning the charm would lead to anything good. For the time being, it would be best to continue along the path Grandfather had planned.

The boy wrapped fresh bandages around his arm and propped it into a makeshift sling. He then cleaned up the old bandages and left his room to find Grandfather.

Ben poked his head in the dining room, the kitchen, and the parlor before standing at the front door. Peering through the windows, he hoped Grandfather was not out somewhere in the rain. Ben was not fond of getting his bandages soaked, but more than anything, he did not want to be around the Hill's residents. A feeling of shame welled up in his chest, and he feared what the hundreds of spirits would say to him for leading to the demise of one of their companions.

The boy walked into the living room and sighed at the sight of Mely. The zombie aimlessly dusted the fireplace mantle, with her skirts drifting dangerously close to the flames.

"Have you seen Grandfather?" Ben asked, warily eyeing the yellow flames of the fire and the white hem of Mely's skirt. Mely did not need to see Grandfather to know where he was. As his familiar, she always knew where he was, and she had no problem telling Ben.

"He is in his study," she said, her voice as monotone as ever. Ben looked down the hallway with trepidation. Did he really need to talk to Grandfather now? Would his presence in the study ignite a well-deserved flame of anger in the necromancer? Ben gulped, knowing he had no choice.

He walked down the hallway, feeling the weight of his steps bear down upon the creaking floorboards. He arrived at the door too soon, but it felt more like a wall than a door. Ben sucked in a deep breath and pressed his palm on the silver handle.

"Grandfather?" Ben squeaked as his head poked into the study.

Grandfather sat at his desk, holding a small purple ledger and twirling a pen in his hand. He wore a pair of reading spectacles and lifted his gaze to look upon Ben. His eyebrows raised, creating five fresh heavy wrinkles, and his nose sneered, adding one more.

"Take a seat, Benjamin."

Ben closed the door as softly as possible behind him and sat in the single wooden chair across from Grandfather's desk. The wooden legs pressed into the plush red carpet, reminding Ben of what was hidden underneath. The room was silent spare Ben and Grandfather's breathing and the slight rustle of paper as Grandfather flipped through the ledger. It was a rare moment Ben could enjoy such sweet silence, but it was short lived.

Grandfather set the ledger down with a gentle thud and folded his spectacles, placing them on top of it. "How is your sight?"

Grandfather asked with a steady tone.

Ben looked down at his knees. His dress pants were scuffed and torn. Nearly all his clothes were damaged from the weeks of turmoil fighting the ghosts. "I can't see them," Ben muttered. "It didn't work."

"No, it did not." *Tap tap.* Grandfather tapped his desk with his index finger. "We must attempt another method of *fixing* your sight immediately."

"Did Erwys Ellandor tell you how to fix it?" Ben said, lifting his gaze. "I promise I can do whatever I need to-"

"You shall not!" Grandfather scowled, eyes flaring a brilliant gold. "You have done enough on your own. Do not listen to that witch! We are Stones, Gravekeepers. We do not take advice from the likes of her."

Ben gulped and shrank in his seat. "But she healed my arm," he protested. Wouldn't she be just as willing to help Ben gain the sight? He contemplated telling Grandfather about the charm.

"She owed me a favor. But we will not owe her a favor. Not one so grievous as the cost to give you the sight. There are other ways, Benjamin. The lantern was an attempt to understand the severity of your condition-"

"An attempt... My condition? If she knows how to fix it-"

Grandfather's glare stopped Ben mid-sentence. "There are other ways," he hissed. He picked up a green ledger and tapped the cover. "There are other methods on which we must focus. Not all answers are given to us. Sometimes the best solutions come only with hard work and research."

Grandfather opened the ledger with the emerald green cover and handed it to Ben, thumb pressed on a worn page.

"What is this?"

"This is a list of every necromancer household that has employed the Stone family and every necromancer protected by the Gravekeepers," Grandfather explained. "Your rite has been scheduled a month from now, so we have until then to prepare you to become the next Gravekeeper, and more importantly, fix your sight."

Ben looked down at the ledger. He opened the first page with care and stared wide eyed at the first subcontract page. There was the name *Jonathan Stone* followed by *Michel Lumons 1532*. The page listed a set of bloody fingerprints and a following list of names with dates. Ben flipped the page to discover a similar contract, and each following page was something almost identical for the first ten pages. At some point, the contracts changed to not include a Stone family member's name and instead just a red thumbprint. Some pages were ashen and nearly illegible, others looked as if they had been scrawled over furiously with a sharpened quill.

Ben looked up at Grandfather who had been patiently watching him absorb the family heirloom. "That is our lineage and our duty," Grandfather explained. "As the next Gravekeeper, you will be bound to honor every page of those contracts. As a Gravekeeper, you are the line that which necromancers cannot cross. You must be able to protect a graveyard at all costs, and the Hill is always, no matter what, our top priority."

Ben lowered the ledger. "Aren't we a family of necromancers? How does just protecting graves make us necromancers?" Ben looked at the books and scrolls surrounding him. He always knew that being a Gravekeeper was his responsibility as a necromancer in the Stone family, but he thought of it as something tied only to the Hill. Ben never imagined the extent of a Gravekeeper's responsibilities to expand beyond the Hill to all the necromancer families and graveyards. How many families were they bound to?

Grandfather sighed. "There are checks and balances to everything, Benjamin. Not all wizards know the extent of necromancy and to ensure that there is not mass carnage between us, we exist to limit necromancy before it steps beyond the line of tolerance."

Ben nodded, looking down at the ledger in his hands. "Then what about this? Why do we need to protect graves?" Ben already cared about protecting the Hill's residents, but he did not see the reason in taking care of other necromancers' graves. That should be their responsibility after all.

"Imagine what will happen when Erwys Ellandor dies. Do you think her spirit or remains will rest in peace? There are many necromancers who would kill to have her as a zombie or undead minion, to enslave her soul just so they can hear her fortunes. As an oracle, she would be invaluable and worth the effort to ensnare. Many necromancers cross the line of respect with the dead, so what do you think happens when their final bell tolls?"

Ben gulped. The magic of a necromancer entirely dealt with death. Grandfather made it clear they only dealt with mutual contracts, but Ben knew there were other ways of practicing necromancy. "What happens?" he asked.

"Imagine the number of spirits you once bound to your every will and whim now on equal ground as you," Grandfather hissed. "You may have the power to control the dead now, but no one living person can evade death forever. Part of our duty is to protect necromancers from each other as well as those in the afterlife. This is only a job that can be performed by a Gravekeeper. A Gravekeeper that can see the dead at that."

Ben winced, feeling the bitter sting of Grandfather's words. "Why does it have to be our family? Why can't we just be normal necromancers?" Ben really wished to know why *he* had to be a Gravekeeper and could not just settle for learning necromancy at his own will and pace.

Grandfather sighed. "Order, Benjamin. It all comes down to order.... Now flip to the near end of the ledger, there is an important name for our next lesson. *Wraithright.*"

Ben bobbed his head and flipped through the ledger until he found the name of Wraithright with roughly fifteen pages to spare. He eyed the date and coughed. The contract was written over two hundred years ago!

"What is this?" Ben asked, reading the contract's contents. They were supposed to check the gravesite of the Wraithright estate every thirty years to ensure that there were no unwanted dead. "Why would they care about *unwanted* dead? What does that mean?"

Grandfather rolled his eyes. "This is one of those contracts our family should have never made. You see, the Wraithrights amongst many other necromancers have their own graveyards. Sure, we are employed to protect many corpses, spirits, and graveyards, but many necromancer families chose to protect their own, and for good or very bad cause. The Wraithrights are an example of the latter."

He shuffled through some books on the side of his desk. These were books Ben recognized as all part of his curriculum. Grandfather lifted a slim black book that was so wide and glossy, it looked like a black tile more than a book. The spine creaked as Grandfather opened it, quickly flipping through intricately drawn pages until he landed on one with an awful ink drawing.

It looked like something close to the grim reaper. There was an ink blot covering nearly the whole page, but somehow the skeleton of a hand appeared in the folds of darkness and a hollowed skeletal face appeared beneath the hood of a cloak. There were no legs, only torn shreds of a cloak, and heavy chains wrapped around the black blotting, highlighting the page with a stark white. Ben could feel the weight of the chains in the drawing bear down on the creature. The shackles anchored themselves to the spirit's soul.

"Now tell me what you know about wraiths?" Grandfather asked.

"A wraith?" Ben asked, eyes stuck on the empty holes where a set of eyes should have been. This drawing looked nearly as horrific as the vetala. Ben shivered. "They are violent spirits," Ben muttered. He looked at Grandfather. "Is there something I should know about them that I don't?"

Grandfather cleared his throat. "The Wraithrights specialize in producing the correct conditions for wraiths to be created. Their graveyard is a hub of wraiths, and typically it is our job to clean up when too many undead spawn because wraiths have a tendency to kill anything in their path."

"There is a reason we have no wraiths on the Hill, and there is a reason why the Wraithrights have hundreds. They hold a grudge and are bound to our world against their own wills. It does not take a tragedy to create a wraith, instead it takes a will of malevolence strong enough to defy the natural course of life and death. They are not spirits that can be reasoned with, contracted with, and they only exist trapped within our realm."

"The Wraithright's activities are an exact reason why the job of a Gravekeeper is so critical to our society," Grandfather explained while twirling a pen. "It has not been exactly thirty years, but due to some concerns, we will be heading there tomorrow."

"We?"

Grandfather's golden eyes met with Ben's. "You are coming with me on this trip."

Ben's eyes widened. The ledger slipped through his fingers

and fell on the ground with the agonizing sound of paper ripping. "You are taking me on a business trip?!"

Grandfather winced and reached out, motioning for Ben to return the ledger to him. "I find it wiser to bring you along than leave you here to your own devices." He took the ledger out of Ben's hand, sneered at the damaged pages, and placed it in the drawer of his desk.

Ben tucked in his chin and looked down at his knees. He did not know whether to be excited or disappointed. If Grandfather were gone, he certainly would have the opportunity to continue investigating a way to gain the sight permanently. Ben chewed on his lip, knowing Grandfather harbored little trust in him for good reason.

"My arm is not fully healed," Ben said.

"I will give you a potion. Now that the curse is gone, there is no need to delay that further. I believe you have learned your lesson on summonings?" Grandfather inquired.

Ben solemnly nodded.

"I shall meet with the Wraithrights to discuss the condition of their catacombs and other matters. You will not be sitting in on these conversations. I have another task for you. This one is twofold and critical to developing your sight."

"What do you want me to do?" Ben asked, wondering what he could personally gain out of assisting in investigating the Wraithrights. Wraiths were not desirable spirits to be around, and Ben did not see how such spirits could possibly improve his sight.

"While I meet with the Wraithrights, you will be responsible for investigating the catacombs," Grandfather said with a raised brow. Before Ben could protest, Grandfather added, "Since you love exploring crypts so much, it is the perfect task for you to do."

Ben's mouth opened and closed as he sought a way to protest. There was something cold in Grandfather's golden eyes, making Ben feel as though anything he said would lack significance. Silently, the apprentice nodded, realizing Grandfather was punishing him for exploring the crypts a few weeks ago.

Grandfather's hands pressed on his desk, and he stood, towering over Ben. "We will be leaving tomorrow midday. Pack yourself a bag. Be prepared for an evening and some rather undesirable catacombs. They don't clean them often enough."

Ben stood and begrudgingly walked out of Grandfather's study with the necromancer looming behind him, wondering how he could protest this. If he did not speak now, he would be in a foreign graveyard by tomorrow afternoon! "I don't think a conversation with him would be something I should miss. Maybe it-"

"No."

Ben gulped. Wraiths were some of the nastiest kinds of spirits. Sure, the vetala was a wicked undead, but vetalas had to be summoned from the underworld. Wraiths, on the other hand, were the kind of creatures that could only be created from horrific curses and tragic fates. Ben shivered, knowing exactly the practices the family like the Wraithrights performed to earn their title and notoriety.

He could not help but protest. "Is it really necessary for me to come along on your trip?" He spun on his toe. "Think about how the graves could use some sprucing up. The grass needs a trim, and the front gates could be oiled. The rotunda also needs to be cleaned-"

"Why do you think it is that the rotunda needs to be cleaned and the graves need sprucing up?" Grandfather asked, stopping Ben dead in his series of complaints. "It is about time you come along with me to one of my business trips. You will be just as responsible for these in the future, and it is time you learn what sorts of spirits you must deal with beyond the Hill. As you have seen yourself, the Hill's residents are an exception, not the rule." Grandfather's eyes glinted something fierce as his lips spread into a sinister smile. "If you thought a revenant was worth creating, I want you to think long and hard about the wraiths you will see."

"But that is not all," Grandfather added, handing Ben a purple ledger. "Along with every contract is a list of names we must protect. The Wraithrights are a special case as not all of their family members fall in line with our protection, but there are a few and one of those names can be found in that ledger. Look for Hubert Mortise Wraithright."

Ben flipped through the first couple of pages, realizing the entire ledger detailed out the Wraithright account. There was a list, *Protected Souls,* followed by a short number of names not exceeding half a page, Hubert's name was scrawled at the bottom in a different color of ink as if an afterthought.

"There is an individual, Hubert Wraithright, slumbering within the catacombs of the Wraithright's who once found himself in a predicament similar to your own."

"A similar predicament? Was he not born with the sight?" Ben could not imagine another necromancer family considering putting in the effort of protecting a family member with a defect. Ben was fortunate enough to be the only heir to the Stone family.

"He was adopted into the family," Ben's eyes widened with shock. "He was not born with the sight. He also could not hear spirits, yet he acted as a necromancer for forty-two years before his demise."

"What did he do?" Ben asked as the wheels in his mind began to spin.

"It is uncommon for someone in such a bloodline to be born

without the inherent abilities of a necromancer. He never became anything beyond an embarrassment, that is until one day, he gained such abilities." Grandfather's index finger tapped on his desk to an unknown cadence as he explained. "The Wraithrights undoubtedly know how he developed such abilities; however, it would take a great deal of effort to encourage them in disclosing such information. If we were to pursue such knowledge, it would also expose your current condition to our entire society..." Grandfather paused and sighed, and Ben knew deep down Grandfather knew that the elites in their society already knew of his defects. "No more necromancers can be privy to such information. If we may discover how Hubert gained the spectral sight and hearing, there may be a possibility that you can gain it as well."

"How do we do that?" Ben asked.

"While you are in the catacombs, you must find where he resides and speak to him, assuming he has not been transformed into a wraith," Grandfather said. "I take it you know how to do a simple enough summons to speak to him?"

Ben bit his lip, thinking about his activities in the past few weeks. He never tried to summon a spirit from its corpse, but that was supposed to be an elementary task that ordinary people could perform. He knew how to do it if only he were given the proper materials.

"Can I actually perform a summons like this? I thought you didn't want me doing any more summons," Ben argued. He was not entirely sure he could speak to the departed.

"I will give you a bell that will help call his spirit," Grandfather said. "With that, and a properly drawn charm, you should be capable enough to do this alone. He is connected to the Gravekeepers, so he should heed your summons if little else."

"Am I to do this by myself?" Ben asked. This task would take place in the Wraithright's catacombs where hordes of wraiths lurked. The boy imagined what dangers would be drawn if he rang a summoning bell in the catacombs.

"Yes, this is not a complicated task, and you will already be in the catacombs, so the Wraithrights will never know."

Ben's eyes narrowed. He was less worried about what the Wraithrights would know and more concerned about the ethics behind his task at hand. Was it right to perform a summonings in another necromancer's graveyard? "How can we violate their graveyard?"

Grandfather scoffed. "Violate the graveyard? The Wraithrights are a violation to everything natural. Their graveyard is nothing but a patch of hell stitched into this world."

"Isn't it wrong to take advantage of our access to their graveyard?" Ben asked, brows knit with concern. As an apprentice Gravekeeper, his job had always been to maintain graves and respect the spirits on the Hill. Now, Grandfather wanted him to awaken a slumbering soul against the family's will for his own sake. It felt... wrong.

Grandfather seemed to understand Ben's concerns. "Benjamin," he said with a solemn tone. "Nothing you are doing will violate their graveyard. I have not taught you how to go against the wills of the dead. If Hubert does not wish to speak with you, at worst he will spit ectoplasm at you." Ben cringed and nodded, resting his argument about the morality of the task at hand. As for his mortality, Ben did not believe going anywhere near the Wraithright catacombs was an easy task.

"How am I to survive amongst hundreds of wraiths?" Ben asked with a quaver in his voice.

"This is not the first time I have walked through those halls," Grandfather said. "So long as you are in the catacombs during the day, the wraiths will not be an issue. However, if the sun sets and you are deep within the catacombs, I do have an *insurance* you will take along. But enough of that, you'll not need it."

"What in-" Ben watched as Grandfather lifted a case with three vials of bright purple liquid. He carefully handed them over to Ben, and the boy's hands shook as he struggled to grab and hold it. "Be sure to drink this tonight. Your arm needs to be fully healed before we leave."

Ben reluctantly nodded, looking down at the vials. Their contents sloshed about, splashing at the edges of their wooden caps and fizzing a white foam. Knowing what the potions were like, he almost preferred the months it would take to naturally heal.

"There are other potions to select from if you do not wish to use these," Grandfather said, reaching for the case of violet vials.

"...it's fine." Ben hurried out of the office before Grandfather could take the case of potions. While the purple potions were unpleasant, they were not cheap and performed better than any other healing potions Grandfather had to offer. Ben wished Grandfather would teach him how to heal himself, but there simply was not enough time to waste hoping Ben would be able to do it. Unlike magic, potions were reliable.

The potions rattled in their case as Ben clambered up the stairs, carefully carrying them in the crook of his good arm. He would have to take the potion immediately to receive its full effects before tomorrow which meant he had little time to prepare for going to the Wraithrights. Once he used the potions, he would be in no condition to do anything.

He stowed the potion case on his desk and looked at his pile of study materials with dismay. He knew enough about wraiths to know they were dangerous and only silver, iron, and other spirits could fend them off. He needed the ability to summon a spirit if necessary, and the only one he could think would be reliable was Elaine.

The first spirit he had ever summoned, Elaine the poltergeist, would be the perfect spirit to bring along to the catacombs if he needed a ghost's aid. He dug through some of his supplies and looked under his bed and in the back of his dresser for her contract. His face paled as he realized it sat under the rotunda along with the other remaining summoning supplies he had stowed away, assuming Grandfather had not found them yet.

Ben looked out the window to the murky gray sky. Rain pounded against the glass with a fervent rhythm, not hinting at letting up. He would not be able to wait for it to cease. He pulled on his jacket and boots and tiptoed down the stairs. He paused at the front door, casting a sideways glance down the hallway to the closed door leading into Grandfather's study. His eyes squeezed shut, and he pushed away his concerns about disappointing Grandfather. He had to be prepared no matter what.

He slipped outside into the rain. Pulling the jacket on as closely as possible, Ben paced down the porch's stairs and into the graveyard. The ground squelched under his feet as he rushed to the gardens.

"Where are youuu going?" a spirit wailed after Ben.

"Probably to summon another monster. This is why I say never trust a necromancer."

"Who will be next to die?!"

The spirits moaned and wailed behind Ben, following him as he hurried through the gardens. He pulled on his hood, pressing it tightly to his ears to try and block out the sound of their wails, but it was to no avail. They cried and whispered in his ears, demanding he return to them Henry Jefferson, pleading he not create another monster, hissing that he was the worst monster on the Hill.

Ben regretted going outside. He knew the spirits were upset with him, but the cries and moans of two hundred ghosts was overwhelming. Ben arrived at the rotunda, and his heart sank to see it completely cleaned. Grandfather had seen every inch of the circle he made and every mistake. He jogged to the back and looked underneath the rotunda, finding his stash untouched.

"Where's the lantern you promised us," a spirit hissed. Ben swatted it away like a fly. A chorus of spirits boo'd at him, heckling him for his attitude. They demanded an apology with the lantern as the prize.

Ben ignored the ghosts as he pulled out a bag of summoning supplies along with a slightly damp set of contracts. He stowed the contracts in his inner jacket pocket, careful to keep them protected from the rain and scooped up the bag with his good arm.

As Ben lifted himself and proceeded to leave the rotunda, the gardens oddly drew silent. Rain thundered upon gravel and shrubbery. The wind howled with only the slightest hints of ghastly laughter.

"What is it?" Ben asked. The eerie silence sent goosebumps up his arms and neck.

"SKREEEEEEE!" A horde of spirits screamed around Ben, mimicking the revenant.

"Agh!" Ben jumped backwards, into the throngs of a rose bush. The bag of summoning supplies flew from his arm, toppling on the gravel. A couple of candles toppled out of the bag at his feet as he stared into the shadowy rain with wide eyes. A flash of terror filled the boy as the memories of the revenant swarmed his mind.

After a long painful moment, he deeply inhaled and peeled

himself off the bush, crouching down to pick up the supplies. His body trembled, and he looked over his shoulder and ahead, expecting to see the revenant.

"HA HA HA..." the spirits hooted and howled. Ben scooped up the bag and hurried down the gravel path, racing to get in the house. He gritted his teeth and glared through the rain, wishing to scream back at the spirits. But a feeling of guilt tore into him. He had led to the demise of Henry Jefferson's spirit. This was the only way the Hill's spirits could enact their revenge.

He made it inside and closed the door, cutting off the howling laughter of the dead. Sopping wet, Ben leaned his head against the wooden panel in exhaustion. His mind filled with the memories of the revenant, and he could not stop shaking. Could he really face a horde of wraiths?

Ben let out a final exhausted sign, knowing he had no choice.

Composing himself, he returned to his room. He locked the door and tore off his soaking jacket before tossing it over his desk chair. Carefully, he stowed away the summoning scrolls in the bottom drawer of his desk beneath a basic book on spirits Ben had read years ago.

The boy hid the bag of summoning supplies beneath his bed, looping its fabric around the frame to keep it off the floor in case Mely investigated his room at the behest of Grandfather. Once the boy finished, he plopped down and studied how to speak to the dead, hoping there would be something to gain out of this trip.

Hours passed, and Ben's time was up.

Knock knock.

Mely entered his room, holding a fresh set of linens. "Benjamin, I am here to witness you drink the potion," the zombie maid said flatly.

"You don't need to do that Mely," Ben said, peeling his hand off his forehead and closing his book. He turned and watched as the maid adjusted fresh linens over his normal bedding. He cringed, knowing what they were for.

"It is time you take the potion, Ben," Mely said, lifting her head at an unnatural angle to look at him while still adjusting the sheets.

Ben sighed and clicked open the case with the vials. He picked up a singular tube and popped the wooden cap off. The purple contents fizzed, foaming over at the rim. Ben cringed as the foam spilled onto his fingers, causing them to burn instantly. He looked at Mely with a stale frown. "Is it really necessary for you to watch me drink this?"

"Yes."

If he could, he would have pinched his nose. He turned the vial upwards and chugged the potion's murky purple contents before he could stop. His eyes turned into saucers, and he chucked the vial aside, shattering it against the wall. He coughed and leaned forward, gasping as the liquid moved down his throat, leaving behind a trail of fiery pain.

Ben did not notice Mely move over to him and lift him. He did not care as she dropped him on his bed and removed his shoes. Soon, a swarm of ants crawled over his skin. The room spun as the concoction's effects spread through his entire being. "*I will* come in the *morning*," Mely said before turning off the lights and closing the door, leaving Ben in a shifting, twisting room of shadows. It did not take long before the potion fully took effect, rendering him unconscious.

Ten

The Catacombs

At dawn on the day of their departure, Ben awoke in a fit. His pajamas and linens were soaked in sweat, and the bandages on his arms were seeping a strange purple muck. He groaned, rolling off his bed while holding his arm in the air, trying to remove the disgusting medical scraps.

Underneath, his arm could almost be glowing. His skin was a pasty white with a faint purple hue, but the wound was completely gone. There was no sign his arm had been nearly torn to ribbons, and not a scar or scratch remained upon his gleaming skin.

Ben ripped off his shirt and bundled it with the ruined bed linens and the bandages. There was no point keeping any of it with the mix of magical excrement the potion had created. Ben sneered while placing them in a bin for Mely to retrieve later. If he could cast flames, he would have burned it all on the spot.

He knew he did not have much time left to prepare for the trip to the Wraithright estate. He hurriedly got ready, noting how his whole body had a strange, glistening purple hue and not a single scar. Ben grabbed a bag and scavenged a few items from his room including some candles, a bag of salt, and the poltergeist contract he stole from Grandfather's study. Ben stuffed away the contract and rushed down the hallway, hoping to beat Grandfather to the front door, but as he reached the staircase, his heart dropped.

Grandfather stood at the base of the stairs, looking at his

watch. He wore one of his standard black suits with a black coat, and a top hat. Beside him was a massive tan suitcase with pink and yellow lotus flowers stitched into its fabric. Atop the suitcase was a smaller matching bag with a similar atrocious pattern.

"Is that all you need?" Grandfather asked as Ben came down the stairs.

Ben looked at his rather worn out bookbag filled with summoning trinkets. "I should be fine," Ben said with a crack in his voice.

Grandfather nodded and looked at Melly who was standing before them with a dazed look in her milky eyes. "Be sure to NOT burn the house down. Do not allow for anyone to enter the property while we are absent..." Grandfather tilted his head and added for good measure, "and do not kill anyone either."

Melly nodded with little expression, and Ben feared she may misunderstand any of Grandfather's orders. He could only hope that she would be bound by her master's intent and perhaps not do something typical of a zombie home alone.

Grandfather eyed Ben with a stern gaze. "You are not to speak unless you are spoken to... by me."

Ben gulped and nodded.

"I have some things to give you before we go," Grandfather said. Ben watched as Grandfather pulled out a thin black leather case from his pocket. He handed the case to Ben, and the apprentice promptly opened it revealing a familiar set of specter spectacles.

"I thought you didn't want me wearing these," Ben said feeling rather stunned as he twisted the spindly frames in his hands and slid the glasses over the bridge of his nose. Instantly, he could see a swirl of fog outside the front window morph into three ghosts peering inside with their fingers pressed against the glass. One was licking the window in a rather obscene manor.

"It is important that you are prepared for this trip. I will not be with you the entire time, and it is dangerous to be around a single wraith. There will be far more than just one, so you must be able to see them." Grandfather reached around his suitcase to a side pocket and pulled out a small silver dagger. He handed it to Ben, pressing it into his hands.

"Silver is the only effective weapon against a wraith. Under no circumstances are you to use it against one unless the wraith is targeting you. Once you attack a wraith, they will all be aware of your presence and hunt you to no end."

As Ben stowed away the dagger, Grandfather hoisted his suitcase and motioned for Ben to follow along. He opened the front door, and they left the house. Behind them, the spirits whispered and gossiped, sharply glaring at Ben. This was the first time he ever joined Grandfather on a trip beyond the Hill, and he was glad to be leaving the Hill's residents for a while. As they went down the mossy stairs, the complaints of the spirits faded into a faint background noise. He could hear a few ghosts near him, but as they reached the iron gates of the Hill, those too died away.

Grandfather opened the gate and motioned for Ben to follow him outside. Ben assisted Grandfather in closing the gate, and they walked around the exterior of the Hill's property until they came to a small parking lot around the corner nestled within a patch of trees. Grandfather's car sat on the cobbled lot. The hearse's black paint gleamed as if it had just been washed.

It had been a long time since Ben had ridden in the hearse. Grandfather twisted the keys and locked the car doors. The passenger door opened with a subtle metallic pop. Ben sat down on the leather seat, placing his bag on his lap. Grandfather closed the door on his end and brought the car to life.

"Are the Wraithrights nearby?" Ben asked.

"They are only about three hours away. It's not a lengthy drive, unless you prefer an unconventional method of travel?"

Ben looked out the window as they passed the cookie-cutter neighborhood of St. Vincent. The white picket fences blurred with the tree line and pastel-colored houses as Grandfather picked up speed. "Like the mirror? Is that something I can do?"

Grandfather shrugged. "The mirror is a way sometimes. For our family, we also have a simple summons. If necessary, I can show you the scroll. The spirit, *Nomas*, can do the job if you are prepared to traverse through the netherworld instead of the highway."

Ben had yet to travel through the means of the netherworld. He had never even witnessed the netherworld. He was horrifically unprepared for taking on the role of a necromancer let alone a Gravekeeper. He wondered how many more lessons Grandfather had planned for him to succeed the role of becoming a Gravekeeper. Traversing the underworld felt like a very advanced task to the minor arts Ben had yet to master.

Grandfather was no stranger to this issue, likely also pondering over their dilemma. Ben was unprepared to become the next Gravekeeper in more ways than one.

As Ben watched houses be replaced by rolling plains and groves, he asked, "Grandfather, is there another reason you want me to come along with you?"

The sound of the hearse's engine humming and the tires rolling over a gravel road painfully emphasized Grandfather's silence. It felt like nearly an hour had passed before Grandfather cleared his throat and said, "While we are at the Wraithright estate, it will be critical you fulfill the task at hand."

Ben merely nodded, feeling uneasy as they drove under the

forest's light speckled canopies. With the glasses, he could see the spirits of fauna drifting through the trees, standing alongside the road, staring back at them. He wondered how they compared to the Hill's ghosts and feared what the wraiths would be like.

Three hours passed, the hearse pulled up to an iron gate. Ben noted the grass around the gate was well trimmed, and the iron glistened with a fresh layer of oil. A security box sat aside the gate with a man in a well pressed suit sitting at the window, back straight. The guard studied the hearse for a brief moment before pulling on a lever. The gate rattled as gears spun, and it slowly creaked inward. The car's engine hummed as it drove through and cruised along a brick driveway.

Off in the distance, Ben could see the Wraithright manor. It looked like it belonged amongst the mansions in St. Vincent. The vinyl siding of the house was a bright blue, the fencing balusters and roof coping and trim were a stark white. Baby blue hydrangea shrubs grew around the house, and patches of pansies and daffodils flourished down the driveway. One would never know this was the house of one of the most violent necromancer families in history, but as Ben looked onward towards the rolling hills within the iron fence's confines, he could see an endless line of gravestones replacing what may have been fields for horses or cattle.

Not so far from the driveway, the flowers stopped growing and were replaced by neatly trimmed grass. Just a few yards further, a thick row of gravel marked off the grass from the start of an unlively graveyard. Not a single sprout grew amidst the tombstones that spanned throughout the estate.

The car stopped in front of the house, looping around a large patch of flowers that brought a smile to Ben's face. The front door opened, and a man walked out onto his front porch sucking on a cigarette. He wore corduroy pants and a white button-down shirt layered with a tan blazer. His ashy blonde hair was cropped short, and his face clean-shaven. He looked like an ordinary salary man, not the head of a necromancer family. Grandfather sat very still in his seat, keeping the car's engine humming. His eyes steadily watched as the head of the Wraithrights approached the vehicle. "Benjamin, no matter what, you mustn't reveal that you cannot see spirits."

Ben nodded, wishing Grandfather would trust him to hide his own embarrassing secret. He watched as Grandfather grunted and turned off the car. The old man struggled to climb out of the vehicle and walked towards Mr. Wraithright with a slight hobble. Ben followed suit, popping open the side door and trailing behind Grandfather's crooked shadow.

"Ernest, it is a surprise to see you," the man said. He stepped forward and reached out a hand to Grandfather.

Grandfather took his hand and shook it firmly. "You were due for a visit, Winston."

"Not for another seven years, I don't believe. Did something change?" Winston Wraithright asked, scratching the top of his head innocently.

"Nothing of pertinence, but everything of timing. I've heard you may have had some intruders in recent months," Grandfather said, while motioning for Ben to come forward. "I have brought my apprentice, Benjamin, along with me today. He will be investigating your catacombs while we discuss matters related to the intrusions and the council."

Winston's face twitched. "Oh the intruders... I believe they all have been taken care of, but yes... I suppose it makes sense for you to visit with that news hovering about."

The head of the Wraithright family then turned his attention to Ben. Ben noted the man's gentle features and soft, careening eyebrows. Ben found it hard to believe he was the leader of the largest wraith producing necromancer family.

"It is a pleasure to meet you, Benjamin. The last time Ernest came here, he had another apprentice... was it Susan who came along with you?" Ben noticed Grandfather scowl.

"I see..." Winston muttered, realizing Grandfather's previous apprentice was a sore subject. His eyes then lit up, and he entirely focused his attention on Ben. "Would you like to come in and have lunch before you head into the catacombs?"

Grandfather tapped Ben's shoulder, looking fiercely down at him, but Ben's stomach was growling. "That would be delightful," Ben said, grinning at Winston and avoiding Grandfather's gaze. If Grandfather wanted him to scavenge through an entire catacomb, Ben wanted to have a proper meal.

"Very well, thank you," Grandfather said reluctantly.

"Wonderful," Winston Wraithright said, clapping his hands. "Come along, now!"

They followed the head of the Wraithrights up to the front porch of their manor. The man popped open the front doors, and they entered a well-lit foyer with canary yellow armchairs, baby blue cushions and drapes, and abstract artworks of things that might be considered flowers. The stairwell found itself down into the foyer, and beneath that, a hallway tunneled itself into the kitchen and dining areas. On the way to the dining room, they passed a large library decorated with white painted bookshelves and chairs and cushions selected with a pastel palette.

They entered the dining room and interrupted a woman wearing an apron cleaning up the remnants of an already consumed brunch. Ben's jaw dropped. A woman, a real living human maid. He glowered at Grandfather for a second. Why did they have to have a zombie maid? Why did the Hill have to be aged well beyond five hundred years with little renovation to speak of? Ben imagined reading in a library instead of his cramped desk in his room or not being concerned with the ineptitude of a zombie maid. He doubted Wraithrights were hated amongst their neighbors or had children sneaking into their property for tests of courage. They had such a respectable estate, people most likely only visited on scheduled appointments!

"Could you bring out some sandwiches and tea for our guests?" Winston asked. The maid nodded gently and stepped out of the room carrying a stack of plates. Winston patted Ben's back and gently smiled, "I hope you like turkey. We just had one delivered."

Grandfather glared at Winston, and he stepped away from Ben. The necromancer fretted about, tidying up the sprawled-out chairs around the table and motioning for Grandfather and Ben to take a seat. "Sorry, we were not anticipating your presence. Has it been thirty years? It's rather hard to keep track of time."

Grandfather refrained from taking a seat and he glowered at Ben as his apprentice gladly plopped down. Grandfather grumbled, "Thirty years is not a lengthy period of time given the circumstances. It may be necessary to make a trip here annually to ensure no one is going missing in the area."

"We put up the new fence since your last visit," Winston said frightfully. "We have a guard in place... Only during the day, but I am sure you can understand why. From what I have seen, we've had no unwanted guests, visitors, grave robbers-"

"-Who would dare want to rob your graveyard?" Grandfather interjected with a sharp laugh. A shiver went down Ben's spine as he imagined what he was getting himself into.

"Is the fence a problem? It's iron. Is it not enough? We've had intruders, and a few mishaps, but our operation is on such a... What is the Council concerned with?" Winston looked at Ben and then Grandfather, eagerly. To Ben, it looked as if the man desperately wanted to do the right thing.

Winston looked at Ben's perplexed expression and a small smile spread across his lips. "Perhaps it would be best if Benjamin enjoyed our library while he waits on lunch if this discussion is beyond him."

Grandfather raised his hand and shook his head. "His tasks will take long enough for us to have the proper conversation about the Council's concerns without him involved. Regardless, as my apprentice and the next Gravekeeper, he has the privilege to listen to our conversation."

"You don't say?" Winston tilted his head. "Well, I insist you take a seat." He watched Ben as he sat down and folded his hands on the table. "What is it like being an apprentice of the Gravekeeper? It was incredibly challenging to find a good tutor for my daughters. Not many necromancers are prolific or have the sensibilities of a good instructor. Does he send you to a school or have a tutor for you?"

Ben glanced at Grandfather, wondering what to say, but as the seconds passed and Grandfather merely glowered at him, screaming through his gaze to say nothing. He blurted, "Grandfather teaches me everything about necromancy."

"Aha, I see. One could say you don't practice traditional necromancy-"

"There is no need to speak to my apprentice," Grandfather growled. His eyes shot daggers at the necromancer hosting them, and a shiver ran down Ben's spine. He normally experienced Grandfather's ire directed towards him, but something felt odd seeing Grandfather mad at such an amicable person. Ben's eyes narrowed, wondering if Winston Wraithright's gentle expressions were merely a guise.

The kitchen door opened, interrupting the tension. The maid returned to the dining room carrying plates loaded with sandwiches and freshly cut vegetables. She placed a plate down in front of Ben and beside Grandfather and quickly left only to return within a matter of seconds with a pitcher of tea and three tall glasses. Ben's stomach growled at the sight of food. He did not wait to start eating while the two necromancers continued to bicker about general politics and curriculum agenda.

Ben wondered what vendetta the Council had against the Wraithrights, and why Winston Wraithright expressed an interest in his studies. But he found it difficult to focus on the conversation as his fear of the wraith infested catacombs grew in strength with each bite. The moment Ben finished his food, Grandfather motioned for him to stand.

"I will come back in a moment to join you, Winston. Let me get my apprentice settled so that he can do his investigation while there is still daylight."

"If that is how you must conduct it, I will be waiting in my study," Winston said. His eyes looked drained, and his voice was devoid of energy. They then lifted to Ben's face. "Oh, you will need this!" He shuffled around in his pockets and pulled out a singular key. "To avoid any unwanted guests, we've been keeping the mausoleum locked. That will lead you into the crypt."

He pressed the key into Ben's palm. Ben noted Winston's fingers were long and frail, constantly trembling to the touch. As the necromancer moved away from Ben, he looked to Grandfather and said, "The maid will guide you to my office when you return."

"I know where your study is, Winston." Grandfather's cold voice made the necromancer shiver. Ben could only sympathize with the man as grandfather ushered him down the hall and back outside.

They walked to the car, and Ben grabbed his bag from the front seat while Grandfather pulled out the gaudy satchel and handed it to Ben. Ben shuffled with the bag a little bit, finding a zipper hidden within the folds. "What is in this?" he asked starting to unzip the bag.

Grandfather reached out and grabbed Ben's hand, pulling it into the air and away from the zipper. "Don't open it!"

Grandfather looked about and crouched in so he was eye to eye with Ben. "If this is exposed to sunlight, it will disappear. No matter what, do not expose this to the light. It is far too valuable and far too dangerous. Do not open this bag unless you are in the shadows of the crypt or after dusk."

"I don't see why I'd be there so late," Ben muttered, frowning and looking at the sky. It was barely reaching noon.

"It is better to have this and not need it than not have it and die," Grandfather said gravely. "Now do you have your watch?"

Ben raised his arm, revealing a silver watch on his wrist. "Yes, sir."

"Be mindful of the time. It is easy to lose track underground. Be careful, and don't forget," Grandfather leaned in and whispered in Ben's ear, *"Hubert Wraithright."*

Grandfather quickly turned and returned to the house, leaving Ben alone by the hearse. The boy's shoulders slumped, and he sighed, looking sideways at the house. The boy hoped to finish the job quickly and gain the opportunity of divulging in the Wraithright library. There were probably things about necromancy he could learn there that Grandfather would never dare teach him.

He shuffled around with his bags, inventorying everything he had. Ben hoped this was enough to keep him safe, but no one said necromancy was a safe job anyway. He turned towards the graveyard and started his walk along the driveway towards the mausoleum.

After a while, a narrow sidewalk branched off into the graveyards. A line of dying, leafless shrubs defined the difference between the graveyard and normal rolling hills of grass. That, and the rows of identical, tall tombstones sticking out of the earth like crooked teeth.

Ben walked along the concrete path towards the stone mausoleum off in the distance. It cut against the overcast skyline, with nothing behind it except rolling hills of graves. The sidewalk leading towards it was cracked and stained. Large chunks of concrete stuck out of the edges, and dried lichens clung to the sidewalk, pleading for life. The grass surrounding the sidewalk was once long, but it laid so lifelessly to the ground, it appeared short. The base of the tombstones were entirely devoid of vegetation, harboring patches of dried earth.

Ben's brows knit as he looked upon the Wraithright graveyard and its abysmal condition. Did they not care about how the spirits felt? He doubted they actually did, knowing the sort of spirits they harbored. A wraith was no joyous spirit, and it would take a great deal of effort to keep any sort of living plant around them. This was no cemetery but a site harboring monsters.

Eventually, the sidewalk ended, drowning into the earth. The grass crunched with each step just like leaves in the fall. As he approached the mausoleum, a chill ran down Ben's spine. A yellowed sign hung on the door with the bold red text: 'Do not enter'. A heavy set of iron chains with a silver padlock wrapped themselves around the door handles securing the mausoleum from anyone willing to disregard the sign. Ben reached into his pocket and pulled out the large iron key Winston had given him. His hands noticeably shook as he twisted the key into the lock, and he flinched as the padlock fell with a heavy thud into the dirt.

The doors creaked open inward an inch with a hollow moan. He slid the chains off the door handles, struggling to lift them as they caught every few links in the narrow handles. After a few minutes, he managed to loosen the chains, and they fell on the ground in a heap.

Ben looked over his shoulder one last time, gauging the position of the sun with the horizon. It was nearing noon, but Ben imagined he would have plenty of time to do his job and be out before dusk. He looked down at his watch, noting it to be eleven thirty in the morning. By seven, if he were not out of the catacombs, he would have no choice but to use the wraith cloak.

Ben sucked in a deep, nerve-settling breath and stepped forward into the mausoleum. There were a couple stone benches and small memorials inset on the walls along with half burned candlesticks caked in dust and grime. The majority of the space was consumed by two towering statues whose shoulders scraped the arched stone ceiling, and their heads bowed, looking down at Ben with heavyset glares and gaping mouths. They bordered a small archway that steeply descended into the crypts.

Ben shuffled in his bag as he approached the bone-chilling staircase. He stopped at the edge of the archway, staring into the abyss. His hand wrapped around the cold metal of the flashlight, and he pulled it out of the bag.

Click

A brilliant beam of white washed over the walls and down the steep stone treads. Waving the flashlight about, Ben watched his steps and studied the walls. Drooping cobwebs lit up like sparkling silver wires, and a deep shadow fled to the very base of the stairs. He sneered at the spiderwebs with disgust. Grandfather was right to call these catacombs undesirable. Having a catacomb without proper maintenance just felt wrong.

The air drew dank the deeper he went until the ground leveled out and a steady, cold humidity fell upon Ben's skin. The air was still and heavy, thick with must and mold. The flashlight highlighted a heavy mist drifting in the air, and the light faded before it reached another wall, dying in the shadows.

He swept the flashlight across the deep rectangular hallway to its nearest edges. Stone caskets were stacked atop each other from floor to ceiling in rows, creating walls between massive columns that formed vaults across the open hall. Sporadically there were gaps between the caskets, leading into deep hallways.

Clang... Clang...

The flashlight flicked to a massive statue near Ben at the entrance to the stairs. It had a twin standing beside it, but unlike the statues in the mausoleum, these stood straight with their arms hidden behind the stone mimicry of cloaks. The cloaks hung over their shoulders and produced cowls that just barely revealed the tops of their chins. Pale blue chains rattled at their feet. He feared to know what would happen if such ethereal bindings broke.

Trying to ignore the glowing blue chains, Ben walked deeper into the main hall. He studied a few caskets, noting several iron chains wrapped about them. Some were rusting and on the verge of complete disintegration. Others were glistening with oil and appeared as if they had been placed just hours ago. He paused in front of the standing caskets wrapped in so many chains that it was hard to read the epitaph. The longer Ben stared at the chains, the easier it was to spot the faintest blue light. Each set of chains were seals to the spirits residing in their caskets, trapping them within the tiny confines of their coffins.

Ben stepped away from the standing casket and rubbed his forehead. If he found Hubert's coffin amongst the masses, he would likely have to unravel a slew of chains and destroy the coffin's seal. After that, there was no telling what the ghost inside would do after having been trapped for over a century. Ben could not believe Grandfather's dismissal to such an idea. What if Hubert himself had become a wraith?!

Unfortunately, he did not have much time to dwell upon his concerns. If he waited and feared for the risk of Hubert being a wraith, he would soon find himself surrounded by hundreds. He needed to spend every minute searching for Hubert and worry about the consequences of finding him afterward. Looking around just the sheer size of the entrance alone, he knew he needed to be quick if he wanted to leave before dusk.

The apprentice started his search with each casket in the main hall, disappointed to not find Hubert's name. He then took the first hole on the left and hurried down the path, Searching for Hubert's epitaph. Ben did not feel guilty about focusing his search on the deceased necromancer. If he found the remains of any unfortunate souls in the catacombs, he would likely trip over them or easily spot them through the beam of his flashlight. Finding a singular name in such an expanse of a maze, on the other hand, was like searching for a specific bone in a catacomb.

After three hours of searching the catacombs through a maddening meandering, he feared his efforts would not be fruitful. If he did not find Hubert, would Grandfather come into the catacombs and assist him? He doubted Grandfather would garner an excuse to leave the Wraithrights. How could he tell him in front of Winston that his search was to no avail? They would have to leave and try again in another thirty years! If he wanted to gain the insight Hubert Wraithright could offer, he would have to find Hubert now while he still had a chance.

But it was particularly hard to focus on his search. Unlike their own crypt, the Wraithright's catacombs were a massive nesting ground for spiders. Every time he studied a casket, he found them wrapped in just as many webs as chains. Some webs spanned across the narrow pathways, being completely unavoidable. He found the condition of the catacombs extremely disgusting and aggravating, and each filthy coffin and cobweb marred his mind. As he delved deeper, he found it harder to avoid the cobwebs that expanded across the narrow halls.

A large circular web spread itself across a hallway, like an invisible net. It stuck against Ben's face, tangling in his hair, and pressing onto his mouth. He sputtered and spat, waving his arms frantically to remove the web and whatever critters might be attached to it. He dropped his flashlight with a painful crack as the metal device fell and rolled under a stack of caskets.

Still covered in the net of webs, Ben crouched down and reached for the light source. It threateningly blinked, daring to submerge Ben in a sea of darkness.

"Come on," Ben muttered as he pressed himself on the earthen floor and stretched his arm through the gap of the caskets. His fingers tapped the metal flashlight, and the beam shifted, flickering again, and tilting just enough to point right in Ben's eyes. He flinched and turned away, tapping the flashlight further into the crevice to the point it was completely unreachable.

He laid there for several minutes, hopelessly wondering what to do next. He attempted to snag the light a couple more times, even using his knife to gain reach, but it was too far under the caskets. Sighing, Ben picked himself up off the ground and sat on his knees, staring at the patch of illuminated dirt. He might be able to find his way back out of the catacombs with the flashlight, but without any light, he was hopeless.

If only Grandfather had taught him how to procure a flame! The only magic Ben could perform was summon. He shuffled in his bag and pulled out the scroll. Perhaps a spirit could help him retrieve the flashlight?

Ben unfurled Elaine's scroll on the illuminated patch of

ground and read over the document. He sighed, thankful he could summon the poltergeist. If any spirit could reach the flashlight, it would be her.

Ben tilted the knife and sliced a sliver of his wrist before allowing it to bleed over the contract signatures as he read out the terms. As he read, the air drew cold, and the moisture around his eyes and lips froze while the icy dew on his skin from the damp air made his skin prickle with pain. He shivered as he read. "E-E-laine."

There was a second delay before the familiar poltergeist appeared directly above Ben. Her icy presence was so close, Ben could feel his ears burning with newfound frostbite. He snagged the contract and clambered away from the spirit's aura, pressing his back against a stack of coffins.

Elaine looked about with concern. *"What is this dreadful place?"*

Even a spirit found the Wraithright's catacombs terrible. Ben adjusted his glasses, wondering if she could see something he could not. He had felt uneasy ever since they entered the Wraithright estate, so it would be hard for him to know if that was simply his nerves or something intuitive. It did not take much thought on the issue given he knew what the Wraithrights harbored in their cursed land.

"Elaine, I need your help!"

"Yes?"

"I dropped my flashlight." Ben pointed across from him towards the pile of caskets where the flashlight was buried. The light flickered incessantly now, but thankfully Elaine's glowing figure allowed him to see as if the hall were basked in moonlight. The boy lowered the specters, and surely enough, he could only see the faint flickering of a yellow light on a bloodied dirt floor

"You dropped... your flashlight?" Elaine tilted her head towards the flickering light. *"That is why you summoned me?"*

"Y-yes," Ben stammered. His cheeks blushed. How often did a necromancer summon a spirit for such a trivial task?

Ben hoped the spirit would simply reach through the caskets and pull the flashlight out of the gap. The spirit's skirts and hair flowed against the breeze of a maelstrom and her face contorted into something fiendish. Her wispy arms seemed to spread out like glowing white veils, sweeping over the pile of caskets.

RUMBLE

As the caskets shuddered, Ben clambered away from Elaine as fast as he could until he pressed up against the stone legs of a statue.

WHAM!

Faster than a blink, the middle casket flew across the passageway, through the poltergeist, and into the pile of caskets on the other side. Ben cried, grabbing his head and falling prone, as three more caskets followed suit, flying in every direction including over where his head was only a moment ago. The heavy wooden coffins collapsed, wood splintered, and a single casket precariously creaked, threatening to topple over. He winced. The poltergeist's ethereal light exposed strewn about and disassembled skeletal remains. How would he explain this to Grandfather and Winston Wraithright?

The apprentice gulped, knowing he could never mention this. As he started to stand, something silver flashed before his eyes, hitting him straight in the forehead with a beam of yellow light.

+X+

Cold. It's so cold…

"Stone," Elaine's voice echoed through the halls and into Ben's ears.

He groaned and opened his eyes. The spectral specter frames were bent, and Elaine's hovering face appeared slightly warped as she floated over Ben.

His eyes widened and he waved his arms forward. "Back away!" he griped, motioning for the poltergeist to move away from him. His hands were completely numb, he could not feel his cheeks. His nose, ears, and lungs burned from the icy air the spirit produced. Once she backed away, the cold quickly subsided, revealing a sharp, painful headache.

Ben grasped his forehead, feeling a knot form and looked down at the source of the pain. A sturdy metal flashlight sat in his lap, blinking with light every few seconds. "Ugh… Lovely."

"Stone," Elaine whispered, bringing back Ben's attention to the poltergeist as she drifted slightly closer to him. Concern wrought her eyebrows together and she constantly was looking about as if she were a girl in a haunted house. Luckily for her, she was a poltergeist in a crypt. She fit right in!

"Yes?" Ben asked halfheartedly as he clambered to his feet and smacked the flashlight, trying to bring it back to life.

"They are coming," she hissed. *"Please, unsummon me."*

"What?" Ben looked directly at the poltergeist. She was not just looking around admiring the catacomb's filthiness. The spirit was visibly shaking, causing her apparition to turn into clouds of fog.

"They are coming…. I feel them, I hear them. You must run!"

she cried, voice raising an octave. Ice formed along the ceiling of the catacombs and threaded itself on the broken caskets as she could not hold in her panic anymore. *"UNSUMMON ME!"*

Ben's eyes widened, and he instinctively took a step back to avoid the dropping temperature. "Okay, okay. *Elaine*, you are dismissed," Ben said. Not half a second passed before her figure dissipated into the air.

They are coming, her words poisoned Ben's mind. The apprentice thought over them, over and over while rubbing his aching head. What could make a poltergeist tremble in fear?

Ching... clang....

Ben's mouth went dry. The wraiths were coming.

The boy clambered for his bags in a panic. His personal bag was under one of the caskets. He doubted he had the time to retrieve it. The other bag with Grandfather's item was half torn under another casket. Ben could see a black silky cloth spilling out of the torn seams.

He looked up at the piles of coffins around him. They would not slow the wraiths, but they certainly would slow him. He did not have a chance of escaping. He hoped the wraith cloak would do its job and protect him. He reached for the bag and snagged at the black cloth stuck beneath the splintered casket.

The moment his fingers grazed the cloth, a feeling of dread enveloped him. He gritted his teeth and tugged on the cloth, freeing it from the bag. Ben lifted it and felt a nasty energy emanating from the cloak. Every instinct in Ben's body screamed to toss the thing on the ground, but something even more dreadful was coming his way.

Ben tossed the cloak over his shoulders. His skin prickled with discomfort, and the hairs on the back of his neck stood. The sickening feeling the cloak created made his stomach churn and limbs weaken. Ben's breaths were light and rapid, and he shivered uncontrollably to the point where the flashlight slipped from his fingers. It clattered on the ground. Ben quickly crouched down to grab it before it could roll away.

Reaching out, he gasped. In the pale light, a rotted hand reached for the flashlight. His suit jacket sleeve was tattered, rapidly withering. His own flesh was rotting away by the second!

He choked down a scream. He was not dying, he was not dying, he told himself. This was part of the cloak's magic. As soon as he took it off, he would be fine. He had to be fine! Grandfather would not have given something that would kill him... he hoped. Ben wanted to pull off the cloak, but he did not have the time to test his theory. The rattle of chains was drawing nearer and nearer. Bony fingers snatched the flashlight and flicked it off. His only chance of fooling the wraiths was to become one.

Clang....

The chains rattled right behind Ben, clamoring against the damaged caskets. The boy slowly turned, careful to draw the cloak around his body as tightly as possible. He wheezed as he watched the pale blue glow of the wraith move through the caskets and investigate the scene. The wraith looked directly at him, and the boy nearly lost control of his bowels.

The spirit's face was warped and rotted. Hollowed eyes filled with a deep darkness that screamed misery stared into his very being. Ben shuddered under the wraith's gaze. The creature stayed still and opened an elongated jaw that stretched past the length of its neck. Ben was sure it would screech out, yet the creature released a soft wail and drifted towards where Ben had summoned Elaine. It stooped its head and stared at the spot the contract had originally been and where there were still fresh drops of Ben's blood. Ben shivered and watched the wraith careen its body towards the ground until its head drifted a mere inch from the earth.

He had to move. Now.

The boy attempted to walk towards the smaller pile of caskets where the wraith had come from, but his legs were heavier than usual. He shuffled forward, fearing the wraith behind him would catch on. After all, that wraith did not have legs. Would it not notice his belabored footsteps?

The apprentice did not care to wait and find out. He climbed over a couple of caskets and hurried down the hall away from the wraith. He looked back at the pale blue light source of the wraith nearly sticking its face into the earth now. It then arched its neck and twisted its skeletal hands outward. A shrill shriek filled the air.

Ben stumbled to his knees and grabbed his ears, refraining from crying out. His throat croaked out strangled gasps.

The sound was soul splitting. The apprentice clenched his teeth. This was not the first time he heard the howl of an undead. If he did not keep his wits now, it would only get worse. Especially with the echo of chains down the halls and the faint retaliatory cries filling the catacombs. The apprentice only had one agenda: to escape.

Eleven

Wraiths

Ben sprinted down the hall, crumpling Elaine's scroll into his inner jacket pocket. He did not look back to see if the wraith was following. He feared more for the horde ahead. His body moved as if he were running on sand. Ben felt like every step would be his last. His lungs drew little to no air. Ben feared his next breath would not come. He understood why Grandfather considered the artifact an 'insurance.' It was something only to be used in a worst-case scenario, a situation bringing forth the risk of a fate worse than death. In no other situation would one desire the persisting pain of the brink of death.

The further Ben ran away from the wraith, the darker the catacombs became. Deep shadows engulfed Ben. His sprinting slowed to a creep as the apprentice stretched his hand to feel for the stacks of caskets, the dusty texture of an earthen wall, or the smooth grit of a stone statue. Instead of feeling anything, Ben's fingers pressed against something with a hollow clack.

The apprentice shivered. He could imagine the flesh from his hands gone with only bones to remain. Not a single wraith was known to have flesh and skin. If Ben were to fit in enough to fool such life hungry fiends, he himself would have to look like the definition of death.

And feel like it to, Ben thought begrudgingly. If only he could see in the dark, just like any spirit. The cloak was just a disguise and perhaps a torture device, nothing more.

The apprentice's hands shook as he treaded down the hall. He debated on if it was safe enough to turn on the flashlight. A bright beam of light in these halls of darkness would surely give him away, but how else was he to find his way out? After several minutes, Ben pressed his finger against the flashlight's switch, preparing to light his path for just a second.

The heavy moan of a spirit ahead, not so far in the distance, along with the clanking and thudding of chains against stone and earth echoed in his ears. He stopped moving and lowered the flashlight, breathing in sharp breaths through his nose. Instinctively, he wrapped the cloak around his shoulders, making sure the approaching wraith would not see any semblance of life. In a matter of seconds, it turned around a curve in the catacombs, illuminating the hall in a faint blue light only detectable with the spectral specters.

He blinked and watched as the wraith drifted forward. A soul rattling breath seeped from its hood. The apprentice held his own breath as the spirit drew near. Slowly, Ben shuffled forward, pressing himself as close to the walls as possible. If the wraith touched him, his waning life force would vanish completely.

They were mere feet away from each other. The source of the pale blue light came from the chains wrapped around the wraith. They weaved through the spirit's tattered cloak and fell and dragged behind it. Ben gulped, knowing he did not have chains on himself. Would the wraith recognize that?

Inches away, he avoided making eye contact with the wraith as it drifted forward, passing him. It seemed to have no interest in Ben and instead focused on the distressed wail from the wraith ahead. The apprentices' eyes lowered to the glowing blue chain dragging on the earth. It slowly slithered past him, rattling as it snagged on lumps of earth and small stones. As the last link in the chain passed, Ben exhaled.

The chains whipped around, smacking the nearest set of coffins. The wraith released a startled screech that echoed down the hallway, sending a shiver down his spine. The apprentice froze, holding his breath, not daring to move an inch. The wraith twisted about, looking for the source of life. It only needed to feel a warm breath.

Ben closed his eyes, trying not to think about the wraith as it drew near him. He hardly had the strength to run or fight the spirit in his current condition. A cold breeze and an unnatural onslaught of immense sorrow enveloped the helpless apprentice.

Ben opened his eyes and choked down a cry, looking face-to-face with the wraith. Sunken black pits stared back at him. A gossamer layer of ashen gray skin mottled from undying decay wrapped around the skeletal face. Its mouth, full of aged teeth, released a rattling breath that promised only death.

To survive, Ben could only play dead.

The wraith drifted away, turning back towards the still screeching wraith down the hall. The chain rattled behind it with a chilling tempo as the wraith floated in the direction of its fellow eternal prisoner.

He shuddered, body screaming for air. He finally sucked in the quietest of breaths. He tilted his head and watched the wraith's blue light draw fainter in the distance, and he released a heavy sigh. While thankful the wraith could not see through his guise, he wondered just how effective the wraith cloak was. He reached towards his face, and bone fingers tapped the bent frames of his spectral specters.

A small cry bubbled in Ben's throat, but the boy furiously fought it down with the brimming terror of knowing what lurked down the hall. His fingers were indeed entirely bone. His face undoubtedly appeared as something similar to the wraith. Perhaps he was now a reflection of the spirit spare the chains binding his soul to this forsaken graveyard. Ben shivered and stepped forward, shaking his head. He had to escape.

Determined to not spend any more time than necessary in the wraith cloak *and* the catacombs, Ben pulled out his flashlight and turned it on, shining a flickering beam down the narrow corridor. While the light only came out in weak spurts, it was enough to guide Ben down the hall without fear of running into a wall or some other unknown undead.

He learned his fate was not entirely sealed. The wraiths filled the catacombs, but they had several disadvantages to finding Ben. To start, the apprentice was completely hidden amongst them. So long as he kept the cloak on and turned off the flashlight as the wraiths neared, they would never detect him.

Alternatively, the wraiths themselves were easy to find. They screeched every time there was a sound including their own cries, filling the catacombs with the echoes of the screaming undead. If a wraith was not howling, its chains still rattled and clanged against everything the wraith passed by. The chains themselves were also physical, and Ben realized they could not pass through objects, preventing the wraiths from traveling though the catacombs in unconventional ways. He did not have to worry about a spirit reaching through the walls or drifting from above or below. So long as he stayed pressed to the walls or slid into the gaps between wall and casket stacks when a wraith passed by, he may stay alive.

These conclusions allowed Ben to navigate the catacombs with a sliver of confidence. He turned the flashlight off as needed and altered his pace as the wraiths appeared. It was not until Ben arrived at the main hall near the entrance did his confidence vanish.

Wraiths filled the hall. Like a snake nest, the wraiths' chains slithered over one another, entangling the horde. They floated aimlessly, heads tilted in different directions. When one screamed, it triggered the rest to join in a chorus of unintelligible cries. Ben's insides twisted, threatening to turn inside out.

The apprentice cowered next to one of the piles of caskets, eyeing the base of the stairs through the pale blue mist of undead. The boy strategized how he could get across without bumping into any of the wraiths or somehow revealing he was an imposter. He settled on moving as close to the walls as possible where the wraiths seemed to keep some distance.

Ben moved as steadily as possible. His hips were creaking, knees shaking, and ankles threatening to snap. If he stayed here any longer, the cloak would kill him before the wraiths. The blood in his head flowed slowly, but he could hear his heart beat heavy thuds like an echoing drum slowing in tempo. If a single wraith picked up this sound, he would be torn to pieces.

He padded down the hallway, towards the stairs. His hands and body leaned against the caskets for support and to be as far away from the wraiths as possible. With each shuffle of a step, Ben tugged the vile cloak to stay wrapped around him, fearing the slightest exposure of his body in this well-lit room would seal his fate.

The echoing moans of the wraiths only built onto the terror churning in Ben's chest. His life force shook, at risk of being devoured. In the pale light, he could see his bony fingers and skeletal arms press upon the caskets. If he died now, would all that remain be a skeleton or not even bones?

As he shuffled towards the stairwell, Ben listened to the endless moans and rattles produced by the wraiths. He wondered who would be enticed to enter the mausoleum and descend into the catacombs by such sounds? No rite of passage could summon such an amount of courage. The wails made his head spin, his heart flutter in dizzying patterns, and his hands rattle in rhythm with the chains dancing across the floor.

He blinked, and the tip of a wraith cloak drifted past him, clearing the path ahead. There were no wraiths in his way. He stumbled forward, reaching the base of the steps. He took a couple quick steps to catch himself and looked back at the horde of wraiths slinking around the main hall of the catacombs. They were drifting without order, without purpose, and their entire attention was on everything and nothing. The cursed beings failed to notice their sole enemy as the boy watched them with sheer hope.

His arms and stomach trembled, holding in the uneven breathing. He clenched his waist as sharp pains shot up from the depths of his stomach. He still needed to leave the underground. He was almost there.

Turning his shoulder, he smacked into the wall and the flashlight slipped from his weakened hands.

Clack – Click – CLANG

Ben froze, listening to the silver flashlight roll. Its light flickered on as it rolled further and further towards the direction of the horde of wraiths until it stopped with a clang against a chain.

No.

His mind emptied. The wraith looked down at the foreign object that had rolled into its chain.

Stop.

It reached down in agonizing slowness and ensnared the flashlight within its long bony fingers.

Don't.

It lifted the flashlight as if it were a critical piece of evidence from a crime scene and looked directly at the culprit.

The apprentice gritted his teeth and stepped backward. He forced himself to turn onto the stairs and run at full speed. Behind him the wraith cried something damning, and it was echoed with a chorus from the deepest of nightmares and horrors.

Ben ran with all his might up the steep flight of stone stairs. His lungs screamed, his bones cracked and creaked with every movement on the verge of snapping. The wraith cloak billowed around him, producing nauseating waves of necrotic energy. Any step along the staircase could have been his last, but somehow, he reached the heart of the mausoleum still breathing and listening to the screams down below crescendo and near.

Ben leapt forward and pressed two skeletal hands against the mausoleum doors. He did his best not to ogle over the sight or scream and focused on pushing with every ounce of strength left in his decrepit body. The doors swung forward with a loud moan, slamming shut.

"DAMNIT!" Ben clawed at the doors, pushing his bony fingers at the seams and grabbing on anything worth holding to pull the doors inward. With immense struggle, the doors creaked inward and Ben pulled them as far as possible until his body could slip through the narrow gap. Ben stumbled forward, tripping over the pile of abandoned chains, and he rolled in a ball onto the withered grass.

As he rolled, his vision cascaded with the sight of a periwinkle sky, the black fabric of the cloak, and the grey stone walls of the mausoleum. Then Ben landed on his bum and stared at a sea of gravestones blanketed by the gently departing sun and the faint light of a crescent moon carving into the fuchsia sunset. The boy blinked for a second, feeling weary and thankful for the sight of the sky.

Phssssssss....

Something hissed.

Ben twisted around and scrambled to his feet. Not a single wraith had followed him outside of the mausoleum, although he could feel their energy near and hear their screams just beyond the doors. He squinted and spied bony hands and hollowed out faces leering at him with immense loathing. The boy stepped backwards slowly, knowing the only thing keeping them at bay was the sunlight.

Sunlight. The wraith cloak could not be exposed to the light.

Ben looked down. His eyes widened as he watched the source of the hissing fade away like dust in the wind. The cloak evaporated into smoke, lifting off Ben, and somehow leaving behind skin and flesh unharmed. He stared at his hands with tears in his eyes. In the sunset, he could see the calluses, his fingernails, the wrinkles of his knuckles, and the smallest of scrapes. It was as if the cloak had never existed.

Sucking in a deep breath, Ben recognized he was still in immense danger. Less than ten feet away waited a horde of wraiths. Unwilling to spend another second in their presence, he spun on his heel and ran towards Wraithright's manor.

Without the cloak, he felt alive. His skin felt the soft texture of his clothing. His lungs inhaled deep satisfying breaths, and his heart pumped furiously. Ben could taste the air- it tasted like fresh tilled soil, and a freshly trimmed meadow. Did he ever pay attention to such things? Was the feeling of being alive something so fleeting?

It did not take him long before he arrived at the house. To his surprise, Grandfather stood on the porch with his arms crossed and his foot tapping away the seconds. Ben stopped running as he reached the side of the hearse, and he shifted his pace to a swift walk.

"Grandfather," Ben called.

"Benjamin Stone," Grandfather hissed through his teeth. He stepped off the porch and towards Ben, closing the distance in two seconds. Grandfather looked Ben over with concern. "What took you so long? It is nearly dusk. Did you speak to him?" He leaned down and hissed, "Where is the item I gave you?"

Ben looked down at his torn suit. Unlike his body, the suit did not recover from the cloak's decaying enchantment. The fabric's color was faded, and the hems were thinned and threading. Chin tucked, Ben stumbled over his words. "G-grandfather, the wraiths appeared in the catacombs before the evening. I didn't have a choice-"

"Ah, Ernest!" A weary voice interrupted Ben and Grandfather. The Stones looked towards the house to Winston Wraithright.

The necromancer waved as he hurried off the porch towards the two. He stepped between Grandfather and Ben and grabbed the apprentice's hands. "How is the condition of the catacombs? Please tell me, there were no unwanted guests?" He pleaded looking into Ben's eyes. "We can't afford any accidental deaths."

Pulling his hands away from Winston, Ben softly stammered, "T-there wasn't a-anyone."

"Are you certain? I keep the doors locked, but are you really sure?"

"I didn't see any bodies." Except for the ones he accidentally had thrown out of their own coffins. The boy bit his lip and refrained from looking away, fearing that Winston would read his mind.

The necromancer leaned away from Ben, patting his shoulder. "Oh, that is good then." His grasp tightened on Ben's shoulder as he looked at Grandfather. "See, Ernest? There is nothing to worry about with our wraiths. You don't have to fear for anyone's safety. We keep our graveyard very secure."

Ben was not so sure about that given he had minimal difficulty getting into the mausoleum. Although, he supposed if the wrong person was going in there, it was not entirely Wraithright's fault the intruder would have to face such a horrible demise. They had been warned.

"Perhaps," Grandfather said, eyeing Ben. "I believe since that is the case, our buisness is done here for the day."

"Really?" Winston asked, feigning disappointment. His hand still clung onto Ben's shoulder, pinching into his sore muscles. "Did you not wish to stay for dinner? My wife and daughters will be available to join us." His voice lowered to a whisper. "But *please* keep the necromancy talk to a minimum. It upsets Avery."

"I'm afraid Benjamin still has chores to do back at the Hill," Grandfather said. "You see, we have our own graveyard to manage."

Winston looked at Ben with dismay and released his shoulder. Ben shrugged it, feeling the sharp discomfort slowly fade. "Ah, I see," Winston said, looking down. Ben could see the slightest of smirks spread across the necromancer's face. He lifted his chin and softly smiled at Grandfather. He reached to pat his back, but a sharp glower haltered Winston's hand. "Be sure to visit another time. Your estate is not quite so far away."

Grandfather nodded. "Yes, another time."

Winston walked back towards the porch and Grandfather ushered Ben to go to the car. Ben paused to listen to Grandfather call, "Do not forget what we discussed, Winston. It will not be me who visits next time."

Ben turned and looked to see the color from the

necromancer's face fade as if he had seen a ghost.

He climbed into the hearse, and Grandfather joined him shortly after, turning the car on and bringing the engine humming to life. As he pulled the car around and drove down the long road out of the Wraithright estate, he consistently shot Ben glances dripping heavy with concern.

"Where is the cloak?" he asked. "What happened, Benjamin? *Where is the cloak?*"

"The wraiths appeared in the catacombs and I had to use it, but it wasn't enough and I had to get out of the catacombs. I didn't know the sun was still out!" Ben exclaimed.

"It got exposed to sunlight," Grandfather groaned, pinching his nose, realizing what had happened to his precious artifact.

"It's gone. I'm sorry," Ben said, looking down at his knees. The fabric of his pants had thinned and frayed. He could only imagine how valuable the wraith cloak was.

"Please tell me you were not wearing the cloak in the light." Grandfather's voice was soft, but Ben knew the danger underlining his calm tone.

He gulped and slowly nodded, keeping his gaze down. "I didn't have time to take it off," he muttered. "It vanished."

The car jerked and swerved as Grandfather turned in his seat to gawk at Ben. "You didn't take it off!" His golden eyes flared like two suns. Grandfather quickly corrected his posture and forced himself to stare at the road, but Ben knew he was in deep trouble.

"Benjamin, this will be a long night for you," Grandfather said. His voice was hollow and grim. "Listen to my words closely. No matter what you do, do not fall asleep."

"What?" Ben asked, wondering if this was his punishment for

losing the cloak.

"If you do, you will turn into a wraith."

Twelve

The Wraith Cloak

Grandfather's words rang in Ben's ears. He sank deep into a pond with Grandfather's words echoing through the water in dizzying waves. "What?!" he managed to ask after a long minute of silence as the panic sank in. "A wraith? I will turn into a wraith?!"

Grandfather clenched his jaw. "I did not anticipate the wraiths would appear in the catacombs while the sun was still up. Benjamin, that cloak is not only the artifact of a wraith. It is also a tool to create one."

Ben felt like his head was spinning. Grandfather had knowingly given him such a cursed item, and he even put it on! A sickening feeling sowed itself into Ben's stomach. He tried to push it away, knowing the cloak was necessary under the circumstance, but the worst of Grandfather's words haunted him. He could not sleep now. Why? The only reason the cloak had any effect on him now was if it still existed.

To answer his concerns, an intense weight pressed on his shoulders and chest, and his breaths drew light. Ben watched as a deep black shadow enveloped him. An astonished cry slipped from his throat. "Grandfather!"

"The cloak is a cursed item. It can be taken on and off whenever, but if worn into the light, it will bind itself to the soul of its wearer until the sun sets once more. The moment you fall asleep wearing the cloak at night or in shadow, it will succeed in completely absorbing your lifeforce and transforming you into a wraith."

"Why didn't you tell me this sooner?!" Ben cried. He pulled at the sleeves of the cloak, but it no longer felt like the same cloak of just an hour ago. In all essence, it was the same item, but now the cloth had an ethereal texture to it. As Ben tried to pull on the black fabric, it vaporized like roiling smoke and twisted around his fingers only to reform the moment he moved his hand away. "It won't come off!"

"No Benjamin, it cannot come off. The cloak is no longer of this world. It is bound to your soul," Grandfather explained with a morose expression.

Ben's eyes widened and he trembled something fierce. In every sense, the cloak behaved like a possessive spirit ready to consume him at his greatest moment of weakness. Ben shifted his glasses downward. The thin metal frames shook with Ben's bony hands. Removing the glasses, his vision blurred, and Ben could see his worn out clothes and his flesh. He looked almost normal, making Ben's breaths waver, yearning to heave a sigh of relief.

Without the glasses, he could *hear* the glasses metal frames *clack* on the bones of his fingers. He could *feel* the looming presence of death's embrace. His breathing was haggard, and his heartbeat pounded in a staggard rhythm. The presence of a curse beseeching death was undeniable.

"W-what do I do?" Ben pleaded.

"Stay awake. If you become a wraith now, not even I will make it out of this car alive."

Ben nodded and stared ahead, focusing his attention on the illuminated road. How could he fall asleep in such circumstances? Terror built in his chest, making his heart pace faster, and he feared before the night's end, it may give out. How could he fall asleep, knowing he would never awaken? No, not waking up was not the worst outcome of this situation. Death itself was not so foul. However, the cloak embracing his being promised something far worse than death. He was cursed to endure an endless existence as a violent, mindless spirit ensnared to the world. And his first victim would be Grandfather.

The drive was terribly long, but as they pulled into St. Vincent and parked the hearse at the bottom of The Hill, Ben hardly felt relieved. The hum of the hearse's engine died, and the subtle rattle of Ben's bones ceased. It was a maddening sound that made Ben want to pull out his hair, but he feared he hardly had any to pull.

He clambered out of the car. "What are we going to do!" he cried. Nearly the whole car ride had been silent, but he knew there had to be a solution to this beyond simply staying awake.

Grandfather closed the car door with a heavy slam. "There's nothing *I* can do-"

Ben groaned, fearing for the worst. Sure, he could hold off sleeping tonight. Ben was used to staying awake until mid morning. Except, the toll of the cloak weighed on him, and all the apprentice wanted to do was curl up in a ball and rest... Maybe he would not make it the night, and if not this night, not tomorrow. "Grandfather, there must be something!"

"I'm afraid this is another call for Erwys," Grandfather said through his teeth as he locked the car and motioned for Ben to follow him.

They walked around the parking lot to the Hill's entrance, only to face another problem. A milk crate sat on the side of the gate, and a torn yellow jacket hung on the spike at the top of the fence, flowing in the breeze like a defeated flag.

"Not now," Grandfather grumbled. "Benjamin, while I contact

Erwys, take care of *them*."

Ben eyed the yellow jacket with dismay. "Yes, Grandfather."

Grandfather unlocked the gate while Ben looked across the sidewalk towards the nearest neighborhood. Some kids had been watching and waiting for the hearse to leave. Someone must have noticed it was gone all day. Whenever Grandfather drove away, it was a tell-tale sign the Hill's necromancer might be gone and a perfect time for a test of courage. Naturally, Ben never left, so the kids never got far before being shooed away. That was, until today.

They hurried up the stairs to the top of the hill. Grandfather left Ben behind as the boy struggled with every step, wheezing constantly. Ben, however, was not alone.

"What happened?!" the voice of a familiar spirit cried.

"There are children here! They are absolutely adorable, so much sweeter than you," the voice of a female ghost sneered.

Ben sneered back at her, triggering an eruption of cackles.

One of the ghosts hissed, *"Can't you see he is unwell? Our Gravekeeper is dying."*

"You look a little wan my dear. Your face is gone," another spirit cooed, followed by the agreement of many more.

Ben paused climbing the mossy stairs and pulled the spectacles out of his coat pocket and placed them back on his face to look at the crowd of spirits circling around him. All the spirits stayed far away from him, being wary of the curling black mist emanating from the wraith cloak. Some of them watched Ben behind the trees, poking their heads through shrubs and tree branches. The ones closest to him were the typical group of spirits that were oddly fond of Ben and normally followed him everywhere.

One of the spirits wept. *"His youthful face is gone! Why must the good die young!"* Another spirit joined in, patting her back and acting as if it were blowing its nose with a summoned tissue of ectoplasm.

"I'm still alive," Ben muttered with a scowl.

The spirits started an intense debate over his statement, remarking some of them looked far more alive than him. Ben waved his hands wearily, barely able to even swat a fly. "Enough," he groaned, only adding fuel to the heavy debate of the ensemble of spirits. Ben glowered at the ghosts arguing about whether Ben was alive or not and focused on the ones deeply focused on him.

"There are unwanted visitors on the Hill. Where are they?" he struggled to ask through several weak breaths. The cool night air did not help the effort, and Ben felt like ice water was being forced down his throat every time he inhaled.

"They are in the gardens," one spirit cooed.

"Last I saw, they were in the house."

"In the kitchen!"

Ben groaned, knowing that the spirits were nearly useless. They knew where the children were, but each spirit had their own tale to tell, and it was nearly impossible to discern the truth from fiction. Ben could only rely on the most common snippet of information. *They are inside the house.*

Ben made his way up the rest of the stairs, reaching the graveyard. The graveyard basked in the faint silver moonlight, and a low fog hung over the tombstones. Up in the windows of the house, Ben spotted the pale flickering of flashlights. He marched towards the house, each step dragging. "Don't they know they can turn on the lights?" Ben grumbled.

Grandfather had already entered the house, but the lit

hallway that led down to the study proved his course of action and priorities. He was in the study hopefully figuring out how to save Ben from the wraith cloak. In the meantime, Ben decided to take advantage of the nasty thing to scare away the children and maybe give them a good lesson to not break into a necromancer's home.

The staircase creaked as he went upstairs. He could hear floorboards moaning and the shuffling of footsteps as the kids hurried around, aware that the necromancers were home. Ben lowered his voice and growled, "Who goes there?!"

Perhaps that was a little too demanding, the apprentice thought as he heaved in deep breaths to make up for the effort of yelling. He reached the top of the staircase and leaned on the handrails, ready to collapse.

Slam

Ben's eyes lifted, focusing on the door at the end of the hallway. A bright light flickered from underneath the doorway. That room led to the loft where Grandfather sometimes did summonings and other magical activities. Of course the children would choose to go there. Unfortunately for them, that was also where Mely resided when she had nothing to do.

Ben only managed to get a few feet past the stairs when a couple of high pitched screams erupted down the hall. The door knob twisted and shuddered for two desperate seconds. The door swung open, and three kids ran out of the loft for pure life. Just in the shadows beyond them, Ben could see Mely's glowing eyes.

The children ran only to freeze halfway in the hall and stare at Ben. "Don't you know its wrong to break into houses?" Ben asked, looking at the three children huddling together. He was sure he had seen them before when he opened the gates in the morning. He reached up to rub his forehead, but this motion caused the children to scream in fear and scramble away from the shrouded entity standing before them.

The children had a major dilemma. Mely lurked behind them, stepping out of the loft with an irritated look in her eyes, if a zombie could show emotion that is. Ben, the necromancer apprentice, stood before them presenting the lethal aura of a wraith. Whether they could see the curse or not, they could feel it.

One of the kids fell on their knees and the other clambered with a door to their side. Ben watched with annoyance as the door swung open, only revealing a closet full of linens, toiletries, and basic cleaning supplies.

"Get out and go home," Ben growled, moving away from the stairs and pointing his finger.

The kid who had stayed still seemed to have the most wits about him. He patted his friend on the floor's back two times and whispered, "Get up," all the while keeping eye contact with Ben. Without blinking, he pulled his friend up and tugged on the sleeve of the kid who had opened the closet door.

"If you come here again, I'll send a ghost after you," Ben warned, forcing as much power in his voice as possible. His words came out in weak huffs.

The kids scrambled down the stairs, and Ben made an effort to follow them, causing them only to dart away faster in pure terror. By the time Ben followed them outside, they were sprinting down the stairs of the hill back towards the gate. Ben listened to the hooting and hollering of the Hill's spirits as the intruders fled. The children could not possibly hear the ghosts, but if they did, Ben imagined they would never dare return. Unfortunately, the only undead they found was Mely... Perhaps they would not come back after all.

The apprentice made his way to the porch's steps and sat down. He looked out over the graveyard. The tombstones popped up like dull gray teeth. The grass was longer than usual, looking shaggy and unkempt under the moonlight. Ben told himself to tend to the yard once he could and had the energy. Ben imagined having energy to do anything, but the only thing he could fathom doing was sleeping.

A shiver went down his spine.

After a couple of minutes of sitting and focusing on labored breathing, Ben stood and entered the house. He made a beeline for Grandfather's study. How long must he wait to have an answer, a cure, anything to keep him alive and break the curse? The boy knocked on the heavy wooden door leading to Grandfather's office. It seemed different, but Ben knew that the texture of the door had never changed. With the cloak, his memory seemed foggy, his ability to physically feel with his hands was non-existent- the air seemed to shudder and twist as if a curling fog was smothering Ben's connection to the living realm.

The apprentice waited a few seconds before Grandfather opened the door. The old man's eyes were in narrow slits and his brows furled into a singular thick gray caterpillar. His shoulders were hunched lower than normal, and his movements were quick and jerky as he hurried back to his desk. Or perhaps, Ben thought as he squinted his own eyes, he himself was losing focus and could not quite track Grandfather's movements.

"Erwys is on her way," Grandfather said while prodding at his watch. "She should be here within the hour."

"Erwys Ellandor?" Ben asked. The same necromancer who had offered a solution for seeing spirits if he ever called upon her again. She seemed like the most reliable person to help him, and he was glad she was coming.

"Wipe that smirk off your face," Grandfather glowered. "I now owe her, and that is a precarious position, Benjamin. Your life is in her hands, and she *knows* it."

Ben gulped and nodded. His vision blurred as he did so, and the room spun for a moment. Undoubtedly, his life was in her hands. If they waited too long, he would pass out and kiss his life goodbye. He feared an hour would be too long of a wait.

"I will wait outside," Ben said. "Just in case." He winced as pain traced across his heart. If he were to turn into a wraith, the house was no place to do it. He would be within the protective spells Grandfather set upon the house, and Grandfather would have to fend him off and destroy him instantly.

Grandfather nodded, eyes focused on his desk. Ben paused, staring at his only family member for a long moment before walking out of the study and back down the hall. The floorboards creaked under his unsteady footsteps. Ben's knees cracked and popped as he walked. Down the hall. His hand reached out and fingers slid along the wallpaper, keeping himself from toppling over. Ben knew Grandfather would not follow him outside. He entirely expected the apprentice to stay alive until Erwys Ellandor arrived.

Ben moved to the porch and stopped at the stairs. He leaned against one of the columns supporting the canopy above and stared out into the graveyard. With the glasses, the graveyard appeared very much alive. Pale blue swirls of ethereal light danced along the tombstones, and the figures of spirits meandered about. It looked like a mystical garden party as the hundreds of ghosts socialized in the night.

Some spirits played games and sports. They kicked around balls of ectoplasm and ran through trees and shrubs as if they did not exist. Others floated in the air as if they were drifting off in a pool or sunbathing. Many spirits huddled around their respective tombstones, deep in discussion. Naturally, a large quantity of them were watching Ben with utmost interest. He was the number one source of entertainment on the Hill, and the idea of him joining their ranks was too tasty to ignore. The suspension filled the air with an onslaught of gossip.

Ben gritted his teeth listening to the spirits discuss his oncoming demise. They could sense the presence of death upon him or perhaps see his body wither away. He was not entirely sure what the ghosts could see. He knew they had the ability to sense far more than anyone with the sight could see. Necromancers relied on spirits to see things of the beyond, and only special necromancers like Erwys Ellandor could see things like the threads of souls and spiritual bonds. Surely the spirits on the Hill saw the deep entwinement between the wraith cloak and Ben's spirit. They probably saw his life fading away by the second. Some of them were gambling, and if he could set aside his pride, he would have placed a bet against himself.

Unfortunately for the Hill's residents, they did not live their lives as necromancers and had no idea of how dire Ben's situation was or their own. A bitter smirk lifted Ben's lips at the thought of him turning into a wraith. He would be the least desirable spirit on the Hill. No one would talk to him, everyone would avoid him, and some of the spirits may try to attack him. After all, with a wraith around, no one would have fresh flowers ever again.

"Do you smile as you feel the touch of death?" A familiar voice asked.

Ben's golden eyes flitted to his right. He flinched, but his body hardly moved. Erwys Ellandor stood beside him, wrapped in a patchwork blanket and holding a large satchel in the crook of her arm. Her eyes analyzed Ben with penetrating judgement. He gulped and wheezed, fearing she would simply turn around and walk away.

"It appears you get yourself into trouble quite often," Erwys Ellandor said, clicking her tongue.

Ben refrained from leaping out of desperation and grasping onto her sleeve. He did not know what would happen if he touched the necromancer, whether he would suck the life from her or she merely kill him. His eyes darted down towards his skeletal hands and back to match Erwys Ellandor's lavender gaze. He had no pride left in his withering state. While cloaked, he felt naked. Stripped away from his skin, his flesh, down to his bones and fading soul.

"Please help me," Ben squeaked.

"There, there child," Erwys said as she shuffled into her large canvas bag. "To earn a favor from the Gravekeeper is no minor feat."

Ben watched earnestly as she pulled out a long thin needle from the bag. The needle was stark white, and Ben realized it was made of bone. She held it in the air as if she were appraising an artifact. "This one should do," Erwys said with squinted eyes.

She then pulled out a small pair of silver scissors. They looked completely ordinary, and the blades were no longer than her thumb. The wizened necromancer looked to Ben, and the apprentice shifted, sliding his foot until it hit the canopy's column, stopping him in place.

"Unfortunately, this is a task far more intricate than removing a necrotic curse from a vetala. Benjamin, I will be unweaving the cloak from your soul, and it is... deeply intertwined with your essence. You must be prepared that this may not succeed."

Ben shivered and nodded. He did not need her to say that, for he could feel the sickening feeling of death down to his core. A feeling that was only ever paired with abysmal odds. "Please," he whispered. There could be no worse fate than turning into a wraith.

Erwys nodded and placed her canvas bag on the ground. The top straps folded over the opening and she stepped forward with her skirts sweeping over the bag. The white needle in her hand rested like a sacrificial dagger upon her palm, and a sliver of fear sent a shiver down Ben's spine. Maybe there was something worse than turning into a wraith.

"It is best you take a seat, child," she said just a foot away from Ben, motioning for him to sit on the porch's staircase. Ben looked at the wooden steps and nervously back at the Soulweaver. A heavy-set look forced him to shakily crouch towards the ground, fingers tracing across the aged wooden steps and up to the base of the baluster.

"Can this be done inside?" he asked as he found his seat, looking out towards the Hill's ghosts. They were still mad at him, but they could not refrain from being curious, swooping in closer and closer to take a look at what the necromancer would do to Ben. Some looked eerily excited.

"And risk you turning into a wraith within the house? No," Erwys Ellandor said as she slowly stepped down the stairs to be level with Ben. "If you are to turn into a wraith, I promise you, for the favors the Gravekeepers have granted my family, I will not allow you to suffer a single second as such an undead."

Before Ben could protest, she reached towards him. He pushed his head back against the baluster, watching through the lens of the specter spectacles as a glimmer of something happening in her hand. The air shimmered and wavered like the radiating heat above pavement in the summer, yet the rippling air warped with the movements of her fingers as if it were as fluid as water. Her fingers grabbed the hem of the wraith cloak. Ben was certain the cursed fabric would slip through her grasp like smoke. Instead, she pulled the black fabric taut.

"Be certain to return, Gravekeeper," she whispered, steadily staring deep into his eyes for a split second. She then raised the tiny silver sewing scissors and snipped the hem of his sleeve.

It was only a snip of a sleeve, but Erwys may as well have

submerged him in a bottomless pool of ice water. His body jolted stiff, and eyes flashed wide open. A freezing, skin prickling, body aching pain flashed through his entire being. He opened his mouth to breathe, but his lungs inhaled fruitlessly. His eyes gaped, searching for light, yet the omnipresent moonlight, the swirling figures of the pale blue ghosts, and the front porch's warm lights blinked out like dying stars. The subtle glint of purple in Erwys Ellandor's eyes was the last thing he saw as the remaining warmth in his body vanished.

+**X**+

It was quiet. Terribly quiet. Ben listened for something, the sound of the wind, the sound of the spirits crying and talking and cheering. The sound of his breath or the blood in his head. Something. Anything. Yet there was only oblivion.

He opened his eyes and gazed into an inky room. He was sitting, but the ground was like black ice. Only a singular ebony door hung in the abyss. Ben looked down at himself and found his own body mixed in with the darkness. His arms were dripping inky waves of shadows, threatening to dissipate at any given moment. He was nothing compared to that door- his existence had no bearing in this realm. The longer he stared at the door, the darker it became- a hallowed beacon. Maybe there was no door at all, Ben thought as he stared at the pitch surface, squinting his eyes and doubting its existence. It expanded and deepened, opening an avenue to the abyss. Or perhaps it remained stagnant, Ben hardly knew.

Picking himself up, Ben stepped towards the door, drawn towards the vastness. His limbs dragged as if submersed in tar, but he had to move forward. From the door, he could feel something. Life perhaps? His mouth watered. The ghosts always said life was warm. And he was very, *very*, cold. The door promised anything but warmth. Strangely enough, it was not cold either. The feeling of death did not seep from this path. It was just... *different.*

Then it struck Ben. He knew what that door was; he had seen it before, detailed in many necromantic tomes. He was on the verge of death, perhaps past it, but was he on the right side? Was the door to the entrance to the underworld or the path to the living realm?

If he was here, then his own body was... His eyes moved naturally, going from the door, turning to look at where he had laid. There, a body was crumpled on the shadowy ground, wrapped in equally deep shadows that slithered like snakes. They threatened to swallow him whole.

He wanted to gag. His face was sunken, almost skeletal. His skin was pallid and wrinkled, sticking to his cheek and jaw bones, having lost all fat and nearly all muscle. The color in his blood red hair had greyed, and his eyes were bulging, empty orbs. It was his corpse. He was dead.

Ben struggled to turn and look at the door and then return his gaze to the corpse. What was he supposed to do?! He hurried back to his body, and just as he neared it, the weight of his steps sent him tumbling. He blinked, face to face with his corpse.

The shadows wrapping around the body slithered across its face, and Ben jolted backwards as the corpse shivered and moved on its own. Ben struggled to move away, watching as the body's head lifted and turned to look at him with wide, white orbs and a gaping grin.

No, this was not him. Ben scrambled to his feet, clambering away from the body. It was purely wrapped in the dark essence of the abyss and lifted itself with ease. The shadows billowing around it could be nothing other than the wraith cloak's remnants.

Ben moved away from his corpse, stumbling towards the door. He had no means of fighting the cloak's curse in this realm. All he could do was flee.

It walked slowly, feeling no desire to rush. But it walked towards Ben with a confidence that made him sick.

He reached the door, and now it was just the height of the top hairs of his head and as wide as the breadth of his shoulders. Ben reached for the ornate black handle and looked back at the body walking towards him, only a couple of yards away. He twisted the handle and closed his eyes, hoping he was on the right side of existence.

His eyes remained closed.

Thirteen

A Mother's Curse

"Huuuah!" Benjamin Stone gasped, opening his eyes with a start.

He stared out into the Hill's moonlit graveyard. Pale blue light dusted the tops of tombstones and turned the grass a luminescent green amidst deep navy shadows. In the bleak landscape there was so much color, so much life. The humid air clung to his cheeks and sweat soaked his clothing through. Ben looked down at his withered suit and admired the movement of his gut as he breathed.

"Ah, *you* have returned," Erwys Ellandor said softly.

Ben jerked his head upwards. She sat on the other side of him, at the top of the porch's stairs, knitting a long red scarf with a pair of needles made from bone.

"It appears to be a success," Erwys said with a sideways glance at Ben.

He looked down once more, searching for the cloak, but there was nothing at all. He grabbed his own hands, feeling the roughness of calluses and the sharp edges of his fingernails and the fine hairs on the backs of his wrists. They were indeed no longer bone.

He looked back up at Erwys Ellandor as tears welled in his eyes, blurring his vision.

"There, there child," she said as she pulled her scarf together and stuffed it into her bag. "As a necromancer, you will have many bouts with death."

She stuffed the last few inches of the scarf in her bag and heaved herself to her feet with minor difficulty. "Ah, but no necromancer would envy the curse of a wraith cloak."

Ben attempted to get on his feet, but instead he fell sideways, stumbling against the baluster for support. His whole body ached, and each movement came with a great deal of effort. It felt like his body had not moved in months or as if each mental command he gave to his limbs was met with only a small percentage of reception. After a couple of minutes, he managed to get onto his feet, balancing on the fencing of the front porch.

"Careful there, child. Your soul was separated from your body." Erwys Ellandor clicked her tongue. She walked over to Ben and patted his shoulder. "It will take time for you to regain your bearings."

Ben gave her a stunned look, although his facial muscles failed to twist the way he had hoped, and his eyebrows cramped. He tried to say '*What do you mean? Why did that happen?*' but instead the effort to speak words somehow jumbled into a confused and exhausted moan. Ben attempted to speak again, but his body was simply too exhausted to comply and instead he let out a heavy and loud moan that stretched itself into a yawn. His face burned with embarrassment. He was behaving like some newly raised zombie!

"It will take a few hours for you to recover, don't you worry dear." Erwys said as she helped adjust Ben so that he was standing straight, albeit using the porch's railings for support. "The wraith cloak is gone, and your soul is intact."

Ben's mind raced as Erwys made her way to the front door. He did not want to think about the true reason Erwys Ellandor waited to see if he would wake up. He did not want to think about what would have happened otherwise. The strange dream he had in his unconsciousness only whispered of the dangers he faced in the pinnacle moments of her unweaving the cloak from his spirit. Yet again, this necromancer was able to help him in a dire situation brought on by his own foolishness.

This was now the second time Grandfather had called upon Erwys Ellandor to help save Ben. How many more times would he need to call her if they continued searching for answers? Ben did not want to waste the time searching for a cure to his sight. He did not want to return to the Wraithright estate to speak to Hubert or attempt some other training regimen Grandfather had configured. He needed to ask her for help now while he still had the chance.

"W-wait," Ben stammered, forcing himself to push out the words.

She paused and shifted her body away from the front door of the house and towards Ben. "Yes?"

Ben stared deep into Erwys Ellandor's purple eyes. "C-can you... help me..." he started.

The Soulweaver patiently waited as Ben struggled to continue forming his words. He feared she would walk away as she began to move, but the necromancer instead moved towards him, and her aged hands grabbed his shoulders, squaring them up. She leaned in close so that her lips hung near his ear and whispered, "The Stone family owes me a great debt already. If you wish to gain the sight, it will depend upon Ernest Stone's capabilities to fulfill his debts. If you still wish to offer your debt be paid by your very own hands, I will consider removing your curse."

"A currr-" Ben's words slurred, but the panic in his face shined true.

A look of knowing crossed over Erwys Ellandor, and she smiled softly. She moved away from Ben, releasing his shoulders. They slumped instantly. "Rest well, Benjamin Stone. Perhaps you can stay clear of trouble so no more debts are incurred? It is dangerous, you know, to tip the scale in another house's favor."

With that, she pulled open the front door of the house and stepped inside. Ben caught a glimpse of Mely waiting at the door. The zombie maid motioned for the necromancer to go down the hall and the two left Ben at the porch alone to figure out how to walk once more.

His eyes drifted to the ground in dismay when a slight red glint of light caught his attention. At first, he believed it to be a hint of the sunrise reflecting off the front door's window. Blinking, Ben realized it was not quite dawn yet. The red strand of light gently flowing through the door itself and towards Ben was in fact its very own ethereal entity. The light pierced his chest with a sharp degree of intention, intensifying immensely as it reached him. He sucked in a deep breath and reached to grab the strand of light. His hand wrapped around it, but he stopped himself from touching it any further as the rhythm of a steady beat pulsed against his palm and curled fingers.

Slowly and shakily, he crept away from the support of the front porch's fence and towards the door. The light wavered in the air and moved with him. The moment he touched the front door handle, a foreign thought slipped into his mind.

"It is called a soul strand, dear child," the thought whispered. The voice sounded similar to Erwys Ellandor's except it was crisper and clearer without the bodily limitations of an aging throat. *"Yes, this is me. With the string attached, you can hear my thoughts projected to you. As the weaver, I control this, and yes, I can hear all of your thoughts as well."*

Ben's mind raced, but at the same time he tried to control his mind to staying focused on the string and the idea that Erwys Ellandor could read his mind. What if she learned something she should not know? What if she- Ben shook his head and struggled to open the front door. He needed to stay focused on the string. Buy why was it connected?

"There you go, child. For me to wholistically allow you to make a deal with me, you must know everything. I fear Ernest is not telling you enough, so consider this a favor on my part. Perhaps you may determine for yourself what it shall take to aid me and my family in our time of need-"

Ben wondered what another necromancer family could need from them or, at least, from him.

"The abilities of the Gravekeeper far exceed the precedent your Grandfather has introduced to you. As you listen, I will be sure to enlighten you as well. It is imperative for you to learn what ails you and your competence as a protector of the dead."

Ben gulped and slowly nodded even though the Soulweaver was not watching him. She was down the hall in Grandfather's study. The image of the room was fresh in Ben's mind. He imagined her sitting on one of the plush velvet guest chairs across from Grandfather's desk while he took his time taking his seat. In fact, Ben was not imagining this at all. He saw through the eyes of Erwys Ellandor. Along with something he had never seen before.

A strange golden light emanated from Grandfather's skin, glowing more intensely at his eyes. Around him were faint red strings poking out of his heart and threading off into every direction yet fading quickly. As if to answer Ben's questions, he heard Erwys think, *"You are seeing what I can see. This is something beyond the standard sight but not beyond a Gravekeeper's properly attuned abilities. To this, you and I are special. The red strings here are threads of fate, something I can see. The gold aura is his spirit, something you could see. You have a similar aura as per your birthright."*

Ben's mouth was agape. Was this what he was missing? There was a level to the innate ability of a necromancer that the spectral specters could pick u-

THUMP

CRASH!

A vase shattered across the wooden floor in every direction. Entirely focused on what Erwys Ellandor was seeing, Ben failed to pay attention to the small side table and urn near the front stairs of the house. He steadied himself on the table but his upper torso merely flopped onto the surface. Still weak and uncoordinated, Ben helplessly looked at the shattered vase and the plume of ash falling onto the floor like ashen snow.

The distraction allowed his mind to drift into his own head long enough to decide the mess was a task for Melly, and he had to sit down. The boy wobbled over to the living room and threw himself onto a thick evergreen couch with golden embroidery and caramel pillows. Two seconds into landing on the couch, his vision shuttered and flickered back to Grandfather's study.

"She is my *granddaughter*, Ernest," Erwys pleaded to Grandfather. She sat comfortably in her seat with her back against the chair and hands folded on her lap, but Ben could feel the anxiousness deep in her heart.

"I'm afraid there is little I can do. You know the circumstances our family is in and what your daughter has done-"

"My daughter, not my granddaughter," she argued. "*She* did nothing wrong, yet they still plan to send her into the netherworld. They *will* send her there."

Grandfather stroked his chin, looking down at his desk. Erwys felt as if he were ignoring her or wished to push away the problem. Knowing Grandfather, Ben felt similarly, and this feeling only strengthened and reaffirmed itself for Erwys as she knew Ben's thoughts. Grandfather had no clue he was being double teamed.

"The council has taken a step too far. Just as your grandson is your only heir, she is mine. They are trying to eradicate my family. Do you think they won't try the same with you? Do you not see what is upon us?!" Erwys hissed.

"Delore Ellandor transformed herself into a lich. Her actions violate every rule the council has followed for the past two centuries! You are lucky you aren't being sent to the netherworld. The council wanted to eradicate your whole family from the moment it occurred. Every uncle, nephew, aunt, niece, and so forth!" Grandfather's face was red, but the anger in his eyes did not shoot towards Erwys. It festered and boiled, brimming his eyes with a raging golden aura. His rage was deep, reserved for someone more deserving of his wrath.

Erwys shook her head. "I cannot condone my daughter's actions, they were foolish." Her eyes squinted, and Ben imagined she cocked her head to the side. "But do you think it wasn't necessary? Do you know *why* she did it?"

Grandfather waved his hand. "It doesn't matter why. She is a lich, she is gone, and the only one left to be punished in the order of things is your granddaughter-"

"The one individual in my family who is the most innocent of all. Ernest, I implore you. You must demand to the council she be saved from the netherworld. They will send her to the prison of Tophet. You *know* that is in your domain. If she is sent there, my line will end. If the crimes our ancestors ever step beyond their graves, we all will selectively be ruined."

Grandfather's lips thinned, and he stayed silent for some time. Erwys directly thought to Ben, *"Pay attention, Benjamin."*

Grandfather lowered his hands to his desk and looked aside. "There is little that can be done officially against the council. As a former member, you know this Erwys. I can put forth a word. If they do not heed it, there is nothing that will stop the process of her being sent into the netherworld. Putting my word against this decision will have dire consequences for my own position. I'm afraid pushing any further could end the Gravekeeper line at this rate."

Erwys eyed Grandfather with disappointment. Ben could feel it in his gut. It was a strange sickening feeling not unlike disgust but with remnants of hope and sorrow twisted into the mix. Ben had never felt like this towards Grandfather, but he now felt embarrassed for him, adding a sour flavor of emotion into the mix.

A nasty feeling arose in Ben's stomach, and it pained him as Erwys's mood darkened. "The Stone family may risk being ruined, but without my aid, you would have already lost your only heir. I am losing mine. I know your grandson cannot see spirits, Ernest. Have you ever considered investigating the crimes of your own daughter?"

Grandfather grit his teeth. "Susan has nothing-"

Erwys leaned forward and hissed, "Our families are at the brink of ruin, and you are more concerned about me squandering your daughter's name? There is a reason your grandson does not have the sight, yet you are too blind to see it."

She leaned back and smirked at Grandfather's befuddled face. "I am reluctant to put faith in your persuasiveness with the council given they are very aware of the incompetency of your own heir-" Ben winced, "-but it appears we are in not so different predicaments."

The Soulweaver stood and leaned in close over Grandfather's desk so their noses were nearly touching. Ben could see the pores on his grandfather's large nose and the crow's feet that stretched out from his golden eyes. This close, his golden light zapped and crackled with energy. Erwys whispered, "If you are to save my granddaughter from my daughter's crimes, I will save your grandson from yours." She tilted her head and spoke with a bitter smirk, "This is the closest and farthest we can be to both serenity and collapse. The decision for what will happen to our families is entirely in your hands."

"I will do what I can," Grandfather said with a grim tone. He eyed Erwys heavily, and Ben feared that somehow Grandfather would know he was listening in on the conversation.

"There are far worse things than becoming a lich in our world, Ernest," Erwys said as she moved backwards and picked up her canvas bag. "Do not forget the Gravekeeper is no friend of the council or any necromancer of high ambitions."

She turned and walked out of Grandfather's office. Ben's vision blackened, and it took a long moment for him to realize all he needed to do was open his eyes.

"See, Benjamin," Erwys said to Ben while she walked down the hall. *"If he can do nothing for my granddaughter, the only one who can help me save her will be you. For that, I will return to you your sight."*

Ben's mind raced over the conversation he had just witnessed. It was hard to trust Erwys, but with their minds connected, it was also hard to feel anything but trust. Everything she said felt sincere in Ben's heart. Worst of all, he could not get over what she said about his mother.

"My mother cursed me?" he thought, his gut twisting with pangs of nausea.

Erwys sighed, but a wave of pity in her heart told Ben all he needed to know. Still, she thought, *"This, Benjamin, is the extent of my goodwill. Your mother has blocked every ability she could of yours. I will not undo that until I know my granddaughter is safe. Forgive me or detest me if you must."*

With that, Ben felt a sharp pain in his chest and the connection between him and Erwys broke. Ben was left alone in the living room with the ailing inability to properly move his limbs and a crucial piece of information he had never heard of before.

His mother, Susan Blair Stone, had cursed him. She was the reason he could not see ghosts. No matter how hard they tried to cure his ineptitude, it would be to no avail. Ben already knew the only way to remove a curse was at its source. Ben gritted his teeth. It was about time he had a conversation with her.

Fourteen

A Conversation with the Dead

With much difficulty, Ben managed to return to his bedroom. His body felt disconnected from his mind, and each effort of movement resulted in a full spasm or jerky yet successful movements. It took several attempts to do basic tasks, and changing clothes was of monstrous difficulty.

Just like a zombie, he collapsed upon his bed in a haphazard form and fell asleep within seconds.

It was deep into the following night when he awoke with his face in a puddle of drool. Ben stirred about, groaning to the intense muscular aches and pains that throbbed across his body. He moved his hand forward, and it moved naturally with no difficulty. Ben blinked and pushed himself up off his bed with no trouble. The boy stretched, testing out his movements and finding everything to be correct. Sleeping allowed his body and soul to reset, and he could move with ease as if the removal of the cloak had not caused any damage at all.

Sighing, he flopped back on his bed and stared at the plaster ceiling. No longer focusing all his energy on merely existing, He dwelled on the conversation the evening prior between Erwys Ellandor and Grandfather and the entire politics of the necromancer society. If Grandfather succeeded in saving her granddaughter, she would help Ben regain his sight. If he failed, Ben would have to save her granddaughter instead. From Grandfather's tone of voice and reaction to Erwys's request, Ben already knew Grandfather had little expectation of succeeding. If he were right, he would have to put his own head on the chopping block for the Ellandors.

Ben gazed at the ceiling basked in soft moonlight. He knew an entire day had passed by with him struggling to survive just because of an ectoplasmic piece of clothing. If he had not been so foolish to drop the flashlight and summon Elaine or if he had just remembered to take off the wraith cloak before stepping outside, he would not have been in another near-death situation. He nearly died if it were not for Grandfather and Erwys Ellandor. Was he capable of saving Erwys's granddaughter? If Grandfather could not do it, he certainly would be of no help.

The boy questioned how he could possibly be of use. Maybe Grandfather would help him regain his sight without Erwys's aid, but Ben entirely doubted that, tossing the idea aside. Grandfather never told Ben his mother had cursed him and treated his lack of sight as a genetic flaw instead. This whole time, they needed to be searching for a cure to a curse, not trying to expose Ben to the ethereal world.

If he waited to try curing the curse until after the Ellandor's trial, Ben knew it would be too late. By then, she would likely present to Ben an ultimatum. He needed to cure the curse before the trial or else, she would make him help her by negotiating with his own future as the collateral.

Ben gulped, knowing he had little choice. He would have to summon his mother's spirit, even if it were against Grandfather's will. Between summoning her and saving a lich's daughter, he preferred summoning his mother. The thought may have been soothing to him, but now it tasted bittersweet. She was not just his mother, but the necromancer who cursed him. He feared the conversation would not be a kind reunion.

But it had to be done.

He sighed and clambered out of bed. He got ready for the day, noticing some disjointed mobility issues with minor movements, but he shrugged them off.

Wishing to waste no more time, Ben slipped on a thick pair of socks and loafers and left his room. He crept down the hallway, tiptoeing as slowly as possible to the point where his legs ached to avoid causing the floorboards to creak. He crossed down the hall and softly pressed his ear against the door of Grandfather's bedroom.

Inside, Grandfather's released weighted and gargled snores. Ben closed his eyes for a second and exhaled. Grandfather was fast asleep and likely would not wake again until morning. So long as he carefully put away everything as it was and be back in his room by dawn, Grandfather would not suspect a thing.

He crept back through the hall and made his way down the staircase. He cursed under his breath every time a floorboard creaked. He flinched and froze, waiting several seconds with his ears intently listening for the stirring of another resident of the house. Luckily, each time the floorboards moaned, there was no matching echo of a similar sound. Not even Mely was awake- zombies could not sleep, but they loved to act like they did.

Ben made it to Grandfather's study and paused at the door, staring at its wooden panel. He knew it was wrong to step into Grandfather's study without permission, but what choice did he have? It was wrong for Grandfather to lie to him about his sight. His fists clenched. Any wrongdoings between them would cease if he could remove the issue of contention: the curse.

Ben grabbed the door handle and twisted it, closing his eyes and sucking in a breath. It shifted just a hair before freezing with an annoying click. Ben rattled the handle a few times, releasing a frustrated groan. Grandfather was no fool, and Ben's face burned, knowing he had every right not to trust his apprentice.

But trust went two ways. Between the choices of betraying

Grandfather's dwindling trust now and betraying his bloodline later, Ben preferred the former.

Ben stepped down the hallway and went into the kitchen. Underneath the sink, he shuffled around with a bin of miscellaneous knick knacks until he found a metal stick perfect for situations like this. He snagged the flashlight from the bin as well and hurried back to the door. Grandfather was no fool, but he also did not feel the need to magically seal his study. Ben picked the lock with ease and listened to the satisfying click as the door unlocked and creaked inward.

He slipped into the study and pressed the door shut. His fingers found the lock and twisted it, seemingly sealing the door once more. Ben felt an immense pressure of stress alleviate. He was already in the study, there was only one more place to go. As the flat of his palm slid down the wooden door panel, his golden eyes lowered to the plush red carpet concealing the entrance to the crypt.

Grandfather had never told him about the crypt, had never mentioned the singular most important casket residing in its depths. He never spoke of where their family was buried, and now Ben knew why. He never wanted him to know the truth of his mother's burial and the chance he may know of what happened to her and Ben.

His mother was buried down there, and Ben had every intent to have a conversation with her. It was not something he could ever dream Grandfather would allow, but Ben doubted there was any other way to solve his inability to see spirits. The cure to every curse started with the source.

But this was about more than just curing his curse. Ben wanted to know why his mother cursed him. Just maybe, Erwys was wrong. Ben hoped the necromancer was wrong. She had to be wrong! But the feeling he felt in her heart while their souls were tied together betrayed Ben's hopes. When she spoke of Susan, everything she felt was honest and true. Grandfather's reaction to her also backed that truth. But he needed to know his mother's truth.

If it were true that she had cursed Ben, he did not know what to say. He had no memories of his mother. Still, the idea that she would have cursed him felt sickening. He deserved to know why, and the only way to know was to ask her directly.

Ben scrounged around Grandfather's office, searching for what he needed to summon a spirit. He wished he had not left behind his satchel in the Wraithright catacombs so that he would already have everything he needed in one place. Instead, the boy risked exposing his actions by ransacking Grandfather's unusually tidy office for the required items.

It took nearly thirty minutes for the apprentice to find all of the items necessary for evoking a spirit from its corpse. Once he gathered everything, he snatched one of Grandfather's book bags, emptied it on his desk without a second thought, and shoved everything he gathered inside.

Confident, Ben lifted the rug and opened the silver trap door. He clambered to his knees and looked down the familiar shadowy tunnel. The silver rungs of the ladder gleamed with the glow of his flashlight, but only a few steps down, they faded into the deep shadows. He clenched onto the flashlight's handle tightly, hoping not to lose it once more. He then hoisted the bag of supplies over his shoulder and swung his leg into the chase.

As he inhaled the musty air of the crypt's stone walls, he trembled with fear. It was too familiar to the smell that permeated the Wraithright catacombs, and the shadows invoked phantom memories of wraiths. He did not have time to fear what may be lurking in the crypt. It was his family crypt- there would be no wraiths or revenants.

Ben climbed down the familiar ladder as quickly as possible. Unlike before, his goal was to get down to his mother's grave, speak to her, and leave. There was no time to waste. For every second in the crypt was a second Grandfather could awaken and discover he was breaking the rules once again.

Ben's leather dress shoes landed with a soft thud on the dusty earthen floor of the crypt. Ben waved the flashlight and looked down a shadowy hallway. Stone statues lined the hall with beautiful stone archways. It was so much nicer than the Wraithright catacombs he thought.

"Stupid spiders," he grumbled just a few seconds into the crypt as he noticed a plethora of spider webs weaved within every gap between stones. He would have to find a chance to dust the crypt later or somehow convince Mely to do it.

Ben treaded through the tunnels. He passed familiar stone caskets, keeping an eye on the marks on the walls, guiding him to the circular room with the central sarcophagus. Having been in the crypt once before, it was easy for him to quickly find that final space, different from all the others. His hand slid along the stone wall as he approached his mother's tomb.

The casket was leaning into its crevice like an ancient offset puzzle piece. The stone cover had a fresh layer of dust resting over it. His fingers slid across the cover, wiping away a layer of dust. He felt bad opening the casket and disturbing the dead, but it was not his fault she cursed him.

Resolved to speak to the dead, Ben whispered, "Sorry, mom."

He placed the flashlight facing upward on the flat casket in the center of the room and returned to put his fingers around his mother's coffin lid. They curved around the cold stone, and Ben took several deep, slow breaths to steady himself and his resolve. What he was planning to do probably was not the right choice, but it was necessary. He pulled on the lid and listened to the hollow scraping of rock as the lid shifted off the casket's frame. It was incredibly heavy, and Ben nearly collapsed trying to keep it from falling flat on the ground.

Ben shifted the lid ajar. His eyes rested upon the contents of the coffin, and he nearly dropped the lid altogether.

There was nothing inside the casket except a massive cobweb and a singular black widow. He stared at the web and the spider's bulbous body with disgust. The red hourglass on its thorax gleamed like a ruby in the flashlight's faint light. His mouth went dry. His eyes scanned the casket repeatedly looking for something different or strange. But the strangest thing of all was the undeniable fact his mother's grave was empty.

He wondered and feared if perhaps she had been taken away by some wicked necromancer. What if her body was elsewhere? Would Grandfather have buried her in another graveyard? Or, maybe... Maybe she was still alive?

THUD

The boy's fingers weakened, allowing the lid to slip through his grasp. The stone lid cracked as it smacked against the stone walls and floor. He ignored it and hurried to grab the flashlight as it fell sideways and began to roll. Where was his mother? Susan was supposed to be dead! For as long as he could remember, Ben always believed she had passed away. Grandfather had said so... but could Ben trust Grandfather?

Ben waived the flashlight's beam over the casket for good measure. Still, there was nothing different about it. She really was not there. His heart skipped a beat. Did this mean she was alive? Or did something happen to her far worse than death?

There was only one way of knowing, and the answer did not reside within the Stone family crypt. He left behind the fallen lid and sprinted down the halls back towards the singular ladder leading to the surface. He reached the ladder breathless and began his ascent as quickly as possible. His breaths were ragged and limbs shaking from the excursion, but the toll on his body did not slow him from seeking an answer.

Questions danced back and forth in an eerie waltz. Was she dead or alive? Was his mother hostage to another necromancer family? Did Grandfather neglect to tell him something this critical no matter the fact that Susan was Ben's mother? Regardless of whether she was alive or dead, she still had cursed him, and now her status mattered little compared to what she was like as a person and what led to her disappearance. In some sense, Ben felt a sickening sadness at the idea that he was abandoned and unwanted. Why else would she have disappeared to live a life not as his mother? Why else would she not be buried in the family crypt?

Ben reached the top of the ladder and clambered onto the wooden floor, clawing into the panels and out of the tunnel. The boy set the flashlight aside and lowered the silver trapdoor with a harsh speed that made it slam shut. Ben flinched, but in his mind a deep resolve sparked. Why be afraid if Grandfather heard the trapdoor slam? Ben would wake him up one way or another.

He angrily tossed the bag of summoning supplies. The bag tipped sideways, and its contents spilled across his desk, but Ben paid it no heed. He stormed out of the study, down the hall, and up the stairs towards Grandfather's bedroom, wanting answers.

He paused just feet away from the door leading into Grandfather's room. What good would it be to demand where his mother was? Ben had lived with Grandfather for years and never once was he told any other tale than his mother was dead. Why would Grandfather change that narrative? Would he tell Ben where his mother was buried if she were dead? Would it matter to him for Ben to know, or would he lie to him again?

Ben doubted Grandfather would care about how mad he was or the severity of the situation that her body might have been stolen. Opening the door to confront Grandfather would only lead to one true outcome. He would be tattling on himself for going into the crypt once again, and he would not have the opportunity to ever step foot in the study or find the truth.

Sucking in multiple deep breaths, Ben focused on calming himself down and thinking clearly. His mother's body was missing. This did not stop him from talking to her. If she were dead, all he needed to do was find her corpse and summon her spirit to have a conversation. If she was alive, he had many more questions to ask her but most importantly Ben needed to know why she had cursed him. Why did she abandon him? Why was there an empty casket with her name on it in the family crypt? Why did Grandfather claim her to be dead?

Ben softly turned on his toes and treaded back down the stairs and into the study. He closed the door behind him with a soft thud and looked around the office for a particular scroll. He wished the contract would naturally highlight itself, but there were hundreds of scrolls stuffed in every crevice of the study. Sighing, he began the task of hunting for the scroll for Nomas, the spirit that could take him to whoever he asked for by means of the Netherworld.

In a fit of anger, he picked up scroll after scroll, opened them to see if they were the right one and tossed each of them aside on the floor. Deep yellow paper unfurled like rows of ribbons onto the ground around him. He shifted through heavy books covered in thick layers of dust. It was not until he made his way to Grandfather's desk, and all the shelves were in disarray, that he found a small scroll tucked in one of the drawers sealed with a silver clasp.

He unfurled the scroll to its very edges, revealing an intricate contract in an archaic language Ben did not recognize. It did not matter as he spotted the one word that mattered most at the bottom of the page. _Nomas_.

Like a madman, Ben laid the scroll flat on Grandfather's table. He pressed his hands on the page, soothing out the frayed corners. Leaning forward, he scoured the scroll for any legible context other than the spirit's name.

In his silence, Ben could hear the slight creaking down the hall. He stood straight and stared at the thick wooden door. The undeniable creaking sound above him could signal nothing other than Grandfather was coming.

Without thinking, Ben hurried around the table and turned the lock on Grandfather's door. He paused for a second feeling relieved but knew it would do little to stop an angry necromancer from entering his own office. Ben looked back at the scroll on the desk and then stared at all of the scrolls spread throughout the study. The bookshelves were so empty that Ben could see the backboards of each one. The plush red rug could not be seen beneath the sea of tossed contracts and books. Ben realized in his anger he had failed himself. Grandfather's rage at the sight of his trashed study would far outweigh any rationalization for Ben's own behavior.

Sweat beaded down Ben's forehead as he listened to the footsteps stop in front of the door. He had seconds to do something.

His eyes flitted to the unfurled scroll on Grandfather's desk. There was only one thing he could do.

Ben ignored the rattling of the doorknob and ran around the desk to stand before the scroll. He had no idea what it said, but it did not matter. Ben clearly remembered the name Nomas, and that was enough. He lifted the small letter opener Grandfather had displayed on his desk and sliced the thick of his palm over the contract. Thick drops of blood fell from his hand and onto the parchment, blotching dark red over Nomas's name.

"Nomas, I evoke thee. Take me to my mother, Susan Blair Stone." Ben's voice shook as he spoke, but there was no turning back. In the last second, Grandfather's voice could be heard yelling behind the door.

SLAM

The door swung open so hard it smacked against the bookshelf directly behind it, tearing contracts in its path. Ben's eyes met Grandfather's glowing fiendish gaze. A flash of lightning appeared to cross between the two of them. Grandfather looked about his trashed study and roared, "BENJAMIN!"

But he was too late.

Ben winced, shutting his eyes. When he opened them, he was no longer in the study. Everything was black. As black as a moonless night sky and blacker still. Ben's eyes narrowed.

"Grandfather?" He dared ask, but there was no response.

And then came the crackling sound of teeth chomping together with sharp clacks and grinds like two pieces of ivory colliding in a machine. Louder yet, hooves thundered, shaking the ground and smacking on shallow pools of ice. Ben blinked again. His shadowy surroundings swirled and twisted, making way for stark white tendrils of ash. They curved and twirled into themselves, congealing into the form of a horse's skeleton.

The undead steed stomped its hooves and bowed its head at Ben.

He searched the darkness for something. He had no ability to see depth or space. Without the spirit, he would be in a true endless sea of nothing. To test this theory, Ben lowered his glasses just enough to watch the skeleton disappear from existence.

Surprisingly, its form did not shift or vanish at all. Ben blinked and realized it must be still visible because Ben was no longer in Grandfather's study or the living world. He stood in a plane somewhere within the netherworld where Nomas existed. Ben's eyes widened as he realized he had summoned himself to Nomas and not the other way around.

The horse snorted with agitation. Ben was taking too long looking around its inky domain. He approached the skeletal horse and climbed onto a leather black saddle. Having never ridden a horse or seen one besides the ones from pictures, he had little knowledge about what else to do with the creature. Luckily for Ben, the horse had dealt with many masters and knew just what to do. It kicked its front legs, nearly sending Ben off its back, and charged through the darkness.

Ben held onto the horse's neck for his life, but the spine was not quite comfortable. He tried finding a better handhold and settled for the saddle's horn. He only hoped he would not fall off the steed and be trapped within this shadowy interim layer of the netherworld.

The longer the horse ran, the more familiar Ben became with its rhythm. After what felt like an hour, he no longer worried about falling off. And after what seemed like two, the idea of falling never crossed his mind. He watched the horse's bone white head bob up and down. Ahead there was darkness, behind darkness. It was an endless sea of onyx.

After an un-chartable length of time, the horse stopped running.

Clack clack clack.

The steed's teeth chattered.

"What is it?" Ben asked. He tilted his head, trying to understand what Nomas may have been saying. Unfortunately, he was at his wits end. Who could understand a skeletal horse anyways!

It was as if Nomas heard Ben's thoughts. The steed shook its boney neck and kicked its front legs before jumping and springing its hind legs in the air. The apprentice flew from the horse and tumbled through the darkness in a puff of inky smoke.

Ben tumbled onto the ground and stopped against a flat wall with his legs in the air bent over his head. He twisted and picked himself up to find himself inside a quaint living room. His hands pressed on a soft shaggy carpet as he slowly got to his knees. A singular light lit the living room belonging to a deep copper painted lamp that sat on and nearly took over an entire wooden end table beside a corduroy yellow couch. The light glowed a soft orange, casting deep shadows over a white wooden mantal and a painting of the rolling hills of a wheat farm in autumn.

Aside the mantal sat a stout white table with a heavy wooden television sitting atop it. Ben blinked in awe. He had only seen them in window shops when he and grandfather went into town. They never had one because they couldn't get a proper signal at the Hill.

Crash!

He jerked in his crouched position only to look at a shattered mug. Coffee bled from the mug's large jagged white shards, spilling dangerously near a soft white slipper. Ben lifted his gaze to a woman wearing a long lavender night gown. Blood red hair spilled over her shoulders and down to her slender waist. Her hands remained frozen as if she were still holding the cup.

"Benny?"

Fifteen

Reunion

Ben stared at his mother with trepidation. He slowly stood, sliding his feet in a way where he was as far from her as possible without taking a step. If her red hair, a striking color identical to his was not enough, her golden eyes told this was undeniably his mother. The boy's heart raced as he tried to collect his thoughts. He could not look away as his eyes scanned every inch of her face, seeking everything familiar to his own face and to Grandfather's and looking for anything that might deny the truth standing before him. His mother really was alive.

She was in an equal state of shock. Her fingers trembled as they searched for the ghost of the mug in her hands. Her lips parted and a whisper of something slipped from her lips. She glanced down, barely realizing the mug now decorated the floor in pieces.

Her hands found each other and glided along her forearms. "Benny, is that really you?" she said while her face twisted as if she were suffering a stomachache.

Ben blinked and slid his feet further away from his mother. She was alive and well. She called him Benny. She knew who he was. She really was his mother, why else would she call him Benny? Ben opened his mouth, but he did not know what to say. He thought he was prepared, but this was his mother in the flesh whom he believed to be dead.

"It really is you," she said, stepping towards him.

Her feet crunched on the ceramic shards, but she did not flinch. Before Ben could react, she embraced him. Ben kept his hands to his sides, unsure of what to do. Part of him desired to sink into his mother's hug, yet his back stiffened, and his fists clenched.

She held onto him for several minutes, shoulders shaking as she grasped the back of his head and tucked her face into the crook of his shoulder. Slowly, his shoulder dampened. "It's been so long since I've seen you," she said, pulling away from Ben to look him in the eyes. Her eyes were bloodshot and brimming with tears. She grabbed his cheek, "You've grown so tall."

Ben gulped. His eyes stung, and he feared he would lose all reason. This was his mother standing before him. She found joy in his growth despite never having been there for him and despite having cursed him from using his magical abilities. Yet she cared about his height?

His teeth clenched, and Ben shifted out of his mother's touch. His legs pressed against the back of the couch, and the boy looked into his mother's bleary golden eyes seeking answers he knew he would never know.

"Susan, I cam-"

"No, no," she interrupted Ben. "I am your mother, call me mom." She reached towards Ben, but he stepped to the side, wary of another endless embrace. If she hugged him once more, he feared he would give up on his hunt and forget why he was there. Why, whether she was alive or dead, they had to talk.

"Mother, I came to talk to you. I need your help," he begged, looking down at her the thin slippers protecting her feet from the mug's shards.

"Anything, Benny. It has been so long, you must have been so scared," she said, putting a hand on Ben's shoulder and guiding him to take a seat on the couch. "Please, take a seat my child. You were very brave to come here."

Ben gulped and wavered before sitting down and sinking into the couch cushions. It was impossible not to feel comfortable in the plush seat, making Ben only more uncomfortable as he struggled to maintain a rigid posture as his mother sat beside him, angling herself to look at him.

"Please, tell me, Benny. What can I do for you? Does father-Ernest know you are here? Do I need to hide you? Have you gone to school? What has he done these many years with you?"

She continued on, fretting over the life Ben had lived for the past seventeen years. He stared at her coldly, scraping his mind for a way to tell her what help he was really seeking. He was seeking help to be free *of her*. Not of Grandfather. But as she continued on, it was clear to Ben that she believed he had ran away from the Hill and rejected necromancy outright. The longer he listened, the larger her statements became and the more convinced she was that Grandfather was after him.

"Mother, enough!" Ben snapped, standing. She stared at him blankly as if he had flashed a beam of light in her eyes. "I'm not running away from home. I'm not leaving the Hill. I came to ask of you for one thing, that is all." He grabbed his forehead, feeling the oncoming prongs of a sharp headache

She blinked. "What do you mean?"

"I don't wish to *leave* the study of necromancy. I came here through the netherworld. I have-"

There was a sudden shift in the air. She sharply stood.

"The netherworld?!" she hissed, grabbing Ben's elbow. "Do not speak of such things. Surely you came here to escape it?" Her breath was low and eyes pleading.

"How else would I come here? I thought you were dead!" Ben said, glaring at her.

Her eyes widened and her jaw slackened. Ben grabbed his forehead, trying to organize his thoughts. "I have every intention of being a necromancer," he said firmly.

He lowered his hand, looking at his mother, and he flinched.

She stared at Ben with a twisted expression. He could have been a slavering ghoul. "Benjamin, I have lost everything to save you. You mustn't pursue necromancy. Please tell me you came here to be free of it," she said, eyes darting back and forth, scanning every inch of Ben for a hint of compliance.

Ben's eyes steeled over. "Why do you care what I wish to do? You never gave me a choice." She shuddered, and Ben pressed on. "I know what you did to me. I am only here to ask for you to undo the curse you have placed on me. That is *all* I ask."

His fists remained clenched at his sides, and his eyes narrowed as he stared at his mother, searching for a glimmer of acceptance. She looked shocked, but as he finished speaking, her hands folded gently and she sighed, composing herself. Then she raised her gaze to Ben, and a fire flared behind her golden eyes.

"Benjamin. When I had you, it was a miracle. Such a blessing of life is undeniably so precious and meaningful. As your mother, you must understand why I did it. Your curse is no curse, Benny, it is a blessing. You mustn't fall to the dangers of necromancy. There is no cure or way to be free from the curse of death and what follows those who tarnish it."

"That's not your place to decide," Ben growled. "You chose to not be a part of my life long ago."

"I was forced to go," she cried, waving an arm. "Oh, no this can't be!" His mother grabbed her forehead and locks of deep red hair billowed around her hand and forearm. "After everything

I sacrificed for you." She lifted her gaze to Ben and reached towards him, clambering onto Ben's shoulders.

"Please tell me you do not plan to go back to Ernest. You came here to get away from him!" she cried, delirious.

Ben's eyes darted examining his mother's face. Crow's feet marked her eyes along with soft gray shadows. Her cheeks were hollow, clearly defining the high ridges of her cheek bones. The longer Ben stared at her face, the easier it was to imagine the defining contours of her skeleton. He blinked in shock. "M-mother, I-"

"No, no," she pulled him in a deep hug, placing her hand on the back of his head. Ben stood stunned, not knowing what to do.

Fearing she would never let go, Ben scrambled to produce something soothing for his estranged mother and whispered, "I came to see you, Su- mother."

She nodded and patted his head. "Oh my child," she whispered with a crack in her voice. Her body shook, and Ben could hear her breathing waver like a quivering violin. "I feared I had lost you forever."

"...can I ask you a question?" Ben asked. He wanted to know why she cursed him, but the question was too daunting in their current situation. Ben feared to know the truth, so he wished to take a lesser truth that was not so damning of him. "Why did you leave?"

His mother froze. Any color in her face rapidly drained away, making her skin nearly the color of bone- she was very pale to a point Ben imagined her to be sickly. She closed her eyes slowly and lifted her brows half an inch. "Benny, I never wanted to leave you-"

"No, why did you leave the Stone family?"

His mother scowled and leered at the fireplace mantle where the farm painting sat. Her lips pursed. "The Stone family, the Hill... Ernest..." she paused. Ben wondered if she would stop completely as a minute passed thick with silence. She then continued.

"Benny, magic means so little in this world. Whether you turn on a light bulb with the flick of a switch or cast a spell, it makes no difference. Whether you shoot someone with a gun or curse them to their grave, murder is still murder. But can we, with science, bring someone back from the grave? Maybe within the minute, while they are still part of the living realm, but an hour? A day? A hundred years? What happens when you tether one back into the living realm, and they are not who you sought to *save*? Is it saving to ensnare a soul to our realm? And what if you bring back not a who, but a *what*?"

She looked deep in Ben's eyes, and Ben could see the undisputable sanity in the weight of her gaze. "Do you know what happens to necromancers when they die, Benny? Undoubtedly, Ernest has told you that much if he is even caring to give you a warning."

"When necromancers die, their spirits are devoured by the dead whom they tormented when alive. They persist in a cursed existence. Your body may be torn apart into a thousand pieces, and that may be the end. But if your spirit is torn, the tearing never ends. And then, another necromancer will one day find your body and bring back those shattered remnants of you and use you as a puppet against your will. Your short time alive will be labored by an eternity of torture. That is your future as a necromancer. It is the path I cannot bear you to suffer."

Ben gulped. Grandfather had explained the dangers of being a necromancer to him, but there was a reason rules and the Council of the Dead existed as well as the Gravekeeper. Gravekeepers were different. Their jobs were to stop that endless suffering from happening. She was supposed to be a Gravekeeper as well. Ben muttered, "So you were scared."

His mother's eyes widened by a fraction. "No," she hissed, leaning forward. "I did not want such an end for my child."

Gears moved in Ben's mind. Was she really trying to help him? "Is that why you took away my ability to see spirits?"

"Benny," she cooed, sliding her hand on his shoulder, "seeing spirits is a cursed, vile thing. It is a blessing to not see the dead."

"I did not ask for that!" he yelled. His fists clenched at his sides. "I didn't ask to be crippled!"

"Crippled?!" Her eyes were wide with shock. "You were born to become a slave to the dead. I saved you!"

Ben stood. "I didn't ask to be saved. I will be a necromancer."

"You can never be a necromancer," his mother hissed through her teeth. She stepped towards Ben, and the boy watched in a turmoil of emotions as his mother's fingers dug into his shoulders. "You cannot become a Gravekeeper. The Stone line of necromancers must end!" she cried in his face. Tears brimmed and spilled over her eyelids, streaming down her cheeks.

Ben was at a loss of words. It was clear she had no intent on removing the curse. His hands slid to his pockets, searching for the scroll to summon Nomas.

Warmth drained away from Ben's face, and his eyes widened in terror. His pockets were empty. He never picked up the bag of summoning items or the scroll. He had no means of returning to the Hill.

"It will be okay, Benny," his mother said. "Life is much brighter without necromancy. Here, you can enjoy what it means to be alive, go to a school, learn about the world you live in!"

Ben scowled. "Mother... do you still see ghosts?"

She smiled sweetly, but she failed to hide the pain and disgust in her eyes. "I wish I couldn't," she said softly, stroking Ben's hair. "But you, my child, you don't have to."

Ben's eyes narrowed and a fit of anger swirled in his gut. If there was a chance she would remove the curse, it was completely gone. She was proud of her curse on him and had every intent to keep it. There was no point in talking to her any longer. He clenched his teeth looking into his mother's golden eyes and blurted, "I am returning to the Hill."

His taunt did more damage than he hoped. Her eyes widened with a fierce golden fire. Her hand viciously snatched his head, grabbing hold of his hair. His mouth went dry as his mother glared into his eyes as if she were staring directly into his soul, all the while firmly clenching onto the back of his head like a sack of rotten potatoes.

"*Return to the Hill?*" she hissed. "Benny, you came here to live with your mother. You came here to be free of *the Hill*," she spat. "You *can't* return to the Hill!" Her eyes rolled and she laughed. "I won't allow it!"

Blood drained from Ben's face. He tried to move away, but she moved quicker. Faster than a striking viper, she pushed her other hand over Ben's eyes and hissed a line of words Ben recognized as the beginnings of a spell. Before he could protest, his eyes rolled back, and his mind slipped into a deep slumber.

Sixteen

Family Matters

A dull aching pain resounded on the back of Ben's head and towards his eyes. The throbbing worsened, and Ben's eyes flitted open to stare at a shadowy plaster ceiling. Faint warm lights sourced from candles flickered, casting long, sporadically dancing circular shadows onto the ceiling. Ben arched his chin upwards, stretching his head. His neck felt horribly stiff. He reached to rub his forehead, but his hand never left his side.

Ben jerked his arms and joggled his head, but his head only barely shifted on the ground, and his arms stayed flat to his sides as if they were tied to his waist. A tight feeling welled in his chest. He was frozen in an enchantment.

"Shhh... undo time, remove the marrings of this life... Spare the living..."

A soft chant echoed through the room like the flutter of a moth. It prickled Ben's ears, developing goosebumps on the back of his neck and arms.

His throat cracked. "M-mother?"

The chanting stopped, sinking the dark room into an unnerving silence spare the sound of the candles' dancing flames. The shadows flickered on the ceiling, showing Ben that his mother knelt near him. There was a strange energy pulsing through the room, causing the candlelight to dance sporadically in a dizzying cadence. There was something very wrong, but Ben just could not see it.

He could not move his head enough to writhe against the discomfort. His back arched to the feeling as a strange tingling sensation built up over his skin. A thousand bugs were crawling onto his hands and feet, to his ankles, knees, elbows, and shoulders. Their spindly little prods were followed by the searing pain of fire, and Ben choked as if he were inhaling smoke.

"Stop it!" he cried, hearing her chant resume over the roar of blood pounding in his ears.

This time, her chant stopped and the terrible burning, itching feeling vanished instantaneously. Ben clenched his teeth, confirming her chanting was in fact the source of his suffering. Before he could say anything else, her voice carried on with the spell, and he groaned in agony as the feeling encroached upon his face.

Ben did not know what she was doing, but he recognized the language enough to know it was a curse. If he did not stop her soon, it would be complete. He imagined what Susan would do to curse him. She may be stealing away his soul in a worst case scenario. Best case scenario, she would return his sight to him. Ben gasped as he realized that would never be the case. Most likely, she was cursing him once again.

"Stop it!" he screamed with half a breath. His voice broke with pained sobs as the fiery agony moved into his mouth and down his throat. Ben could see dark shadows swirling against the candlelight, and then the red locks of his mother's head.

She loomed over him with a face of disdain. She stopped chanting, and the pain from the curse vanished. In the candlelight, long and deep shadows stretched over her face, aging her fifty years. Susan's eyes narrowed for a split second. She then reached down and stroked Ben's hair, pushing it off his forehead and away from his eyes.

"Oh, Benny," she cooed. "I am doing this for you. Don't be afraid, my child. This will all end, and you will be eternally safe."

Ben's eyes widened, and his chest rapidly sank and rose as his lungs heaved for precious air. Through his teeth, he growled, "This is not for me."

"Tsk." Her eyes narrowed, and she swiped her hand down on Ben's head rather harshly. Retracting her hand, she moved away and out of Ben's sight. But he could tell she had not left the room. He knew what he had said only added fuel to the fire, but he was too terrified to plot out an escape.

She took away his sight, and now she was performing another ritual! Ben cursed under his breath. How stupid could he be trusting her to be kind to him given she had taken his sight. If she genuinely cared about what was best for him, she would have allowed him to see spirits but taught him to ignore them or use magic to hide them. Instead, she settled on crippling her son.

As if to enforce these conclusions, she began chanting once more. This time, there was a rushed and angry fervor in her voice. Ben trembled against the burning, itching pain that spread across his skin as she chanted off in the distance of the room. She then appeared once more at Ben's waist with a look of deep concern on her face.

"It will all end soon, my child. It is much better for you..." she mumbled incoherently, "I will make sure your spirit is safe..."

She pulled forth a foot long black blade. Ben winced at the sight of the blade. Why did she need that?!

Ben's mind raced to understand what she was doing. This was no form of magic or necromancy Grandfather had ever taught him. From everything she was saying and the position he was in, she undeniably was planning to ensnare his soul. If he stayed here any longer, he would be worse than dead. Yet, Ben shuddered, he could do nothing.

She lowered the blade, and Ben winced, but she only gently slit the palm of her hand so that blood could drip upon his forehead. A painful shiver went down Ben's spine as he realized this was far worse.

She continued chanting as she reached down to smear her blood over Ben's face. He jerked his head away, but a magical force held him still. Realizing he could not do anything, Ben settled for glaring deep into his mother's golden glowing eyes.

She paused and whispered, "I must do this, my child. It is best your spirit rest in serenity. Do not resent me."

"You have no right to call me your child," Ben hissed through his teeth. This made her freeze for a long moment, and a look of sorrow appeared on her face. In a blink, her emotions vanished, and she continued to chant. There was no way of stopping her from finishing whatever curse she was casting. A terrible gut feeling told Ben just what it may be.

"STOP THIS AT ONCE!" a familiar voice bellowed over Susan's chanting and the whooshing sound of blood flowing through Ben's ears. He flinched and attempted to look at the source, but it was no use.

Susan looked up and opened her mouth to scream, raising the knife in her hand.

Fwoosh!

Thud

"AGH!"

Something bright flashed above Ben, pushing Susan back and away from him. The knife clattered on the ground beside him, and Ben felt a strange weight lift from his body. He clambered into a sitting position and looked at Susan pressed flat against her living room wall.

"Hello, Ernest!" Susan cried through her teeth and the foggy entity muffling her. "This line will come to an end!"

"Benjamin!" Grandfather yelled from the other side of the room.

Ben scrambled to his feet and ran to Grandfather, wrapping his arms around the old man's waist. He buried his head into the folds of his black cloak, burying his shame and fear. "I'm sorry Grandfather!" Ben cried.

"What? Why are you running to him?! There is nothing there for you as a necromancer!" He could not block out the sound of his mother yelling. "You cannot return to the Hill! You cannot be a necromancer!"

"Susan, I am afraid Benjamin is in line to be the next Gravekeeper. There is nothing you can do about it," Grandfather said as he moved one arm over Ben's shoulders and the other was held out, more than likely directing the spirit holding Susan against the wall to keep her in place.

Loud, manic laughter burst from Susan's mouth. It was so sporadic and misplaced, Ben recoiled to the idea that just seconds ago, she was holding a knife over his head.

"Ha! You are too late! He will never become a necromancer!"

Grandfather tightened his grasp around Ben and whispered, "Do not listen to her, Benjamin. Hold on tight."

"I will save y-" Her voice cut out instantly as if she had submerged her face into water.

Ben blinked and moved his head just enough to see only darkness so deep Grandfather's cloak nearly appeared gray.

There was the familiar sound of hooves and the crackle of bones striking stone as the familiar spirit, Nomas, approached.

Ben pulled himself from Grandfather slowly, trembling, and blinking away the memories of what happened moments ago. This time, the horse was paired with a second, identical skeletal horse, and a carriage. The carriage was made of deep purple panels with an ashen black door. Gold lined the base of it, curling along the edges and the carriage's hardware. The seat of the carriage was a deep violet. Ben wondered how Grandfather's summon of the spirit procured such luxuries.

"I assume you are familiar with Nomas," Grandfather grumbled. "Climb aboard. We have much to discuss."

Ben nodded blankly and climbed onto the carriage. Grandfather followed suit, sitting beside him. The boy's eyes rested on the stark white spines of the horses and the back of their skulls. The skulls bobbed up and down as the horses galloped through the inky sea of darkness. Beyond the sound of their chattering and clacking bones, Ben sat in silence, quivering.

He abruptly wiped his forehead, attempting to clean the blood sticking to his brows. He looked away from Grandfather and the horses, but there was nothing to see. Ben settled on staring at his lap, replaying what had just occurred.

"Benjamin."

Ben shivered and looked at Grandfather.

"I cannot condone your actions for breaking into my study once again," he grumbled. "But why did you go to Susan?"

Ben's frown sank deeply, and his stomach twisted. He looked away from his grandfather, knowing there was little he could argue. But he also knew, if he were ever to say or ask anything, now would be the time.

He did not want answers. Ben wished to sit in silence and not think about what had transpired. But he needed to know why his mother cursed him, why she behaved the way she did, why Grandfather exiled her from the family, and why he was not to know anything about it.

"Grandfather," he whispered.

"Yes, Benjamin?" Grandfather's voice was solemn.

"Why...why did you hide that my mother was alive? Why is she dead to the Stone family?"

"Because she no longer is a necromancer," Grandfather explained simply without hesitation.

Ben bit his lip. "If I fail to become a necromancer, will I be exiled too?"

Grandfather hesitated to respond, convincing Ben the truth was still wrapped in layers he would not willingly unravel. "Well, no that won't happen..."

Ben winced. "Then what did she do that stopped her from being a necromancer? I know what she did to me, Grandfather. I know she is the reason I cannot see spirits or harness magic."

Grandfather scowled. The rhythmic sound of bones rattling and wheels spinning over a slate-like texture filled the silence.

"Why did she do it?" Ben pressed, looking right at Grandfather. "Why did you not tell me?!"

Grandfather's jaw tightened, and he kept his face forward, looking onward into the abyss. "Some things are best left unknown and unsaid. Her reasonings do not matter, she is no longer a part of the family. Her goals mean nothing."

"But she still succeeds, Grandfather." Ben stomped his foot on the carriage floor, blinking away tears and gulping down the burning sensation in the back of his throat. "Her curse still stands, and she nearly *killed* me. Why would she do that now whether she be exiled or not?!"

Grandfather turned his head and growled. "Benjamin, there is a time to know everything, and that is not now. You should have never sought out your mother. The cure to your curse will not be found in seeking out her aid!"

He looked straight ahead once more. "We will find a way to cure you, it just may take more time than what we have. But that... that is not the way."

"Did you know about this?" Ben asked through his teeth as a knot twisted in his stomach. "Did you know that she cursed me this whole time?"

"...Yes."

Seventeen

The Trial of a Lich

The carriage slowed to a steady stop, and Nomas clicked its teeth announcing their arrival. Grandfather climbed off the carriage with ease and stroked the skull of the steed, talking to it as if the horse was an old friend. While Grandfather thanked Nomas, Ben carefully climbed off the carriage.

His hands trembled as he grasped around the cold curved frame, and his dress shoes slipped no matter where he stepped. Shivering and shaking, the boy struggled to mangle his way out of the cart as if he were immensely ill. As his feet plopped onto the lightless ground and a cloud of darkness seemed to plume at his heels, Ben felt a wave of vertigo nearly overcome him.

"Benjamin," Grandfather hissed, drawing him back to the strange light illuminating the necromancer and his steed.

"Coming," Ben said, wading his way around the cart and to Grandfather. He stood behind him and stared up at Grandfather in distress.

"Follow me," Grandfather said while granting the horse one final pat. He then stepped forward, and his leg seemed to move like the pendulum of a clock. As he swung his foot forward, the air shifted backward, it drew colder and warmth prickled Ben's skin. Was it like this before? Ben remembered only tumbling through the shadows in a dizzying array of black fabric. This was how it felt to control the shift between realms, Ben told himself as he mimicked Grandfather's long, steady strides. The necromancer's crooked back was like a tall, oddly shaped wall that blocked Ben's vision as they stepped smoothly into the living realm.

They took their final steps through the inky passage from the netherworld. Ben flinched as his shoes tapped onto a smooth surface unfamiliar to the wooden floors and plush carpet belonging to Grandfather's study. Where was the crunch of the scrolls? The shuffling sound of crumpling paper!

The wisps of darkness subsided, revealing a long hallway unfamiliar to the Hill or anywhere Ben had ever been. Most striking were the artifacts and curiosities displayed under every artificial archway along the hall. There were tall glass cases with horridly configured skeletons, suits of devilish armor belonging to knights of old, pedestals holding haunting artifacts, and statues resembling fiendish gargoyles and undead. Ben gulped and took a step back.

The floor was a black marble with veins of white crossing in every direction like a spider's web. The marble gleamed under the warm lights from the scones hanging over each curiosity on lavish walnut walls embossed with silver runes. This was a place belonging only to those who had mastered the dead. To any undead being, this hall would have been synonymous with a prison.

"Where are we?" Ben asked as Grandfather turned to look at him whilst unclipping his cloak.

Grandfather crouched down enough to almost be eye to eye with Ben, and Ben was certain Grandfather was ready to reprimand him for running away. Instead, Grandfather tossed the cloak over Ben's shoulders and pulled it tight, clipping the silver brooch in a way that made the cloak completely cover Ben's attire.

"Keep this on and make sure no one sees those unruly

pajamas," Grandfather said while looking deep into Ben's golden eyes. Ben blushed at the thought someone other than Grandfather would see him in the pajamas, and he hurriedly nodded. He normally would never be seen anywhere except in his suit, but emotions and urgency had taken priority over appearances. Now, his clothes were covered in blood stains and torn by the nefarious curse his mother had attempted to cast.

Ben looked down at the cloak with dismay, remembering his most recent experience in a similar article of clothing. He shivered with fear as the weight of the fabric felt the same, and the long black swaths of fabric flowed identically to the wraith's cloak.

"It is a normal cloak, Benjamin," Grandfather said with a flat tone that made the boy flinch.

Pulling the cloak tight to his body, he looked around and hissed, "Grandfather, this isn't the Hill."

"I haven't the time to return you to the Hill. Do you know how much time it takes to travel through the netherworld? Our journey back was two days!"

"H-how long was I gone?" Ben asked.

Grandfather shook his head. "Do you think it was easy for Nomas to follow your request? It took the spirit three and a half days to find Susan for you. Once you were deposited, it only took the spirit a few hours to return me to your location, but this time has passed without the world waiting for us to pick up yesterday like it hadn't already happened."

Ben gulped, and his face paled. He had been gone for days, but not a day had passed. He did not know the spirit's travel was not instantaneous, and he feared what would have happened if the spirit could not find Susan at all. How long would he have ridden the horse in the shadows of the netherworld before changing his command?

A shiver ran down his spine as he realized it was only due to a strike of luck that Grandfather arrived when he did. If another hour had passed, Ben feared to know what would have happened to him. He doubted his mother would have killed him, but a gut feeling told him she likely believed death was better than living as a necromancer. If it came to that, he could easily imagine what she would have done with her knife.

"Grandfather, I-"

"Not now, Benjamin. You *must* stay silent now. I hadn't the time to send you home, but now you cannot leave my side, and of all things, it is imperative you stay silent. We are in the chamber of the dead. If another second is delayed due to my absence, I fear the trial upon us will proceed with an undesired outcome. Bear witness to this, Benjamin. One day, you will be guiding these proceedings too."

If there was any color remaining in Ben's face, it surely had drained away. "A trial?!" Ben remembered Erwy's conversation with him, and a gut feeling told him he already knew what the subject of the trial was.

"Yes, Benjamin. Now silence. And keep those pajamas hidden, they are a disgrace," Grandfather urged as they approached the door.

Ben looked down at the collar of his pajamas and squeezed the edges of the cloak together in a fit of embarrassment. They were only a few strides away from it now, and Ben dreaded taking another step. The last time he had seen the Council of the Dead, they were discussing his failings and lack of ability to be a necromancer. Would they let him walk into a trial? Ben wondered if Grandfather's presence would be enough to spare Ben from necromancers like Jacob Withertomb.

They reached the door, and Ben never felt so small. It towered two times Grandfather's height. Massive golden rings hung on the door with circumferences so large Ben could easily fit his head through them. He watched as Grandfather reached out and lifted a ring with moderate effort just enough to let go halfway. The ring swung sharply and slammed against the door.

Dong

The boy quivered as the sound echoed and resonated throughout the corridor. A lock clicked, and the door moved inward just a hair. Grandfather pushed his hand forward, and an aggravated moan erupted from the heavy wooden panels as they opened, revealing the council's court room.

Ben's mouth dropped, and he hurriedly wrapped the cloak around himself even tighter. Just ten feet away from them sat three council members. Ben looked backwards and realized this hallway was explicitly only for the Council of the Dead's use. Grandfather yanked him along the line of tables towards his own seat.

The council sat in a large hall with a line of tables covering half of the width. There was a minor half wall below the tables, leading to a lower level where a couple of chairs were placed for an audience with the council. Ben noted the silver glimmer of runes and magic circles drawn across the floor. There, he could see Erwys Ellandor sitting in one of the chairs towards the back of the hall along with a few others. Their attention was entirely focused on a young girl standing in the heart of the circles and runes.

The girl looked entirely distraught. She had long black hair that rippled down her back and stopped flowing just at her knees. The hair covered half her face, but her hands were pressed to her mouth as she shamelessly gnawed at her nails. She wore a modest purple dress with white stockings and black loafers.

Black ribbons adorned the dress; some of them were haphazard as if she had dressed in a flurry. The girl's lavender eyes were wide and focused on the ground, occasionally flitting from necromancer to necromancer before settling back on her feet.

Grandfather's hand curled over Ben's shoulder, and he moved him along. Ben followed Grandfather past the necromancers in the council, being sure to avoid looking at anyone and settling on staring at the back of Grandfather's suit jacket.

Grandfather arrived at his seat. He pulled out a tall wooden chair with a velvet cushion. He sat down, and Ben stood behind him, feeling awkward and wishing he could sink away into the shadows. Grandfather's cloak draped over his entire being and pooled at his feet, making him feel like he was cowering in an oversized blanket.

"Wow, I am shocked! Ernest, you brought the next *Gravekeeper* here," a semi-familiar voice said with a snicker.

Ben glanced at the necromancer and quickly realized that it was Jacob Withertomb himself.

"Has he gained the sight? Or does he wear those silly glasses for fashion?" Withertomb blatantly said with a smirk as he leaned back in his chair and picked up a cup of tea. His brows raised with mirth as he sipped loudly. It was the loudest sound in the room as everyone stopped whispering to focus on Ben.

The boy's shoulders hunched forward as he tried to hide himself in the cloak. His ears burned red, and he wanted to yell at Withertomb, but nothing could hide the fact that he was wearing a classic set of spectral specters atop his nose.

"He will be prepared to be the next Gravekeeper. That is none of your concern," Grandfather said.

The necromancer noticed this, and his lips parted into a slight grimace. His eyes moved to focus solely on Ben, and Ben noticed a glint in his bright red gaze. "Not my concern? I train our future necromancers, and I promise you *any* of my apprentices can best yours. If he cannot see the dead, how will he stop them? How will he control them-" Jacob Withertomb laughed abruptly. "I digress, Ernest, I forgot. Your family does not believe in controlling the dead. You are not capable of it."

A deep chuckle emerged from Grandfather's throat, causing Ben to flinch. "As the Gravekeeper, he will be entirely capable of handling any one of your apprentices that you *think* can become true necromancers. In due time, Jacob."

Jacob Withertomb's lips drew thin, but after a long second, their corners lifted with a vile smirk. "The time due is fast approaching. If he is not prepared by then, be prepared for one of my *apprentices* to replace yours."

Grandfather stood, and his chair screeched against the marble floor. Before he could yell at Jacob Withertomb, another voice from the center of the tables roared, "Enough!"

It was the voice of Isabelle Nightshade. He did not expect her to be seated at the foremost table, but there she was. Her blonde hair billowed around a black dress down to her waist. Her face appeared petrified in a state of eternal youth. Beside her stood two skeletons clad in armor and carrying halberds. Their heads turned to stare at Grandfather and Withertomb, and Ben could see the glow of two spirits animating the skeletons through the glasses, but that glow was a mere whisper to what he should be capable of seeing.

Jacob Withertomb shot Grandfather a sideways sneer, and Grandfather harumphed and shook his shoulders.

"Jacob, there is no harm in teaching the next Gravekeeper on our proceedings, unless you oppose the Gravekeeper himself?" the speaker challenged with a clear voice that resonated throughout the hall, ringing directly in Ben's ears.

"No, I do not," Withertomb said through his teeth.

"Very well," Nightshade smiled, and a chill went down Ben's spine. Her skeletons looked forward as she said, "Let us proceed with the trial of the Ellandors. Any objections?"

The room was met with heavy silence. Nightshade's gaze dropped down upon the family sitting in the heart of the room. Ben looked over Grandfather's shoulder and down at the entire family. It was clear they were on trial, but with the girl in the center of the room standing in a series of rings and runes, he could not help but feel like he was witnessing a slaughter. How could this family possibly walk away from a trial in this position unscathed when they were already standing at the gallows?

Erwys's purple eyes met with Ben's and his stomach churned. She kept her gaze locked on him as the necromancer at the front of the room began.

"We are here tonight to determine the punishment of Delore Ellandor for her undeniable crime of becoming a lich and every succinct crime leading up to this detestable act," the speaker began, all the while, smiling softly as if she were equally presenting a commendation and not a condemnation.

"Is Delore here to defend herself or deny this?" she asked, looking once amongst the Council of the Dead before lowering her gaze to Delore's family.

The Ellandor family had seven in attendance. A couple sitting furthest away from the girl were trembling in pure terror. An old man sat beside them, glaring deeply at the council speaker. Another man, young yet noticeably frail, looked at his knees and did not acknowledge the council's claims as if he were asleep. Three women including Erwys sat beside each other, staring hard at the speaker while the girl stood there with her shoulders straight and eyes fierce.

"She is not here," Erwys said, and her voice echoed through the room just as loudly as the speaker's, causing Ben to wonder if the room were enchanted.

"Then she is guilty," the speaker said, cold and dry. None of the family members reacted to this as if they were already aware of her fate. They only stood there hoping, just maybe, the lich would appear. But Delore would never hand herself in to the Council of the Dead. So the only ones the council could punish were the only people a lich could still care for. Those tied to her blood.

The speaker's eyes settled on the girl. "The Ellandor family will be forbidden from applying for council for the next century, will be banned from Gravekeeper services for the deaths every family member equal to the number that was sacrificed for the lich. We count five thousand immediately afflicted. As Delore Ellandor is not here to receive her punishment, the rules state that her closest kin, her offspring, Igraine Ellandor, shall be punished in her stead."

Igraine's shoulders visibly shook. She shot a look of pure terror towards Ben and Grandfather. Ben looked at the back of Grandfather's gray hair, wondering what the current Gravekeeper would do. Would he actually make an effort to save the Ellandors? If five thousand people died for the sake of Delore Ellandor becoming a lich, did Igraine deserve to be saved?

Ben's stomach roiled with disgust, but as he looked at the girl, a sense of guilt washed the disgust away. His own mother wished to drag him out of the necromancy world meanwhile hers pushed her into the darkest parts of it. Why did she deserve to be punished for her mother's actions?

Igraine looked right at Ben, and her purple gaze stayed steady. Locked in, the two apprentices stared at each other. As the speaker continued to list the milder punishments of the

Ellandor family acting as secondary accomplices for Delore's behavior, Igraine continued to look in Ben's eyes. She was hollow. Defeated.

"-Igraine Ellandor will be sent to the underworld as punishment for Delore Ellandor's crimes. Her spirit shall reside within the prison of Tophet until Delore Ellandor turns herself in for her crimes and succumbs to death."

Igraine looked away from Ben as a sob escaped her throat. She crouched down and pressed her hands over her face to hide and muffle out her sobs. Erwys flinched but did not move to aid her granddaughter. There was nothing she could do in this moment to save her against the crimes of Delore and the judgement of the council. She settled on glaring at Grandfather with a look that could light him aflame.

"Are there any objections to this punishment?" the speaker asked.

"I find it not severe enough," one necromancer said on the opposite side of the room directly across from Grandfather. He looked to be older than Grandfather, and his hair fell over his shoulder in a thick, white braid.

"How so?" the council speaker asked, tilting her chin with curiosity as something wicked glinted in her venomous eyes.

"They should all be revoked of their rights as necromancers and their entire family, including those passed, should lose all services from the Gravekeepers. They must suffer the fear and endless pain Delore's victims have suffered!"

A couple of necromancers nodded in agreement. Jacob Withertomb jauntily clapped, standing in support. Grandfather stayed seated, but Ben noted his clenched fists at his side and his knuckles turning bone white.

"Are you suggesting an entire purge of the Ellandor line?" the speaker asked, only to cause Erwys Ellandor to spring from her seat.

"This is incredulous! Delore did not do these acts with our family. She does not have the right to call herself an Ellandor!" Erwys cried. "How dare you suggest our entire family, a family tied to the fates themselves, be eradicated for a crime we did not commit nor were in collusion with!"

"Do you believe you do not need to be punished?" the speaker hissed. "It is your lack of diligence for allowing this to come. As an heir of the fates, you should have known this whole time what she would do and what she was to become-"

"Excuse you, Nightshade," Erwys growled, voice echoing like thunder in the chamber. "The only fate we cannot see is our own."

Grandfather coughed and cleared his throat, causing the conversation to cease. The speaker looked at him with a questioning gaze and asked, "Perhaps the Gravekeeper himself should have a say?" she asked, resting her chin upon folded hands. "It is you who's job is equally critical to stopping such crimes."

'Thank you, Isabella," Grandfather said. "Do not fail to recognize my duties solely focus on graves, and Delore's actions did not violate any existing graves." Grandfather paused long enough for a low murmur to erupt amongst the necromancers. "That being said, the banning of the Gravekeeper services from the Ellandors at any scale should entirely be up to my personal determination."

"So how will you see this out? Will you follow the recommended punishment?" Isabella Nightshade asked, no longer smiling. Ben doubted she appreciated opposition during a trial public to the necromancy world. If the Gravekeeper rejected her authority, who else would reject the punishment?

Ben thought about the conversation between Erwys and Grandfather, and he wondered what it really meant to remove the services of the Gravekeeper. Technically, that would allow other necromancers to violate the graves of the Ellandors on their own accords, adding more consequential punishment. In turn, this also symbolized an allowance for other necromancers to behave in such a way. Ben doubted removing a Gravekeeper's protection could be done in any name of true justice.

"I will not revoke any protection from the Ellandors," Grandfather said simply, mirroring Ben's thoughts. "That is a power only my family holds, and there is no reason to allow their family to receive further retaliation from those seeking revenge for Delore's actions."

The speaker nodded. "And of the other punishments?"

"I believe the only individual that ought to be punished for creating the lich is Delore and her catalyst," Grandfather said simply, pointing out the only people who actively participated in creating the lich. The lich themselves was clearly at fault, but there always one other who assisted in creating the lich by gathering the appropriate items and drawings the runes and casting the spell upon the lich. They, in a sense, were more guilty than the lich. But it appeared no one knew who that catalyst was.

This led to an uproar in the chamber, with several necromancers standing and arguing in protest. Ben shook and pulled the cloak tightly around him at the sight of powerful necromancers throwing fits, but the calmest of them all were Grandfather and the speaker, causing the boy to be more afraid. The speaker had a cold calculating look reflected from her gaze, and Ben could not tell if she agreed with Grandfather or not. It did not matter, however, as the council's dissent became deafening, making it clear what the majority of the council believed.

"Enough!" the speaker cried, causing the council to silence. "Very well! The Ellandors will not lose the services of the Gravekeeper, but otherwise their punishment shall stand!" She slammed down a gavel, and again, instead of producing the sound of wood slamming, the sound of a deep bell rang throughout the chamber.

The girl, Igraine, screamed out in horror, unable to hold back her sobs any further. Erwys stood along with the two other women, and the man who had kept his head down the whole time. They ran for the girl, but an invisible force stopped them.

"Grandma!" the girl cried as she spun to face Erwys. In that moment, Ben wished he had closed his eyes. The silver runes on the ground glimmered with a strange light, and a flame erupted from the floor, covering Igraine in a torrent of fire. She screamed at the top of her lungs, but in seconds her voice disappeared, and within the minute, the fire vanished along with every trace of the girl.

Erwys looked up at Ben with a tear filled, daring gaze. Grandfather had failed to save her granddaughter. If Ben wanted to gain the spectral sight, he would have to save Igraine.

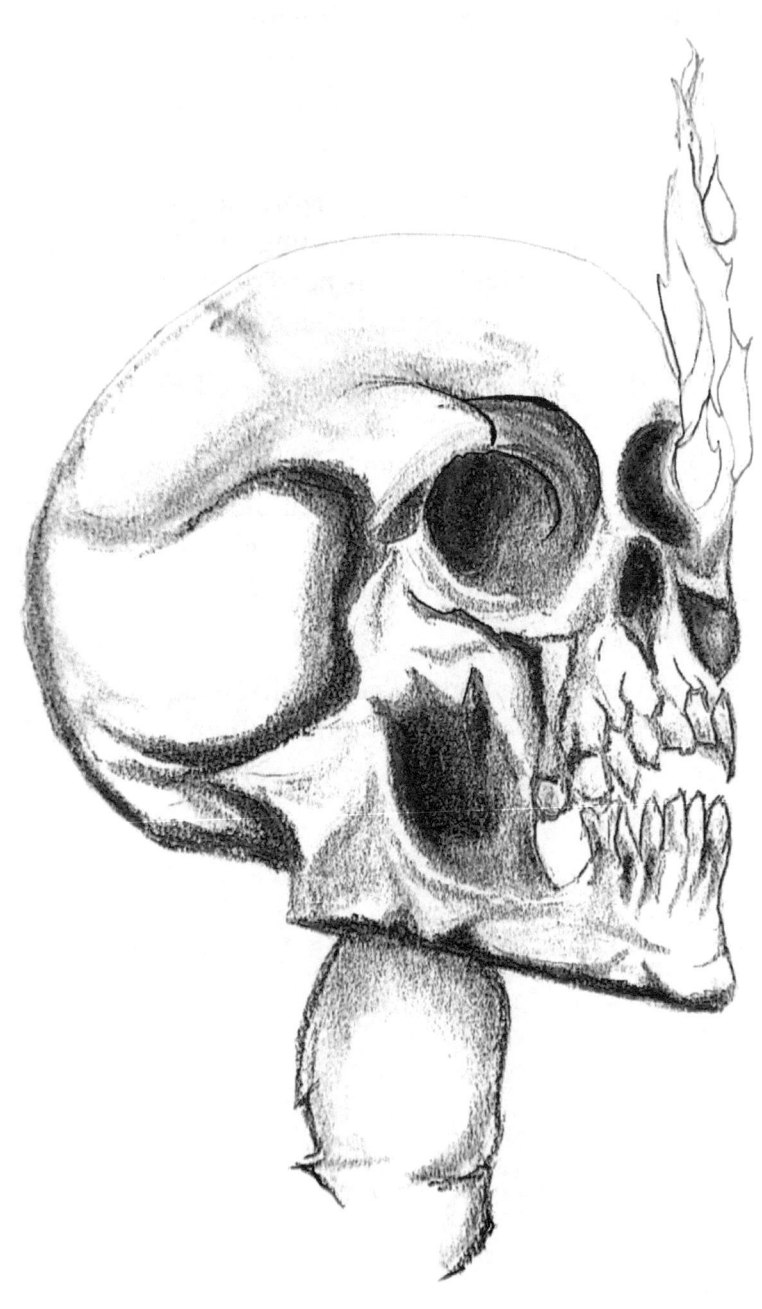

Eighteen

In the Council's Hands

After the trial finished, Grandfather swept Ben out of the council room in a flurry. He hurried him down the long hallway and through a door wedged between two statues. They entered a large, luxurious office, outfitted with a mezzanine study, a brewing station, and two tall, floor to ceiling stained glass windows. The office was furnished with a massive rectangular desk sitting before the windows. In front of the desk, a brilliant red flame floated in the air, magically hanging over a small dish potted with ash. Around the flame sat two red upholstered chairs and behind them a large couch made of red leather and brass fittings. Books covered the walls, and Ben caught on to the uncanny style similar to that of Grandfather's study.

"Follow along, we can return to the Hill quickly from here," Grandfather said as he stepped around his desk to open a small chest sitting on its corner.

"What *was* that?!" Ben blurted, causing Grandfather to pause and lift his gaze.

"*That* was none of your concern. That was a normal trial for the-"

"They burned her alive!" Ben cried, ripping Grandfather's cloak off his person and crumpling it in his arms. "What are they doing, witch hunting?! Since when did necromancers burn their own people alive!"

Grandfather laughed, but there was no mirth in his voice. "Necromancers have done far worse to our own kind. The only thing preventing us from becoming our entire demise is the law of the council and the protection of the Gravekeeper."

Ben shook his head. "How does that law help anyone? She was innocent! Erwys asked you for your help, and you did nothing to stop them!"

Grandfather froze and his eyes narrowed. "Erwys," he muttered, eyes darting back and forth. "How do you know she asked for my help? What has she told you?"

Ben's mouth went dry. Grandfather shuffled around his desk, approaching Ben in a frenzied manner.

"I- I... She connected me to her soul-"

Grandfather's brows twisted as Ben explained what happened. "This all makes sense now," he grumbled in a deep, solemn tone while rubbing his forehead. "She is the reason you sought out Susan."

"She was just trying to help me."

"No, Benjamin, there is no such thing as just trying to help a Gravekeeper. What has she asked in return for divulging such information to you?"

Ben gulped, thinking about the string charm she had given him. She never charged him for the information she shared, but she did propose a solution to his problems for his aid, if he was willing to make the trade. Ben knew Grandfather would not approve, and he knew that it would be wise to not mention the red string.

He sighed. "She took pity-"

Click

"Shhh," Grandfather hissed, smacking his hand over Ben's mouth. His eyes darted to the door of his office. "We wasted too much time! Quickly, redraw the cloak." He then looked deep in Ben's eyes, hand still pressed against the boy's mouth, and whispered, *"Do not speak of Erwys or Susan."*

Ben nodded, eyes wide. Grandfather released the apprentice's face, and Ben gasped for air. He hurriedly tossed the cloak over himself as three necromancers from the council entered Grandfather's office.

One of them was Jacob Withertomb to Ben's dismay. There was the speaker, Isabella Nightshade, and she walked with a cold confidence that made Ben wish to cower. But the most striking of the three was the third necromancer.

The third necromancer stood at just half Grandfather's height and was seemingly twice his age. He paced into the office with a bone white cane that struggled to hold him up. His limbs trembled horribly, causing the cane to rapidly tap on the ground as he dragged it across the marble floor. He looked like he could have been wearing a wraith cloak from how his skin clung to his skeletal frame. The old necromancer looked at Ben, and the boy withheld a cry. His eyes were missing entirely.

"Running away so fast, Ernest?" Isabella asked, slowly walking to one of the plush upholstered chairs. Her hand slid along its back before she languidly sat down.

"I was," Grandfather grumbled. "But I am in no rush." He nodded at the old man, "Hector Ashrot, I haven't enjoyed your presence in quite some time."

"If you find it enjoyable," the old man rasped as he tapped his cane and made his way to the couch.

"Not many do," Isabella scoffed, crossing her legs and allowing the folds of her black robes to swoop in the air as they re-draped her slender figure.

"Have a seat, Jacob," Grandfather said, motioning for the first necromancer who had intruded into the office to sit on the remaining chair. She glanced at Ben and smiled softly. His hands clenched tightly upon Grandfather's robe in trepidation.

Jacob Withertomb shook his hand and stood near the open flame, arms crossed. His eyes focused on Ben and the boy looked away, stepping closer to the comfort of Grandfather's shadow.

"What can I do for you?" Grandfather asked with an irritated sigh.

"Such a wonderful host, as always," Isabella said with a curt laugh.

"Igraine Ellandor has been sent to the underworld. The Ellandors have been punished. The lich is still at large. What else is there to discuss?" Grandfather asked as he took his time sitting in his own seat.

"Indeed, that issue is addressed, for now," Hector Ashrot stated.

Isabella Nightshade sighed. "Hector and Jacob are both in charge of the educational disciplines of necromancy, you see, Ernest. It just so happens, they are equally concerned about the future of the Gravekeeper."

"Are you to say an Ashrot is concerned about the capabilities of a Gravekeeper?" Grandfather inquired with a mocking tone as he folded his hands upon his desk. "Or am I mistaken to believe that your specialties are far from the maintenance of the dead?"

Hector Ashrot was the head of the necromancer family entirely focused on necrosis and its reversal. Many of their family members never aged, and they were often responsible for many massive plagues. In speculation, Ben had read theories that they were allegedly responsible for the first Bubonic plague and the origination of Yellow Fever. If one was lucky, their plague doctor may have been an Ashrot attempting to undo the disease they caused.

Hector Ashrot harumphed and shook his head. "I have no intention of contributing to the development of a Gravekeeper. I merely care about continuing to use their assistance. How behind are you on your tasks, Ernest? Can you do enough in our region? Is it time to move the Gravekeeper responsibility to another family?"

"Who would take that on?" Grandfather asked. "There is not a single necromancer family except our own who can handle the job."

"Mine can," Jacob Withertomb proposed. Ben could imagine the smirk on the man's face, and his blood boiled with contempt.

Grandfather snorted.

"Enough," Isabella said, faking a yawn. "That is only speculation, and there is no true need for you to offer that, is there Jacob? You have enough to keep you busy with the academy."

Jacob turned around in his seat to protest to Isabella, but his eyes caught Ben's and they lingered. He grinned. "My duties to the academy are of no concern, Isabella. You see, my school can produce hundreds of potential Gravekeepers. I can ensure they develop a fitting curriculum with Stone's input. Potentially develop it into a paid profession. However, I do not see this young man here even slightly capable of becoming *the* Gravekeeper. Not compared to the tier my students boast. It is simply impossible!"

Grandfather glowered at the back of Jacob Withertomb's head, but if the man knew of this, he did not pretend to care.

Isabella frowned. "Is there a reason, Ernest, that your grandson would not be able to continue the line of being a Gravekeeper? Has he yet to develop his sight?"

"Why else would he be wearing spectral specters?" Withertomb interjected, causing Ben's face to burn. He looked down at his lap, and his hand absently slid along the glasses' spindly frame. He wished he could not see or hear anything at all. They acted as if he were not in the room. He wanted to say 'they were working on it' or 'he is capable of being the next Gravekeeper' but the pressure Ben felt being in a room with the world's most powerful necromancers kept his voice trapped within his throat.

"Ernest, you are aware there are merely three weeks before his rite is scheduled to take place?" Isabella asked.

Grandfather cleared his throat and looked aside with bemusement. "Yes, I am *well* aware. Benjamin will entirely be prepared for his ceremony. He is not just a perfect candidate as the next Gravekeeper. He is the only candidate." Grandfather took a moment to glower at Withertomb. "There is no need for any of your apprentices to pretend they could inherit such a role."

Jacob Withertomb scoffed.

Ben swayed. Would Grandfather believe Ben could succeed in becoming a Gravekeeper? Ben could not even perform enough magic to be qualified as an apprentice wizard. As for a necromancer, he could summon spirits, but that had proven to go poorly without the spectral sight.

If Ben had the proper sight, he wondered what more he would be capable of. Would he see the world like Erwys Ellandor through a myriad of ribbons or have the sensibilities that Elaine, the poltergeist, possessed? There was so much to see and know, and he knew his lack of sense inhibited his capabilities to the point no one needed to pretend he could be the next Gravekeeper.

He did not believe it himself.

"I do not believe he is the wrong candidate. I simply fear the child is not prepared to be the next Gravekeeper," Isabella said. "Perhaps training him under Jacob Withertomb's wing would allow him to gain some alternative insight?"

"Absolutely not," Grandfather said, slamming his hand flat on the desk and causing Ben to jump.

Hector Ashrot shook his head. "There is no level of training that can assist an apprentice without the sight. I have not a single potion that could cure him of his ailment unless he wishes to experience death itself. Even that is only a temporary solution!"

"Fear not, Benjamin's ailment will be resolved," Grandfather said, nodding at Ben. "And if you fear he is not capable, even blind, the boy has already perfected summoning techniques. He summoned a vetala not so long ago successfully, mind you blind."

"A vetala?" Isabella mused, eyes widening.

Ben blushed and looked down. He did not feel the slightest bit proud about the evil spirit he summoned, but in this moment, Grandfather would pick any piece needed to convince his fellow council members to let them be.

"That shouldn't be possible," Jacob Withertomb said. "Have you contracted with-"

"No," Grandfather said coldly, eyeing the necromancer with distaste. "The boy will be prepared. You have no reason to worry. Now," he stood and waved an arm towards the door. "If that is all, my grandson and I have much to discuss. Instead of spending his time on his flaws, it is better to use it to learn, don't you think?"

Isabella shrugged as she stood. Hector took his time standing, but he joined her and was the first to leave. Jacob Withertomb followed Hector Ashrot, but Isabella lingered behind, allowing the office door to close in front of her face.

She turned back and looked at Grandfather with a cold, sharp gaze. The air in the room seemed to decrease ten degrees, and Ben cowered deeper into Grandfather's cloak, stepping behind the necromancer.

"Have you no sense of self-preservation? Do you wish death upon yourself?" Isabella hissed with a flash of venomous light in her green eyes.

Grandfather glared at her. "I haven't a clue what you-"

"The Ellandors! *The lich!*" she said through her teeth. She paced towards Grandfather. "How can you defend them? Do you know what this means as the Gravekeeper?"

Grandfather sighed and pinched the ridge of his nose. "I did not defend the Ellandors. I simply refuse to revoke my services to a family for the crime of an individual."

"Ha! Your actions may have lost you your right to make such decisions. You do not need to worry about the next Gravekeeper's lack of sight. If he fails to become a Gravekeeper, there will be no reason to keep the Stone family in such a privileged position."

"*Isabella Nightshade,*" Grandfather growled, causing the hair on Ben's arms to stand, "The authority of the Gravekeeper is not to be challenged, or do you forget why I hold my place in the council?"

Isabella's lips pursed. She studied the two members of the Stone family for a long moment. "I only hope you are aware of the storm you are brewing."

She left abruptly with the door clicking shut behind her. Ben stared at his cloak covered knees, trembling. He could not bring his eyes to Grandfather's. He had done everything he knew how to do, and yet he still had not gained the sight. The rite to become a Gravekeeper was fast approaching, and there was no solution for his lack of senses to speak of.

He had to help Erwys Ellandor save Igraine Ellandor. The popular opinion of the council did not support the Ellandors. If some necromancers had their ways, they would have completely executed the family. He imagined Grandfather had done nothing for her family given her granddaughter was now imprisoned in the underworld, but there was a limit to what Grandfather could have done. With that limitation, the council still had called him out, and now he sat in an unfavorable seat. With Ben's own rite fast approaching, it was in their worst interest to be in such a precarious position.

Ben chewed on his lip as he came to the realization that he would have to help Erwys without Grandfather's knowing. He did not want to betray Grandfather again, but he also feared for him. If the council wanted to hurt him or get rid of him for not condemning the Ellandors, how would they feel about him supporting his grandson in removing the punishment? He could not participate in sending someone to jail only to break them out the next day. The only person with little input and thus commitment on the issue was Ben. No one would notice if he went to the underworld to save Igraine. No one would care if the *blind* Gravekeeper went to the underworld.

Grandfather ushered Ben to come around the desk. Ben joined him as he pulled out the small silver mirror. Ben caught sight of Grandfather's golden eyes along with his own. They looked incredibly intense as if they belonged to something inhuman, and then they were gone, replaced by a murky silver glass.

The apprentice blinked, feeling his eyes now to be heavier than before. He turned away from the mirror and realized they were in fact back in Grandfather's office on the Hill. Ben watched as Grandfather stuffed the hand mirror into his desk. He then pulled out a little brass key and locked the drawer, and the boy blushed knowing he was locking it specifically to keep him out.

"Now then..." Grandfather pushed Ben's shoulders to force the boy to move away from the back of the desk. The boy stumbled and felt his feet crunch upon tossed around scrolls. "Get to cleaning this up."

Ben gulped and nodded. He crouched down and picked up scrolls as Grandfather sat at his desk and focused on mending a torn parchment. He had a small spool of thread, a needle, and a couple of vials of liquids Ben knew to be oils and ectoplasm. Ben stared at the necromancer a second too long, and the old man slammed his hand on his desk, causing the vials to violently rattle. "What are you staring at me for? Did you think you would get away with this?!"

"No, Grandfather!" Ben turned his head back to the sea of scrolls that covered the floor and hurried in picking them up. His face burned with shame.

"If any scroll is damaged, set it up here," Grandfather said and tapped a clear area on his desk as he continued to mend the scroll before him. He grumbled, "a torn contract is as useless as a filth riddled tissue."

Ben frowned as he looked down at the pile of scrolls in his hands, feeling his face burn. So many of them were frayed on the edges, but a substantial number of them harbored nasty rips thanks to his tantrum.

He crouched down and unfurled a scroll, inspecting it for damage when an idea came to mind. He looked at the shelves, smirking to see them empty spare a few heavy tomes and trinkets. He would have to examine each scroll for damage if he were to do his job well, and then he might as well organize them into *his* desired locations. Ben looked back down at the unfurled document before him with a new agenda. If the integrity of the contract was damaged, he would hand it to Grandfather, but if not, he would spend just an extra second scouring the contents to determine what use the scroll may have and sort them accordingly.

Grandfather never seemed to care about how Ben stowed away the scrolls as he had plenty of work to do with the towering stack of parchment that continued to pile up. He wished he had been more careful with the scrolls as he continued to stack the ones he found most interesting on Grandfather's desk. One was a contract with a spirit belonging to an ancient will' o wisp and another belonged to an actual djinn.

When Ben finished cleaning the study, he stepped in front of Grandfather. Massive piles of torn scrolls surrounded Grandfather, causing Ben to blush. He sheepishly looked away and said, "I'm done."

Grandfather looked at him with a sharp, cold gaze. "Benjamin, if I had my wits about me, I would send you off for what you have done here. After summoning the revenant, I had thought you learned your lesson, but here you went off, ransacked my office, and summoned a spirit you are not supposed to summon until your rite let alone without my permission."

Ben's jaw clenched. He wished to leave, but a sickening gut feeling kept his feet still. Despite better judgement, he muttered, "Then what." Grandfather's brows twisted. Ben continued. "What should I do? What would you do if you learned what I know? Nothing? You have known this whole time of my curse, yet you have done nothing to resolve it."

Anger made Ben's heart race. "You heard Nightshade. My rite is only three weeks away, and I'm hardly qualified to be a necromancer. You've done nothing about this, not even now. And now, the Council of the Dead is preparing to be rid of me! What will you do then when you have no heir?"

Ben glowered at Grandfather, waiting for a response, but no matter what he thought Grandfather might say, he was prepared to reject his answer. He was too mad to accept anything Grandfather had to say. A painful piece of logic whispered in his mind that Grandfather would not say what he wanted to hear. There would be no apologies or retributions.

Grandfather blinked and scowled. "Benjamin, there is a process to-"

"I just witnessed the Council's opinion of me firsthand. What process produces positive results when I will be condemned before I even have a fighting chance?!" Ben's eyes searched for sympathy from his grandfather. No matter what he did, whether it broke the rules or not, he saw no future with himself as a necromancer following Grandfather's will. He hoped his grandfather would acknowledge this. If he could not save Erwys Ellandor's granddaughter, perhaps he would have the courage to save his own grandson.

But Ben could see as Grandfather solemnly shook his head that he did not have the desire to strive for such success. "A curse of this caliber is no minor thing," Grandfather said under his voice. "There is nothing I currently can do short of convincing Susan to reverse the curse. You know how that went. If you haven't learned your lesson from that-"

"You told me she was dead," Ben said through his teeth. "I saw her grave."

"To the world of necromancers and to our family, she is. As for her grave, every Gravekeeper earns their grave once they complete their rite. It is a reminder to us all that we also will die, and our graves are to be protected. She was no exception," Grandfather coldly explained. The feet of his chair screeched against the wooden floor as he stood. "The only fraying tie she has to this family is the curse she has cast upon you and the place she will one day rest."

"And yet you can't break that either?" Ben asked. "You can sever the ties of your own family, but you can't break a curse or at the very least, be honest? She's my mom, Grandfather!"

"The only way to remove the curse is to destroy her!" Grandfather slammed his hand on the table. Ben's mouth went dry.

"Destroy her?" Ben whispered. She was still his mother. The idea of killing her was gut wrenching, but Grandfather explicitly said *destroy* and that was far worse than kill. "You can't mean... is that the only way? Curses are so common, and Erwys can remove-"

"Not even Erwys Ellandor can remove the curse of a mother cast upon her own child. Not one of this severity," Grandfather said softly. "I'm sorry, Benjamin. I do not know if there is a way to regain your sight."

Ben's heart sank. The air in the room froze, and his ears rang with a hollow sound. The edges of his vision blackened, and Ben felt as if he were sinking into himself. A deep, aching pain resounded in his chest, and his breaths came and went in sharp bursts. "Y-you," he stammered, failing to procure his own words while the heavy weight of shock crushed his spirit. "You knew this w-whole time.... This whole time, you never planned to help me. Y-you never expected me to be-"

"No, Benjamin," Grandfather said, shaking his head.

Ben stepped backward and shook his own head. From the beginning, ever since the council meeting in the garden, he knew that Grandfather was the one to suggest finding a new heir. Ever since then, he knew the risks of failing to become a Gravekeeper if he could not prove himself. But now, it all made sense. Grandfather had cast his mother out of the Stone family, and his mother had in turn barred him from ever having an heir. Grandfather was simply too ashamed to face the truth and see it real by telling Ben. This whole time, he never was capable, yet he had been raised to believe he in fact was the next Gravekeeper.

Ben stepped backwards, shaking his head and whispering no under his breath. Grandfather tried to explain himself, but the ringing in Ben's ears along with the swirling thoughts in his head drowned the necromancer out. The boy's hand grabbed the study doorknob and twisted it sharply as Grandfather moved to step around his desk. He would not let the necromancer come near him. He swung the door open and sprinted down the hallway.

He ran out the front door and descended the front stairs of the porch into a swarm of ghosts. Hot tears shamelessly streamed down Ben's face, and he pulled off the spectral specters to wipe the tears away while effectively ridding the ghosts from his vision. He stepped into the graveyard, feeling ready to be bombarded with taunts and laughter for crying, and his sprint morphed into a weakened shuffle as his breaths turned into aggravated heaves and his body trembled with anguish.

The spirits seemed to watch him in silence as he stumbled through the graveyard, looking at the graves with dismay and disappointment. As long as he could remember, he worked tirelessly to maintain the graves, but now, it was all for nothing. They did not care to poke fun at him or ask why he was upset. The silence was mocking.

He kicked a tombstone. "Go ahead and say something!" he screamed. "Go ahead! Oh, the groundskeeper is crying. He's just a ghost whisperer. Go on!" He kicked another tombstone in a fit of furry as no one decided to speak.

"So what, now you think it's funny to shun me? Is it because I can't see you? Is it because you've known all along as well, I'll only ever be your groundskeeper?!" Ben laughed sharply and pulled on the glasses once more. He wanted to look at the bewildered faces of the ghosts and see if they could really refrain from responding while looking him in the eyes.

Ben blinked. A massive horde of spirits surrounded him with a mixture of expressions, but none of them hinted at being silent. Some spirits had their mouths wide open as they sang in a chorus of boo's and moans, a couple were screaming at Ben, as he had kicked *their* tombstones. Many more chattered around him, but nothing of what they said reached him.

The apprentice fell to his knees in shock.

The Hill's residents were in a full uproar, but he could not hear a sound.

Nineteen

A Deal for the Dead

Ben fled the graveyard as quickly as possible, face burning, eyes blurred with tears. Grandfather had not followed him outside, and he was thankful for it as he stormed up the porch's steps and back into the solace of the house. Inside, he did not have to concern himself with the impending silence. It was naturally quiet indoors.

The boy treaded up the staircase and into his room while his mind swirled. Grandfather never expected him to become a necromancer due to his lack of sight. Now, he could no longer hear spirits. How would he reveal this to Grandfather?! Ben gulped as a sickening wave of nausea washed through his body, and he slammed the door behind him, swiftly turning the lock.

His heart raced as he thought over the consequences behind losing his hearing. If only he had not summoned Nomas to visit his mother, she never would have reinforced the curse. His fist slammed on the door. Of course, she had to reinforce the curse, but Grandfather could not even break it! This whole time, he was aware of the curse and yet he played Ben along, allowing him to believe there was another way.

And now, Ben did not have the chance to be a Gravekeeper in the slightest. The spectral specters could relatively assist him with sight, but nothing except an inherited talent would allow him to hear the ghosts. Even ordinary children often could tune in to such an ability, but Ben knew his abilities were not gone, simply blocked, meaning no matter how hard he trained and tried, the senses would never surface.

His heart raced, but his breaths were faint as he stared into his bedroom, a place of comfort yet a prison of complacency. The bed was made with tightly tucked corners and fluffed pillows. His shoes were lined up, one pair of work boots, one spare pair of dress shoes. Ben looked down at his shoes, the ones he had worn for the past few weeks. Now they were scuffed and scratched and peeling at the heels.

The desk near the window was organized with his latest study material gently placed in a stack, untouched in days yet hosting little to no dust. Ben approached the desk and slid his hands on the books. It seemed so long ago since he had last studied Latin or basic contracts or how to summon a spirit. Now there was no need to study this material. He would never be a necromancer.

Was it best to put everything away? To run from the Hill? To let the council officially condemn him? Just the thought of Jacob Withertomb's smirking face as he declared Ben a mere groundskeeper, not even a ghost whisperer, made Ben shiver with anger.

Shunning the destructive desire to throw his study material across his room, he opened his desk drawer to stow away the smaller notebooks properly. The drawer squeaked and dragged as it opened. It was mostly empty. There were only a few bottles of ink, a couple quills, a pouch of salt, and lastly a red knot of yarn. Ben's arm froze, and he stared at the yarn, his mind drawing blank.

Erwys Ellandor...

His hand trembled as he lifted the knot of yarn from the desk drawer. He collapsed upon his desk chair and cradled the yarn in his palms. It looked like an ordinary clump of yarn with many intricate knots tied in haphazard chains and loops, creating an unruly form. It had little semblance of any magical origin, but this object was the only link Ben had to her.

In a daze, Ben lifted his gaze out the window to the black, silky sky. An endless abyss with not a speck of the spectral light he so deeply desired to see. There were enough ghosts on the Hill that their presence should have created a consistent lunar glow, but without the spectral specters, Ben found himself yearning for the slightest hint of an unnatural shimmer or orb.

If he ever wished to see the spirits, he had no other choice but to make the deal with Erwys Ellandor. Grandfather had shut her down, but perhaps he was wrong. What was the harm in him being wrong anyway?

The boy set the yarn charm down and hurriedly changed into a full-dress suit topped with a black cloak curling just at his heels. If he were ever to be a Gravekeeper, this was the proper attire, he thought as he tied on his nicer dress shoes and adjusted his tie. "Not an if," he muttered to himself. This was his first task as a Gravekeeper whether he had the ceremony or not. He did not need Grandfather's approval to perform, and he could prove he did not need the sight, hearing, or any magical abilities to succeed. He would save Igraine Ellandor.

After stowing away his silver dagger into his inner pocket, Ben cleared his mind through deep breathing and picked up the strange little yarn charm and a box of matches. He slid the matchstick against the rough edge of the box, igniting a spark and a violent red flame. The apprentice sucked in a deep breath and held the flame to the charm. The red string singed and blackened as it caught aflame. Then the whole charm combusted into a singular ember. It curled and charred away into a pile of ash in Ben's palm while the flame rose nearly a foot as if the charm was soaked in kerosene.

The boy yelped as the fire burned his palm, jerking his hand away. The ember fell to the ground as it flared upward.

The smoke from the charm lifted like a thick red smog unlike anything Ben had seen before, clearly hinting that this was no ordinary item as he had hoped. He choked in the smoke, tasting the scent of dried herbs, flowers, and a dash of rosemary that seemed all too strange of a smell to originate from fire. His eyes burned from the thick ash, but as he tried to blink and swat it away, the smoke seemed to only thicken.

Ben refrained from stepping away from the fire. It was not burning the floor or expanding in any direction. Only the smoke funneled into the room, and he knew to not resist it. He coughed and wheezed as the red smoke thickened and thickened, stinging his eyes and blurring his vision. Ben stayed still until he could no longer gasp in any breath at all. He collapsed to his knees in a fit of strangled coughs while his vision spotted and blackened and hot tears marked his flushed cheeks.

And in the moment when he believed the charm was nothing but a cruel curse, and he was doomed to die, the endless smoke vanished in a singular harmless plume that dissipated like steam, revealing an unfamiliar room and the soothing scent of lavender and eucalyptus.

Ben heaved and gasped for air. He wiped loose saliva from his mouth, feeling his lips tingle as if they had been brushed with sandpaper. He rubbed his stinging eyes, blinking tears that felt like they harbored glass dust. The tips of his ears burned from the persistent plume of ash, but as Ben sharply inhaled the fresh breezy scent of eucalyptus, the irritation in his ears and eyes resolved.

Ben clambered to his feet and looked around, shocked to find himself no longer in his bedroom or anywhere close to the Hill. He stood in the middle of a small living room that was a third the size of his own living room. There was a singular brown leather couch crammed against one of the walls, riddled with ancient cracks and discoloration. The walls were covered in peeling, yellowed wallpaper that shamelessly revealing the wooden shiplap hidden behind them. A fireplace sat in the opposite corner of the couch, topped with a stone chimney and mantle that extruded from the wall. Beside the lit fire sat Erwys Ellandor in a tall, spindly wooden rocking chair. The room could have aged along with her, living the same extent of an endless lifetime with every scar of time and no hint of ever dying.

She slowly rocked in her chair- it creaked softly, as she knit together a half-formed sweater made of royal purple yarn, the richest color in the room. The knitting needles moved with no hesitation and at an astounding rate to the point Ben could see the sweater grow in the passing minutes. Erwys did not look up, but her chair stopped rocking, gifting an eerie silence.

"So it appears you have made a decision."

Ben blinked and coughed lightly to clear any remnants of the smoke from his blistered lungs. "I will help your granddaughter, Igraine Ellandor, so long as you return to me my ability to sense the dead."

"Ah... sense? Are you to say you are lacking more than the sight?" Erwys nailed the head on the coffin, causing Ben to flinch. He felt naked under her narrowed gaze as she stared deep into the knots and strings tied to his soul. "The curse has strengthened significantly. Did you search for another way? Did you fear the netherworld and the trouble your assistance to my family will cause yours?"

"Grandfather does not know I am here," Ben said through his teeth, looking at the smoldering fireplace with discomfort. "Unlike Grandfather, you told me of my mother and what she had done. I spoke to her to try and persuade her to remove the curse...."

"I see your conversation did not go as planned," Erwys said. She set the ball of purple yarn, her knitting needles, and the half-finished sweater in a basket beside the rocking chair. The old necromancer then pushed herself onto her feet in a slow steady manner. "Fear not, if you free Igraine, I shall ensure your senses are fully restored."

"Really?!" Ben's eyes lit up. "It can be done?!"

Erwys laughed. "Of course, it can!" She then solemnly glared at Ben. "It is no minor price to cure you of your curse. I shall only remove it in exchange for your help. I shan't lift a finger until Igraine is back in our realm, safe and sound."

Ben could have cried. He lowered his gaze and said, "I'll do anything if it means I can become the next Gravekeeper."

Erwys stepped close to Ben so that they were only half an arm's length away from each other. She patted his shoulder in a gruff, comforting manner. "That is a dangerous statement to make, child. Never say you are willing to do anything, or someone will take away from you everything. Are you prepared for the oath you are offering my family? The netherworld is an unforgiving place for those who still wish to breathe."

The boy raised his chin to nod, but then he paused. He had never been to the netherworld before. Maybe traveling with the spirit Nomas counted to a certain degree, but that was the greatest extent of such an experience. Ben had no idea how to navigate such a place beyond the general knowledge he had acquired through some of his books. The netherworld could be described in many manners, ranging from a hellscape, to a desolate vastness the living realm could never rival. No matter the description, it was entirely unearthly and toxic to the living for nothing that sustained life existed in such a realm.

"I... I don't know how to save her entirely," Ben stammered. "How do I find her? How do I succeed?"

Erwys patted Ben's shoulder reassuringly. "There are many

ways to navigate the underworld, child. I do not need your help to go there myself, however you see, there are limits to *who* are allowed to enter the netherworld freely and return to the living realm just as freely. And there are places in the netherworld only the Gravekeeper has a right to enter. The *Prison of Tophet* is one such place forged by necromancers. It is your right to navigate it."

Ben shook his head gently, wishing Grandfather had taught him more on this topic. His lack of confidence did not dissuade Erwys Ellandor as she sighed softly and said, "However, for finding Igraine.... You will have no difficulty tracking her. If you find her and free her, she knows of how to return."

Ben's face paled as he realized if he did not find Igraine, he would be equally trapped within the netherworld.

She turned away from Ben and moved towards a narrow door next to the leather couch. "Come along," she said as she pushed the door open with a loud creak. Ben gulped and followed the necromancer down a smaller hallway that turned at a sharp angle, down a flight of stairs made of uneven wooden steps, and into a basement. When she opened the door at the bottom of the stairs, Ben was hit with the unpleasant dampness of mildew.

The basement was much larger than the living room or the length of the hallway. It extended in a linear direction, and on each stone wall were long wooden tables with trinkets and potions and strange contraptions made of bone and yarn. Erwys Ellandor walked into the middle of the room, and Ben followed closely behind her.

His neck turned as his eyes scanned over the tables' contents. Some of the trinkets made with yarn hung from the ceiling's wooden beams. Others sat in haphazard piles on the tables, and others hung halfway off the tables, just barely scraping the floor. The floor was made of long wooden boards, but where they were missing was packed earth. Across the boards, symbols and circles were painted into the ground with fading white paint. It reminded Ben of a less refined version of the silver runes in Grandfather's study.

"What is this place?" Ben blurted.

"Every necromancer has a place to practice their arts and make their wares. Our family is known for predicting fate and telling of destinies, and this is where those tools of fortune were originally crafted, long ago," Erwys lightly explained as she strolled through the long rectangular room.

"What about now?"

"We have a shop in Salem," Erwys said with a shrug.

She walked up to one of the tables in the middle of the room. A silver stand cradled a long white bone. She lifted the thin bone with care. It had a sharp curve and looked as if it came from the ribcage of a bird. Only one bird came to mind, that being a creature from the underworld.

Ben shivered.

"The Stone family is a family of their word," Erwys Ellandor said with a heavy gaze on the bone. She looked at Ben and turned to him, revealing the full length of the slender bone that undeniably belonged to one of the underworld's crows.

She then stepped towards Ben, pulling his thoughts away from the bone, as she said, "If you complete this task, it is enough proof to me that you are the rightful heir to the Gravekeeper line."

Ben's face burned, but as she whispered a spell under her breath and nicked her skin with the sharp edge of the bone, his face drained of color.

A stream of blood flowed from her palm with the elegance of

a cobra's dance. It slithered in the air and twisted as it made its way to Ben's. "Your soul shall be tied to mine and my bloodline until the end of this contract is met. I, Erwys Ellandor, promise to resolve and return to you the sight and sound of the dead so long as you, Benjamin Stone, return to me my granddaughter, Igraine Ellandor, safely and alive. Do you agree to these terms?"

Benjamin nodded, eyeing the thread of blood as it connected to him similarly to how Erwys performed magic on him before. Without the glasses, he could not see the greater effects of the spell, but Ben already knew its implications. "I, Benjamin Stone, agree to your terms."

His heart suddenly raced with a violent fervor. Ben coughed and grabbed his chest in agony but in the split moment his palm reached his shirt, the pain was gone. Erwys Ellandor nodded solemnly and took a step towards Ben. She moved so closely to Ben that they were noses apart. The boy shifted uncomfortably as the necromancer leaned towards him. Her breath stung hot on his cheek and up to his ear as she whispered, "Save my granddaughter, Gravekeeper."

"*Ugh,*" Ben gasped as a sharp deep pain filled his chest. Unlike before, it permeated from his burning skin to his spine. He looked down at a piece of the bird's ribcage as it stuck through him, deep into his heart. His eyes flitted to Erwys Ellandor's steady gaze. She released the bone and instead grabbed Ben's shoulders, easing him down as his body slumped.

Ben's body trembled in horror. His hands moved towards the bone stabbing into his heart, but his arms had no more strength, falling limply at his sides. He tried to speak, but only a frustrated gurgle slipped through his lips as his lungs quickly filled with blood.

A deep cold permeated Ben's bones, more piercing than a wraith's icy touch. His vision blurred and darkened, and his mind slipped away. The last thing he saw was the deep purple gaze of Erwys Ellandor. A steady gaze filled with an ocean of determination and a star of hope.

Twenty

The Netherworld

Ben laid on the ground, staring up at something that could be compared to the sky. It was inky black, but there was no moon nor a single star. Clouds drifted slowly far above. The air was thick with fog, making it hard to see clearly anywhere beyond the thick blackness. It seemed like a roof belonged somewhere far above the fog, but there was no cap to be seen. A place with no sky nor ceiling. The underworld.

Ben blinked, knowing a strange amount of time had passed. He sat up and groaned. His body ached as if he had slept for several days.

He ducked his chin and stared at his chest where a sharp pain lingered. He resisted screaming at the sight of a red stain over his split dress shirt. Some skin was exposed, pasty and pale with a brick red stain that permeated through the ruined shirt. His skin almost appeared luminescent in the deep surrounding darkness. To top it off, a horribly familiar black cloak swayed around his body.

Ben rolled to his knees and grabbed the sleeves to pull the cloak off. He tugged at them in a futile attempt, heaving heavy breaths on the verge of morphing into choked sobs. He stopped once his eyes laid back on the red stain. The cloak did not absorb his flesh, emanate the scent of death, or consume his lifeforce. The cloak was not killing him. He was already dead. The stain proved it. It proved Erwys Ellandor had betrayed him.

"Why," Ben whispered. His voice was sharp and clear, and it echoed through the empty landscape. He sat for a long moment, shocked by the clarity of sound compared to the harsh silence surrounding him. Beyond his own voice, everything was quiet. He could not hear the thuds of his heartbeat.

A shaking, pallid hand reached for his torn shirt. His fingers felt a thin cut, but he knew it went all the way through. Ben's stomach churned. He had not come to the underworld just by means of a portal or contract. He was here by the most natural of methods: death.

Ben patted his chest as he yearned for a beat but there was nothing to be felt or heard. Painfully aware he was dead, Ben slowly got to his feet and swayed. There was a slight draft pushing him backwards, empty like a hollow breath. Erwys Ellandor had killed him to send him to the underworld. *What a dirty trick.* He scowled at his chest, but his eyes widened with shock and relief. From the stab wound in his heart was the faint light of a red string. It flowed weakly out of the wound like a ribbon, drifting off into the fog.

The longer he stared at the ribbon, the opaquer it became and the further he could see it. The ribbon floated in a specific direction rather than tangling itself haphazardly through the air. He reached down to grab it, but it crossed through his hand in an ethereal manner. He wondered if his own body was something of an ectoplasmic consistency in the underworld, for as he looked back into the abyss, he knew his unease was a telling sign he did not belong to this plane just yet.

Ben watched the ribbon as his mind churned over Erwys Ellandor's actions. He felt betrayed for being stabbed without warning, but he knew she would send him to the underworld one way or another. Logically, killing him was an easy way to succeed in this task. If she had only meant to kill him, they would not have created the contract nor would he have a red string tied to his soul, reaching out towards her.

Or towards Igraine. Ben smacked himself in the forehead. This was the way to find Igraine Ellandor and return to the world of the living! He stepped forward, feeling his legs move as if he were swimming. His movements were slow and steady, behaving at a pace he was unfamiliar with. Just as if he were submerged in water, he felt like his weight had changed. In a sense, he moved as if he weighed the same, yet weight had no matter in the underworld. Ben wondered that if he willed it, he may have been able to float, but there was no time to play around with the physics of an ethereal world.

He focused on following the ribbon, walking through an inky landscape unlike anything he had witnessed before. His surroundings were desolate, and the ground appeared like obsidian hills belonging to the ruins of a field beneath a volcano. The ground shifted and crunched under Ben's dress shoes as he followed the red string. The odd cloak drifting over his figure only ruffled to the movement of his legs. There was not a single breeze, yet the air felt fresh and cool.

The murky landscape extended on forever with no sign of any changes. After what could have been hours or days, Ben wondered if the string would flow endlessly towards nothing, and that he was following a red herring. He could not tell the passage of time, and the lack of feeling in his body made it harder to detect. He felt no hunger, thirst, or exhaustion as he walked, and the sky never changed. He could have been standing still and felt the same the whole time, and Ben feared that while he could not sense time, it still very much existed in the living realm and there was a link between the two.

As this thought appeared in his mind, so did the landscape change as if his very will manifested it. The land had been sloping upward as he walked, and he could see the very edge of the land before him as if he had reached the end of the underworld. As he stepped towards it, something gleamed off in the distance and a gust of air that felt dreadfully cold tore against Ben's cloak, sending a chill to his bones.

The ground sloped steeply below Ben, revealing a massive crater in the charcoal earth. Inside the crater resided a town that beheld an appearance of ruins. Some houses were stacked on top of each other, layer by layer from foundation to roof, creating unsettling towers of timber frames and twisting brick walls. Other areas were desolate, spare a singular arch or abandoned chimney and the bare footprints of where a home once was. There was little color to the buildings. They all appeared gray with hints of purple and deep blue shadows. A town belonging to the underworld, lost to a timeless era of reconstruction and desolation.

His feet skidded against the ground as he made a desperate descent down the steep valley, towards the town. At some point, he feared he would fall over and roll along the steep earth but somehow he managed to safely make his way to the outskirts. When the ground leveled out, Ben brushed off his knees and stared into the town more closely, watching as the red string weaved itself between buildings.

Igraine Ellandor would not be here, but this was a hint that there were places to be, making Ben feel slightly saner. He was not wandering an endless landscape. This town was a testament to time and place. And it was not empty.

Ben spotted the shifting figure of a person move through one of the busted windows of a house four stories high. It was just enough to catch a strange blue aura typically hosted by a spirit. He stepped forward, walking past a couple of houses and noting the imprints of skeletal feet and shoes alike in the ashen dirt.

He paused and listened to the faint breath of wind and then watched for the slightest hints of movement, fearing to witness a horde of spirits. This town was not empty, but it was undeniably devoid of the living. Everything from the powdery, cracked earth to the creaking and crumbling houses symbolized the fossils and memories of an era. This place in the underworld Ben could only recognize as a place of intermittence in passing, a place to grasp onto.

He waded his way through the streets, following the red string with desperate determination. Ben never imagined himself traveling to the underworld, but now that he was here, he could not risk being foolishly curious if he ever wanted to leave. The netherworld was no place for the living, and if it were not for the cloak that pressed tightly over his skin, it would be clear to every being here that he did not belong.

Worst of all, necromancers were incredibly unwelcome in such a place. They used the undead as tools or slaves, and no undead spirit would view Ben any differently in their realm. He would not have a chance in such a town if they rang bells or cried out in anger. If such an event were to occur, Ben would be torn to pieces or devoured here with no hope of return.

He pulled on the hood of his cloak, willing it to cover his face and shadow his eyes as he treaded forward. Ben stepped over a small bridge atop a dried out creek, and the wooden planks groaned under the weight of his feet. As he walked, he shivered to the sound in agony. It was far too loud, and this town was far too quiet.

Skitch skitch skitch

There was a strange dragging sound coming from behind Ben. He ducked his head and turned his shoulder just enough to watch a slowly approaching figure. It was of a young man in a pair of overalls dragging an ethereal burlap sack. The sack had a subtle glow to it, hinting it entirely belonged to the man's existence, but there was a tear in the bag, and as it moved onto the bridge, what appeared to be grain spilled behind and remained, creating a very real trail.

Skitch skitch sk- "*What do you want?*" The spirit drawled stopping before Ben.

Ben flinched and straightened, turning away from the farmer spirit. "N-nothing. I was... impressed seeing you work so hard," Ben stumbled over his words, but he was used to talking to spirits. He told himself repeatedly, this was just like talking to another one of the Hill's residents. Except, here, he was in their domain.

"*Impressed?*" *Skitch Skitch Skitch.* The spirit moved, dragging the sack along with him until he was close to Ben. Oddly, Ben did not feel the sickening chill he normally expected from ghosts. It felt as if another person were standing behind him. The farmer shifted to be at Ben's side and leaned to stare at the corner of his face.

"*Ohhhh, you are not of this place,*" the spirit said, mouth agape and eyes narrowed. Ben froze and darted his eyes downward at the bare feet of the spirit. Faintly, Ben could see the outline of a skeleton, but the longer he stared, the more the feet looked like ordinary feet, covered in ash.

The ghost leaned forward further, taking a longer look at Ben's face. "*What are you doing here, wanderer?*"

Ben kept his face down. The spirit knew he did not belong, but it may not have known the extent of it. So long as Ben hid his eyes, there was a chance the spirit would not realize that Ben was still tied to the living realm. "I am searching for the prison of Tophet," Ben said.

Skitch... "*The prison of Tophet....*" The spirit mulled over Ben's words and shook its head. "*I know not of any prisons. But if you chose to wander beyond this town, you will find that prisons may be something you wish to find for those who find you should not roam freely. Now I need to take care of my farm..."*

With that, the spirit dragged his sack of grain across the bridge and down a pathway before taking a sharp turn into a small two-story stack of houses. He watched the grain trickle from the bag as the spirit left while he mused over the name *wanderer*. He wondered if that title was due to the black cloak clinging to him or if it was because he obviously did not belong.

Thankful the spirit was kind, Ben continued following the red string. However, as he reached the other edge of the valley and the slope picked up to a steep rising hill, he feared that the spirit's warning hinted at the many foul spirits lurking in the underworld that necromancers so often desired. If an ordinary ghost found the spirits off in the hills to be vile, then what could these spirits be like towards Ben?

After passing through the valley, Ben found himself to be in something less than a wasteland. Houses and ruins scattered the land sporadically, marking the homes of the undead in this temporal plane. Ben kept his hood low as the spirit's words played through his mind. There were violent spirits in the plains. If he were not careful, they would not hesitate to strike.

Twenty One

Igraine Ellandor

The ashen earth crunched under Ben's shoes. The sound was familiar now. It soothed Ben's mind, telling him there was something solid and real to this ethereal plane. The realm of the undead was a layer in the underworld where many spirits still linked to the living realm resided. It only seemed natural Ben would arrive in such a plane, not being quite dead, or so he told himself. Something about the red string convinced Ben Erwys had not killed him.

The only reason Ben would not be dead was entirely linked to the other end of that red string. It was the only way for Ben to return, so in every respect, he was trapped to fulfill his contract with Erwys.

"She's rather cruel," he bleakly mumbled to himself. Without any sense of time, Ben had begun to talk to himself. Just like the soft crunching sound of the earth, his own voice sounded sweet in the silence. His voice cracked a little as he spoke. Something perhaps related to the fact that Ben had not drank water ever since he awoke in the underworld.

The idea of drinking made Ben's throat feel parched, but the moment he focused his attention to the soft crunching of the earth and the shifting ashen soil or the strange ripples of gray shadows in the sky, the ache in his throat perished, and he felt virtually nothing. And then Ben would think about being thirsty, and the cycle would repeat.

This went on endlessly through the plains, until Ben noticed something odd.

The red string no longer faded off in the distance like a flame in smoke. It had a very direct end, leading right towards a massive looming shadow belonging to a hill. Ben hastened his pace, stumbling over himself as he outright picked up to a sprint. He did not worry about startling the nearby wandering spirits as he ran towards the end of the line.

It appeared miles away, and as he approached it, everything became clearer, and hotter. The ground cracked and hardened under his steps, and the ashen dirt transformed into solid, sturdy patches of cracked earth that felt harder than rock, making his knees and ankles ache. It was the first time he felt fatigued in the underworld, and his sprint faltered.

But the end of the line was *so* clear now, weaving itself through this new landscape where the earth seemed starved of water. He licked his lips, finding them cracked as well, and his mouth was as dry as the dirt.

"What is this place?" he whispered as his desperate sprint morphed into a steady, curious stroll. There were several dead trees sprouting amidst the landscape, each one of them charred black and appearing like hands clawing out of the ground and frozen in an eternal curse. The red line ended before one of the trees just beyond a tall black fence.

He approached the iron fence and inspected it intently. In all respects, it looked like iron. It was such a strange thing to witness in the underworld as iron was a well-known element for repelling spirits. He placed his hands on the bars and felt a little uneasy, but that was all. He supposed since he was still alive, the gate would not affect him as it would an undead being. It was, in fact, a highly effective barrier in the underworld.

He strolled along the fence until he came to a tall sturdy gate.

The gate was sealed but with no apparent lock. On the other side, the red string weaved its way amongst barren trees, pointing to an entity within the confines of the fence. He realized that this fence was truthfully a barrier placed in the underworld on purpose to trap the spirits inside the prison of Tophet.

Ben grabbed the gate and shook it, and while the iron bars trembled slightly, they did not budge. He pressed his forehead against the gate and sighed. Wasn't it enough that he was not dead to be able to open the gate? He stared through the bars, peering for the end of the red line in desperation. He had been wandering through the underworld for ages now, and he was so close to Igraine and his opportunity to regain his senses. He could not let something like this stop him.

The fence and gate surrounding the prison were beyond welcoming. The iron bars were four inches apart and impossible to squeeze through. At the gate, they twisted toward the top arch, stabbing through two ornate curves and poking up into the air as sharp spikes with no rhyme or reason. The spikes multiplied and jutted in haphazard ways, and as Ben looked closely, he spotted serrated edges on the spikes. It would be impossible to climb over the gate or fence without being torn to shreds.

But the gate had to open somehow, Ben thought as he stared at its central iron lock. There was a symbol written in Latin: *per viam ad vivum*. A path for the living. It was simple enough, yet as Ben shook the gate's bars, he felt foolish. Who could be in the netherworld and still classify as *the living*? Existing in this realm could only imply one's death except for a necromancer.

Ben stared at the central piece of the gate. Between the text was an open eye, and in the eye, a sharp spike had replaced the iris. Ben swallowed hard and pressed his hand against the eye. A sudden prick, followed by a strange sensation as blood streamed from his palm and down the gate's plate. It appeared as if the eye were crying. Deep red filled the iris and spilled over the words *viam ad.*

The gate then trembled and split. The iron creaked and groaned as the doors moved forward just enough to create a narrow gap for Ben to squeeze through. The boy pressed his bleeding palm against his sleeve and slid through the gap in the gate, pushing into the prison of Tophet.

The prison looked the same from the outside except now an intense wave of heat billowed up from jagged crevices in the earth. As Ben dodged the cracks, black dust plumed beneath his steps. Deeper into the prison, the trees were thicker and more twisted than before. Some trees were so contorted their branches clawed against the earth. Others had completely snapped, leaving behind tall, ashen spikes.

The most terrifying thing in the prison was not the heat or the trees. It was the presence of something wicked that Ben could not shake. He looked over his shoulder, feeling as if something were following in his shadow. A heavy spiritual presence existed in this prison, but no matter where Ben looked, he did not see any ghosts. There were only the snapped and decaying trees, but Ben could not shake the feeling as if he were surrounded by a storm of spirits.

He forced himself to look forward and follow the string. He treaded carefully to ensure he would not trip over any fallen branches or step into the ground's cracks. He made his way up the hill and through a denser grove of dead trees before arriving in a clearing with a singular tree before him.

The red string stabbed straight forward into the central stump of a twisted black tree. There were leaves still on this one, although gray and withered. The trunk looked as if it had been in a fire, charred completely black, but the branches furthest from the trunk still preserved hints of color and life.

Ben approached the tree slowly as his mind raced to

understand what this could mean, and what this prison was. Part of him knew this tree was tied to Igraine Ellandor. Another part of him feared what this meant for every tree he passed. How many were trapped in this prison to suffer such torment?

"Igraine?" Ben whispered as he was a breath away from the trunk, wondering what to do and how to save her. He could not speak to a tree nor carry it. She was rooted within her prison.

He reached out and touched the ashen bark, and a sharp pain stabbed into his chest. It was the same feeling as when Erwys Ellandor stabbed him in the heart. Ben pressed his hand on the tree for support and grasped his chest in agony. His vision darkened, and Ben sank to his knees in shock. Was he dying in the underworld? Could this be possible!? Ben gasped as his vision flickered. A dizzying wave of exhaustion overcame him, but just as he pulled away from the tree, something grabbed his hand.

Two hands held his, emerging like branches from the tree. They glowed like ivory beneath a midsummer sun. They tugged Ben's hand with a fervor. The boy stumbled backwards away from the tree, unable to stand any longer as his energy rapidly faded.

The girl's form shifted through the bark as if she had been trapped inside. She grasped Ben's shoulders, desperate to flee her cell. His heart raced as the agonizing burning filled his chest, followed by an unbearable cold. His skin burned everywhere the girl touched, and as she wrapped her arms around his shoulders, Ben lost his breath.

He fell onto his back, and the girl pulled away from the tree, falling atop of him. Ben gasped in agony and his vision blackened completely.

+X+

"-ake up…. Hey, wake up," a soft voice whispered like a cool breeze. Ben opened his eyes and stared at a set of determined purple saucers. The purple eyes blinked with satisfaction as they stared back at him. They belonged to the porcelain face of Igraine Ellandor, not a tree nor a corpse. The girl's long black hair showered around her face, curtaining their surroundings from his vision.

The boy grabbed his chest. "I'm alive," he whispered.

"Relatively," the girl said, clambering off him and offering a hand. "We need to leave before it is too late."

Ben ignored her and quickly stood and grabbed his chest where he had been stabbed. He patted his chest, inspecting it. There was no longer a wound, and the red string had completely vanished. His eyes shot towards Igraine. No string connected to the girl.

"Come on, come on, before *it* finds us," the girl said, urging Ben to follow her. She grabbed Ben's hand and pulled him in the direction of the gate.

Ben paused, studying the withering tree Igraine had been trapped within moments ago. "Hold on," he said, leaning closely and ducking his head to whisper, "How do you know where the exit is? Weren't you in that tree?" He tried to wrap his mind around how the prison worked. If someone were burned alive and sent here, he imagined they would just die, but that was not the case here. Ben could not shake the strange feeling that there were many eyes within the trees. If Igraine knew where to go, then there was a chance the gazes he felt belonged to many prisoners with deep knowledge of this prison and deep resentment. If he has touched the wrong tree, who knew who or what he may have released. Ben shivered.

"You do not come here as a tree," Igraine said, looking back at the dying tree with distress knitting her brows. She tugged on

Ben's arm again, but he was stubborn enough to stay still. She looked down at his hand and back in his eyes. "If we don't hurry, you may be cursed as well."

"Be cursed?"

"There are spirits here to ensure you are trapped forever. They feed off your energy and curse you to serve as nutrients for these damned plants. If they find us, we will both be bound to this nightmare forever," Igraine hissed.

Ben could sense Igraine's palpable fear and nodded. If what she said was true, then there was indeed a horrible guardian in this prison he did not wish to encounter. He followed Igraine briefly before stepping ahead of her and more swiftly guiding her to the gate. Her hand trembled in his, and the girl stumbled to match Ben's pace. Ben looked back at her on occasion with growing concern for her wellbeing.

Erwys Ellandor's granddaughter was very unlike Erwys. She was small and frail and looked as if the slightest fall would be her last. Her limbs were bone thin, and her frame was so small, Ben could easily see her clavicles and her rib bones. She looked as if, at any second, she may wither away, and Ben feared the underworld had taken a fatal toll on her whether he saved her from the prison or not.

He also noted that she wore the same black dress he saw during the trial. It wrapped loosely around her frame, hinting that indeed she had lost vitality during her time in the underworld. She did not have a black cloak over her shoulders, and Ben feared the implications behind the cloak sewn to his soul. Was it a remnant of the wraith cloak after all?

"Pay attention to where you are going," Igraine groaned and jerked on Ben's arm to stop him before he nearly stepped right into another one of the twisted trees.

Ben turned and stepped back, wheezing. The trunk of the tree before him showed the imprint of a hollowed face moaning in pure terror. He stepped away from the face, as an energy of pure sorrow emanated from the tree. He shivered. Was this what would have happened to Igraine?

"It is too late for them," Igraine whispered, her voice hoarse. "That is the fate of those who remain here."

He gulped and nodded, seeing why Erwys was so desperate to save her granddaughter. If she knew this was where Igraine was going, he was be surprised she had not gone to the underworld to save her directly.

"Igraine," Ben whispered as they carefully treaded through a thicker grove of trees. "Erwys says you know how to leave the underworld. Why haven't you left on your own accord?"

"I can't touch the gate," Igraine said with a scowl. "There is no way to leave this place so long as you are within the gates. I hope you opened it."

Ben nodded. She likely had tried to escape, but knowing the power iron had over the undead, she had no chance of freedom until now. He pulled Igraine along. In a few minutes they could see the open field and the surrounding fence and gate. He picked up his pace and nearly dragged Igraine towards the exit. Despite her desperation, she did not have the energy to match Ben's pace, and she stumbled and fell on the cracked earth.

Ben turned and grabbed Igraine, swiftly picking her up. He helped her get to her feet and mumbled, "Sorry," before continuing to run at a gentler pace towards the gate.

"There - is – something - at the gate," Igraine said through heavy breaths, weakly pointing ahead.

Ben blinked and saw a figure standing before the gates on the outside. It had a twisted form, and its flesh was dark red. Ben stumbled and slowed down, just yards away from the gate. It was none other than the spirit of a vetala, and Ben feared he knew exactly the one.

"Benjamin Stone," the spirit hissed. It had no intention of crossing through the iron, but it stood, waiting, blocking their path of retreat. *"It is a delight to see you in the flesshhhh..."*

"Do you know this spirit?" Igraine asked, giving Ben an incredulous look. "You were followed?!"

"No, I-" Ben gulped, feeling a terrible presence behind him. It was as if all the eyes he felt watching him were right behind him within an arm's length away. He turned his head slowly and stared at the line of trees. Amongst them stood a tall shadowy figure that emulated the trees, twisting its limbs in unnatural directions. Its fingers were long like branches, black and spindly like the thorns of a dead rose bush.

"R-run," Igraine hissed. She pulled on Ben's sleeve. "W-we need to run." Ben could not move his gaze away from the entity in the tree line. The spirit looked as if it had once been engulfed in flame and its shadows now stretched and moved like smoke. It had no physical merit, but everything in Ben's soul screamed this creature was very real.

Its long fingers spread outward and forward towards Ben and Igraine. The legs of the creature multiplied, stemming out into the ground, and then divided, vanishing at random. It had no formal method of movement, yet it raced towards them.

Ben's heart skipped a beat. He could not see the creature's eyes, but he feared he knew what would happen if he ever gained such an opportunity. His foot shuffled backwards, sliding on cracked earth and pushing up dust.

"Keep moving!" Igraine cried, pulling him. "We must get past the gate!"

He moved his foot although it felt as heavy as lead. He stumbled backwards, towards the gate with Igraine's pull. He turned and followed her, sprinting towards the vetala.

The vetala shrieked with laughter. It raised its massive claws in the air, prepared to strike the fleeing apprentices. Igraine did not hesitate to run through the gate, but Ben faltered as pure terror filled him at the sight of the spindly spirit. Memories of the revenant filled his mind. But the unbearable, undeniable demise he would face if he lingered another second forced him to move forward towards the lesser fiend.

Ben stepped through the gate and withdrew his dagger and pushed it forward, stabbing at the vetala's chest while its claws hung in the air. The silver dagger's blade met with the vetala's ribs, stabbing past them into its chest. The spirit had no heart, but its very essence burned beneath the silver blade.

The spirit screeched in Ben's face, its jaw unhinging, revealing a sharp set of teeth that seemed to grow in the wicked shadows of the underworld. The spirit's claws raked down on Ben's back in a painful embrace as its teeth sank furiously into his shoulder. Ben screamed in agony and withdrew his dagger only to pull it upwards into the underside of the fiend's neck.

Igraine screamed something indiscernible in the background of the roar of blood in Ben's head as it flowed through his ears in a furious torrent.

THUD

The vetala fell upon the ground, writhing with the silver dagger lodged in its head. Ben collapsed on his knees staring at the undead creature in terror and agony while it started to fade like crumbling ash in a flame. Fiery pain burned along his back and his shoulder felt as if it were decaying rapidly.

"THE GATE!" Igraine screamed, grabbing Ben and

attempting to pull him to his feet. "Close the gate!"

Ben stumbled to his feet and turned.

No matter the heat radiating through the ground nor the burning sensation in Ben's flesh, the boy froze. It was as if an icy waterfall poured over his head, and his vision glazed over. The shadowy fiend trampled across the field. In a matter of seconds, it would be upon them. Ben could feel the looming sensation of death permeating from the sinister being.

"The gate!" Igraine screamed, pushing Ben's shoulders. He blinked and grabbed the iron bars and pulled them inward, swinging the gate until the lock clicked in place.

The shadowy entity appeared at the edge of the gate, looming several feet above the apprentices' heads. It looked down at them like a shadowy spike that stabbed the air, inches from their faces. Ben could not see through the entity. The longer he stared, the sicker he became. Deep within the shadows, Ben *sensed* something vile and wicked.

He stumbled backwards, and Igraine reached out and grabbed his shoulder. "Look away," she whispered, placing her hand on his face and gently moving him to turn. "It is not safe to stay here, even with the gate closed," Igraine said, looking at the ashen remains of the vetala. The silver dagger laid on the ground, covered in the remnants of the forlorn spirit.

She crouched down and studied the knife. She tapped it and quickly withdrew her hand as if it were striking hot.

Ben bent down and picked up the blade, hands shaking. Igraine watched him with curiosity as he stowed the knife away. "That spirit had cursed you," Igraine said. Ben looked at her briefly and nodded. He did not know how the vetala had tracked him in the underworld, but it was incapacitated for now.

They quickly walked away from the prison. Ben had no

direction in mind, so he relied on Igraine. She walked with a quick, determined gait, and Ben wondered if there was a certain place in the underworld she needed to go or if she just wanted to be as far away from the prison as possible. As the prison faded in the shadowy air and the ground ceased radiating heat, Igraine faltered.

Igraine looked at Ben with exhaustion and concern wrinkling her face. "Why did you save me?"

Ben frowned, unsure of how much she knew about his deal with Erwys Ellandor and of what he could safely tell her.

Igraine seemed to know his doubts and pressed on. "I saw you during my family's trial. And that spirit said your name... you are the gravekeep-"

"No. I'm not," Ben snapped.

"How else could you open the gate?" Igraine asked. "Everyone knows, only the Gravekeeper can free someone from the prison, so you must be it."

"Only the Gravekeeper can open the prison gate?"

Igraine nodded.

Ben fretfully looked behind them and at the prison off in the distance. The tall shadowy guardian still stood at the prison edge like a black pillar striking the sky. Ben bit his lip, wondering what it would mean to the council when they learned of Igraine's freedom. Erwys must have known this all along. He cursed under his breath. So that was why she wanted him of all people to save Igraine. Grandfather would never have agreed to it- only Ben would because he had something to gain.

"What's wrong?" Igraine looked at him pointedly, tapping his shoulder. "You don't mean to tell me, you, *the Gravekeeper*, didn't know you could free the prisoners of Tophet?"

"Okay, for one, I'm not the Gravekeeper," Ben snapped, brushing away Igraine's hand and looking at the open expanse of nothingness ahead. "I might *become* the next Gravekeeper. But I saved you for that reason, and that reason alone."

He stopped and looked at her. "And two, I do not support your mother being a lich, or you bring imprisoned here. I'm here just to bring you home safely so I can become the Gravekeeper."

"Is saving me your rite?" Igraine sneered. "Don't tell me they sent me there for your rite. Ugh, that means you aren't a full-fledged necromancer yet."

Ben crossed his arms. "Are you?"

Igraine scowled. "Okay, so you aren't a Gravekeeper yet. So, when did a necromancer apprentice save someone for no benefits of their own? What are you after? My mother? Do you think she cares if I rot here for an eternity?" There was a distinct bitterness in Igraine's violet eyes that made Ben's chest ache.

"I'm not after your mother," Ben protested. He was not like the council or Grandfather.

"Then, what? I must be a bargaining chip to catch her," Igraine said through her teeth. "Or do you plan to use my spirit and force me to find her?"

"I don't care about where the lich is."

Igraine laughed and prodded Ben in the chest right where Erwys had stabbed him. "Do you think I believe that? You may be the Gravekeeper, but you are still a-"

Ben grabbed Igraine's hand, causing her to freeze. "I told you, I'm not the Gravekeeper." His eyes blazed with anger. "Don't you have the same abilities as Erwys? Can't you tell, I'm cursed?! I can't wield magic, I can't see spirits, and now I can't even hear them. How in the world can I be a Gravekeeper when I can't even procure a single flame or wisp?!"

Igraine jerked her hand from Ben's and cradled it. Concern warped her brows. "You know grandma?" Her eyes darted back and forth. "You were at the trial... you freed me... did grandma send you here?"

Ben pinched his nose. "Yes."

"Why would she send you?" Igraine grabbed her forehead and muttered something to herself. "This is bad," she mumbled, and she continued to mutter a stream of concerns. Her eyes then pointedly glared at Ben. "Why did you agree to come here?"

Ben frowned. "Because we made a deal."

"What deal?"

Ben's eyes narrowed. He told her plenty of information, but Igraine was too distressed to put the pieces together. He did not care to withhold it anymore, he was tired of secrets, and it felt good to talk to someone in a similar situation to him.

"In exchange for freeing you, she will remove my curse," Ben explained simply.

Igraine glared at Ben intensely, and first Ben planned to answer her question, but he quickly realized she was not looking at him but at his very essence. He shifted uncomfortably as she studied the knots in his spirit and his mother's curse in some tethered form. "Oh," Igraine whispered, recognizing what ailed Ben. Her brows knit, but she nodded and looked at Ben with an intense degree of concern. "Your mother cursed you."

"Yes," Ben said uncomfortably, although he could say the same for Igraine. She was only in the underworld because of her mother's crimes.

"I'm sorry," Igraine said, shaking her head with a look of pity on her face.

"What are you sorry for?" Ben asked, frowning.

"Removing such a curse is impossible for grandma."

Twenty Two

The Lich

Ben glared at Igraine with his teeth clenched. "What do you mean that is something she can't do. She did not just promise it. She swore to those terms!"

Igraine's eyes darted back and forth. "I- I don't know how she swore to those terms, but it isn't something even an Soulweaver can do. No one can..."

"Then who can?" Ben sneered. "If not her then who? If she lied in our contract, are you saying I should bring you back to the prison and give up?"

"NO!" Igraine roared, eyes fierce. "That's not what I mean! And my life is no bartering item either!"

As Igraine glowered at Ben, he turned away and looked ahead. Through their discussion, they had garnered the attention of a few wandering spirits, but so far, none had chosen to approach them. He sighed and looked upwards at the wispy abyss. There was no need to be mad at Igraine. It was not her fault she was sent to the Prison of Tophet, and it certainly was not her fault if Erwys had lied to him or not.

But something felt off about what Igraine said, because no matter how much she sounded like she was telling the truth, Erwys could not have lied in the contract. She had to be able to return to him his abilities.

They walked for a while in silence. Neither apprentice wished to speak to the other, and while Ben was enticed in meeting the fellow apprentice, she was still the daughter of a lich, and he now had a bone to pick with Erwys Ellandor. Glancing at the petite lich's daughter, Ben knew she was also fuming with anger for what her family and the council had done to her.

He sighed. He could not and would not blame Igraine for anything.

"Erwys said you knew how to leave the underworld. Do you know how, or are we to continue wandering this plane endlessly?"

Igraine's steps ceased, and she nodded slowly. She nearly whispered, "I've never been here before... I've only seen this in dreams but I may know a way in which we can leave... It just is not safe to do it near that prison... and you mustn't panic no matter what happens, or I... I won't do it."

Ben gulped. He did not care what happened so long as he could return to the realm of the living. Although he wondered if her concern brought a solid reason he *should* be afraid. "I-I promise I won't panic."

Igraine turned to face Ben with a sharp look of determination in her violet eyes. "We can leave now," she said as if it was just that simple. She stepped towards him so that her feet nearly stepped upon Ben's. She reached forward into Ben's pocket and pulled out the silver knife. The girl flinched as the silver seared her. Ben quickly stepped back.

"What?" she asked with an annoyed look on her face.

Remembering what Erwys Ellandor did to him, Ben shook his head, not taking any chances. "What do you need that for?"

"I need to call her somehow," Igraine said before pricking her finger with the knife. She tossed the blade aside, and Ben quickly stooped down to pick it up.

Wiping the blade on his pant leg and tucking it back into his pocket, Ben stood and watched Igraine. Her finger was bleeding, but the stream of blood behaved strangely, acting like the red ribbon Ben had so desperately followed.

The ribbon streamed downward, and then it curled and flowed, forming a pattern in the air that defied all physics. Igraine began to whisper so softly Ben could hardly understand what she was saying. Her whisper was filled with hissing and drawn out words in Greek.

Ben crossed his arms and leaned forward to examine the floating rune. "Who are you summoning? Shouldn't you be doing something the opposite?" He spun his finger around, tracing the circle's pattern trying to make sense of it. "Like form a pathway that interjects another summon to the living realm?"

Igraine glanced at Ben and glowered, and he refrained from speaking. He watched the girl do her work in awe. He never interacted or practiced with another apprentice, but he could tell she was leagues ahead of him.

He knelt to look at the flow of blood in the air from an alternate angle. It did not look like a typical summoning circle, in fact, it was hardly comparable. The ribbon traced down and branched out, forming a complex pattern resembling a tree. Ben shifted his head and stumbled backward, avoiding the ribbon as it traced further from its core, nearly touching him. Despite his curiosity, he did not want to interrupt the spell and risk his way back to the living realm.

"*Mother,*" Igraine whispered the last word, and the ribbon froze, drifting midair with a weight of tension.

Igraine looked at Ben, and he felt as if she were moving through frozen time. "Grab my hand. Quickly, now," she said.

Ben stood and wrapped his hand in hers. Her hand was

ice cold, but in the strange emptiness of the underworld, he imagined the chill as some form of warmth and could not imagine the girl being anything but alive.

Shhhhhhhh

The ribbon moved again, but this time it slithered in the air at a rapid pace, creating a strange breeze as it spun and twisted, repeating its pattern. The ribbon intensified, doubling, tripling in size. Ben stepped backward, but Igraine kept her stance firm and tightened her grip on his hand.

"Say nothing," she hissed as a strange light split through the ribbon, shining in the shadowy air of the underworld like an unearthly blade.

Ben shivered as the light expanded, slicing more through the ribbons. The entire tree now glowed with a brilliant light, blinding him. He imagined how any creature nearby would be able to see this unnatural presence. The light itself was a symbol of the living realm, and Ben wished to reach forward and grasp it, but Igraine's mannerisms told him that was the wrong thing to do.

And then a shadowy hand appeared, twisting in contrast to the light and looking as if it were caught aflame. The hand appeared nearly skeletal, and Ben blinked only to see half an arm, a torso, and the entire figure of a woman appearing from the core of the tree symbol.

The light vanished, swallowed up by the presence of the woman. She stood before them in a long black, lacy dress with a violet shawl that unnaturally glimmered in the surrounding inky darkness. Her black hair hung down in a curtain past the middle of her waist. Several small braids looped at her ears and adorned her hair like a veil. Her face was a ghostly white, but it looked very similar to Igraine's and Erwys. She was undeniably beautiful.

"Delore Ellandor," Ben whispered. Igraine squeezed his hand sharply, but it was too late.

The lich turned and looked at Ben, revealing a deadly smile. She looked like her daughter, however her bone structure was more prominent, she stood two feet taller, and her eyes were entirely black.

"The Gravekeeper," Delore said with a soft smile that sent chills down Ben's spine. She stepped forward, closing the distance between them. Igraine's hand squeezed Ben's to the point where his hand ached under the pressure.

"You succeeded in retrieving my daughter from the Prison of Tophet. For that, I hold much gratitude," the lich said.

"Why did you need me to retrieve her if you can come here yourself?" Ben asked.

"And confirm her crimes? No, if I had saved her, the council would only commit a more concrete punishment. It had to be you. Only the Gravekeeper has the right to enter such a place, but do not think that one needs the right to enter," she said with a smirk. "You will learn, child. I pity the council dearly."

"Mother, we must go," Igraine said weakly.

"Hush, Raine," Delore said, hissing at her daughter, while keeping her eyes locked on Ben. "This boy has saved your life, be grateful. If I am to repay your debt, it must be here where the balance of life and death intertwines. Do you not feel it? We stand in the realm of power."

Igraine's hand slackened, and Ben looked through the corner of his eye. Her cheeks filled with color and eyes brimmed with angry tears.

"Benjamin Stone."

He looked back up at the lich, and goosebumps trailed across his arms. This time, his grip tightened on Igraine's hand, seeking support. He was not entirely certain what the lich wanted. Such a being was the most powerful undead and the most dangerous necromancer of all. The amount of people she had to sacrifice, the cost to attain immortality... Ben's mouth went dry as he stared at the woman with fear and a deep ingrained hatred dancing across his mind. He did not want a monster like this to be thankful to him.

The lich laughed, making Ben shudder. "Do not be afraid, Gravekeeper. I will return you to your home, but that alone will not repay my family's debt to you for saving my daughter. Allow me to resolve what ails you most."

She crouched down slightly so that they were face to face, noses just inches apart. "You wish to commune with the dead and be a stellar necromancer, correct? You wish to prove to the council your worth. I shall grant your wish for you have saved my daughter's life."

Igraine flinched.

Ben attempted to move away, but he was frozen stiff. The longer he stared into the lich's face, the more he could see her skeletal structure. Her flesh was slightly transparent, showing her bones and dark red runes etched into them that Ben had never seen before. His eyes then landed on hers. The black orbs were darker than the sky in the underworld. They reminded Ben of the fiend in the prison, and he could see deep into the shadows the whispers of the souls she had consumed to become the most powerful and vile of monsters.

"To stare into my eyes so deeply... What do you think of my eyes, Gravekeeper? What do you see in them?" the lich asked with a soft smile and a morose chuckle.

"T-they..." Ben stammered, not knowing what to say. The

wrong thing, despite her gratitude, could have him killed. Her eyes were deadly, vile, a sign of her tradeoff from humanity. "I see the dead."

"Yes, and with them, you will be able to see much more. This is my gift."

"Mother, no!" Igraine cried.

Ben attempted to turn to look at her, but it was as if something were holding him still. He felt her hand squeeze his so tightly he almost cried out, but something far more frightening drew his attention away from Igraine.

A pale white hand blacked his entire vision. Ben flinched as the lich embraced his face, sliding her palm over his eyes and along his cheek in a gentle gesture. Her other hand then reached upwards and held her own face and a saddened smile curled her lips upwards. Her hand then crept along her face, and her fingers wrapped around her right eye, mirroring what she was doing along his forehead.

Ben felt her fingers curl around his eyes, stroking his eyebrow while watching her do it to her own. He wished to turn away, and he squeezed Igraine's hand tightly, pleading for something to happen. Igraine's hand was frozen, and her breathing was ragged next to Ben.

A dizzying sensation overcame Ben that made the air shimmer and his body sway. It did not hinder the lich's movements, and he begged his body to collapse his knees, but they were locked in place. His mind screamed to break out of the lich's trance, but his mouth stayed shut. Not even a sound could croak from his throat.

A dull pain pressed into the side of his eyes, followed by a sharp pain Ben had never felt before. His whole head ached as if it were to explode. He needed no means of imagination to know what was happening. He tearfully watched as the lich cupped her own eye with her hand, proceeding to scoop it out of her head.

Ben could not scream as hot blood trickled down his face. He could only stand still and watch as the lich pulled back her palm, retrieving his eye and presenting hers. Then, with grace, Ben witnessed through tears as she cupped her hand over her own face, smiling all the while.

His stomach churned as she reached forward again, and the apprentice screamed in his mind, but no ounce of his will could stop the lich from her spell. Just as gently, she stroked his face. His eye stung and blurred, watching in agony as she stroked her own eye with just as much care and feeling it upon his brow, sliding along his lashes, hooking underneath the lid…

For a long moment, he saw nothing, and all he could feel was the pain. Fear bubbled in Ben, forcing his breathing to quicken. His heart began to race, following the command of his body once more. The boy shuddered, and at last, his knees collapsed, striking hard against the dusty earth.

"Open your eyes, Gravekeeper," the lich commanded from above.

Ben laughed harshly and opened his eyes to present whatever hideous work the lich had committed. His eyes burned as he did so. He blinked. And blinked again, staring at the lich's long, lacy black skirts.

His arms shook and hands pressed onto his cheeks, feeling around his eyelids and the orbs fit underneath. He looked up at the lich and gasped, "What did you do?"

"Mother!" Igraine cried, looking down at Ben's face with horror and fear. She grabbed her mother's arm. "What have you done?!"

The lich smiled at Igraine and down at Ben. Her own face had streams of black blood trickling down her cheeks, mocking tears. Her eyes blinked, but they were not hers. They glowed gold, just like Ben's always had and everyone in his family.

"I have given the Gravekeeper what he desired. You now have the ability to sense the dead and every aspect of the other realms, child." She crouched down and stroked Ben's face. Ben trembled with terror at her touch. It was nearly impossible to discern her face from a skeleton, and the longer he stared, the more he saw the swirling spirits of hundreds of souls making up the fabric of her flesh. He could hear them scream in agony. He ducked his head and vomited.

"Ugh. Help him stand," the lich said, snapping her fingers.

Ben felt Igraine's hands wrap around his shoulders and attempt to pull him up. She was horribly weak and could not move him an inch. Forcing himself to push away the disturbing memory of the lich's making, Ben stood and brushed off Igraine's grasp.

"You have my eyes," Ben said, firmly and angrily.

"And you have mine. I am aware you did not wish to give away any more than you already had. Think of this as the toll for returning you to the living realm... unless you believe there is another way to return on your own?"

Delore Ellandor chuckled but then her eyes widened as if she had just received an extravagant gift, and she clapped her hands before pulling a necklace from her chest. She looped it over Ben's head, causing the boy to glower at her as their faces came nose to nose. For a split-second Ben saw himself with glowing purple eyes, and his head spun with dizzying agony. As the necklace landed on his chest, the dizzying sensation faded and was replaced with the icy cold touch of metal on his chest.

"Keep this on your person, and your eyes will continue to look like your own. I am certain you are aware it will not be received well by the council if they are to learn you bear the eyes of a lich. No matter how generous an act this is, they will not allow you to keep your head let alone your sight."

Ben gulped, looking down at the amulet. It had a silver chain that ended just past his collarbone. The amulet was flat and round and looked entirely black with a singular silver crescent.

"It also tells you what the current moon phase is," Delore laughed. "Pretty clever right?"

Ben gritted his teeth and looked away. He could not argue with the lich. Deep down, a strange feeling tickled his heart. Undeniably, his heart was racing. He would see spirits again. He could be a necromancer! A small smile cracked his lips.

Igraine looked at Ben with disdain and then back at her mother. "Mother, I wish to return home. I am exhausted," she whined.

"Very well, my child... Benjamin Stone, be sure to tell no one of what has transpired today. Remember, your eyes are in my possession," the lich said with a soft hiss. She then reached forward and tapped him on the forehead with the tip of her long black, and blood-stained nail. Ben collapsed.

Twenty Three

Deception

"Gah!"

Ben awoke, gasping for breath. He laid on the wooden floor in his room, staring up at the plaster ceiling. A sharp pain stabbed under his rib. Ben grasped his side, feeling the edge of his knife poking him through his suit pocket. He slid his hand into his pocket and shifted his body, tossing the dagger aside. It clanged against the edge of his desk and landed with a heavy thud.

The memories of the underworld poured into his mind like an unwelcome dream. Ben grabbed his chest, patting for the wound from when Erwys Ellandor had stabbed him. His shirt was still torn, but as Ben traced his fingers along his chest, he could not find the slightest hint of a scratch. It was as if Erwys Ellandor's assault was only but a nightmare, and the entire journey in the underworld was a strange figment of his imagination.

He laughed under his breath. Maybe it never happened, and he was dreaming! His laughter brought on a fit of severe coughs that made his lungs burn, and he shuddered in agony as the sharp pain from the stab wound on his side escalated. Not everything could be a dream, he thought with a strangled sigh.

He clambered to his feet and stepped into the hallway, crossing over into the bathroom. He gently pressed the door shut, clicking the lock in place. He shuffled under the sink cabinet for a package of bandages and medical supplies, foraging for everything he needed to treat the knife wound from the bin of medicine 'for the living.' He placed a bottle of alcohol and bandages on the vanity and paused at the sight of silver as the pendant dangled from his neck.

The glass bottle of alcohol slipped from his fingers and fell to the ground with a sharp clack.

The silver pendant swung at his neck, gleaming under the warm vanity light. His hand trembled as he clutched it and pressed it against the base of his neck. The netherworld was no dream nor figment of his imagination. Every part of his appearance was a testament to that. His hair was disheveled and skin a sickly pale under the vanity's pale blue light. Deep shadows hung under his eyes and stretched along his hollowed cheeks. His jacket was torn and dirty as if he had been buried underground. Most strikingly, his shirt was stained deep red, although the cut on his chest was nowhere to be found.

Ben prodded at the tear in his white dress shirt, contemplating how he had healed. There was not a drop of blood on the shirt, alluding to the concept that he had never been stabbed at all. Even the shoulder wound from the vetala had vanished.

He could clean himself up, smack his face to regain some color if he had to, and Grandfather would never know he had been to the underworld. If anything, it simply looked as if he had spent the night rolling in the dirt instead of sleeping. However, there was one physical change he feared would be far too permanent to hide.

Ben stepped closer to the mirror, fingers curling around his cheek bones and at the base of his eye sockets. The tip of his nose tapped the glass, and his eyes widened and fingers pulled on his cheeks, opening them wider for inspection. His eyes were slightly bloodshot with burning red veins of blood splitting the white of his eyes into faint pink shards. He otherwise could not see anything out of the ordinary. His iris's appeared like the petals of a sunflower basking beneath a brilliant midday sun and reflected his own concerned expression. Ben blinked and squinted, searching for something strange. The soft sound of metal clinking on glass brought the boy's attention back down to the pendant dangling from his throat.

The pendant tapped against the mirror like a foreboding metronome. His mouth went dry as he lifted the pendant and resumed an air of quiet. This was the key to the truth and the lies. He shut his eyes and pulled the silver chain over his neck, feeling it tug at the back of his ears and scrape beneath his jaw. Once it was off his person, he held it tightly in a fist for a long while before placing it upon the vanity. He counted to three before opening his eyes.

His eyes were entirely black. There was not a trace of gold nor white. The normally pale blue veins around his eye lids were now black and spread like vines of inky ichor. Ben stopped breathing, staring at his reflection with horror. It was undeniable. Without knowing the events that had transpired in the past several hours, he could tell that these were the eyes of a lich.

He slowly leaned forward. Deep in the black orbs, he could see an inky emptiness that absorbed light. It once again reminded him of the spirit in the prison, but Ben could not trace the souls he saw swimming in Delore Ellandor's eyes before the transfer.

Ben blinked and trembled, wishing the black would go away and his own irises return. No matter how long he stared and blinked and wished something to change, his eyes stayed the same. Cursed. A sign of the evilest necromantic act possible. If Grandfather saw this, he would believe Ben had been bewitched by the lich or was some imposter.

With that thought, the boy hurriedly draped the necklace over his head. He watched as the black pooled into his pupils as if draining away to reveal his normal eyes once more. It was a magical act of deception Ben hoped could fool Grandfather and the rest of the council. His hand tightly clenched on the necklace knowing no matter what, he could never reveal this to Grandfather.

Ben intensely washed up, being sure to scrub away any hint of blood or dirt on his skin. He splashed and slapped cold water on his face, hoping to draw some color back to his cheeks. Even if no time had passed in the living realm, he could see the toll the underworld had taken on his body and spirit. Unfortunately, the past few weeks of events were harrowing enough, Grandfather would never notice the subtle changes in his appearance. With that realization, he decided there was nothing more he could do.

As he pulled on a fresh suit jacket, Ben noticed a few new, neat patches of thread from where Mely had attempted to repair his suit. He did not have many that were fully intact, but her handiwork truthfully only made them more ragged. Ben told himself to make the effort to repair his clothes later, but there were more pressing issues than sewing.

He hurried out of his room and trampled down the stairway, into the foyer. The early morning sun shined through the transom, kissing the wooden steps with a dusty dew. He pressed his hands on the glass, peering outside. A thick, unnatural fog shrouded the salmon tones of sunrise. He gripped the door handle when a sharp cough sounded from the dining table.

"Where are you going?" Grandfather asked, sitting at the table with a mug of coffee and a plate of jam slathered toast.

Ben paused and looked at Grandfather. His eyes then dropped to the plate of toast, and his stomach growled like a ghoul. He was so hungry, he had to push down the urge to run across the room and steal Grandfather's breakfast. When was the last time he had eaten?!

"I-I need to get a head start on the tombstones. They need to be scrubbed," Ben said, eyes helplessly flitting between Grandfather's plate of food and the window.

"You are banned from your duties until you make up with the residents," Grandfather said calmly with a clear, sharp voice.

While Grandfather's words brought Ben a sharp feeling of remorse, a wave of relief filled Ben. In the underworld, he felt as if he were there for years. Grandfather's reaction told him he had only been gone for an evening at most.

"I forgot," Ben whispered. The weight of Grandfather's words sank in, but as he looked out the window, he was certain he could make amends with the spirits.

But first... He stepped backwards and slinked away into the kitchen. His heart sharply leapt to the sight of the remaining bread loaf still sitting on the kitchen counter. He ran over to the counter and grabbed at the bread, eating as quickly as he could. It felt as if he had not eaten in years, but he had no knowledge on how being in the underworld would impact his body. Clearly his physical body had changed even though what entered the underworld could not be called his entire physical self. Some part of him had to have remained in the living realm in Erwys's basement, he thought while he ate. The more he thought about what the Ellandors did, the more confused he became, and his appetite transformed into disgust. He wished he could ask Grandfather to explain everything to him, but to do so would risk a quick return to the underworld he was not prepared for.

Ben finished eating and turned on the sink faucet to drink. The kitchen door creaked open as Grandfather returned with his dishes only to witness his grandson drinking from the sink like a madman.

"What in the world are you doing?" Grandfather asked, causing Ben to jump and choke on the water.

Ben gasped. "Drinking."

Grandfather's arm flailed towards the cabinets with the dishes. "Do you live in a barn? Where's your manners?!" His eyes moved to the crumby remains atop the flattened bread bag.

Ben gulped, wishing he had controlled himself as he stared at the empty bread loaf bag and felt his stomach queasily churn from overeating. He should have at least used a plate and some jam.

"I was hungry," Ben muttered, allowing his gaze to drift above the kitchen sink, and away from Grandfather's stern glare. His jaw slackened as he stared into the eyes of a very curious spirit.

There were a number of spirits staring through the window, pressing their hands on the glass as if they were watching something intriguing on the television.

"Benjamin what are you..." Grandfather followed Ben's gaze to the window. His brows knit and he looked back at Ben and then returned his attention to the window. And back to Ben. He leapt forward, grabbing Ben's shoulders. "You can see them!"

Ben blankly nodded. "Uh huh."

"You can see them!" Grandfather yelled again. He reached his arm out towards the window, pointing at the group of very concerned faces. "How many- how many are there!"

Ben looked to the window, trying to count while Grandfather shook his shoulders. "Thre—five."

Grandfather turned and looked, counting for himself, but more spirits were joining in at the window. He looked back at Ben, and his gleaming eyes narrowed. "How can this be?" he whispered.

Ben gulped, scraping his mind for an excuse. A heavy lump

formed in his throat. "Wraithright!"

"What?"

An idea formed in Ben's mind. It was either this or the truth. He looked in Grandfather's eyes, forcing down a lump of guilt, and said, "Hubert Wraithright. I did not tell you, there was too much going on with the wraith cloak... he told me how he gained the sight."

Ben did not need to tell Grandfather the extent of his curse. He did not need to know that he had lost his hearing with his mother's visit. All he needed to know was that he was cured.

"How could you not tell me something so important?" Grandfather shook his head and grabbed Ben's shoulders. "How? How did you fix it? What did he say?!"

He looked equally confused as excited. It was undeniable he could see spirits, so he knew his story did not need to explain everything. He looked out the window and said, "Because my curse was because of my mother, I needed to counter the curse with a spell... He taught me what to do and made a spirit imprint... and I did not believe it would work... but it did."

Grandfather paused, thinking hard about what Ben had said. The apprentice was sweating, fearing Grandfather would pick his story apart. If he had met Hubert Wraithright, there was no saying, he would help him. And no spirit would create a spirit imprint on a whim with nothing in exchange, and no spirit imprint could undo such a curse... but, Ben could see. The plausibility did not matter. He just needed enough for Grandfather to move on.

Grandfather pulled the boy into a massive hug. "I knew this day would come! I knew you'd overcome the curse!"

Ben shuddered, thinking about what had happened. He never overcame any curse. His actions only gave his mother every right to reinforce the curse. Instead, he had to sacrifice his own eyes and risk everything to save the lich's daughter. He wanted to smile in Grandfather's grasp and celebrate. He could finally be recognized as a true necromancer apprentice, but the cost wrought a twisted feeling in his gut not resultant from the quantity of bread he had just consumed. He sucked in a sharp breath and forced his expression to remain neutral.

Grandfather pulled back from the hug. Tears formed at the brims of his golden eyes and he looked down at Ben with an undeniable pride that made Ben's stomach twist. How long had it been since Grandfather was proud of him for something? He could not remember the last time Grandfather looked at him like this.

Grandfather hugged Ben one final time, patting the boy's shoulders proudly. He shut his eyes, suddenly nauseous. He had wanted this for so long. He desperately craved Grandfather's pride and approval. Yet, now receiving it, his stomach twisted with the weight of his deceit. If only Grandfather knew the cost he had paid for this embrace. He clenched his teeth and openly scowled into the nook of Grandfather's hunched shoulder.

"Come along," Grandfather said, pulling away from Ben whilst grabbing his shoulder and pulling out of the kitchen, towards the front door. As the doorknob twisted, Ben's heart raced with anticipation and skipped beats as he choked back the urge to cry. They stepped outside on the porch, and Grandfather waved his arms about. "What do you see, Benjamin?" He looked at Ben keenly, eyes sparkling with anticipation.

Ben looked over the hill and felt his heart pound in his chest with excitement and panic, but no matter how terrible he felt internally, it could not overwhelm the emotions brought on by what he saw.

The clouds he saw earlier were not clouds at all. They were

everything Ben could never see and what he dreamt of seeing every second. A swarm of spirits filled the hill, and a massive amount of ethereal energy thickened the air, creating a fog. He could also see the faint line work of a spell tracing over their heads in the air, tendrils of magical ether and golden ribbons of runes drifting like leaves in autumn. He did not know if this was something he normally should see or if it was an enhanced ability thanks to the lich.

The apprentice then lowered his gaze to the tombstones. The Hill's residents looked just like normal when he had worn the glasses, but this time he could see remnants of their presence and behaviors as if he were witnessing their actions in the past from seconds to hours to years ago. He had no way of knowing how far back the traces went, and the more he focused on them, the harder it was to know the difference between past and present.

Ben rubbed his eyes and focused on one of the spirits. The longer he focused on it, the deeper the trail became, until Ben could clearly see everywhere the spirit had floated for the past several days. The spirit then paused and stared right at him, dumbfounded. He realized he was being invasive and looked away.

"What is it?" Grandfather asked. "What do you see?"

"All of them," Ben blurted as his heart raced. "Grandfather, I can see memories of the spirits. Like... traces from where they were. What is that?"

Grandfather's mouth went ajar and then twisted into a beaming smile. His hand tightened on Ben's shoulder. "*You can see the spirit remnants?*" Grandfather lifted his head and laughed with his gut. Ben shivered as Grandfather rejoiced over his newfound ability. If only he knew its source.

Grandfather's hand patted Ben's back. "That, my boy, means you can sense the tendrils of time. That is a very *very* special skill to have!" He looked down and mumbled, "How dare she withhold such abilities..."

Ben's face turned hot as Grandfather shook his head and looked at him with fervor in his gaze. "This is a game changer my boy! There is much to be done, Benjamin. Your rite is three weeks away. There is much to prepare even with your sight! Ohhh, we must focus on preparing for your rite immediately!"

Grandfather was so giddy, he nearly danced as he turned and made his way back into the house. Ben nodded, unable to hold back his excitement. But as he followed him, his stomach twisted. Would it be okay to deceive Grandfather like this and not tell him about the lich? Would the council know that he had saved the girl from the underworld? As he followed behind Grandfather's tall, crooked back, he decided it was best to push those concerns aside for now. Grandfather was going to teach him how to be a proper necromancer. Everything else could wait.

Twenty Four

Preparation

Over the next two weeks, Ben focused all his energy on preparing for his rite. He did everything Grandfather told him to, and thankfully, Grandfather did not withhold his instruction. However, as Grandfather strived to teach Ben the makings of a necromancer, one critical issue was apparent. Ben could see spirits, see the ether, see the very essence of magic, yet he could not harness magic no matter how hard he tried.

They both knew he was ill-prepared to become the Gravekeeper. Forget about aspiring to be a druid or wizard. He would never have a chance to be a street magician. But now, Ben had the sight, and that was enough to make a difference as a necromancer.

Necromancers did not need to harness the ether of magic to create spells, at least, not for someone like Ben. He had inherited magic in his blood, and no curse could fully deflect that. If he had to summon a spirit, it was possible through the blood in his veins. Grandfather taught him how to properly dispel a spirit and summon one without the ability to harness magic. But, as they focused on other forms of magic beyond summoning, they realized Ben's talents ran dry.

The final straw that proved Ben had no magical aptitude to speak of was the night the boy stared at a candle flame. From dawn to dusk, he sat at his desk in his room and gazed into the thumb sized fire, willing it to vanish. Instead, it flickered lightly to the rhythm of his breaths and only died when the candle's wax completely melted away.

"Enough, Benjamin," Grandfather said, grabbing his shoulder. "Your rite is a week away. Let us focus on what you can do, and not what you cannot. You can just use a matchstick during the rite."

"Can I?"

Grandfather harrumphed. "Who said you need to conjure fire to be a necromancer? A measly flame means nothing compared to summoning a powerful spirit or a horde of skeletons!"

Ben gulped, thinking back on when he was in the Wraithright's catacombs. He certainly could have benefited from the ability to conjure a tiny flame then.

Ben stared at the pool of melted wax with dismay. Somehow, he had convinced himself everything was better. That he could earn the title of Gravekeeper. But the lich had only granted him the ability to sense the dead. She did not recover his ability to cast spells or harness the ether that he saw. No matter how hard he willed it and chanted spells, the magic in the air was so unresponsive.

Ben clenched his fists, knowing his mother's curse still deeply bore into his being. However, with the lich's eyes, he would be fine. Just maybe, if he could attain the proper title of Gravekeeper, he would have the time to properly remove her curse and harness his true potential.

"We shouldn't worry about fire... I need to prepare you to summon your own familiar after you get some rest," Grandfather explained, stepping away.

"I'm not tired," Ben said while withholding a yawn. "What do I need to do?"

Grandfather paused. "Very well." He pulled up his chair and

sat down next to Ben. "During your rite, you have three tasks you must complete. You first must summon a spirit, secondly, you must succeed in making it your familiar. And lastly, you must defeat your opponent with the familiar. In that order."

Ben nodded slowly. He chewed his lip. "I can summon a spirit..."

"Correct, but you must be careful with who you conjure. You can only summon once."

Ben nodded, thinking about the vetala and how easy it would be to summon the wrong thing. "Can't I just make a familiar now?"

"No."

"But I almost did with the vetala," Ben said, looking down at his notebook beside the pool of wax. It was full of notes on which spirit to summon in different circumstances and the pros and cons of each. If he tried to summon a poltergeist again, would he succeed or beckon upon something more sinister?

"If you had contracted with a spirit to be your familiar before your rite, your right as a Gravekeeper would have been suspended," Grandfather said with a shake of his head. "This is how things must be done. I can only prepare you so much before the rite, but your first familiar must be created during your rite. You could do a simple contract now as practice, but we are too close to the rite to waste your energy on producing singular contracts."

Ben frowned. "How is that any different from summoning a familiar? Couldn't I make a contract now for them to appear then and become a true familiar then?"

"Absolutely not."

Ben groaned.

"Not all formalities are logical. The rite is as equally political as it is a testament to your skills," Grandfather said and pointed at Ben's notebook. "Now what do you think is different between a normal contract and a familiar?"

Ben imagined any contract he made with a spirit would be the same as a familiar, but then Elaine and Gasped should have been considered familiars tied to their family. He knew familiars were not quite the same. They did not require consistent rituals, redrawn circles, or paperwork. He looked down at his notebook and grumbled, "It can be summoned at any time by will."

"Correct and incorrect." Grandfather tapped Ben's desk. The setting sun's rays crept over the horizon, basking Grandfather's wrinkled hand in pink and golden hues.

"During your trial, you will summon your first familiar spirit. They will accompany you everywhere and be intrinsically tied to you. Unlike other families, we do not force our familiars to do our bidding against their will. It is critical that when you make this summons, you summon a spirit that will agree to work along with you. Or else, you will fail. If not then, later."

Ben gulped, feeling the pen in his hand slip from his fingers. "So, how do I do that?"

"Think about it, Benjamin. What did the vetala want when you summoned it?"

Ben shuddered, and the blood drained from his face as the memory of the fiend appeared in his mind. The vetala desired a body, something Ben was not willing to give. Additionally, it wanted to kill him. It craved violence and more bloodshed than he could ever mutually offer.

"Grandfather, what if I summon another vetala? What do I do?"

"That would be a very unfortunate thing, Benjamin. You can

give it what it wants or send it away, but you can only summon one spirit in the rite, so whatever you summon, if you do not contract with it, you will fail. We must focus on how to summon the spirit of your choice properly, so the same mistake is not made twice."

Ben nodded, glad Grandfather was giving him the instruction he so deeply desired. He rubbed his eyes, determined to do anything to succeed.

"Is there a limit to the items I am allowed for the summoning?" Ben asked. "I mean, if I can have a match, certainly I can summon whatever is prescribed for the spirit of my choice."

Grandfather nodded. "You will be allowed a selection of standard items and one artifact item of your choice. Everything will be available for you. So, what spirit do you want to summon as your familiar?"

Ben blinked. He found it difficult to breathe with the weight of Grandfather's question. When was the last time Grandfather asked him about what he wanted to do? He bit his lip, hoping his decision would not disappoint him, and hoping to prove that vouching for him this whole time was worth it.

He pulled on his notebook and studied it, thinking about what spirit he wished to summon and how he would successfully contract with it. He never contracted a spirit before, and if it were something like a vetala or a wraith, there was no hope for him successfully completing his rite. He needed a dedicated spirit who also could win a fight.

"What was your familiar?" Ben asked.

"Oh, ha, I did not summon a familiar for my rite," Grandfather said with a chuckle. "The rules changed after my rite... Now your mother, she summoned a banshee."

"A banshee..." Ben flipped through the pages of his notebook until they fell upon a clipped in drawing of a woman screaming. Ben quickly tilted the page away from Grandfather, hoping he would not notice that the page had once belonged to one of his tomes. Ben scanned it and closed the notebook.

A banshee was not a terrible spirit to have a contract with. They could foretell death and sense when the future appeared bleak. Their cries were also crippling and very powerful against other spirits and living beings alike. But... they cried a lot, and Ben would have to suffer solacing such a tearful spirit constantly. He did not think of himself as someone with the best temperament to deal with such a spirit. If they got in a screaming match, he would lose.

"Maybe not a banshee," Ben mumbled.

"Perhaps, think about what you can offer and what you need. A poltergeist may wish for closure, which you can provide. There are many spirits seeking just that..."

Ben nodded, but everyone knew spirits looking for closure had no desire to become familiars and add more tethers to the living realm. He needed a familiar that would be sticking around for a while and did not mind assisting a necromancer.

"What about a Will O Wisp?" Ben asked, thinking about the mysterious spirits that often caused people to disappear. "You got your lantern from one. What are they like?"

Grandfather frowned. "Benjamin, a Will O Wisp is not a good spirit for a familiar."

"Why not? They are powerful and they travel freely. It seems like-"

"Would a spirit that travels freely wish to be tied to a necromancer?" Grandfather interjected. "There are many reasons a-"

Knock Knock

Grandfather flinched but continued. "Will O Wisps are trickster spirits who solely seek out causing mischief. Even at the expense of killing those they lead astray. But even then, Benjamin, that is only the knowledge shared for those who have not met-"

KNOCK KNOCK KNOCK

The two turned their heads and looked to Ben's bedroom door. Mely stood in the doorway with one arm limply at her side and the other hanging in the air, fist loosely clenched, and ready to knock on the door again if they continued to ignore her.

"Yes Mely?" Ben asked as Grandfather sighed.

The zombie turned her head, looking at Grandfather with drooping eyes, and said, "There are guests."

"Guests?" Ben asked as Grandfather stood.

"Lead the way, Mely," Grandfather said, ushering Mely to show him to where the Hill's guests were. They may have just been some normal graveyard visitors, but Mely never bothered with them. They had to be someone important or problematic.

Ben started to stand, but Grandfather urged him to stay seated and continue looking over his notes. Ben watched as the two left. He sighed and turned his head back to his notebook, flipping the pages until he came upon one about Will O Wisps.

He truthfully knew little about the mischievous spirits. They were classified more on temperament than on distinguishable characteristics. In fact, it was nearly impossible to find one. They were clever, capable of traveling quickly, and masters of illusions. They also were attuned to the element of fire... Ben liked the idea of having a familiar that could procure a flame.

But he had no written information on how to summon one.

He looked at his stack of books and then shuffled through the drawers of his desk, finding a book he snagged from Grandfather's study. *Advanced Conjuring for the Curious* was exactly what he needed. He lifted the heavy text, plopped it onto his desk, and divulged into the contents, searching for summoning circles for trickster spirits and Will O Wisps.

An hour had passed before the irksome feeling of something being wrong pulled Ben out of his focus. He shifted in his seat and looked towards his bedroom door. Grandfather should have returned by now.

Ben stood, stretched, and left his room. As he walked down the stairs, he could hear the faintest sounds of people talking on the front porch. Mely stood near the front door, watching out the transom windows with the guarded gaze of a watch dog. Her black hair hung around her face, and she awkwardly careened towards the front door. Ben stepped down the hall and whispered, "What are you looking at?"

The zombie turned her head, looking at Ben with drooping eyes, and said, "There are guests."

"Guests?"

Still looking at Ben, Mely raised her arm, limply pointing towards the front door. "Ernest is speaking with them outside. They are not welcome in the house."

There was a hint of malicious energy in Mely's last words. It was not an opinion of hers. Grandfather had ordered Mely that no one else was welcome in the house. If they entered, they would have to deal with a very violent maid. While Mely was not the best of maids, she still was a zombie and a force to be reckoned with.

Ben nodded and stepped towards the front door. He peered

through the window, seeing a couple of people dressed in black cloaks talking with Grandfather at the foot of the stairs. They were undoubtedly people from the council. A sickening feeling twisted in Ben's stomach as he knew something was horribly wrong.

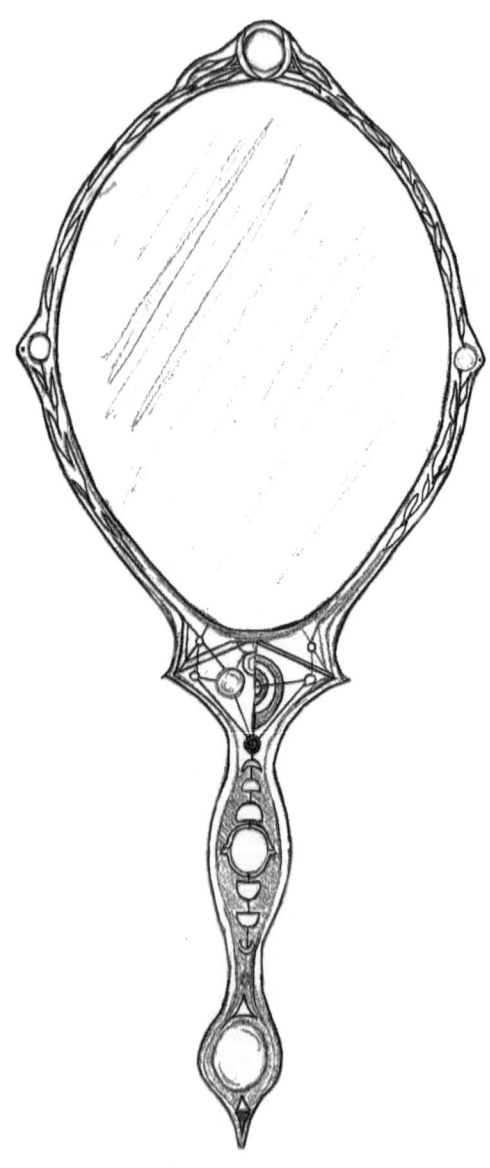

Twenty Five

A Warning

"You should have stayed inside, Benjamin," Grandfather said as Ben stepped onto the porch.

"Oh, no this is important information for the apprentice," Isabella Nightshade said with a soft smile directed towards Ben.

She then looked at Grandfather, keeping that same gentle smile that made the hairs on Ben's arms stand. "But we do not need to discuss here, Ernest. It would be better if we spoke in my office. I am afraid you have far too many ears floating around."

"The gossip stays within the Hill's vicinity," Grandfather said, looking aside.

"There is no such thing as stagnant gossip amongst the dead," Isabella retorted. She reached in her pocket and pulled out a silver framed mirror, similar to the one Grandfather had used. "If you may?" she asked while reaching out her hand.

Grandfather looked down at Ben reluctantly before taking his hand and grabbing a hold of Isabella's.

Ben watched as Grandfather gently grasped Isabella's hand. He looked down at Ben with a concerned gaze Ben returned. Then there was a dark flash, and they stood in an office belonging to the Council of the Dead's chamber.

The floors were black marble, and the walls were a deep purple as dark as midnight with golden diamonds laced from floor to ceiling. Two couches sat across from each other in the center of the room, each made with bright green snakeskin and imprinted with golden studs. Before the couches sat a wide wooden desk made of dark walnut, and behind it hung a tall window that cast a foggy array of moonlight upon the desk's piles of papers and ledgers.

Isabella paced across the study to her desk and leaned against it, crossing her arms. "You're welcome to take a seat."

Grandfather looked over his shoulder towards the door, and Ben followed his gaze. Two skeletons stood at the doors with their arms crossed, holding slick daggers that gleamed in the candlelight. He jabbed a thumb towards the skeletons. "And you were concerned about my ghosts, but you can have skeletons here?"

"Ugh, if you wish, they will leave," Isabella grumbled, waving her hand. The skeletons shifted and lowered their arms. One of them clacked their teeth while the other picked at a rib before they shuffled their way out of the office.

Once the skeletons left, Ben took a seat on the couch. The other necromancer sat across from him, comfortably kicking a pair of black leather boots onto the table. Despite being a member of the council, he was shorter and younger than Ben in appearance. Ben recognized the necromancer right away as one of the oldest living members of the council, striking an age somewhere around seven centuries. If vampires could be considered living.

Augustus Moroti looked at Ben with a set of deep, blood red eyes through the glowing face of a child. His face was soft and round, and his olive skin gleamed with youthful energy. If Ben did not know better, he could easily have mistaken Augustus for one of the children that passed by the Hill in the mornings.

He was significantly shorter than Ben, standing nearly

four feet tall. The head of his cloak had been drawn back since her arrival, revealing a pale face and thick black hair. Ben remembered him from the initial Council meeting, and he was still shocked to see the council member who looked as if he were ten years old standing before him.

"Must you put your shoes on the table?" Isabella moaned, but the vampire simply turned his head and looked towards the door nonchalantly.

"What is your reason for bringing us here? We have a meeting tomorrow evening," Grandfather said.

"That is why our meeting is pertinent," Isabella said. She looked at Augustus and added, "Tell them what you discovered."

Augustus sighed. "I have received a report that Igraine Ellandor has returned to the living realm. Additionally, there is a trace of Gravekeeper blood on the Prison of Tophet's gate."

A shiver went down Ben's spine, and he sharply looked at Grandfather. He appeared shocked, and of course, he would be. He knew nothing about what Ben had done. The boy absentmindedly grabbed the silver pendant hidden beneath his dress shirt.

Isabella paid Ben no heed and looked at Grandfather with a disappointed gaze. "Did you help them?"

Grandfather froze, and Ben felt the room grow around him. His head buzzed with a million thoughts as he helplessly stared at the head of the Moroti family, jaw slackened. He never considered that someone in the underworld would check for his blood, but he knew deep down he would not have changed his mind if he did. Whether they found his blood on the gate or not would not have stopped him from making the deal with Erwys.

Ben's fist clenched. He was glad grandfather knew nothing about the deal. They would never guess a blind apprentice could traverse to the underworld let alone succeed in returning. Hopefully, their suspicions of Grandfather would distinguish.

"I know nothing about it," Grandfather said, folding his hands. "Are you certain it is my family's blood?"

"I know blood," Augustus said firmly. "It never lies."

Isabella stepped towards the group. "I am afraid this is an incredibly concerning matter. There is nothing holding the lich to her place. Per the rules of the trial, if it is truly the Gravekeeper's blood on the gate, we do not have the authority to return Igraine Ellandor to the prison. But, tell me Ernest, is it true you saved her?"

"No," Grandfather said. "I have not saved the Ellandor child."

"This is a grave matter, Stone. You said in the trial yourself that you would not revoke the services of the Gravekeeper. Was it for this reason that you refused to remove it? So you could enter the underworld and save her yourself?" Isabella asked. "If I don't believe you, who do you think will? If word of this ever spreads to the rest of the council-"

"Do they know she is no longer imprisoned?" Grandfather asked. "This is my first time hearing of it, certainly the rest would not be the first to know."

"Only those in this room are aware as of now," Isabella said. "But knowing the Ellandors, this won't stay hidden for long. I give it hours at best."

Augustus coughed. "I have no intention of creating a storm and informing the council of your blood, but if it was not you, this issue must be investigated. They will know of her freedom whether by my word or yours. Whether we announce it now or later will not change the outcome. But if I am to say what I know, an irrefutable truth that *your* blood is on the gate, the very title of Gravekeeper is at risk. Mimicking the Gravekeeper's blood is no small crime nor easy task."

Ben gulped, but his mouth was horribly dry. He felt faint, and as the necromancers discussed what to do, all he could do was sit still and stay silent. If they even slightly suspected him of going to the underworld, he would be done for.

"What of your apprentice?" Augustus asked, causing Ben to flinch. "Was he the one to release the girl?"

Grandfather froze and then laughed. His laugh echoed against the tall ceilings and made Ben wince. He bellowed, "You think Benjamin went to the underworld?! He is but a mere apprentice. Not even a fledgling out of the nest, and you believe he succeeded in releasing the Ellandor's child?!"

"If he did not, then who would have?"

"Blood is a fickle thing, is it not?" Grandfather shook his head. "How difficult would it be to find a cousin or conjure the blood of a deceased distant relative? Benjamin had an incident in the Wraithright estate not long ago. Some of his blood easily could have been confiscated then for all we are aware. Blood may not lie, but how it is retrieved or used does not tell all."

Ben trembled as Grandfather defended him. Isabella's piercing green gaze rested upon him, and Augustus studied him with doubt marked across his face. He looked down, fearing what would happen if they pushed their suspicions any further. Grandfather would disown him if he knew that Ben had indeed gone into the underworld to retrieve Igraine. If they discovered that, then the truth about the lich would become known, and they would learn about his eyes.

He shut his eyes in terror, wishing he were back on the Hill.

"You are right," Isabella said calmly. "We mustn't fret over such minor details. We are up against a lich, after all. I trust you will keep this between us, Augustus?"

"Yes, of course."

"Then it is best to assume this will not be added to the agenda for tomorrow?" Grandfather asked. "Do you mean to tell me you have no intent of divulging this to the rest of the council?"

Isabella shook her head. "It was the Moroti's discovery. If he chooses to share this information to the rest of the council, it will be his prerogative. For now, we believe it is best to monitor and see what will happen. If not the Stone family, another necromancer family must be aligned with the Ellandors, and the lich. Wouldn't you find it wiser to watch and wait whilst allowing them to believe they are ahead?"

Ben pressed his hands on his knees, wondering what would happen. The Ellandors were entirely alone in their actions. They had no support from any of the necromancer families. The only family that cared to help them was his own, and if that information came to light, they would be just as guilty as the rest of the Ellandors for supporting a lich. Ben chewed on his lip, wondering if watching and waiting was intended to track and target another family or if it was to wait until damning evidence appeared against the Stone family.

"Very well," Grandfather said with a soft nod. "We have yet to discover the catalyst of the lich. This may reveal who is assisting Delore Ellandor."

Augustus Moroti sighed, drawing everyone's attention to the vampire necromancer. It took little to gather attention, and Ben could not help but feel a magical energy tracing its way from the creature. In some sense, he was like a lich. However, unlike a lich, he was not entirely dead, and his curse for immortality came at a different cost. "The lich will reveal herself when she is ready," he said. "The catalyst is of no concern. They were simply a pawn to her making... I am more concerned about who is freeing the lich of her chains and restrictions. Without her daughter imprisoned, there is nothing stopping her from doing as she pleases."

"And this, Ernest, is why we came today," Isabella said.

"If we must hide our knowledge of the lich's movements, we cannot restrain our ability to track her. We need the Gravekeeper, and we have no reason to limit our ability to procure one. Tomorrow the council will convene to select the next Gravekeeper whether Benjamin is ready or not. I hope you have selected an alternate heir."

Ben looked down, eyes stinging. He did not have the nerve to say he could see spirits. Despite the effort he put into his training the past few weeks, it could not make up for the years he had lost to fine tuning his ability to use magic, connect with spirits, and perfect spells. If Grandfather supported him, there was no promise that the council would.

"I have not procured another heir," Grandfather said sternly. "Benjamin Stone is the only rightful heir to the title of Gravekeeper."

Augustus Moroti scoffed, and Isabella smacked her forehead with disappointment. Ben wanted to curl up in a ball and disappear. Instead, he kept his gaze at his feet, looking away from the three necromancers entirely.

"If his rite must come sooner, so be it," Grandfather said before Isabella could protest. "But in the end, only I can decide who the next Gravekeeper will be."

"And if he fails the rite?" Augustus Moroti interjected. "Then what will be of the Gravekeeper line?"

Ben lifted his gaze to see the vampire staring directly at him. He shivered, but there was something in Moroti's gaze that was alluring and hard to ignore. He felt trapped in the deep red pools of his eyes, and the longer he looked, the more still he became.

Grandfather grabbed Ben's shoulder, breaking him free from the vampire's gaze. The boy grabbed the pendant on his neck, fearing that Augustus somehow had been able to see through the pendant's charm and his deceit.

"He will not fail."

Twenty Six

The Trial of the Gravekeepers

Knock Knock

Everyone in Isabella's office turned their heads to the door.

Grandfather's eyes narrowed. "Is that your skeletons, Miss. Nightshade?"

She sharply looked at Grandfather and mouthed no before approaching the door. It opened before she could reach it, and a man stood at the threshold, wearing a black cloak and a silver mouth guard that covered half his face. *"Speaker, the council is convening,"* he spoke as if his voice came from everywhere and nowhere. Ben blinked, realizing the man was not human.

"Our meeting is not scheduled until tomorrow," she said, finishing crossing across the office and standing near the undead. She did not stand too close, Ben noted, staying two arm's length away.

"Half of the council has agreed to this session. Will you take part as speaker?"

Isabella looked at the Stones and Augustus Moroti. "It appears, we have less time to prepare than expected," she said with a half-smile. Her posture slackened slightly in defeat as she turned to the thrall. "Very well, we shall follow."

Grandfather grabbed his forehead, cursing under his breath. Before Ben could protest, he grabbed his shoulder, urging him to quickly follow. Augustus Moroti stood and glided out of the room, passing Isabella. She looked at him with a piercing gaze, but he paid her no heed, coolly leaving the room.

"Did you plan this?" Grandfather asked, passing by Isabella.

She glanced at the undead and back at Grandfather. "No."

He smirked and pulled Ben out of the office. They entered the long main hallway full of horrible curiosities. This time, the hall was not quiet. Necromancers in long black cloaks rushed from their offices down the hall and towards the doors.

"Grandfather what is happening?" Ben hissed as they rushed down the hallway, following Augustus and a few other necromancers. Ben spotted a few ghosts drifting in the mix. Three were chained to a necromancer several feet ahead of them, and the sight of it made Ben's stomach churn with disgust.

"The council is convening. Our meeting scheduled for tomorrow is likely happening now due to the information you just learned," Grandfather said, looking ahead. He paused and turned, grabbing Ben's shoulders. "Benjamin, this meeting was intended to be on other matters, but I fear you may be the subject. No matter what you hear and are told, only listen to me, and no matter what, stay silent about your sight."

Ben anxiously nodded, fearing what would occur beyond the heavy set of doors in the chamber. Maybe another necromancer discovered the Gravekeeper's blood on the gate. Maybe another one knew that Ben had colluded with the Ellandors and had gone to the underworld. Maybe someone knew the trade he made with the lich. He lost all color in his face as Grandfather urged him to continue down the hallway. What would happen to him if the council knew the truth?

They passed the group of undead servants holding open the doors and moved through the U arrangement of desks until they arrived at Grandfather's station. Grandfather motioned for one of the undead servants to bring another chair, and soon Ben was sitting beside Grandfather, shoulder to shoulder.

He folded his hands in his lap and twisted his feet over each together, looking down and fearing for what would happen as the necromancers funneled into the room. Nearly everyone was there, but as the doors closed with a heavy slam, Ben peeked upward, noticing a small number of empty seats. The seat to their left was filled with the most loathsome necromancers of all.

Jacob Withertomb sat in his chair, posture tall and straight, watching the room as it filled. His eyes flickered to Ben, and he leered at the apprentice with a crooked smirk.

The boy looked away, focusing his gaze on his dress shoes. At least he was dressed properly this time, he thought. At least, in appearances, he would not embarrass Grandfather. But Ben clenched his teeth and could not refrain from shaking. Two council members had already caught on to the Gravekeeper's involvement releasing Igraine Ellandor. If the rest of the council discovered this, then Ben's actions may cause Grandfather more strife than mere secondhand embarrassment.

"Two thirds of our members are here. This achieves quorum. Are we in agreement to proceed with the meeting?" Isabella asked, her voice echoing over the hubbub of people filtering into the chairs and small side conversations. The room grew quiet until a chorus of voices assented to the premature council meeting.

"Very well, and our meeting topic?" Isabella looked about, eyes narrowed yet posture firm. "Who pushed for this meeting one day sooner, and what is this so called urgent agenda?"

Ben glanced at Jacob Withertomb, but the necromancer was merely smiling and resolute to remain silent.

A chair's iron legs screeched against the marble floors, shooting Ben's attention to a woman with brilliant red hair. She was tall and slender, and her black garbs draped around her being, cinching at her narrow waist. Ben had never seen her before, but something about her, the slightest trace of a malevolent aura engulfing her being, reminded him of Delore Ellandor. He shuddered with revulsion. Ben glanced at Grandfather, dreading what she would say.

"I called for this meeting," the woman said, and Ben so dearly wished she had not.

"Yes, Emile Heatherlay, and for what purpose?" Isabella said with a stern look upon her face. "There are members missing who may have chosen to be here had they received notice."

"Enough of us are here," Emile said with a soft smile and waving a well-manicured hand. "Does that matter now? It is quite urgent we discuss the issue of the Ellandors. If you have not heard, the child of the lich has been freed from her prison."

A rumble of discussion erupted in the chamber. Ben sharply closed his eyes and clenched his fists, wishing for the sound to stop and for himself to appear back in his room. Instead, as the council drew quiet, he opened his gaze to the disgruntled expression of Isabella Nightshade. "Would you care to elaborate on this claim?"

Isabella played ignorant, but concern stitched across her face. Emile knew about the missing child, but it was not due to her involvement in their recent conversation. Perhaps Augustus Moroti had shared his discovery with more council members than he let on, or perhaps the information had already naturally weaved its way through the society of necromancers.

Emile smirked and nodded. "The Prison of Tophet is a nasty prison, one in the underworld on the plane of intermittence. A plane of split existence, if you may, closer to the living realm than the realm of death. Yet, here, we hoped the lich would seek to save her daughter and be trapped by the prison because only a living being can properly enter the prison and successfully leave. The lich went to the underworld and retrieved her daughter, but she did not enter the prison to save the girl."

"Then how do you suppose the girl was freed?" Isabella asked coldly.

Ben did not need to hear the answer to already know the danger he had put his own family in. He looked at Grandfather's face to find it stiff and stern. His jaw was clenched and his skin paler than usual. He already knew what Emile would say, and there was no way of stopping her from proclaiming such damning words.

"The blood of the Gravekeeper was found on the door. It is the only key to opening the prison's gate."

Ben's mouth went dry. His gaze first returned to Grandfather, and the man's expression was so nauseating, he turned it to Augustus Moroti's who looked completely aloof. Ben's eyes skated by Jacob Withertomb, and the necromancer's grin was blatantly larger. The boy's blood boiled as he forced his attention back on Emile.

"I am aware that the daughter of the lich, Igraine Ellandor, has left her prison. If it is true she left due to the aid of the Gravekeeper, by our laws, we are not to return her to the prison," Isabella said although she sounded entirely displeased and pained as she spoke. She looked over to Grandfather, and Ben wished he could simply tell the truth and relieve Grandfather, but this time, he hoped Grandfather had a plan.

"Tell us, Ernest Stone, did you open the gate to the prison of Tophet?"

Grandfather laughed, and his voice echoed through the

306

chamber. A number of necromancers whispered and gossiped as Grandfather continued to roar with laughter.

"Stone?"

"Ha, excuse me..." Grandfather stood, beaming. "I am formally asking, is this meeting about my family as the Gravekeepers or about the lich. Because, even if I were to say I did release the lich's child, I never revoked my protection of the Ellandors and have every right to release her if that was my choice. Now," he sat, folding his hands. "If we are here to discuss the lich and her whereabouts, finding that she did retrieve her daughter is a sign that there is a tie with her and her family, and she is traceable... so who is the subject of this evening's discussion?"

Emile glared at Grandfather, but another necromancer yelled, "Are you alluding to the fact that you opened the prison gate?"

"No."

"Then how else could she-"

"ENOUGH!" Isabella roared. "What is the meaning of this session?"

"To determine the adequacy of the Gravekeeper," Emile said with a sharp grin.

Ben looked to Grandfather, but now the old man's face was as red as Ben's hair. "What is the meaning of this?"

Jacob Withertomb slapped his desk. "Oh please, *Ernest*. You have a singular heir that cannot see spirits. Amongst that, your previous apprentice was a complete failure, and you are a dying line. Atop that, you have gone against the council's will and freed the daughter of a lich."

"I did not claim to do that, and you have no place to speak

given what lurks in the halls of your academy," Grandfather snarled.

"QUIET," Isabella snapped, silencing both Withertomb and Grandfather. The remaining council members broke out in a hushed flurry of whispers and murmurs, but as Isabella spoke, they died down.

"This session has been called early due to the unnerving news that Igraine Ellandor has been released from the Prison of Tophet. This information shall be investigated and confirmed through proper channels. I will not waste our time idling like some gossip party. Because we are here with enough members, we shall continue our conversation onwards. Ernest Stone, is this acceptable to you?"

"Yes," Grandfather said with a harumph.

Ben looked at Emile, but she did not protest. A smirk similar to Withertomb's resided on her lips, and her eyes glimmered with something foul. His stomach churned with unease.

"Very well. Our topic of discussion this night shall be as Emile Heatherlay stated: the Rite of the Gravekeeper. Any objections?"

Ben eyed Grandfather, but Grandfather simply shook his head and crossed his arms. He then looked at Ben with a heavy but confident gaze. Ben's stomach danced with a flurry of moths. Undeniably, Grandfather believed Ben would have no difficulty proving himself now that he had the sight.

"Emile, present your case," Isabella demanded.

"Yes speaker," Emile said, maintaining her smile. She stood, and her voice echoed through the chamber. "In a week's time, the Rite of the Gravekeeper is deemed to take place. Here, Ernest Stone will be retiring from his place as Gravekeeper as he has met the full length of his term. His grandson, Benjamin Stone is determined to be his heir."

"However," her smirk vanished, "if we wait until the clock ticks out, and the heir, Benjamin Stone, fails his rite, Ernest Stone will have no time to select the new Gravekeeper. I propose we push the rite to this evening and provide insurance of a week for the current Gravekeeper to find a replacement if his selected apprentice fails the rite."

Ben was frozen stiff. Perform the rite tonight? He was not ready. He was woefully unprepared! Ben looked at Grandfather and opened his mouth to protest, but the current Gravekeeper maintained that look of confidence that made Ben sick.

"This is unprecedented," Isabella began to protest in Ben's defense while Grandfather remained painfully quiet.

"But it is well known amongst the council that the apprentice Gravekeeper is a mere grave whisperer. Is it to be expected we rely on the expertise of a Gravekeeper who can do nothing more than speak to the dead?" Emile asked.

Hector Ashrot, albeit he was literally missing his eyes, nodded in agreement. "We deserve a Gravekeeper who can maintain the balance of the council. Learning of the news that the Ellandor child has been released from her prison and the lich runs amok, there is no room to allow for failings. I agree with ensuring the current Gravekeeper a week's time to find another heir."

"Is a week's time even a number worth considering?" Isabella asked. "We can extend the Gravekeeper's time of service or perhaps propose an heir and have them attempt the rite next week as well."

"The rite will be tomorrow night." Grandfather's words rang through Ben's ears with a dizzying clarity. Ben's mouth hung open, and it felt as if he had been kicked in the gut.

"Yes, Stone?" Isabella asked, blinking with shock.

Grandfather stood, and as he rose from his seat, Ben felt as if he were shrinking in his, becoming increasingly insignificant as Grandfather sealed his fate. "My apprentice is as ready now as he ever will be to perform his rite. Let us not drag on this discussion and allow the opportunity for meddling with this ceremony. As the Gravekeeper, I am officially declaring the Rite of the Gravekeeper shall commence at midnight tonight."

Twenty Seven

Final Moments

The moment they returned to the Hill, Ben turned on Grandfather in a flurry of anger.

"How could you do that?! How could you agree and push the rite to tonight?" He cried, grabbing his hair, and flailing his arms.

Grandfather solemnly frowned, but he reached and placed a steady hand on Ben's shoulder, grounding his tantrum. "You successfully summoned a vetala whilst blind and only through the magic of your blood. You have survived the Wraithrights catacombs, and you saved the Ellandor's child. You are entirely prepared to become the next Gravekeeper."

Ben froze, and the color in his face drained away. "H-how did you..."

Grandfather smiled softly. "There is a reason Erwys removed the Wraith Cloak without asking for anything in exchange. The favor she owed me did not compare to the weight of your life. And, the only blood of a Gravekeeper belongs to you and me. As far as I am concerned, you bringing Igraine Ellandor back from the underworld solely qualifies you as the Gravekeeper. More so than any silly ceremony the council concocts."

Ben blinked back tears. He had betrayed Grandfather, but Grandfather had known all along what Ben had done and was still proud of him. Perhaps he did not know about the lich's eyes, but he certainly knew about Igraine, and he believed he had done the right thing.

The apprentice nodded, stunned, but it did not change the fact that, if Grandfather saw him as qualified, he still had to properly create a familiar and win in combat. He looked up at Grandfather, blinking away stinging tears. "What must I prepare for before midnight?"

Grandfather grinned, holding his hand on Ben's shoulder for one long moment. He went to his desk and shuffled through its contents, pulling out different items from drawers he never allowed Ben to touch. "First, we must determine what spirit you intend to summon-"

"A Will O Wisp," Ben said firmly.

Grandfather looked up from the trinkets on his desk with his brows raised. His forehead crinkled in waves of wrinkles as he stared at Ben in shock. "Are you certain?" He whispered.

Ben nodded.

"There is no guarantee you will successfully conjure a Will O Wisp or make one your familiar. They are tricksters. If they know how dire your circumstances are, they will reject any and all offerings just to witness you fail."

"I know," Ben said. But if what Grandfather said was true, he did not feel dissuaded. After spending years with the Hill's residents, he felt like any spirit called a trickster would be nothing worse. Every day, the Hill's spirits made it their mission to torment and aggravate Ben just for their entertainment. If there was a temperament Ben knew how to deal with, it was one that preferred aimless fun and mischief. The Will O Wisp was the perfect spirit, and he knew exactly what he needed as an offering to make the mutual contract.

"Grandfather, you said I can pick a singular item to assist with the summons?"

"Er, yes," Grandfather grumbled. "Here are some things that may assist in the circle... this here will increase your ability to bind the circle... this scroll here-"

"I need the lantern," Ben said flatly.

"What?!"

Ben pointed at the Will O Wisp lantern eerily sitting atop the corner of Grandfather's desk. "I need that."

"Of all things! Benjamin, if a spirit gets their hands on that, they can roam the living realm freely. If you summon the wrong spirit, they can steal it from you during the summons. Just think what would happen if you conjured another vetala?!"

Ben recoiled at the thought, but his decision was sound. "Grandfather, you said this is my choice. If I am going to summon the spirit of my choice, I should also be able to select the item necessary to succeed."

Grandfather looked at the lantern while clamping his hand over his bearded chin. Sweat beaded down his forehead as he thought about Ben's request. After several weighted minutes, he wiped his forehead and sighed. "Very well then."

Ben approached the lantern and picked it up. Now with the sight, he could see tendrils of ethereal energy emanating from the ectoplasmic artifact. As he studied the lights, he could almost hear an otherworldly whisper drifting from the lantern, curling up his arm like the hiss of a snake. Ben quickly set the lantern down and brushed his arm. He was not remotely familiar or comfortable with the increased senses the lich had given him.

Grandfather sighed. "If that is the item you choose, let's see you draw your circle. There is not much time..."

Grandfather's words could not be more true. The sun had yet to rise, but time was still not on their side. Grandfather gathered a pile of summoning materials and urged Ben to follow him. They made their way down the hall and outside into the graveyard. Ben followed Grandfather along through the graveyard as they made their way to the gardens.

The spirits hung in the air, watching the two with glowering faces. Ben ducked his head, not wishing to make eye contact with any of the ghosts. He wondered if the Hill's residents would ever forgive him for creating the revenant. He knew he could not afford to fail again, or they would have worse things to be mad about. An imposter would come to the Hill to care for them, someone who may not care about forgiveness or their safety.

They made it into the gardens and came to an earthen clearing near the garden shed. A few sacks of soil and mulch were piled in the corner of the clearing along with a shovel and a rusted wheelbarrow. It was a patch Ben had originally prepared to grow vegetables in, but ever since the council's initial arrival to the Hill, he had neglected such tasks.

"Draw your circle here," Grandfather said, tapping his foot on a patch of newly sprouted weeds. Ben frowned and nodded. He preferred the solid wooden flooring of the rotunda or his bedroom. Drawing circles in the earth was far more tedious.

Still, the apprentice did not protest. He grabbed the shovel from the pile of dirt and carved out the summoning circle necessary for the spirit. Halfway through, Grandfather inspected it, shook his head, and said, "Start over."

Ben groaned, patted the earth flat, and tried again. As hours passed, sweat beaded down his face, his clothes became caked with dirt, and his callused hands ached and blistered from the constant shovel work. The sun was just tipping over the horizon, turning deep shades of orange and fuchsia, when Ben finally drew a circle Grandfather found acceptable.

He collapsed on the ground and looked at the setting sun

while his heart raced and sweat poured along the contours of his brows.

"This will do," Grandfather said sternly. "You must clean yourself up and be prepared. We have but an hour until we need to leave."

"Is the rite not here?" Ben gasped as he picked himself up and brushed the dirt off his clothes.

"No," Grandfather said. "Once you are prepared, grab the lantern, and we will leave."

Ben nodded and hurried to get ready. While he washed, he mentally chanted the summoning contract in his mind over and over again, sometimes whispering crucial terms in repetition. By the time he finished washing and pulled on the nicest suit he owned, he felt comfortable with the summoning.

But, an unnerving feeling could not leave the back of his mind. If he was successful with the summoning and making the spirit his familiar, he still had to defeat an opponent. He never had fought someone with the aid of a spirit. He had only ever ran away from fights. He knew running away was no option during the rite, but he feared what it would take to survive the night.

+X+

"I'm ready," Ben solemnly said as he stepped into Grandfather's study. He was wearing his best dress suit, dress shoes, and a black buttoned-down shirt with a red tie. His red hair was slicked back and combed. It was not the first time Ben had met the council, but it was the first time he would be officially acknowledged. Appearances were everything.

Grandfather sat at his desk with his hands folded on the back of his neck. He looked up and softly sighed, seeing the apprentice standing and waiting. Ben was exhausted, but Grandfather looked far more tired. The bags under his eyes told of many sleepless nights, and the wrinkles carving across his face hinted at a tale beyond normal aging.

But his golden eyes gleamed brilliantly, and now Ben could see that golden energy dancing around Grandfather as if he were standing right in direct sunlight. It was a beautiful energy not marred and corrupted like Emile or Delore. Ben looked down at himself, but his own energy was suppressed by the pendant's charm.

"Very well then." Grandfather stood and pulled on his cloak. "It is best we be off."

Ben nodded and picked up the lantern, cringing as whispers from the object prodded the back of his mind. "Grandfather, what will happen if I fail?"

Grandfather firmly grabbed Ben's shoulder. "You shall not fail. You are more than qualified to be the next Gravekeeper, Benjamin. Now is the time to carry no doubts and believe in yourself."

With that, he pulled Ben close and announced, "*Nomas!*"

The study bubbled into darkness, and the spirit horse appeared alongside its skeletal companion and the ornate carriage. Grandfather ushered Ben into the carriage and whispered to the horse their destination.

Unexpectedly, Grandfather did not climb into the carriage. Instead, he stood in the inky darkness staring at Ben with a look of confidence. "You will do well, Benjamin. Undoubtedly, you are the next Gravekeeper."

Ben blinked and tightened his grip on the lantern. "Aren't you coming with me? Grandfather!"

Grandfather patted the carriage heartily. "You will do great," he said to Ben before yelling, "Go!"

Ben did not have a chance to protest before the horses took off, and the carriage zoomed through the shadowy abyss towards an unknown destination.

Hooves galloped and bones rattled like a metronome. Ben listened to the steady, clattering and clacking rhythm while he absolved himself to the quiet and his restless thoughts. He tried to calm himself, but he continued to think about the what if's. What if he failed to properly summon the spirit? What if he succeeded but the spirit would not agree to be his familiar? What if his opponent defeated him or, what if he succeeded despite everything, but the council then determined he was indeed the one who freed the Lich's daughter and thus could never be the Gravekeeper?

Joining in the chorus of bones clattering, Ben's teeth chattered as he shivered, a bundle of nerves. He wished Grandfather was in the carriage with him so he could project these thoughts. He doubted Grandfather would console him. He knew better than that. The old necromancer would tell him off and to focus on what is ahead, not what may be.

Just as soon as Ben decided it best to take that figment of imaginary advice, the gallop slowed to a canter and then a trot, and Nomas came to a steady halt. The steeds shook their spines from their skulls to their tail bones, rattling like a box of piano keys. Nomas stomped its hoof, impatiently announcing their arrival.

Ben eyed the skeletons for a long time, wishing to stay there forever. The horse on the right turned its head and hissed an unnatural screech that made Ben's ears ring.

"I get it!" the apprentice cried, clambering off the carriage. He barely had time to snag the lantern before the skeletons kicked their legs in the air and sprinted through the abyss. Ben tumbled backwards through a pool of dissipating shadows, landing hard on a patch of mushy, cold grass.

Ben's fingers curled, tightening his grip around the cold handle of the lantern, and clawing up clods of grass and mud. He blinked as the remaining tendrils of the netherworld drifted from his being, dancing in the air like snakes. He watched them as they faded, folding into nothing. If he traced it long enough, he could almost make out the seams in the air that had just been torn- and then they were gone, revealing an unbroken starry sky and the soft white curve of a crescent moon.

Ben grunted, picking himself up off the ground and clambering to his feet. His shoes sank into the mud, making sucking and squelching sounds with every burdened step. He had fallen into a grassy marsh, and the back of his clothes were soggy with water and clods of mud. He brushed at the backs of his suit sleeves, scowling. So much for making a decent appearance.

The boy shivered, looking around the marsh with just the aid of the faint moonlight. The surrounding weeds were tall, reaching well over his head. He could jump to see past them, but he feared he might leave his shoes behind. Ben squinted through the shadows, seeing a few clear paths, but it was nearly impossible to tell what was ahead from pure sight alone. But something was different about the marsh and the night sky.

As he squinted, a flare of blue light appeared, drifting in the air like a bubble before zooming haphazardly back into the weeds. Just as that one vanished, another light drifted in the air, slowly and steadily. It lingered, almost mirroring the moon, before it floated back down. And then more appeared, with different lights, speeds, and personalities. It was not to say they were hiding in the weeds when Ben arrived. He simply was not looking for them and was not choosing to see them.

Now that he noticed the spirit orbs, it was impossible to see anything else. The energy of the spirits filled the field, and Ben could see their lights dance within the grass, within the weeds, and through the cleared pathways. Ben trudged forward, towards an open patch of weeds. He held the lantern tightly to his chest as he meandered along a less muddy path, following the light of the dancing orbs.

They were not guiding him. They did not acknowledge him. The orbs merely existed as dying lights of energy. They only offered an ethereal glow that leaked into the living realm, granting Ben just enough guidance to know what was before him in the marsh's woven shadows.

As the apprentice walked through the clearings, weaving his way around tall patches of weeds and small ponds, he noticed a looming darkness not so far away. It was like a giant sphere of emptiness. Not a single orb drifted in that direction, and as Ben meandered closer to the dark space, he noticed the orbs intently floating away from the void.

Ben stepped just into the edge where no spirits would go further. An unsettling feeling raised the hairs on his arms. He listened to the faint sound of the council members' conversations as their voices carried through the brisk night air and faded through the rustling of grass.

Ben gulped and paused, knowing what was ahead. That was where his rite was to take place. Or perhaps, it had already begun. He looked backwards at the dancing lights. If another week had passed, the moon would be a new moon. He would be wandering in pure darkness, and if he lacked the sight, he would have no earthly guidance. The council fully anticipated he would never make it out of the swamp.

Ben's teeth gritted, and he trekked forward, closing the

distance between himself and the council. As he neared them, the elevation increased and the ground stopped harboring patches of puddles, becoming only damp with the kiss of midnight dew. He stepped into a clearing with the Council of the Dead.

They stood in a half-moon, each holding a candle. They all wore black cloaks with hoods that draped over their heads. Grandfather stood amongst them, and Ben could spot him easily. A golden light gleamed under his hood, one Ben found familiar and comforting. As for the other necromancers, they sent a chill down Ben's spine.

The presence of some spirits were easily discernible as they floated over their masters' shoulders. Behind Isabella stood two skeletons, making it obvious it was her. Her green aura in the night emanated off her cloak and a similar light danced around the bones of her undead minions, telling they belonged to her and not another.

Ben's stomach churned as he spotted Hector Ashrot. The necromancer known for plagues and blight had a nauseating aura. Now that Ben could see it, he could sense the lingering feeling of pestilence, nausea, and the dizzying smell of rot. He quickly turned his attention away from the necromancer to Grandfather to regain some sense of sanity.

"Benjamin Stone. You have been selected as the next heir to the title and responsibility of the Gravekeeper. Step forward if you accept your destiny and prove yourself worthy of your fate."

Isabella's voice pierced Ben's ears like a howling wind.

He trembled and nearly stepped backwards. Goosebumps spread across the nape of his neck as he fretfully wondered what symbol would they treat that as if he suddenly walked away?! Huddling the lantern tightly to his chest, the apprentice stepped forward, into the encompassing ring of the world's most powerful necromancers.

Twenty Eight

Jack O' Lantern

As Ben stepped forward, he could feel the energy in the air shift. The temperature dropped below freezing, and he could feel frost form along his back down to his toes. His fingers went numb.

"You have chosen to undertake the Rite of the Gravekeeper. If you fail this rite, you will be exiled from your family and the privileges as the Gravekeeper will be stripped from you. If you succeed in these trials, you will earn the title Gravekeeper and bear the responsibilities this title holds. If you turn away, surrender, or abandon the rite, you will fail."

As Isabella's voice drifted like a forlorn wind, the necromancers turned one by one and walked in two lines through the marsh. Ben watched as all of them moved, but Grandfather lingered in the back and beckoned for Ben to move forward and walk beside him. The boy hurried to his grandfather's side as they followed the rows of necromancers out of the swamp and into a massive graveyard.

As far as Ben could see, gravestones dotted the landscape. The tombstones stuck out of the rolling earth like jagged teeth. Some once splendid statues now contorted into hacked figures, worn by the elements and damaged by unknown entities. Ben spotted the occasional crumbling remnants of mausoleums.

Amidst the graveyard, Ben could see the lingering energy of spirits wisping away in the shadows of midnight. He sensed them off in the distance, some slumbering near their graves, and others lurking in the surrounding marsh, watching the necromancers warily.

Ben gulped nervously as he watched the backs of Isabella's skeletons and a number of chained spirits drifting over the head of one of the necromancers, not attempting to hide their misery. Once he summoned his familiar, who would he fight? Skeletons, wraiths, a reaper? The boy's stomach churned.

They treaded along through the graveyard until they came to the ruins of a small pavilion. A crumbling stone arch marked the entrance, and the grass shifted into smooth, dewy stone with integral weaving patterns carved into its cold blue surface. As Ben crossed under the arch, he felt another shift in the air, and the temperature returned to something more comfortable. He rubbed his hands and looked around.

A circle of braziers surrounded the pavilion, each alit with a towering flame that lit up the cold blue stone, the surrounding crumbling arches, and nearby tombstones. Thirteen necromancers lined themselves up along between the gaps of each brazier until they stood in a full circle surrounding Ben. Grandfather merely stepped backwards, taking his place and sealing the full circle.

Isabella stepped forward, and her voice echoed and danced through the pavilion as if they were standing within a bubble. "Benjamin Stone, take your place in the center of the circle."

Ben paused, looking around, shoulders hunched, and heart racing. He clenched his eyes closed for a long moment before listening to Isabella's instructions and treading into the center of the pavilion. His eyes lowered to the ground, and he could see trace markings of past summonings. The moonlit stone bore scars- the rakings of claws, the ashen marks of fire, the erosion of salt, the stains of blood.

"-heir to the Gravekeepers. You must summon a spirit and make it your familiar before the flames go out. When the light of the moon is all that touches the ground, you must fight your opponent. Now, chose your opponent amongst us."

Ben looked around, stepping swiftly as he spun to look at everyone. He knew most of the council members, but with their cloaks and concealed faces, he could not fully discern amongst them. Isabella was the only necromancer who so obviously showed herself, but amongst the rest, Ben could only clearly recognize Hector Ashrot and Grandfather. He would never dare to fight his grandfather, and a battle with Hector Ashrot promised certain death.

Ben eyed the skeletons, wondering if he could take them on, but there was nothing dictating that Isabella would use her skeletons in a fight, or only just the skeletons. Ben already knew she could raise the whole graveyard if she so chose. He never had a chance.

His eyes shifted from necromancer to necromancer. They were all the council members of the Council of the Dead for a reason. Neither Erwys Ellandor nor Winston Wraithright qualified for the council! Compared to those two, Ben felt utterly weak and humbled. It would be no fair fight amongst anyone within the ring.

"Can I call a name?" Ben whispered, wishing not to blindly point at a necromancer he did not know.

Isabella cocked her head. "I see no reason not to? Speak out if anyone objects!"

The air fell silent for a long painful moment. Ben watched tearfully as a brazier's flame flickered, threatening to go out.

"Very well," Isabella sighed. "Who do you desire amongst us to be your opponent."

Ben gritted his teeth, thinking of the necromancer who had humiliated him. He was the whole reason Ben had been exposed as a ghost whisperer, and he was the biggest advocate for removing Ben as the heir to the Gravekeeper title.

"Jacob Withertomb," Ben snarled.

"Ha!" Jacob laughed, breaking the heavy silence.

"Silence!" Isabella snapped at Withertomb. "Jacob Withertomb shall be your opponent. Use the items before you, and summon your familiar. The moment the lights fade and the moon takes precedence, your opponent shall be free to strike."

Ben shivered and turned to look at Jacob Withertomb's gleaming red eyes. The necromancer had lowered his hood and stood, staring at Ben with a malevolent grin. Ben hoped he made the correct choice.

But he did not have time to dwell on his decision. He focused on a pile of summoning supplies sitting on a small stone slab in front of Isabella. He shakily stepped towards the items. There was a silver dagger, a large bag of salt, a box of chalk, a matchbox, a jar of ectoplasm, a bottle of hemlock, candles, a small bowl of bird bones, and a stack of parchment and ink amongst several other trinkets. With them, Ben could practically summon anything.

Keeping the lantern hooked in the crook of his elbow, Ben grabbed the chalk and began his work. The apprentice scanned the large, circular stone platform, mentally tracing out the summoning circle for the wisp. He had practiced it enough with Grandfather that he felt comfortable, imagining where every line, arc, and rune should go. The boy stepped into the center of the ring, marked the center with a subtle triangle, and began drawing the lines that stemmed from the core of the circle.

The first brazier flared out.

The boy looked at the smoking brazier, heart racing. He had nine more braziers left. He hurried his pace, drawing as swiftly as possible, not hesitating to mark the ground with the intricate and chaotic pattern of runes that would properly hold the spirit of a wisp.

Once he was finished with the runes, he leapt backwards and hastily scanned the ground for errors. To his delight, the circle seemed correct. It had to be correct.

The flame in the second brazier faded into a plume of smoke.

The boy ran around the circle and grabbed the bag of salt. He poured it along the outer edges of the circle he was to stand in and around the places where the candles would reside. He then grabbed the candles and place them in their fifteen spots, lighting each one with a match. A few necromancers snickered as he did so, and Ben's face burned with embarrassment. Surely they believed he could still not see spirits. The fact that he could not magically conjure a flame was enough damning evidence.

Gritting his teeth, Ben stuffed the matchbox in his pocket and returned to the table. He grabbed the knife and a piece of parchment, but considering what happened when he summoned the vetala, he set the parchment down. He did not need a document to seal his agreement with the familiar. He needed an unbreakable trust that was not as fragile as paper.

He stepped into his ring just as the third brazier's light died. Time was moving too fast.

Ben closed his eyes and listened to the eerie sound of the surrounding necromancers' breathing, a distant howling wind, the crackling of the remaining braziers' flames, the unsteady rhythm of his racing heart, and the shallow, subtle whispers of the dead that drifted through the graveyard, fearing the necromancer's ritual and what curse might befall their unhallowed land.

Ben sucked in a deep breath. "I, Benjamin Stone, summon thee. Will-O-Wisp, you who walk the planes of the living realm and dance in the fray of twilight's dying rays. You who sing the song of what is lost, what must be found, the song of desire- the song of desperation- the song of curiosity. You, Jack O' Lantern who have lost your guiding light- the light you shine to lead astray- the path none chose to take and never know to chart. I summon thee to this place. Heed my call."

Ben pulled the dagger along the side of his forearm and winced as the blade nicked his skin. Blood streamed down the blade, and Ben knelt forward, letting it drip into the sigil's center.

A red light, like a deep, hot, smoky fire full of embers crackled as the blood touched the triangle. The red light weaved itself along the circle's pattern, and gold traced its way between the red lines. Ben blinked in shock, nearly forgetting to step back into his protective circle as he watched for the first time the traces of the magic within his blood.

A brazier's light flared out at the corner of his eye.

Deep red and gold danced like fireflies, lifting into the air and illuminating the sky. A faint golden veil formed along the outer edges of the summoning circle, fully enclosing Ben within the sigil and away from the surrounding necromancers' probing eyes.

"It has been a long time since I was summoned...."

The playful voice of a young man danced through the circle, echoing and fading in and out.

"Benjamin Stone, was it?"

Ben gulped, but his mouth was dry. It worked. It really worked. He looked around searching for the Will O Wisp, but it was completely hidden even with his ability to see spirits. But he could hear it perfectly. The apprentice sighed. "It is hard to have a conversation when you don't reveal yourself."

"Ha! Why would I do that?!" The Will O Wisp laughed, and its laughter danced mirthfully around Ben, causing the apprentice to believe the spirit itself was flying in a loop around him.

"Because I am here to make a deal with you. I want you to be my familiar," Ben said as calmly as he could. He was not afraid of this spirit. It was hardly terrifying compared to the vetala. Instead, sweat beaded down his forehead as he noticed another brazier's light die. It was not the dead he needed to fear.

"Oh, a familiar? I think not. Do you intend to force me against my will, oh necromancer? Is that why all of these necromancers are here? Are you proving yourself to them or something of the like?"

"Something of the like," Ben muttered.

"Then I will not be your familiar. If that is all, it is rather a shame. It has been so long since I've been summoned..."

Ben frowned. This spirit desired to have nothing to do with him. It was just as Grandfather had warned. Will O Wisps were playful spirits. They only cared about their own entertainment and mischief.

The apprentice waved his hand. "So why leave so quickly? At least hear me out. I am the next Gravekeeper. I will not make a deal against your will. In fact, if there is something you want, I can help you achieve it. In exchange, you must be my familiar... at least for today."

"No. I rather be sent away now. This conversation is borrrringgg."

"Even if I were to offer you this?" Ben challenged. He pulled out a match and lit the lantern in his arms.

The wisp let out a low whistle.

"Well... now you have me intrigued..."

The upside down face of a young man appeared, floating right before Ben. He wore a loose pair of overalls and a cotton under shirt. His hair defied the laws of physics, floating in every direction, but his arm pointed at Ben's chest and his pale blue eyes were as round as saucers. *"Where did you get that from?"*

Ben held the lantern so the Will O Wisp could clearly see it. While the spirit inspected the lantern, Ben studied the spirit. He looked like a young farmer's hand. His hair was long and shaggy, and it danced in the ethereal breeze. His eyes were heavy and dark, but his brows remained raised with excitement, and deep creases from years of smiling carved into his cheeks.

The spirit looked Ben in the eye, not smiling in the slightest. *"Where did you get this from, necromancer?"*

"That is for me to know," Ben said. "It can be yours, in exchange for being my familiar."

Jack crossed his arms and drifted in front of Ben, flipping upright. *"So you want me tethered to you until you die for-"*

"Or until I chose to release you," Ben said. "Until I am grounded as the true Gravekeeper and no longer need your help, or be it... a year... that is the term of you being my familiar in exchange for you receiving this lantern at the end of the term upon your release."

He lifted the lantern in the air and waved it, watching the spirit's eyes follow the item hungrily. *"... A year..."* the spirit muttered. He was obviously tempted. The lantern would grant him the freedom to walk the planes of the living realm, and for a Will-O-Wisp, that was something they greatly desired.

"Do we have a deal?" Ben asked, eyeing another dying brazier. Only two remained lit. He was running out of time.

Jack O Lantern tapped his chin. *"This is not enough. How dare you hold something that rightfully belongs to me and barter it for my service."*

Ben groaned. "Look, I will negotiate with you additional terms, and I may agree to them at a later time. I will at least agree to one of your requests in addition to giving you this lantern. But do you wish to make such a request before this audience?" Ben jerked his jaw towards the surrounding circle of necromancers. There was nothing to say they could hear their conversation with the veil over the summoning circle, but amongst a crowd like this, Ben doubted their conversation was private.

"... Very well, you have me sold but make it three things. I've always wanted my own genie," the spirit said with a smirk.

Ben scowled but nodded. "I accept."

Jack O Lantern reached out a hand and Ben took it. Instantly the lantern in his other hand vanished into a mist. Ben glanced at the fading lantern with fear, but the spirit's smirking facial expression never changed. If he was not panicking about his prize, Ben had no reason to panic either. They firmly shook hands and the veil surrounding the summoning circle vanished along with the spirit's appearance.

However, Ben could still *feel* Jack O Lantern's presence as if he were looming right over his shoulder, looking past him. Ben gulped and looked at the last remaining brazier. He swiftly thought out his commands for his newfound familiar, *"Jack O Lantern, once that brazier dies, I will be attacked by the necromancer over there-"* Ben pointedly glared at Withertomb. *"-Your first and primary task is defeat him or whatever spirits he may summon. He is sly, so don't expect him to fight fair."*

The sound of the spirit's voice laughed through Ben's mind. *"Slyer than me? Fighting fair is not even in my books! This is a large demand, but I suppose keeping you alive is worthwhile for those future agreements... Call me Jack by the way."*

Ben blinked in agreement and felt his heart skip a beat as the last brazier flared out.

Twenty Nine

The Gravekeeper's Rite

Ben's shoes slid along the moonlit stone as he shuffled away from Jacob Withertomb. The necromancer slowly stepped forward with a large grin stretched across his face.

"So it appears the Stone's apprentice was successful in summoning a spirit," Withertomb announced, and his voice echoed throughout the pavilion, stinging Ben's ears. "But no matter, this will be quick work."

He ducked his head and pulled out a small, black leather bound notebook from his pocket. Ben could feel a sickening, heavy energy from the book. A gooey, black ectoplasm dripped from its seams as Jacob opened the pages and flitted through each sheet as if he were scanning a high end magazine catalog.

"I don't like the looks of that," Jack hissed.

Ben blinked and looked up to see the faintest appearance of the spirit floating in the air, watching the necromancer before them. Ben knew deep down no other necromancer could see Jack. If he had summoned a wraith, a poltergeist, a banshee, or any normal spirit, the council members had the sensibilities to see it floating over him, but the Will O Wisp was a master of illusions. Ben could not even fully see the ghost as it blended itself with the air and moonlight.

"It looks like he keeps his spirits in the book," Ben thought. *"I will steal the book. You fight off whatever he summons and*

distract him if you can."

"Ah, a strategist."

Ben did not wait for Jack to agree with him. There was no room for negotiation. Jacob already had landed on a page, eyes narrowed, and lips stretched in a sinister smile. Ben ran forward, towards the necromancer. His chest pounded, and his breathing felt strained as he moved against a wall of terror. It was as if Jacob Withertomb were projecting a black cloud of death.

His grip tightened on the hilt of the silver knife, determined to wipe the smirk off Withertomb's annoying face. The necromancer was taunting him and mocking him. If he allowed himself to show fear, it would only bear worse for him in the future. Ben shook his head, pushing away the agonizing fear that screamed DANGER and pleaded for him to run away.

The page ripped from Withertomb's notebook. He was too late. Courage alone could not overcome the fiend unraveling from the necromancer's grimoire.

Tendrils of a ghost unraveled from the page, unfurling around Jacob Withertomb and in front of him, expanding like a plume of smoke from a growing fire. The smoke towered above the necromancer, higher than the pavilion's arches, and it grew higher still until it blackened the stars in the sky. The tendrils then darkened and wrapped around themselves, forming the body of a giant with a single red eye gleaming where its heart may have been. And just above was an empty chasm, so dark, Ben stopped in place, shaking in his shoes. An endless abyss stood before him with a maw wide open, ready to devour him if he took another step forward.

Jacob Withertomb stepped around the spirit and gently flipped through the pages of his book. "Will this be enough? Should I summon another just to get this over quickly?" The necromancer cockily yawned, causing Ben's head to fill with anger and return him his wits.

He locked eyes on Jacob Withertomb. He had to get rid of the book before the necromancer decided it was necessary to continue summoning. Ben ran towards Withertomb, ignoring the monstrosity standing in his path. It moaned something soul shaking, causing his knees to weaken and cave.

"Don't tell me you are a coward!" Jack laughed, floating somewhere ahead of Ben. And then, out of nowhere, a massive golden flame appeared, shrouding the behemoth's head. The monster panicked and swatted at the dancing flames.

The spirit screamed in agony as the flames burned its eye, and a couple of council members stumbled with its cry. Ben grabbed his ears, suffering a fresh wave of nausea while his vision blackened. But he could still feel the ground. He stumbled forward.

He closed the distance as his vision cleared, weaving his way to the side and around the swaying, swatting fiend. Withertomb's eyes focused on the fire engulfing his spirit for a split second before looking back at Ben. "What, you think you can defeat me with that puny blade and a flame?" Withertomb laughed. "Even if you cannot see the spirit, it will devour you!"

Ben did his best to withhold a grin. Withertomb still believed he could not see spirits. Ben rushed forward, but before he could reach Withertomb, the necromancer reached out his hand and screamed. A group of shadowy arms reached from the dark folds of his cloak, punching, slashing, and grabbing Ben.

The apprentice slashed the silver dagger, dissipating the necromantic force. But it was enough time for Withertomb to tear another page from his book and allow another spirit to unfurl from its cursed pages.

"JACK!" Ben mentally shouted!

"Stop crying," Jack groaned, and the flame surrounding the first fiend instantly disappeared, leaving a confused and blinded monstrosity behind.

"Ha ha!" Withertomb laughed as another spirit appeared before Ben in the form of a writhing sludge of ectoplasm. It congealed and split and congealed again, forming into a larger pool of black sludge with the occasional bone and skull floating in its mass. It moved towards Ben at a slow rate, but Ben knew if he got near it, he would not be able to run.

"Is fire all you have? Did you summon a mere orb or a low level djinn?" Withertomb asked. "I'm not surprised, Ernest," he called, jesting, and picking a fight with the Stone family.

But then Ben noticed something strange and elating. Behind Withertomb stood Jack, but Jack did not look like Jack. He looked like Ben although his feet were slightly off the ground. And in his hand, he held what looked like Withertomb's book.

"Is this yours?" the spirit asked with Ben's voice.

Jacob Withertomb's eyes widened with shock. He spun around, and Ben took his chance to run around the edge of the writhing ectoplasmic phantom.

"What are you- how did you get there?!" Jacob roared as Ben's foot stepped into the edge of the ectoplasm. His leg burned as if it were aflame, and he withheld a scream, fearing it would ruin Jack's distraction. He shuffled in his pockets and dumped the remaining bag of salt onto the spirit. It fizzled and jerked away, releasing Ben's bright red foot and his half consumed pant leg. His shoe had already entirely melted away.

"Ha I got your book you old man! And you call yourself a necromancer!" Jack jeered as Ben stepped behind the necromancer. Jacob was still clearly holding his book. Ben only had seconds at best before Withertomb recognized Jack's ploy.

Ben snagged the book, but the necromancer's grip was firm. He turned on Ben and sneered. "Funny."

His other hand grabbed Ben by the knot of his tie. His knuckles were illuminated in the moonlight as his fingers scraped against his neck, digging into his collar. He hooked Ben's collar, holding him still. His other hand slipped the book in his pocket, and he grabbed hold of Ben's neck, strangling him as he lifted Ben and carried him towards the blob of undeniable death.

"This is your only chance to forfeit before you become a pile of bones," Withertomb hissed.

"Let go of me!" Ben wheezed. The apprentice wriggled in Withertomb's grasp, gasping for breath. He pushed on the necromancer's hand, wincing as he felt a sharp pain on the back of his neck.

SNAP!

The necromancer stared deep into Ben's eyes while his red eyes widened in horror. His pupils expanded and glazed over, as if he were placed into a trance, and his grip on Ben slackened.

Ben wriggled free and snatched the pendant loosely hanging in the folds of his collared shirt and tie. The chain had unclasped in the scuffle, and Ben's eyes widened in horror as he realized Withertomb had stared directly into the lich's eyes.

He reached forward while the necromancer was stunned and snagged the book. Instantly, Jack appeared between the two and grabbed hold of the book in Ben's hands. He paused, looking at Ben's eyes, and a slim smirk lifted his lips.

"Allow me," he said before igniting the book into flames.

Ben dropped Withertomb's summoning book and stepped back, trudging into the ectoplasmic spirit. Its form burst into flames, rapidly deteriorating as its contract was devoured by the

Will O Wisp's fire.

He fumbled with the silver chain of the pendant. He pulled it from his neck, ducking his head down while surrounded by the ectoplasmic fire, and reconnected the chain. The boy then looped it over his neck and stuffed it in his shirt, wheezing horribly.

"Get out of the fire!" Jack roared, pushing him.

Because the fire belonged to his own spirit, it had not burned him, but the slime's ectoplasmic smoke entering Ben's lungs was another issue entirely. He stumbled from the force, and fell to his knees, gasping for air as his lungs tightened and spasmed.

"HA HA HA!" Through blurry eyes, Ben looked up at Jacob Withertomb. He had recovered from his trance, but now he was laughing madly, standing just a few feet away from Ben. The boy scrambled to his feet just as the necromancer stepped forward and grabbed his shoulder sleeve.

"I see what you've done here, Stone," Jacob hissed in his ear between convoluting chuckles. He forced Ben's arm in the air while laughing. "I acknowledge Benjamin Stone as the Gravekeeper!"

In an instant, the surrounding braziers flared to life, and the council members each removed the hoods of their cloaks, clapping. Grandfather stepped out of the ring and approached Ben, golden eyes gleaming with pride. He took Ben from Withertomb's grasp and wrapped him in a cloak filled embrace.

"I knew you would succeed me," Grandfather said, stepping back and looking at Ben with a soft, cherishing smile Ben had never seen before.

Isabella Nightshade stepped forward, carrying the black folds of a cloak. There were deep, blood red threads interwoven in the mix that shimmered in the dancing glow of the firelight. "Dawn your cloak, Gravekeeper," Isabella said. She looked at the council and roared. "Let us all welcome the Gravekeeper, Benjamin Stone, to the Council of the Dead!"

The council members applauded, but Ben's ears tuned out the congratulations, the clapping, and his own inner feeling of pride. Instead, his eyes landed on Jacob Withertomb, and his ears rang to the slow, steady sound of his clapping. He laughed sporadically, teetering on the edge of insanity, but his blood red eyes stared at Ben's, looking right through him. As Grandfather lifted the cloak and placed it over Ben's shoulders, Ben could not shake the feeling, despite his succession of the Gravekeeper title, his future had never been in such grave danger.

End of Book 1

A.N. Anderson is the author of the Necromancer Legacies and works as an architectural designer. If she is not writing down her dreams and nightmares, she is drawing buildings or playing with her two dogs, Matcha and Ace.

Learn more at anandersonauthor.com

www.ingramcontent.com/pod-product-compliance
Lightning Source LLC
Chambersburg PA
CBHW020659110726
47901CB00001B/251